D1173446

Candace Camp, a *USA TODAY* bestselling author and former attorney, is married to a Texan, and they have a daughter who has been bitten by the acting bug. Her family and her writing keep her busy, but when she does have free time, she loves to read. In addition to her contemporary romances, she has written a number of historicals, which are currently being published by MIRA Books.

Dallas Schulze loves books, old movies, her husband and her cat, not necessarily in that order. She's a sucker for a happy ending whose writing has given her an outlet for her imagination. Dallas hopes that readers have half as much fun with her books as she does! She has more hobbies than there is space to list them, but is currently working on a doll collection. Dallas writes mainstream novels for MIRA Books in addition to her work for Silhouette, and she loves to hear from her readers. You can write to her at her Web site at www.dallasschulze.com.

Ann Major has written over forty novels for Silhouette Books, many of which have placed on national bestseller lists. She is a founding board member of the Romance Writers of America. She loves to write and considers her ability to do so a gift. Her hobbies include hiking in the mountains, sailing, reading, playing the piano, but most of all, enjoying her family. She lives in Texas with her husband of many years and is the mother of three grown children. She has a master's degree from Texas A&M at Kingsville, Texas.

Raye Morgan has spent almost two decades, while writing over fifty novels, searching for the answer to that elusive question: Just what is that special magic that happens when a man and a woman fall in love? Every time she thinks she has the answer, a new wrinkle pops up, necessitating another book! Meanwhile, after living in Holland, Guam, Japan and Washington, D.C., she currently makes her home in Southern California with her husband and two of her four boys.

Candace Camp
Dallas Schulze
Ann Major
Raye Morgan

small wonders

Silhouette Books

Published by Silhouette Books

America's Publisher of Contemporary Romance

 SILHOUETTE BOOKS

SMALL WONDERS
Copyright © 2004 by Harlequin Books S.A.

ISBN 0-373-21883-4

The publisher acknowledges the copyright holders of the individual works as follows:

TABLOID BABY
Copyright © 1998 by Candace Camp

CULLEN'S CHILD
Copyright © 1994 by Dallas Schulze

THE BABY MACHINE
Copyright © 1994 by Ann Major

THE BABY INVASION
Copyright © 1996 by Raye Morgan

Visit Silhouette at www.eHarlequin.com

Printed in U.S.A.

CONTENTS

TABLOID BABY

Candace Camp

Dear Reader,

I was glad to learn that *Tabloid Baby* was going to be reissued. When I was asked to write a story featuring the birth of a child, the idea for *Tabloid Baby* popped into my head almost immediately (I love it when that happens, as it does all too rarely), and the book was just plain fun to write.

It also turned out to be the first in my A LITTLE TOWN IN TEXAS series, because I fell in love with Beth's family of tall, overprotective brothers and the small town in Texas in which they lived. Beth Sutton's oldest brother, the rancher Daniel, gets his story in *Hard-Headed Texan*, and Quinn, the sexy sheriff, is the hero of *Smooth-Talking Texan*. There are two more brothers and plenty of interesting townfolk, so hopefully I can continue to write about the Suttons and the town of Angel Eye, Texas, for some time to come.

Happy reading!

Candace Camp

Chapter 1

It was not supposed to happen like this.

Beth Sutton scanned the horizon, fighting down panic. It stretched limitlessly all around her, the flat West Texas landscape, dotted with low mesquite bushes and prickly pear cacti. The road beside which she stood bisected the empty landscape, disappearing into the distance like a gray ribbon. She had been standing here for ten minutes, and there hadn't been a car yet.

Another pain gripped her, and she leaned against her crippled car, trying to breathe as she had learned in Lamaze class. *Why hadn't they taught her what she really needed to know now: what to do when you're having labor pains and are stranded in the middle of nowhere?*

The worst of it was, she knew that it was all her own fault. She had been utterly, hopelessly stupid. She had felt two pains this morning, about thirty minutes apart, but after that there had been nothing. She had assumed it was like last week, when she had had a few false labor pains one day and nothing else had happened. Of course, she realized now that it had been foolish to assume it was false labor—and even more foolish to decide to drive into town to get the eggs that she needed for muffins. She understood now—too late—that her sudden burst of energy and the urge to start cleaning and baking were part of the nesting instinct the Lamaze teacher had told them about.

She should have stayed home, should have waited to see if the pains began again. Instead she had driven into town, but as she was returning to the ranch house, a sudden pain had struck her, so much sharper and more severe than the others that when it hit, her hands had jerked on the wheel and the car had wound up in the ditch. So now here she was, miles from anywhere, with her car half in the ditch and one tire blown. Not only that, her water had broken during the accident, soaking her dress. Only a few minutes later, she had had a second pain.

Tears battered at the backs of her eyes. Beth blinked them away. *She had to be strong.* She was all alone, but she told herself that she was used to that. She had always been an independent woman. It was, after all, why she had moved away from the ranch when she was nineteen. She had felt as if she was being smothered by the small town, where everyone knew everything everyone else did, and by her father and three doting older brothers, who were convinced it was their duty to protect her from all life's little bumps and scrapes. She had been living alone in Dallas and taking care of herself for ten years now, and even if she had come back to her dad's ranch for help when she found out she was pregnant, it had been a purely practical move. It did not mean that she was any less capable of taking care of herself.

She drew a calming breath and made herself think. She obviously could not stand there dithering beside an inoperative car and wishing she had brought the cell phone with her. The fact was that she didn't have it; Dad and Cory had taken it when they went out to work on the other side of the ranch today, so that she would be able to get hold of them if she had an emergency. Another fact was that no one had come down this road in almost twenty minutes, and she could easily stand here for another hour before someone did, since it was only a side road.

She took her purse from the car and slung it over her shoulder. Then she set off down the road in the direction in which she had just come. Though it was a good deal farther to the town of Angel Eye than it was to the ranch house—ten miles instead of five—at least in another mile or so she would reach the main highway. While it was not exactly heavily traveled, her chances would be much better of flagging down a ride. She trudged along, refusing to think about the horror tales she had heard about hitching rides. She also tried not to think about how hot the sun was or how thirsty she had become or how far a mile was when one was heavily pregnant and being blasted by pains every ten minutes.

Suddenly there was the sound of a car behind her. It was so faint, and she was concentrating so hard on walking, that for a moment she did not recognize the sound. When it finally dawned on her that she was hearing the purr of an engine in the distance, she whirled and looked behind her, shading her eyes. Sure enough, there was a dark shape on the road. Relief flooded her, leaving her knees so shaky she almost sank onto the ground. She hadn't realized until that moment how tensely she had been holding herself.

As the car drew closer, she could see that it was a large, dark, expensive car, a Mercedes, in fact. In one way, that was reassuring; a Mercedes seemed like the car of a solid citizen, not a psycho serial killer who preyed on hitch-hikers. On the other hand, it also meant that it was not anyone she knew. She could not think of a soul in or around Angel Eye who drove a Mercedes. Just then another pain hit her, and she almost doubled over with it.

The car screeched to a stop beside her, and she heard the car door open and the sound of running feet. She could not look up, could not even open her eyes. It was difficult enough just remembering to breathe right.

"Ma'am? What's the matter?" It was a man's voice, deep and with the faintest tinge of the South in it.

She could see his feet. They halted a few feet from her, then came forward more slowly. "Ma'am?" he repeated, and now, as the pain began to blessedly recede, she could hear the wariness in his tone. "Do you need some help?"

He was close to her now, and the pain was beginning to be almost bearable. She uncoiled from her defensive posture, and for the first time she looked up at him—and found herself staring into the most beautiful blue eyes she had ever seen.

She knew she must look like a fool staring at him, but she could not help it. This was a man who did not belong in Angel Eye, Texas. He wore loafers, off-white linen trousers and a collarless shirt of the same color. It was the sort of casual outfit she had seen on male models in *GQ,* and the clothes suited him to a T. His hair was black, thick, excellently cut and just a fraction too long, giving him a hint of the rebel. His lips were modeled and firm, his jaw strong and his nose straight. A slash of a scar, about an inch long, cut through one of his dark eyebrows and saved his face from perfection.

"Who in the world are you?" she blurted out.

His brows went up at her words, and he replied coolly,

"The man who stopped because you looked as if you were in a great deal of pain."

"I'm sorry. That was rude. I was...just so surprised. I—yes, I was in pain, and I'm extremely glad you stopped." Her hand went instinctively to her swollen stomach. "My car broke down back there."

She turned and pointed and was surprised to see how short a distance she had walked from her automobile. It had seemed like forever. She looked back at him. Those cool blue eyes were still on her assessingly, and Beth realized, embarrassed, how awful she must look: sweating and dusty, her curling red hair, never tame, now blown in every direction by the wind, her stomach huge and pressing against the cloth of her dress.

"I'm sorry. I know this must seem bizarre. But I—you probably guessed. I seem to have gone into labor. Could you possibly take me into town?"

"Of course." He took her arm and guided her toward the car. Beth decided that she must have been wrong in thinking he had been wary a moment earlier. No doubt it had merely been the surprise of finding a woman in this situation.

"Thank you," she said, as he opened the passenger door for her. "This is very kind of you."

He came around and got in on the driver's side. The car started with a smooth purr, and he took off. He glanced toward her and said, "My name is Jackson Prescott."

"I'm Beth Sutton. It's nice to meet you," Beth responded politely. His name sounded faintly familiar, and she wondered if he was someone she was supposed to know. "Have you moved into the area recently?"

His eyes lit up with amusement, and he let out a bark

of laughter. "No. That is, well, I was just looking around. Checking the place out."

"I see." She didn't, really. She supposed he must be considering moving here, and she had the uneasy feeling that his face was one she had seen before. Perhaps he was some politician or well-known businessman or something, someone she should have recognized. It was obvious from the clothes and the car that he was wealthy. A trial lawyer? She supposed he might even be a sports figure—he was tall and well-built, although he didn't have the thickly muscled frame she associated with football. Tennis, perhaps? A swimmer?

At that moment another pain seized her, and she forgot all about Jackson Prescott. Fingers digging into her palm, eyes closed, she concentrated on her breathing.

Prescott glanced over at her. She was in obvious pain and struggling not to show it. There was strength in every taut line of her body. *Beauty and strength.* They were the hallmarks of a Prescott heroine. Indeed, it had become a capsule description in Hollywood to call a gutsy, intelligent female character a "Prescott woman." Looking at her, Jackson felt certain that this woman would someday, someway, work her way into one of his productions.

Her head was back against the seat, and her eyes were closed. Her skin was translucent in the way of some redheads, pale and luminous, with just a sprinkling of light brown freckles across her cheeks. Her mouth was wide, with a full lower lip. Her nose was straight and a trifle short; he suspected that at better moments the combination of the snub nose and freckles gave her face a gamin look, particularly when she smiled. Her hair was a mass of red curls, tied in the back by a ribbon, but a great deal of it had gotten loose and tangled around her face.

Though he could not see them now, he knew that her

eyes were mahogany. He had taken in the detail just as he had taken in all the other details about her. It was part of what made him good, that attention to detail. Another of his assets was his calm, the unruffled attitude that was capable of seeing him through a continual series of crises, and that soothed the frazzled nerves of studio executives and insecure stars alike. It was rare that anyone saw him lose his temper on the set or give way to the gut-gnawing anxiety that dogged every director at one time or another.

But that calm was certainly being tested at this moment. Prescott was accustomed to daily film crises. He was not accustomed to crises being of the life-and-death variety.

He pressed down a little harder on the accelerator, and the speedometer moved up to eighty. It made him feel a trifle queasy to think that he had been tempted not to stop when he first saw Beth Sutton. Fifteen years of living in L.A. had taught him to be wary. Fame had made him even more so.

Of course, he had not driven past her. He could not have ignored the vision of helplessness and pain she had presented, even if it had been on the carjacking streets of L.A. instead of a deserted road in West Texas. However, as he had walked over to her, there had been a niggling suspicion at the back of his mind that this was some sort of setup, a stunt by a would-be actress to meet him, or even one of those bizarre celebrity practical jokes that had been popular on TV a few years back. Then he had seen the panic in her eyes, the remnants of pain on her face, and all such thoughts had fled his mind, replaced only by the instinctive need to help.

He reached the intersection of the highway and turned

right, assuming that the sign pointing toward Angel Eye, 8 Miles was the correct direction. They sped down the road.

"I'm sorry." Beth spoke and Jackson glanced over at his passenger. Her eyes were open again and tinged with the aftermath of pain. Her skin and the hair around her face were damp with sweat.

He raised his brows. "For what?"

She shrugged. "Stopping you. Forcing you to have to deal with this." She fluttered her hand in a vague way.

He smiled faintly. "Don't worry. Don't apologize to me. You're the one who's having to go through this. I'm just driving the car."

Even in the backwash of fatigue that followed her pain, Beth had to smile back at him. There was something quite calming about him, she thought—a sort of sureness, an inner strength that reached out and enveloped her. She could count on him, she sensed, and the thought made her feel stronger.

She sat up straighter. It would be a few more minutes, she reassured herself, before she had to go through that again. "You can drop me off at the sheriff's office in town," she told him.

Her brother Quinn would not be there, of course. He was over in Hammond today, testifying in a district court case. But any of the deputies would take her, sirens blasting, over to the hospital in Hammond. She was, after all, the sheriff's sister, and besides, she had known most of them all her life. But she hated to do it. She didn't like asking favors of anyone, even one of her brother's deputies, and she particularly did not like the thought of having to ride all the way to Hammond with Darryl Hawkes, who apparently had never gotten over his high school crush on her and who, with her luck, would be the very deputy chosen to take her.

But there was little other choice. Cater was out of town, and it would take too long to phone her father and Cory to come in from the ranch and take her to Hammond. Her oldest brother, Daniel, lived just as far out of town. She knew time was of the essence. Already she was beginning to feel the first little twinges that she now knew presaged another contraction.

"The sheriff's office?" her driver repeated, puzzled. "Don't you think you ought to go to the hospital?"

"The hospital isn't in Angel Eye." She frowned and began to do her breathing in preparation for the pang. "It's in Hammond."

"Hammond?" His voice rose a little. "Is that another town? Is that where you're going?"

She nodded and gasped out, "Thirty miles from here." She pointed vaguely east as she tried to stay above the pain.

"Then that's where I'll take you."

Beth nodded again, in too much pain to argue. It would be faster than stopping at the sheriff's office and explaining. Besides, she realized that she would rather have this calm stranger with her than Darryl Hawkes, who would probably drive her to distraction with his chatter as he tried to take her mind off her labor.

"We'd better call ahead—" He reached automatically for his cell phone, then remembered. "Damn! I didn't bring it with me."

He had wanted to be by himself today, away from the people and the distractions. That was why he had insisted on coming to look at the West Texas locations himself, not bringing the assistant director or even his personal assistant. He had been feeling stifled and restless, and he had wanted a day or two of complete peace and silence. So he had left his cell phone lying in his briefcase and set out with only a minimum of clothes, a pad of paper and Kyle's memo about the possible locations for the desert scenes that he had scouted.

"I'm sorry," he said, looking over at her. But her eyes were closed and she was in the midst of her battle with pain.

The contraction subsided before they reached Angel Eye. Beth glanced at her watch to time the next contraction. "Turn left at the stoplight and keep driving till you get to Hammond," she said when they reached the outskirts of the small town of Angel Eye. "The hospital's on the edge of town—on this side, fortunately."

"Will do." His voice was as cool as if they were out for a Sunday drive, but Prescott glanced at Beth anxiously. He didn't know much about labor, but it seemed to him that there had been very little time between her contractions.

He made the turn carefully, not wanting to jar her. "Odd name for a town, Angel Eye."

"Yeah." Beth wiped away the sweat from her forehead with the back of her hand. "Comes from the name the Spanish explorers gave it—Los Ojos de Los Angeles."

"The Eyes of the Angels. Poetic. Referring to the stars, I presume."

"Yeah. They're so bright out here. 'Course, the gringos weren't about to have to say a mouthful like that. They worked the name down to Angel Eye. *Mmmph.*" She let out a muffled noise as the pain started again and glanced at her watch. "Damn! Five minutes."

They were out on a flat, deserted highway again, and Prescott floored it, nerves beginning to dance in his stomach. Five minutes apart sounded way too close to him, particularly when the hospital was thirty miles away.

The contraction left Beth panting, her dress drenched

in sweat. She thought with longing of the ice chips that the Lamaze instructor had said the nurse would give them to chew on in labor. She noticed out of the corner of her eye that Prescott reached over and turned the temperature lower.

"I'm sorry," she said. "You're probably freezing in here."

"No problem." He gave her a slow, reassuring smile. "I've been colder. So tell me, how'd you get stuck in this situation?"

She gave him a wry glance. "The usual way."

A corner of his mouth lifted at her small attempt at humor. *Gutsy.* He liked this lady. "I meant going into labor by the side of the road."

"Stupidity. I was driving back home when I got a contraction, and I went off the road. Got a flat tire. I think I might have hurt the axle, too. The wheel was at a funny angle."

"Is there someone I should notify when we get to the hospital?"

"Yes, if you want to go to the trouble." She looked grateful. "My father. I can write down his number." She glanced around vaguely, and Prescott reached up to his visor, tearing off a piece of paper from a pad there and handing it to her, along with a pen.

Beth wrote down her father's name and the numbers of both the ranch house and the cell phone. Prescott plucked the paper from her fingers and tucked it into his shirt pocket.

"What about your husband?"

"No husband."

"Oh. Well, uh, the father, then. Don't you want—"

Beth let out a harsh laugh. "No, I don't want. He's in

Chicago and he doesn't know a thing about it. And he wouldn't care if he did.''

"Oh."

Her breathing was beginning to sound as if another pain was coming. She put her hand on her stomach and winced. He could see her whole body grow taut. "Damn!"

Prescott knew it hadn't been even five minutes this time. More like three. Surely things weren't supposed to develop this quickly. She groaned, panting. He had never felt so helpless in his life. He was used to controlling things, to making the worlds and people he created move in the direction he wanted. But here, he had absolutely no control over anything.

"I hope Dad and Cory don't come home and go looking for me," she gasped as the wave of pain gripped her.

"Don't worry about them right now. You've got enough on your mind." He looked across at her. Her hands were balled into fists.

He reached out, the only thing he could think of to help, and took her hand. She gripped it gratefully, squeezing it hard as she rode out the pain. When the contraction ended, her hand relaxed in his, but she didn't let go. It felt too good, strong and reassuring, and at the moment she needed those qualities badly.

"Cater was supposed to be my coach," she panted. "But he's gone on a book tour. We thought...we thought it would be all right. I wasn't due for another week. He'll be back the day after tomorrow."

"Your brother's an author?"

She nodded. "Mysteries. Cater Sutton."

"I think I've heard of him." *Hadn't he once optioned a Cater Sutton book? If so, nothing had come of it.*

"Damn! Why did it have to come early?" Beth was

seized with panic at the thought of going into the delivery room by herself. She had counted on having Cater's strong presence by her side. "Cater's the calmest, you see. Quinn—well, he's so easy to fire up. He'll always fight your battles for you, but you can't rely on him to keep everything under control. Daniel's reliable, of course, but everyone knows he can't stand to see a woman in pain, especially his baby sister. Dad's the same, only worse, and Cory's only nineteen." Beth realized that she was babbling, but she couldn't seem to stop.

"It'll be okay." Prescott squeezed her hand comfortingly, feeling inadequate to the occasion. He watched as another contraction gripped her. Her fingers dug into his hand, and he felt her struggle.

"Go ahead. Scream if you want to." It hurt, somehow, to watch her fight her pain.

"I...refuse...to...scream," she panted out, as if it were somehow part of the battle she was waging.

"It's happening so fast," she went on when the pain subsided. "The contractions are coming so close together. I thought I would have more time in between. You know, to sort of gather up my strength for the next one. They kept talking about it taking hours and hours. Now...God, I'm hoping we can make it to Hammond."

Prescott was, too. He was driving too fast for safety. *Where were all the cops?* He would have welcomed seeing flashing red-and-blue lights in his rearview mirror right now. He could feel Beth's rising panic, and it was infectious, but he made himself push down his own uneasiness and keep his voice calm and free of stress.

It was the longest twenty minutes of his life. Beth continued to gabble between contractions, stopping abruptly when the pain seized her and gripping his hand so tightly that her nails dug into his flesh. Jackson held on, trying to impart strength and calm to her; it was all he could do to help. His own nerves were becoming increasingly jangled. It was obvious that her contractions were growing closer together at an alarming rate, until he thought there was no more than a minute between them.

The number of cars on the road increased. There were more billboards, even a building or two. Hope rose in him that they were nearing the town of Hammond. Then, blessedly, right on the edge of town, as she had said, rose a blocky, modernistic white building with the unmistakable look of a hospital.

"Here we are," he told Beth encouragingly. "Just a minute more now."

Beth opened her eyes and looked, and a sob caught in her throat. "Thank God!"

Prescott felt like sending up a few hallelujahs himself. He whipped into the driveway and surged up the long driveway to the emergency entrance. He came to a screeching halt and jumped out, running around to open Beth's door. She was leaning back in the seat, breathing hard, her eyes closed and her face shiny with sweat.

"We're here." He leaned in and unfastened her seat belt, then slid his hands behind her back and beneath her legs and gently pulled her out of the car.

She opened her eyes, murmuring a faint protest as he lifted her up.

"Shh," he said softly, smiling. "Don't spoil my big scene."

Beth gave in gratefully, leaning her head on his shoulder. He hurried toward the automatic doors, which whooshed open before him. Inside, there were three people in the small waiting room, looking bored, and they glanced up with interest at Prescott's entrance. A woman behind a raised, horseshoe-shaped counter looked up, also.

"Can I help you, sir?"

"I need a doctor!" he barked back. "Are you blind?"

"Of course, sir." She pushed a button. "A nurse will be right out. Are you admitting this patient to the hospital?"

"She's having a baby!" His voice escalated to the roar that, though rarely used, sent underlings running.

Fortunately, at that moment, a nurse hurried toward them, pushing a gurney, and he turned toward her. Gently he laid Beth down on the rolling table. The nurse began to take Beth's pulse, asking her questions in a soothing voice. "Now, honey, how far apart are your contractions?"

"If you're admitting your wife to the hospital," the receptionist went on doggedly in her flat voice, "you'll need to fill out some paperwork." She picked up a clipboard stuffed with forms and held it out to him.

"I can't fill that out! Can't it wait? She needs help immediately!"

Beth listened to the bickering, awash in pain and feeling as if she might burst into tears at any moment. She missed Prescott's large, warm hand in hers.

"And she's getting it, sir." The receptionist nodded toward the nurse, who was starting to wheel Beth toward one of the small examining rooms. Then she picked up a pen with an air of resigned patience and held it poised over the top form. "Now, if you would just give me your name, Mr.—"

"Why the hell do you care what my name is?"

"Elizabeth Anne Sutton!" Beth shrieked from the gurney as she disappeared into the examining room. "I'm preregistered, dammit!"

"Oh." The stiff-haired receptionist gave Jackson an exasperated look. "Well, it would have been much easier, Mr. Sutton, if you had simply told me that to begin with. Let's see." She began to type on the keyboard of her computer. "Yes, you are." She pushed another button, and the printer began to click away. Tearing off the sheet of paper, she handed it to him with a practiced smile. "There you go, Mr. Sutton."

"Thank you," he responded with awful politeness. "Now, could you please call this number?" He handed her the slip of paper on which Beth had written her father's numbers. "It's her father. He needs to know that she's here."

"I'm afraid that I can't use the hospital line for—" the woman began officiously.

"Lady." Jackson leaned forward, fixing her with an icy-blue stare that had been known to frighten powerful stars and even studio executives into submission. "You have been a pain in the butt from the minute we walked in. Now, if you don't want everyone in the administration of this hospital, from the top down to your supervisor, not to mention the local press and my attorneys, to be told in great detail of your uncooperative, insensitive, bullheaded, downright inhumane attitude—then I suggest you call this number and very nicely explain to this gentleman that his daughter is here having a baby. Understood?"

The woman nodded mutely. Jackson straightened, taking the hospital printout, and strode away to the admitting room.

He found Beth with a sheet draped over her and a doctor examining her. The nurse had just turned away from a phone on the wall and was saying, "I've called your doctor, honey, and he'll be here in fifteen minutes."

Beth groaned. "I don't think I can make it that long," she growled. The pains were continuous now. She could hardly tell when one ended and the next one began. And now there was this force building in her, this thing that shoved down through her abdomen, demanding release.

She sensed Prescott's presence beside her, and she reached out for him. He slid his hand into hers, and she grasped it as if it were a lifeline. She was scared. She had never thought she would be this scared.

"Just remember to breathe." The nurse began to demonstrate.

The doctor cut in. "She's fully dilated. Get her up to obstetrics. Stat."

The nurse called for an orderly as she shoved the gurney from the room. An orderly appeared and began to roll the cart down the hall toward the elevators. The nurse rushed to push the button for the elevator. Prescott strode beside the gurney, still holding Beth's hand, his heart pounding.

The elevator seemed to take forever to come. Beth squeezed Jackson's hand, letting out a groan, and jackknifed her legs, bracing her feet against the gurney.

"She's bearing down," the orderly commented.

"Don't push," the nurse instructed as the elevator doors opened and they rolled her inside.

"I can't stop!" Beth snapped back.

When the doors opened, they got off the elevator in a rush. Another nurse came toward them, holding out a pile of green clothing with a mask on top. "Here, you'll have to get into your surgicals quick," she said cheerfully to Jackson, "or you'll miss the show."

"What?" He stared at her blankly.

"You have to change," the nurse said patiently, obviously used to dealing with distraught fathers-to-be.

"You have to wear scrubs in the delivery room. So hurry and change."

"But I'm not—"

Beth squeezed his hand tightly, and he looked down at her. "Please..." she said hoarsely. Her eyes were wide and panic-stricken.

"All right," he said and took the clothes. Apparently, he was going to attend a birth today.

Chapter 2

Beth closed her eyes to shut out the sickening movement of the ceiling above her head as the attendants wheeled her down the hall at a trot. Doors banged open, and then they were in a chilled room, bright with lights. There were people and noise around her. Everyone wore green surgical scrubs and masks. They lifted her onto a different table, this one with a back that slanted her up to a half-sitting, half-reclining position. Someone began to put an IV into her arm. A man stopped beside her, looking down at her with kindly brown eyes.

"I'm Dr. Hauser," he told her. "Sorry. Your doctor isn't here yet, but I'm afraid we're going to have to go ahead. You seem to have an eager one there."

"That's fine." Beth was in the grip of the fierce pain again, the force that seemed to be tearing her apart. "I don't care...who delivers it...as long as you do it *now!*"

He smiled, unperturbed, and moved away. "Let's see what we have here."

Beth bore down, the pain ripping through her, panting and almost sobbing. *Where had Jackson gone?* She

wished desperately that he was there. She didn't want to
go through this alone. "Jackson!"

"Right here." His calm voice came from behind her
head, and then he was beside her, taking her hand. A silly-
looking surgical cap covered his hair, and a green mask
hid most of his face, but she could still see his eyes, as
blue as a lake, calm and smiling, and that made her feel
much better. "It took me a while to get into these things.
How are you doing?"

"I'm about ready to kill somebody." She let out a sigh,
relaxing as the intense pain went away. "I'm just not sure
who to start with." She took another gulp of air. "I think
I'm in delivery now."

The pain was vastly different. Much better, she
thought. At least for these few moments of breathing
space, the pain was gone. It was not the constant, unbearable contractions that had plagued her earlier. And
the pain, when it came, had a purpose; it was making her
do something.

A nurse moved around her, handing things to the doctor
and reminding her to breathe. "Bear down," she said
when the pain slammed through Beth again. "Bear
down."

Beth didn't need the instruction. Bearing down was all
she *could* do. She clung to Jackson's hand. He murmured
encouragingly to her, wiping the sweat from her face with
a cool, wet rag. She couldn't really make sense of his
words, but the tone was comforting, something to focus
on in the haze of pain.

"All right, come on, you're doing great," the doctor
was saying. "Just one more push. We're almost there."

It slammed through her again, and then suddenly there
was a blessed release. Beth let out a gasping sob.

"It's a boy!" the doctor announced gleefully, and the
thin wail of a newborn filled the delivery room.

"You did it!" Jackson Prescott beamed down at her, his eyes sparkling with excitement. He pulled down his mask and bent to plant a kiss on her lips. "Congratulations."

"Thank you." Beth was still holding on to his hand, half crying, half laughing in the blessed aftermath of the pain. She gave his hand a squeeze. "Thank you so much."

"Are you kidding? You did all the work."

There was another pain, which the doctor encouragingly told her was the afterbirth. By the time it was over, the nurse was on the other side of her, laying a little bundle, wrapped in a thin blanket, on her chest. Beth's arms went instinctively around the baby, cradling it to her, and she bent her head to it, murmuring gently. The baby was tightened up into a ball, legs hunched up and arms waving around. His face was scrunched up, eyes closed and mouth wide-open. When Beth cuddled him closer, murmuring to him, his tight little body relaxed, and the crying ceased.

"Look. He knows you already." Prescott leaned over them, beaming. He felt almost high with excitement and wonder.

The baby was deep red and wrinkled, wet dark hair plastered across his head, and his eyes were swollen, with bluish patches.

"Looks like he's gone a few rounds," Jackson commented, and Beth chuckled waterily.

"Isn't he beautiful?" she asked, and Jackson agreed.

"Just like his mother."

"Yeah, right." Beth made a face.

But Jackson meant what he had said. It didn't matter that she was sweaty and pale with exhaustion. Beth *was* beautiful, her face glowing as she gazed down at her child.

A nurse stepped in and scooped up the baby, saying, "Now, now, don't worry. We'll bring him back soon. There are just a few things we have to check, and you have a little more to do here." She turned toward Jackson, smiling. "You want to hold him for a minute, Dad?"

"What? Oh. Uh..." The little bundle seemed impossibly small and fragile, and Jackson felt clumsy taking it in his arms. But the urge to do so was far greater than his fear. The baby nestled naturally in the crook of his arm, he found, and he stood for a moment, gazing down into the little red, wrinkled face as if he were viewing the eighth wonder of the world.

Finally, with a smile, the nurse reached for the baby, and with some reluctance, Jackson let her take it. They wheeled Beth first to Recovery and then, since she had been given no anesthetic and was obviously healthy and alert, after only a few minutes they whisked her down to her room. Jackson stayed with her the whole time. They talked and laughed, giddy in the aftermath of the adrenaline-charged experience. They rehashed the events of the morning, chuckling now over the skirmish with the receptionist and the headlong dash to the delivery room. Jackson wondered idly what had happened to his car, left, door open, in front of the emergency room, and they giggled over that, too.

Everything seemed rosy to Beth. Problems did not exist. Even the lingering ache she felt was a minor annoyance, easily borne as she floated on a cloud of euphoria.

It was bizarre, perhaps, for this man was an utter stranger, but at the moment Jackson Prescott was the person closest to her in the world. He had been with her through the most important and intimate event of her life; he had been her rock in the haze of pain. He had shared with her that wondrous moment when they had laid her baby in her arms. It seemed only natural that he stayed with her now.

A nurse brought the baby in, swaddled tightly in a thin blue blanket, and settled him in Beth's waiting arms. The two adults gazed down at the child in awe.

"Look at him," Beth breathed. "Isn't he absolutely perfect?"

"Absolutely."

She pulled the sides of the blanket away, exposing his waving arms and legs. Tenderly she ran her hand down one little arm and tucked a finger into his hand, holding it up to examine each astounding tiny finger and minuscule nail. Jackson bent over the bed, watching with the same kind of wonder as she inspected each finger and toe.

The baby's arms and legs moved ever more frantically. His face started to screw up; then a wail issued forth. Beth looked at him anxiously. Guiltily she decided that he was cold, and she quickly wrapped him back up in the blanket, but that did not stop his cries. She turned to Jackson as if he might have the answer, but he simply stared back at her in consternation. For a moment Beth was swamped with uncertainty. She didn't have a clue what was wrong, and it occurred to her that she was going to be a horrible mother.

Then she felt a sort of tingling in her breasts, a fullness that was not quite pain, and suddenly, she realized what was wrong. "He's hungry."

"Oh." It sank in on Jackson that she needed to breast-feed the baby. "Oh!" He could feel a flush of embarrassment rising in his throat. He almost laughed; he had thought himself incapable any longer of actually blushing. "I—I guess I'll leave now."

Beth felt a little lost. She didn't want him to go. It was awkward. He was a stranger, and yet for the last two hours they had been incredibly close. She wanted to ask

him to come back, yet she knew that she had no hold
on him.

"I—thank you so much. I don't know what to say."
Tears shimmered suddenly in her eyes. "You were my
lifesaver."

Jackson shrugged. "I didn't do anything special. I
should thank you for letting me be a part of it." He
reached out and ran a gentle finger down the baby's soft
cheek. "I've never experienced anything like it."

It was the truth. None of the fancy premieres of his
movies could even begin to compare to this. He knew
studio heads and world-famous actors and actresses on a
first-name basis. He had met the wealthy and the famous,
politicians and rock stars and businessmen. But none of
those people, none of those experiences, had ever filled
him with the sense of awe that he had felt holding Beth's
hand while she gave birth. Nothing had ever seemed as
wondrous as this tiny scrap of flesh in her arms.

The baby made himself known with an even heartier
cry, and Jackson stepped back. "I'd better go."

"Will you come back?"

"Of course!" He smiled. "You couldn't keep me
away."

"Good." Beth smiled back.

He turned away and walked out the door.

A few feet down from Beth's door, the hallway was
blocked by a crowd of enormous men. Jackson stopped,
intrigued. There were only four of them, actually, but as
tall and broad-shouldered as they were, they seemed to
fill the hall. They were all glaring balefully down at one
short, squat nurse, who stood, arms akimbo, facing them.

"Now, blast it!" the oldest of the men said, slapping
a stained, creased Stetson against his leg. "That's my
daughter, and I am going in to see her!"

"Not while she and the father are spending their first time with the baby. We will take the baby out in thirty minutes, when it's visiting hours. You may go in at that time. Until then, you can sit in the waiting room." She pointed toward a small room down the hall.

None of the men even glanced in the direction she pointed.

"The father!" one of them repeated in shocked tones.

"Yes, the father," the nurse repeated, as if they were rather dense. She glanced back over her shoulder and spotted Jackson. "Why, there he is!" Her voice was tinged with relief. "Gentlemen, you can talk to him. He will tell you all about the birth."

With that, she shouldered through the line of men and strode off down the hall. The men all focused on Jackson. They were an imposing group. Their faces were hard, their dark eyes cold and narrowed with emotions ranging from contempt to fury as they looked at Prescott. All of them were dressed in casual Western garb—boots, jeans and sweat-stained shirts—except for the one who was dressed in khaki, with a sheriff's badge pinned to his chest. Jackson was not a short man, standing about six foot one, but all of these men topped him by at least two or three inches. With the heels of their cowboy boots adding to their height, they loomed even taller. One, the youngest-looking, must have been at least six-five. They were, Jackson realized, Beth Sutton's family.

"The local basketball team?" Jackson asked lightly. "You're missing one."

"Cater's not here," the boy responded, as if it had been a serious statement.

"Don't be dense, Cory," the one in the sheriff's uniform snapped. "He's making a joke." He stepped forward, his hands clenching into fists. "No doubt he thinks this is all real funny. Don't you, you little scum-sucking, bottom-feeding, slimy son of a bitch?''

Jackson stared back at him in amazement. "I beg your pardon?''

The others moved forward, too, advancing on him like something out of *High Noon*. Jackson held up his hands in front of his chest, palms out, in a stopping gesture. "Hold on. Wait a minute, fellas. Let me explain.''

"You think you can just get her pregnant and leave her stranded, then come waltzing back into her life when the baby arrives?'' This came from the one with the gray-streaked hair and the most lines in his face.

"I take it you're Beth's father," Jackson began in his calmest voice.

"You're damn right about that. I am also the man who's going to shove that pretty-boy face of yours out the back of your head.''

"I wouldn't—'' Prescott began.

"Yeah, well, I would," said the fourth man, the only one who hadn't spoken yet, and with that he stepped forward and swung, his fist connecting smartly with Jackson's cheek.

Jackson, taken by surprise, stumbled back and crashed into the door of Beth's room. It swung back easily, and he tumbled inside, falling to the floor. Beth let out a shriek, and the baby began to cry. Jackson came up lithely to his feet as the man who had hit him headed toward him again.

"Daniel! Don't!" Beth shrieked.

Jackson punched the man with a short, hard jab in the ribs, surprising him, and followed up on the advantage by grabbing the man's arm and twisting it up behind his back. Hooking his leg across Daniel's shin, he knocked him off balance at the same time that he threw all his weight against him from behind. Daniel crashed into the wall beside the door, and Jackson pinned him there.

For a moment all the other men froze in shock. Then, with a curse, the khaki-clad one started forward. Behind Jackson, Beth scrambled off the bed, laying the baby down on it. "Quinn! Don't you dare! *Daddy!*"

She threw herself into the doorway between the men and Jackson. At that moment the squat nurse came charging down the hall and burst through the men as if she were a linebacker.

"What do you think you're doing?" she snapped. She gave Beth a quick glance and pointed a forefinger at her. "You! Get back in that bed right now. And you!" She turned to glare at Jackson. "Release that man."

Jackson did so, feeling rather like a third-grader who had been caught fighting on the playground.

"Gentlemen—and I use the term loosely—may I remind you that this is a hospital? This woman just had a baby, and I am sure the last thing she needs is to have her family brawling in the corridor like a bunch of yahoos."

"Yes, ma'am," Beth's father answered, and all the Sutton men seemed to find something highly interesting to look at on the floor.

"All right, then, any more outbursts like that and I will have to ask you all to leave."

She took the baby from Beth, cast a last admonitory look around the room and marched off down the hall, shoes squeaking, leaving a much chastened group behind her.

"All right," Beth said in a coldly furious voice. "You three get in here and close the door."

The men, looking disgruntled, shuffled into her room to join Daniel and Jackson. Jackson started to slip away,

but Beth said, "No. You, too. I want you to meet my
family the right way."

With a sigh, Prescott stayed. Beth folded her arms and
gave each of her brothers and her father a hard stare in
turn.

"I can't believe you. Attacking strangers in the hospital!"

"Ah, Beth..."

"What the hell are you doing protecting that sorry—"
Quinn began.

"Shut up, Quinn." Beth shot him a look, and he subsided.

"Now." She took a long look around at her family. "I
would like for all of you to meet the very kind *stranger*
who stopped to help me when my car broke down and I
was stranded by the side of the road. He drove me all the
way into Hammond and stayed with me through the
whole delivery, even though I had no claim on him what-
soever."

"You mean he's not the guy who—"

"No. He's not 'the guy who,'" Beth retorted pointedly.

"But the nurse said..." the youngest one protested.

"She was mistaken, Cory. They all assumed Mr. Prescott was the father of the baby because he brought me in.
We didn't tell them any differently because I was scared
and wanted him to stay with me during the birth. Which
he very kindly did." She cast a significant look at Daniel.
"And he managed to hang in there and not faint, like
some people I could mention when their son was born
sixteen years ago."

Daniel blushed to the roots of his hair. "Ah,
Beth...why'd you have to bring that up? I didn't faint. I
just..."

"Had to leave the room," Quinn, the sheriff, put in,

his brown eyes, so much like Beth's, dancing with unholy amusement.

"Shut up," Daniel told him without heat. "It's different seeing blood when it's *your* wife doing the bleeding. And screaming...damn! I'd rather take a shot to the jaw any day."

Beth cleared her throat ostentatiously. "Now, then, if you guys can conduct yourselves like adults, I would like to introduce you to Jackson Prescott. Jackson, this is my father, Marshall Sutton."

"Mr. Sutton." Jackson, suppressing his amusement at the other men's abashed expressions, reached out and shook the oldest man's hand.

"Mr. Prescott. I can't tell you how grateful I am or how sorry about that—that incident in the hall."

"It's perfectly understandable."

"And this is my oldest brother, Daniel."

Jackson nodded and shook the hand of the man who had hit him, a younger version of Beth's father. Both men were tall and lean, with an impressive set of shoulders and hands roughened from years of hard physical labor. But the resemblance went beyond the similarities of their dark brown hair and brown eyes. There was a kind of stillness, a quiet, in them that wasn't in the other two.

"I'm awfully sorry about that," Daniel said, gesturing vaguely toward Jackson's face and looking embarrassed. "I don't usually lose my temper."

"I know," the redhead added, grinning irrepressibly. "I was real impressed, Daniel."

"The sheriff here is Quinn." Beth cast a smile that was part exasperation, part affection at her quick-tempered brother.

"Sorry. Pleased to meet you." Quinn reached out and shook hands with him. "Thank you for helping my sister."

"I was happy to do it."

"And this—" Beth smiled at the teenage boy with special affection "—is my baby brother, Cory."

"Do you have to call me that?" he protested, but he stepped forward manfully and shook Jackson's hand. "Sorry, sir."

"No problem." Jackson looked up at the towering boy and wondered if he had stopped growing yet. He glanced around at the men. "I'm glad I met all of you. But now I think I'd better go and let you all talk with Beth."

With a nod, he slipped quietly out of the room. For a moment there was an awkward silence. Then Beth sighed and held out her arms. "Oh, you guys. Come here and give me a hug."

She could never stay mad at her family for long.

It had been devastating when her mother had died when she was a teenager, but Beth had managed to get through it with the love of these men. Hardworking, loyal, even a little rough-and-tumble, they had done their best to make sure their little girl had a good life. Their concern had sometimes made her want to scream such as when she was a sophomore in high school and had sat home alone every Friday and Saturday night because Quinn had threatened all the boys at school with the wrath of the Suttons if they tried anything with his sister. But she had never doubted that they loved her or that she could go to any one of them if she was in trouble. It was, after all, one of the reasons she had come home to the ranch when she learned she was pregnant. She had known they would take her in and wrap her around with their rock-hard love.

Finally, after all the hugging was done, her father said, "We called Cater."

"Boy, he was mad as fire about missing everything!" Cory added. "Said he was going to jump the tour and fly down on the first possible plane."

"He shouldn't do that," Beth protested. "He has two more days of it. Besides, it's already over. I'm fine."

"I know, but he's feeling bad because he wimped out and went on the tour," Cory said bluntly.

"Cory!" Beth looked at him reprovingly, but she could not keep the loving light from her eyes. She was close to all her brothers, but she knew that there was a special place in her heart for Cory. Ten years younger than she, he had been only three when their mother died. Beth, at thirteen, had been a little mother to him. The hardest thing about leaving home when she was nineteen had been leaving Cory. "I hope you didn't say anything like that to him!"

"No, but it's what he thinks. And he's right."

"For heaven's sake. He had to go. And we didn't figure it was going to happen this early." She waggled her finger at Cory. "You tell him to stay on that tour and finish it. The baby and I will barely be out of the hospital by the time he's through."

Her father shrugged. "You know Cater. He'll pretty well do what he pleases."

"Mmm." The corner of Beth's mouth quirked in amusement. "So unlike all the rest of you Sutton men."

"I hope you aren't including me in that," Quinn said, grinning. "We all know that *I* am a model of flexibility."

"Uh-huh. Right." Beth rolled her eyes. "Now, tell me. Have you seen the baby yet?"

"Nothing but a glimpse of him when that drill sergeant of a nurse whisked him out of here." Marshall Sutton frowned at the memory.

"Then you'd better get down to the nursery and look at him."

"It's a boy?"

"What else?" Beth answered. "I would probably have

been drummed out of the family if my first hadn't been a boy."

At that moment the door burst open, and a sixteen-year-old boy entered excitedly. "Hey! Hi, Gramps. Hi, Dad. Hey, Cory. Quinn. Aunt Beth. How are you doing?"

"What are you doing here?" Daniel looked suspiciously at his watch. "School isn't out yet."

"They let me out early as soon as Coach Watkins heard about Aunt Beth having the baby."

Quinn shook his head in disgust. "Best spy system in the world," he said. "The CIA ought to come train in Angel Eye."

"It was on the scanner."

"Jimmy." Beth opened her arms, and the boy went to her for a hug. Daniel's son made up the last of her family of men. Daniel's wife had left when James was just a boy, and Daniel had raised James alone. Since Beth had moved back to the ranch, the boy had taken to hanging around their house, confiding in Beth about his teenage problems.

"Have you seen it?" James asked the other men, straightening up from the hug. "It's only about this big." He demonstrated with his hands. "And squalling! Hoowee! Raising hell already."

"It's a 'he,' not an 'it,'" Beth admonished, laughing. "Why don't you take these guys to the nursery and show him to them?"

"Wait. First I want to hear the whole story about how you got here," Quinn said, folding his arms and fixing her with what she called his "cop stare." "Who is this Jackson Prescott guy? Don't get me wrong, I'm grateful to him for stopping to help you. But there was something weird about him."

"Dressed funny," Daniel concurred.

"Just because he doesn't wear cowboy boots and

jeans...'' Beth said disgustedly. ''He dresses very nicely. He's a handsome, sophisticated, perfectly respectable—''

''Who did you say?'' her nephew interrupted, an odd look on his face.

''Jackson Prescott. My car broke down, and I—''

''Jackson Prescott! You're joking, right?'' James glanced around at the others.

''No. What's the matter? You act like you know him.''

''Know him? Well, of course I know him. Everybody does.''

''I don't,'' Daniel said, pointedly.

''Oh, Dad...not you. I mean, anyone who goes to the movies. Except it couldn't be him. What would he be doing in a jerkwater place like Angel Eye?''

''Oh, my God!'' Beth exclaimed, her hands flying to her mouth. Her eyes grew wide. ''I thought I knew that name! I thought there was something familiar about him!''

''You mean it *was* him?'' James gaped at Beth.

''Him, who?'' Beth's father interrupted impatiently. ''What in the devil are you two talking about?''

''Jackson Prescott,'' Beth said numbly. She let out a groan and covered her face with her hands. ''He must think I'm a complete idiot!''

''Oh, yeah!'' Cory slapped his forehead. ''That's the name of the guy who made that movie you and I went to see last month, Jimmy.''

''Right. *Flashpoint*. Also *The Fourth Day*. And *Pursuit*.'' James shook his head in despair at his family's ignorance. ''Jackson Prescott is known all over the world. He's only one of the most famous, most important producers and directors in Hollywood.''

When he left Beth's room, Jackson strolled down the hall, trying to ignore the disapproving gaze of the nurse at the station. Apparently people who got involved in brawls in the hall were not popular here. He stopped in front of the nursery. Baby Boy Sutton lay in a clear crib in the center. He was awake again and obviously displeased. His little red face was screwed up, his mouth wide-open. Jackson couldn't keep the broad grin off his face.

After a moment he turned and walked down to the lobby. The same woman sat at the receptionist desk. It took a few minutes to wangle out of her the information about what had happened to his car, as well as the keys to the vehicle. He was so involved with the bureaucratic struggle that he did not notice that across the room a young woman was staring at him.

"Casey." She jabbed her boyfriend in the side with her elbow. "Casey, look at that man. Do you know who that is?"

The young man with her looked up disinterestedly. "No."

"It's Jackson Prescott."

"Who?"

"The director. *You know*...we went to see *Flash- point*."

Casey turned his head and surveyed her with scorn. "Yeah. Right. A Hollywood director is here in the hospital in Hammond, Texas."

"Well, it could be," she replied defensively. "I just know it's him. Don't you remember those couple of teenage movies he was in before he became a director? I used to watch them on video." Jackson Prescott had, in fact, in his younger incarnation on video, been the focus of her adolescent dreams. *And this man—well, it hardly seemed possible, but it looked like him.*

The woman got up and moved closer, peering around a pillar at Jackson. Her boyfriend, curiosity aroused, followed her. Prescott turned, and she had a full view of his face. "That's got to be him!" she hissed.

Casey, taking in the expensive cut of the man's clothes and hair, was beginning to think that maybe Janine was right for once. This man definitely didn't look as if he came from around here.

Prescott walked out through the front doors. Casey strolled over to the information desk. "Say. Wasn't that Jackson Prescott who just left?"

"No," the woman behind the desk said coldly. "I don't know any Jackson Prescott. That man is Mr. Sutton. His wife just had a baby."

Casey made a noise of disgust and turned away. "See, Janine? It wasn't him."

Janine grimaced and followed him. "It was so. I've seen pictures of him in the papers and magazines."

Hurriedly she thumbed through the magazines on the small table beside her chair, then moved down to the next table. Finally, triumphantly, she returned, holding up an old issue of an entertainment publication. "Here he is. This is an article from last year, when *The Fourth Day* came out. Look."

She held open the magazine, pointing with one long, hot pink nail to a photograph at the top of the article. Her boyfriend stared. "Holy—you're right. That *is* him. But what is he doing here? And why did that lady think his name's Sutton?"

"He's probably going incognito," Janine said knowledgeably. "They do that a lot, you know, famous people."

"Is he married?" Casey asked suddenly.

"No way." She pointed to the article again. "See? 'Hollywood's most eligible bachelor, Jackson Prescott.'" She looked up into her companion's face. "Casey? What are you looking like that for?"

"Just had an idea, Jeeny. Those newspapers like you like, you know, like *Scandal,* they pay for stories, don't they?"

"Oh, yeah. Tons of money." She nodded solemnly. "So they can get an exclusive."

Casey's smile turned predatory. "You know, hon, I think I'm going to go home and get my camera."

"But why?"

"Well, if a man's 'wife' just had a baby, he's going to come back here to see it, isn't he?"

"Yeah. Ooh, Casey, that'd be great, to get his picture."

"Yeah. Great. Especially since I'll have an 'exclusive' about a big shot director who doesn't have a wife but whose girlfriend just had a baby."

Chapter 3

Beth lay on her side, contemplating the vase of twenty-four red roses that sat on her bedside table. The arrangement dominated the table, out of place in the plain little hospital room. Beth had never gotten anything quite like it. The roses were long-stemmed and utterly perfect, each a deep red, and they were set in an elegant crystal vase. Since it had arrived an hour ago, seven nurses and other hospital personnel had popped in to see it. Some of them hadn't even bothered with an excuse.

She turned over the simple, elegant small card that had come with it. It said only, "Jackson." She could not keep a smile from creeping over her lips again. Two dozen bloodred roses had a way of making one smile. Until they had arrived, her day had been less than joyous. The euphoria she had felt yesterday at giving birth had ebbed, leaving behind soreness, pain and a certain sadness. It had been wonderful, of course, when they brought in the baby. There was a kind of bliss in cradling her son in her arms as he nursed avidly that was like nothing she had ever felt before.

But in the middle of the night, when the nurse took the baby away after his feeding, Beth had lain awake, unable to return to sleep, thinking about the loneliness and fear of raising a child by herself. Only a few minutes ago, when she had shuffled down to the nursery, as the nurses kept telling her she needed to, and had stood looking in the window at her baby, she hadn't been able to suppress a pang of envy when she looked at a new mother and father who were looking at their child together.

Impatiently Beth shook her head. She was *not* going to give in to feeling sorry for herself. After all, there were lots of other women who were raising children on their own, and she knew that she was lucky in having the loving support of her family and friends around her. She looked at the roses again and reminded herself that even strangers had been exceedingly kind to her.

A tap on the door interrupted her thoughts, and Jackson Prescott stuck his head inside the room. Beth's spirits rose. "Jackson! Come in."

She gasped, and her hand flew to her mouth as she got a better look at him. There was a blue bruise high on his cheekbone where Daniel had popped him. "Oh, no! I'm so sorry."

He shrugged. "It's all right. I'll live."

"My family really isn't like that usually. It's just that they're so protective of me. I'm the only girl."

"I gather they're not too fond of the baby's father."

"They don't even know him. Obviously, since they thought you were it. All they know is that I'm raising the baby alone, and that's enough to make them hate him."

"I can see their point." He smiled and walked over to the bed.

There was an awkward pause. Beth gestured toward the flowers. "Look. Your flowers came. They're beautiful."

"You like them?" He had been carrying something behind his back, and now he brought his hand around and held out a fluffy white bear toward her. "I brought something for the baby, too. Figured I couldn't leave him out."

"It's beautiful." Smiling, she reached out and took the animal. It was incredibly soft, and she rubbed her cheek against its fur.

He nodded toward a chair in the corner of the room. "I see he's already starting a collection."

Beth chuckled. "Yes." She had had a steady stream of visitors since yesterday afternoon, and it seemed as if at least half of them had brought a little stuffed animal for the baby. "I foresee some serious spoiling going on here."

"He deserves it." Jackson looked down at her. "How about you? How are you doing?"

Beth shrugged. "Not as ecstatic as I was yesterday. I've discovered a few aches and pains I didn't notice then. But I'll be fine."

"A little blue?"

"How did you know?"

He shrugged. "Just guessed. Don't they always talk about postpartum blues?"

"Yeah. But I don't think this is enough to quality for that. I think it's more sleep deprivation. I had the hardest time sleeping last night, and it seemed like every time I'd finally doze off, a nurse would come in with the baby to feed or a pill to give me. Then they woke me up at the crack of dawn to feed me." She rolled her eyes. "I'll be glad to get home so I can get some sleep."

"Well, you're looking good."

"Bless you. I've looked in the mirror today, so I know you're lying, but it's very kind of you to say so."

"No. Just truthful." He smiled.

Beth shifted a little uncomfortably. There was something in his smile that started a strange flutter in her abdomen, a feeling she was sure was most inappropriate for a new mother still lying in the hospital.

Quickly she changed the subject. "Have you seen the baby?"

Jackson nodded. "Yeah. I went by the nursery as I came in. And I stopped by yesterday evening to look at him. I came to see you, too, but you were asleep."

Beth smiled. It pleased her that he had thought of her the evening before, too. "I wanted to ask you something."

"Sure."

"It's about the baby. If it had been a girl, I was going to name it after my mother. She died when I was thirteen. So now, I'm thinking I could name it after my dad, but I always hate to have two people with the same name in a family. Everybody would be calling him 'Little Marshall,' and that's not fair. So I was thinking I'd make Marshall his middle name."

"Sounds good."

"For his first name…well, you did so much for me. I don't know what would have happened to either of us if it hadn't been for you."

"Oh, no." He looked at her with horror. "Don't tell me you're thinking of naming him after me. You don't want to saddle the poor thing with Jackson. Trust me, it's awful. It's caused problems all my life. Everybody's always asking which is your first name and which is your last. This poor kid would have *three* last names—Jackson Marshall Sutton."

Beth giggled. "You're right. That would be awful. But I'd like to, I don't know, acknowledge what you did.

Honor you somehow. What about your father's name? What was it? Would you mind if I used it?''

"It was Joseph.''

"Joseph.'' Beth smiled, and Jackson found himself staring at the way her face glowed. "That's a good name. I like it. Joseph Marshall Sutton. It has a nice ring. Would it be okay with you? I won't use it if you don't want me to.''

"I'd be honored. It's a wonderful name. If you're really sure that that's what you want to name him.''

Beth nodded. "Yes. It's perfect. I've been worrying and wondering what to name him. And the lady from county records has been by twice asking me what I plan to name him. Joseph. Joey. Joe.'' She tried it out, savoring the name. "Joe Sutton.''

Jackson grinned. "I'd say it's an improvement over Baby Boy Sutton.'' He hesitated, then said, "Thank you. I really mean it.''

He could not explain precisely the bond he felt with this baby and this woman. For a brief moment in time he had been connected to them in a way he had never been connected to anyone else. His life had been filled largely with his career until now, and people had perforce taken a back seat. He had had relationships, of course, but he had never thought of marriage, let alone raising a family.

But when he had held Beth's hand during labor, feeling her fingernails scoring the back of his hand and hearing her struggling breaths, almost feeling the waves of pain that came from her, he had been close to her in a powerful and intimate way. When he had heard the baby's cry, it had shaken him. And when the nurse had laid Joseph in his arms, he had experienced a tenderness so profound, a connection so deep, that it had seemed as if the baby actually were his own.

It had been an emotional letdown later when he had realized that he really had no business staying with Beth in her hospital room. He was not connected to her or the baby in any real or important way, not even as close as the men who had crowded into Beth's room yesterday afternoon. He had known that there wasn't any reason for him to hang around today, either, even if he had used the excuse of checking out other locations in the area. He could have looked at them and driven on, he knew, rather than returning to Hammond to spend another night. But he had not been able to leave. He had been drawn back to the hospital and to the nursery, where he had stood gazing at the Sutton baby for at least twenty minutes last night. Nor was he really sure why he had felt the impulse to find a stuffed animal for the baby or to send the roses to Beth.

He had let his assistant in Austin take care of the details of getting the perfect roses delivered, but he had tried to find the stuffed animal on his own. It had been a shock to discover that his selection was pretty much limited to the local discount store. Once he returned to the city, he promised himself, he would find one of those huge lions or elephants or bears, the kind that stood thigh high and were as soft as rabbit fur.

"You stayed in Hammond today?" Beth asked, wondering why the thought pleased her so much. She'd had no interest in men, *any* men, not since that bastard Robert, and this was certainly not the time to start.

He nodded. "I had a few locations around here to check out."

She was aware of a certain disappointment that there was a practical reason for his staying. "Oh. For one of your movies?"

"Yeah. We begin shooting in Austin in two months.

We have some 'barren land' scenes. That's why I'm out here.''

"I see." She paused, then went on, "My nephew Jimmy told me who you were yesterday. I'm sorry. You must think that I'm an idiot for not recognizing your name.''

He smiled, shaking his head. "Actually it was kind of enjoyable. It's good to get away from L.A., get a dose of reality. It's kind of fun to have someone relate to me as a person, not as 'a director.' ''

"I have seen your movies, though," Beth went on. "When he told me, I remembered. And weren't you an actor first?''

He nodded. "For a couple of years. Two teenage movies that made a great deal more money than they had any right making. But I discovered that acting wasn't for me. I wanted to be running the show. Directing, producing.''

"You're obviously quite good at it.''

"What do you do? For a living, I mean. You said something about a ranch house. Is that what you do? Ranch?''

"That's what my father does. He and Cory work the family ranch. Daniel has a horse farm. He runs a few cattle, too, but it's a small operation. But I don't usually live here. I live in Dallas. And I make my living by painting portraits.''

"Really?" He looked amazed.

She nodded. "Yes. You'd be surprised how many people want their portraits painted—or their spouse's or their children's. I've even done a portrait of one lady's dog. It was beautiful, too.''

"So you're good.''

She chuckled. "Of course I am. I've been able to make a living at it for several years. It was a struggle at first, but I do all right now, and it will be a good career for raising a child. My studio's right there at my house. But when I got pregnant, I decided to take a break from it. I didn't think all the fumes I breathe in every day would be good for the baby. And all that standing would have gotten pretty tiring, too. So I moved back to the ranch.''

"You'll return to Dallas?''

"Oh, yes. I rented out my house for a year. When that's up, Joseph and I will go back.''

Jackson found himself wanting to ask about the father of the baby, but he managed to restrain himself. Beth had made it pretty clear the day before that she didn't want to talk about the man.

Soon afterward a hospital volunteer wheeled in the baby in its little rolling plastic cart. "Ready for a visit?''

"Yes.'' Beth held out her hands, her tired expression lightening perceptibly. She gazed at the baby for a long time, stroking his little cheek with her forefinger, letting him curl his hand around her finger, straightening the thin snap top that he wore. "I always have to check him out again,'' she explained sheepishly to Jackson. "Just to make sure he's still perfect.''

"Understandable.'' He leaned closer over the bed.

"You want to hold him?''

"You wouldn't mind?''

"Of course not. I'll have plenty of opportunity to hold him. They'll leave him here for at least an hour. He ought to be getting ready to eat soon.''

"Okay.'' Jackson grinned and reached down to slide his hands under the baby. "I'm an easy sell.''

"So I see.''

Beth watched as he picked up the baby and cradled him against his chest. Jackson bent over Joseph, compelled, as Beth had been, to inspect every detail of his tiny face. He slipped his forefinger beneath the baby's palm and felt the miniature hand grasp his finger. Joe was frowning fiercely, his legs pumping beneath the light blanket in which he was wrapped, and his lips pursed and working as he looked all around in an unfocused way.

"What do you suppose he's thinking?" Jackson asked in an awestruck voice. "Do you suppose he thinks we're all idiots for grinning at him so fatuously?"

Beth chuckled. "I don't think they decide that until they're about twelve or thirteen."

"And nobody's grinning by that time."

Beth watched Jackson smile and talk to the baby. The baby was gazing back at him earnestly. It was a picture that made Beth's heart swell in her chest. *If only someone like this had been her baby's father!* She thought about Joseph growing up, never bonding with a father. She had thought her brothers and father would provide plenty of male role-modeling for the baby, but she could see now that it wasn't the same. There would not be a father who had shared the baby's birth, who would have the same sense of pride, awe and joy that she did.

She sighed. It was useless wishing for something she could not have, and she knew it. Robert Waring would never have been this kind of father, anyway. He was a cheating, sneaky bastard, and she had made the right decision.

Joseph's mouth began to work ever more furiously, and he flailed his arms and legs. By accident his fist landed on his lips, and he sucked it greedily.

"Time to eat, I think," Jackson said, turning and handing the baby back to Beth. "I, uh, I'll go now." No doubt she needed to breast-feed him, and the thought made Jackson feel uncomfortably warm. It was, he thought, peculiar to feel embarrassed at the thought, when he had seen plenty of actresses' bare breasts in any number of shots. Somehow, though, this was very different.

"All right. Goodbye. I'm glad you came back today."

"I have to go back to Austin now." He had stalled here as long as he reasonably could. "I'll be there for two or three more weeks, scouting locations before I go back to L.A. If you need anything, just get in touch with me. Will you do that? We're staying at the Four Seasons." He pulled out a pen and glanced around. Then he saw the small card from the flowers he had sent, and he picked it up and wrote a number on it. "This is my room number there. I'll put your name on the list of callers they should let through. If by chance they screw up and won't put you through, leave a message. I'll call you back. Okay?"

"Sure." Beth took the card, fighting back a giggle. There was something so silly about the idea of such security, as if he were the president or something.

He saw the amusement in her eyes and smiled. "Sure. Go ahead and laugh. You aren't the one who gets calls from every writer and actor anywhere in the vicinity any time you're on location—not to mention all the fans who just want to tell you what you ought to do for your next picture."

"I'm beginning to realize how lucky I was that you stopped."

"I'm always a sucker for a woman with a stomach out to here." He bent and planted a kiss on her forehead in a spontaneous gesture that surprised both of them.

He stepped back, feeling suddenly awkward. Joseph set up a howl.

"All right. I can see he won't wait any longer for his dinner." He turned away, strangely reluctant to leave. At the door he turned back for a last look. "Remember— call if you need anything."

She nodded. "Goodbye. Thank you for everything."
She realized with some astonishment that she was hovering on the edge of tears.

He smiled and waved and was gone.

Of course, Beth had no intention of calling him. Jackson Prescott had done more than enough for her already.
She was capable of doing things herself and, besides, she already had a father and four brothers who were eager to do everything for her.

The hospital sent her and Joseph home the next day, despite her father's protests that it was too soon. Cater, who had left his book tour a day early, was waiting to drive her home in his sparkling blue BMW.

"Cater!" Beth shrieked, momentarily startling the child in her arms into silence.

He bent to kiss her on the cheek, smiling, his dark green eyes warm with affection. "Sorry I missed the main event."

"Don't worry. I had an able substitute."

They talked all the rest of the way home, chuckling over the mad rush to the delivery room and the case of mistaken identity in the hospital corridor. The baby, ensconced in his car seat, promptly fell asleep.

However, he did not remain so. Cranky from the final shots he had received that morning in the hospital, he slept fitfully and cried often. During the next few days, Beth found herself spending most of her time rocking him, feeding him and coaxing him to burp or sleep. She gave her family credit for trying to help her, but they obviously could not feed him, and it seemed that he was already developing a preference for Beth's holding him. Besides, her father and Cory had to work during the day, and they needed their sleep at night. She blessed Cater for taking care of the cooking, cleaning and washing, as well as trying to relieve her of some of her burden with Joseph, but even so, she found herself run ragged.

They were awakened three times that first night by his cries, and though it got better as the days went by, Joseph was still crying to be fed every four hours. Beth had to catch her sleep as best she could in between his feedings. She wondered—panicked—what she would do when Cater went back home to Austin, as surely he was bound to someday.

One afternoon the doorbell rang, and Cater went to answer it. He returned carrying a gray stuffed elephant that had to be at least three feet high. Beth stared at it, then began to laugh delightedly.

"Let me guess. Jackson Prescott."

Her brother looked at the card and nodded. "This thing's huge."

"I don't think Jackson thinks small. He told me he wanted a different stuffed animal for Joseph's room."

Beth went over and stroked the animal. It was plush and soft, even the two tusks. She ran her hands over it and picked it up, hugging it close. She wished suddenly that she could see Jackson. But she knew that was stupid. She hardly knew the man. He just took an interest in Joseph because of what had happened, and no doubt even that would fade with time.

That night Joseph got colic—or so her father pronounced knowledgeably. All Beth knew was that he cried and cried and almost nothing would shut him up. She fed him; she changed his diaper; she walked him; she bounced him; she rocked him. Cory, Cater and her father each tried his hand with him. Nothing seemed to do any good. Joseph occasionally nodded off, but as soon as she laid him down in his bed, he would start to scream again. Finally she gave up and just dozed in the rocking chair, the baby asleep on her chest, and didn't even try to put him to bed. Even that way, however, he slept only fitfully, no more than an hour at a time before his face would screw up and he would begin to wail.

Cory and Marshall went off to work. Cater made her breakfast and tried to take over rocking Joseph. But the baby sensed the change and would have none of it. Beth, bleary-eyed, took the baby back, grinding her teeth. She wondered what had happened to her much-vaunted patience. *Why had she ever thought she would make a good mother?* It was becoming clear to her now that she would in all likelihood go insane after a few more days of this and have to be locked up.

Then, miraculously, Joseph let out a little sigh, burrowed his face deeper against her chest and fell into a deep sleep. Beth sat in stunned amazement, unable to believe that his little body was actually limp in the deep relaxation of sleep. She waited a few more minutes, scared to believe it was real, then tiptoed into Joseph's room. Cautiously she laid him down in his bed, afraid that he would once more wake up and begin to scream, but he was out like a light, and he did no more than let out a shuddering breath and begin to make sucking motions with his mouth.

Beth left the room, closing the door softly behind her and leaned limply against the wall. If anyone wakened him, she thought, she would tear them limb from limb. She walked back into the kitchen, where Cater was rinsing out baby bottles and stacking them in the dishwasher.

Beth collapsed into a chair with a groan. "I'm going to go to bed and sleep for a year."

The telephone rang, and Cater pounced on it. Over the

past few days they had turned off the ringers on all the phones except this one in the kitchen, since it was farthest away from the baby's room, and whenever it rang they all jumped on the nearest phone as if it might explode. The whole world now revolved around Joseph's sleeping habits.

Cater turned to Beth, his brows going up inquisitively. "It's for you. You want to take it?"

She sighed. "Yeah." Friends and neighbors kept calling to ask how she was doing, and she felt guilty for so often trying to get out of talking to them. All she wanted to do these days was sleep.

She took the receiver. "Hello?"

"Elizabeth Sutton?"

"Yes?" She regretted taking the call. It obviously wasn't anyone who knew her.

"This is Julie McCall, with *Scandal*." The speaker's voice went up a little at the end of the sentence, almost as if she were asking a question.

The words made little sense to Beth. What was *Scandal?* It sounded like a perfume.

"I understand that you're the proud new mother of a baby boy," the woman on the other end of the line went on cheerfully. "Congratulations!"

"Thank you." Beth realized that this must be a come-on for some baby product. But what baby product would be named *Scandal?* Maybe she had heard it wrong.

"I wanted you to know that we're very interested in what happened."

Beth could think of nothing to reply to that statement. *What was this woman talking about?* She wished she weren't so sleepy. Perhaps then this conversation would make sense.

"For instance, how did you meet Jackson Prescott?"

"On the road," Beth replied automatically. "I'm sorry. I'm a little confused. Why are you calling me?"

"We're very interested in your story, as I said before, Ms. Sutton. And I imagine that you would enjoy a little extra cash to help out with some of those baby bills, too—unless, of course, Mr. Prescott's taking care of those."

"What?" This whole conversation was surreal. Beth felt as if she were one of those characters in an absurdist play, where none of the conversations made sense. "Of course not. Why would—"

"Well, we here at *Scandal* are prepared to pay you $10,000 for your story."

"My story?" Beth was sure now that the woman was insane—or she herself was. "What in the world are you talking about?"

"Why, the story of you and Jackson Prescott, of course."

There was a long silence. Beth was too stunned to speak. Finally she managed to say, "Are you nuts?"

The woman on the other end of the line chuckled. "No, Ms. Sutton. I'm not. And I'm not joking, either. We would like to publish your story."

"But there's nothing—" Beth shook her head as if to clear it. This whole conversation was making her vaguely uneasy. "No. No, thank you."

"Don't be too hasty. Perhaps I can persuade my editor to give you a little more money."

"I said, *no.*" Beth hung up the phone.

"Who was that?" Cater turned to look at her.

"I don't know. Somebody name Julie Something-or-other from something called *Scandal*. Do you know what that is?"

"Sure. You really have been out of it lately," Cater

teased. "It's a tabloid. You know, 'My baby is a 310-pound alien.' That kind of thing."

"She just offered me $10,000 to tell her my 'story.'"

Cater's straight black brows sailed upward. "What story? 'My baby is a crying alien with colic'?"

A giggle bubbled up out of Beth's throat. "No. I think that's too common. Apparently she wanted me to tell her about Jackson Prescott's rescuing me from the side of the road. Can you imagine?"

He shrugged. "I guess it'd make a fairly interesting story. The human side of a famous person and all that. But it sounds a little tame for a rag like that, I would think."

"But why do they think I would want the story of my delivery in some national scandal sheet?"

"Lots of people would."

Beth shrugged, dismissing the subject. "Well, I'm going to bed now. Don't wake me up unless the house is on fire."

To her astonishment, she was able to sleep for almost six hours before the baby awoke. The awful night of his colic seemed to have been a turning point, for after that, Joseph began to sleep for one good long stretch of six hours each day. At first he had his days and nights all turned around, sleeping during the day and staying awake during the night, but after a couple of days that straightened out. By Friday, two weeks after he'd been released from the hospital, he had awakened Beth only once during the night—about one o'clock—and she had been able to get an almost normal night's sleep. She thought she was beginning to feel almost human again.

She was feeling so chipper, in fact, that after her shower, she put on a bit of lipstick and mascara and tried on some of her prematernity clothes while Joseph lay waving his arms and legs on the bed. She was pleased to find two or three casual, loose-fitting old dresses that looked all right on her. Of course, she still had a few pounds to lose, but she was hopeful that the extra calories she expended daily on breast-feeding would help to take care of that, plus she had managed to fit in the exercises that the hospital had taught her every day—or almost every day.

Beth straightened and regarded herself from every angle in the mirror, smoothing her hand down over her abdomen. She sincerely hoped that little pouch was not here to stay. The worst-fitting part of her dresses, actually, was over her bustline. Her breasts, swollen with milk now, were at least a cup size larger.

The front door slammed, making both Beth and the baby jump. He gave out a little uncertain cry, and she swooped down and picked him up, cuddling him reassuringly. He stopped the beginnings of his wail and simply looked at her.

"Hi, darling." Beth smiled down at him and planted a kiss on his forehead.

"Beth!" came Quinn's roar from the living room. "Where are you?"

"I'm in here," Beth replied tartly, going into the hall. "Would you kindly stop shrieking like a banshee? You're upsetting the baby." She turned away and went into the baby's room to put him down in his crib. Then she walked down the hallway to the den, where Quinn was alternately standing and pacing, fairly vibrating with impatience.

Quinn's face was almost as red as his hair, and his brown eyes crackled with fury. In his hand he held a thin magazine, which he shook agitatedly as he came toward her. "Have you seen this?"

"No. What is it?"

"Lord, Quinn." Cater appeared in the doorway. "What are you yelling about? I could hear you all the way outside."

"Come see."

He thrust the magazine at Beth. She could see now that it was not a magazine but one of the tabloids sold at the checkout counters of grocery stores. Across the top of the front in bright red letters, it read, *Scandal.* Just below that was a headline in bold type: Director's Secret Love Child! Beneath it was a photograph of Jackson Prescott leaving the hospital in Hammond. Beside the photo it read: "Jackson keeps secret mistress and illegitimate son hidden in Texas."

Chapter 4

Beth stared at the cover, blood draining from her face. "Oh, my God."

"Yeah. I found my secretary reading it."

"What is it?" Cater had reached them by now, and Quinn plucked the tabloid from Beth's nerveless fingers and handed it to his brother.

"Holy—" Cater let out a whistle as he perused the cover. "Well, I guess *this* is the story that woman was trying to buy from you the other day."

The phone began to ring, and Quinn went to answer it. "Hello? Yeah, hi, Tina. No, Beth can't talk right now. She's, uh, lying down. Yeah, she saw it. Just now. What? No, of course it's not true! You know how those newspapers are."

He hung up, and almost immediately the phone rang again. "Everybody'll be driving you crazy now," he said and answered it. "Yeah? No, this is her brother. *Sheriff* Sutton. No, she doesn't have any statement to make." He put down the receiver, shaking his head. "Can you believe it? That was a TV station."

Cater opened the tabloid to the article inside and began
to read aloud: "World famous director and producer Jackson Prescott is in Austin, Texas, today, following the birth
of Joseph Marshall Sutton, in tiny Hammond, Texas. Local sources confirm that Prescott, going under the name
of 'Mr. Sutton,' was present at the birth of the baby. Both
baby and mother, Elizabeth Sutton, a statuesque redhead,
are doing fine. Hollywood is all agog at the news. Apparently Prescott had kept the news of his Texas honey
completely under wraps."

"Texas honey!" Beth let out a heartfelt groan. "Cater!"

"I didn't write it, darlin'. I'm just reading it." He continued, "Ms. Sutton told this newspaper that she met the
renowned director while he was on a publicity tour for
his blockbuster movie *Pursuit*."

"I never said that!" Beth protested.

Cater shrugged. "These guys are not known for their
concern with accuracy. Didn't you say something to that
lady about meeting him on the road?"

"Well, yeah. She asked me where we met, and I told
her 'on the road.' I didn't say he was on a publicity tour."

"I guess they figured that was close enough."

"Where did they get this stuff?" Beth moaned. "How
did they even hear about my having a baby? Or his being
there?"

"Probably from him," Quinn said.

"Jackson? Don't be ridiculous! He wouldn't want
something like this spread all over the tabloids."

Quinn made a noise of disgust. "He's from L.A. Those
movie people will do anything for publicity. They don't
care if it's good or bad, just so long as it gets their name
in front of the public. Hell, they hire publicity guys just
to make sure they *are* in the media."

"I don't believe it," Beth replied staunchly. "He was so nice."

Quinn pulled a cynical cop face. Beth turned toward Cater, who shrugged.

"I don't know," Cater admitted. "They got the news somehow. They certainly didn't get it from us. Who else knew that he was Jackson Prescott and that he was in Hammond with you?"

"Well, if it was him, surely they would at least have gotten the facts straight!" Beth said pointedly. "Maybe somebody recognized him at the hospital. After all, someone shot that picture of him. That had to be the day it happened or the next day."

"You think someone just happened to be hanging around the hospital with a camera who saw him, knew who he was and took a picture?" Quinn asked sarcastically.

"He certainly didn't take it himself!" Beth snapped.

"He could have called and gotten one of his guys down there from Austin to take the shot. That's probably why he hung around an extra day and came back to see you."

Quinn's words stung. Beth planted her hands on her hips pugnaciously. It had always been Quinn with whom she had the worst fights. Whenever they got into one of their flaming arguments, the others would turn away, saying, "The redheads are at it again."

"So you think that's the only reason a man would come visit me a second time?"

"I didn't say that." Quinn backtracked, realizing he was treading on dangerous ground. "But think about it, Beth. You had a stomach out to here, and you were in labor. Do you really think he came back because of your looks?"

"Not *all* men are solely interested in a woman's looks. Just macho, chauvinistic—"

"Don't start in with me on that," Quinn warned. "You know that's not what I meant."

"Oh, yeah? Just what *did* you mean, then?"

Cater chuckled and folded his arms, waiting for Quinn's reply with an air of expectation. "Yeah, Quinn, I'd like to hear you get out of this one."

Quinn cursed. "Ah, hell, Bethie, you're just too nice. You believe everybody's good. I don't know that it was Prescott who leaked it. Maybe he *is* a wonderful guy who would never stoop to getting publicity like that. But it's the most obvious choice."

"He came back because he liked Joseph," Beth said stubbornly. "I don't fool myself that he fell for me. But he did fall for the baby. You didn't see him holding Joseph. I did."

"Okay. Okay." Quinn held up his hands in surrender. "The man's a saint."

"I didn't say that, either. Honestly, Quinn, you're as bad about twisting my words as that—that paper!"

Beth took the tabloid from Cater's hands and studied the article. There was little else there. It wasn't surprising, Beth thought, since they had so little to go on. She sighed and handed the newspaper back to Quinn.

"What should I do? Call them and demand a retraction? Threaten to sue?"

"Well…the article doesn't actually say that Joey is this Prescott guy's baby," Cater replied thoughtfully. "All it really says is that he was present at his birth, which is true. It calls you statuesque—no argument there—and says you met him on his publicity tour, which is false, but I'm not sure you want to even get tangled up in a telephone call with them over something as minor as that. There's no telling what else they might trick out of you and twist around for another story."

"But what about the front page? That says that Joseph is his. Doesn't it?"

Quinn and Cater studied the front. "It implies it, sure. It says director's love child right next to a picture of Prescott leaving the hospital. But it doesn't actually say that the director who has the love child is Prescott. I don't know. The thing is, they're used to being threatened all the time by pretty powerful people. They look on lawsuits as part of the cost of doing business. I don't think you're going to scare them with the threat of a suit. Are you willing to actually sue?" Cater asked.

Beth thought of the ordeal of a trial and all the attendant publicity. She shook her head reluctantly. "No. This is bad enough. It just makes me mad, though, to let them say stuff like this and not take any action."

"I know. I'll call them if you want me to," Quinn offered.

"I don't think a sheriff in Texas is going to scare these guys." Beth sighed. "I guess the best thing to do is just to keep quiet and let it all blow over."

Days later, Beth would think back to her words and shake her head over her naiveté. The thing had not blown over at all. They had been deluged by phone calls from more tabloids and several members of the legitimate press, as well as from almost everyone they knew. Even friends of Beth's from Dallas called up to ask her if the story was true. Her father had finally had to give in and buy an answering machine, which he hated. But even worse was the fact that a reporter from one of the tabloids, *The Insider,* showed up at their front door one day.

He came back several times, until finally Beth's father met him at the door with a shotgun and a scowl and pointed out to him that he was trespassing on private property, and that the next time he did so, the sheriff would personally be out to escort him to jail. After that the obnoxious man took to sitting on the side of the road at the entrance to their land, waiting for Beth to come out. As a result, she stayed in the house until she could stand it no longer and finally decided she was going to go stir-crazy, so she set out for the grocery store. Within twenty minutes she was back, muttering imprecations on the man's head.

"I'm trapped!" she exclaimed, as she walked into the kitchen and slammed her purse down on the table. "Trapped! I can't go anywhere or do anything without that guy *stalking* me!"

She walked into the den, where Cory was sitting in the rocker, the baby in his lap gurgling and spitting. Cory was leaning over him, making faces and cooing. "Hi, Beth. I swear, I didn't wake him up. He just started hollering a few minutes ago."

Beth had accused Cory yesterday of tiptoeing into the baby's room to see if he was awake in order to wake him up so he could play with him. He wore a look now of such virtuous innocence that Beth had to smile. "It's okay. As long as you changed his diaper and didn't save it for me."

Cory assumed an even more saintly expression. "I certainly did. It was a stinker, too." He turned his attention back to the baby. "Wasn't it, Joey?" He bent down to rub his nose against the baby's, dissolving into baby talk.

Beth turned away, smiling at Cory's obvious infatuation with Joseph. Cater, sitting on the couch, feet propped up, smiled back at her. "Looks like you've got a permanent baby-sitter."

"At least until he goes back to college." She let out a sigh and plopped down on the couch beside him.

"Rough day?"

She nodded. "That *Insider* reporter followed me all the

way to the grocery store, and when I got out in the parking lot, he came running after me, asking all these questions. I realized that if I went inside, everyone in the whole store would be staring at me, with this guy pursuing me. So I just got back into my car and left.''

She did not add that she had been fighting a bluesy feeling for the past two or three days—or that she kept wondering why Jackson Prescott had not contacted her since the arrival of that stuffed animal ten days before. She supposed it was foolish to feel so bereft—after all, she hardly knew the man. Sure, he had been nice when he was caught up in the emotional aftermath of witnessing Joseph's birth. But it stood to reason that he would cool off after a few days. She had no real place in his life, and it was natural that he would more or less forget about her. Such reasoning, however, only served to make her feel even bluer.

"I'm afraid I'm not going to make you feel any better," Cater said, picking up a tabloid from the table beside him. He tossed it into her lap. "This is what you would have found if you *had* gotten inside the store."

It was yet another tabloid, this one emblazoned with the words "Family Feud—Prescott And Suttons Brawl In Hospital!" Beneath was a fuzzy close-up of Jackson Prescott, a bruise clearly visible on his cheek.

"What!" Beth sat up with a shriek. She tore open the paper and began to read. It was an account of a major brawl in the corridor outside Elizabeth Sutton's hospital room. "Oh, my God, it makes it sound like you all jumped him and beat him to a pulp."

"Mmm."

"It even mentions Quinn by name and says he's the sheriff! Oh, no! He'll be furious!"

"Doesn't look too good for a county sheriff to be brawling," Cater agreed.

"I can't believe they wrote this! It's so untrue, so unfair. Oh! I'd like to get my hands on that Julie Whatsis... Where do they get this stuff? How did they find out?"

"Probably someone at the hospital. You've seen how willing the paper was to grease palms."

"But this isn't what happened. That nurse saw that Daniel just hit Jackson once, and then it was all over."

"It sounds more sensational this way."

"Yeah—it's a lot more sympathetic to Prescott, too," Cory added.

"You're saying it was Prescott who told them? You don't know that. It could have been anyone at the hospital."

Cory just looked at her, and Beth flushed. *Why was she clinging to the thought that Prescott had not let the story leak to the press?* She jumped up from her seat. "Okay. Let's just call him and see."

"Call who? Prescott?" Cater asked.

"Yeah, right," Cory said sarcastically. "Like you can just ring up his hotel and they'll put you through."

"He told me I should call him. He gave me the number. He said he would put my name on a list." She charged into the kitchen, opened her purse and pulled out the card Jackson had given her. Then she marched to the phone and rang the number.

When the hotel operator answered, Beth identified herself and asked for Jackson. There was a moment of silence. Then the operator said, "I'm sorry, ma'am, Mr. Prescott is not accepting phone calls."

Beth's stomach clenched. "He—he said he put my name on a list of approved callers. Did you check it?"

"Yes, ma'am. I'll check it again." She spelled Beth's last name questioningly and when Beth agreed that that was the spelling, she finished, "No, ma'am, I'm sorry, but I do not have your name on that list."

"Oh." Beth hung up the phone with suddenly nerveless fingers. *He had lied to her! He had told her that she could call him and acted as if he were concerned for her, and all the time it had just been an act.*

She stood for a moment staring at the kitchen wall, then slammed her fist down on the counter. "Damn him!"

She marched back into the den, her face pale and her eyes blazing. "I'm going to Austin."

"What? Why?" Cater and Cory stared at her.

"Because I'm going to find Jackson Prescott and tell him exactly what I think of him."

"Uh, Beth..." Cater rose to his feet. He had had some experience with his sister's hot temper. "Do you think that's a good idea?"

"Yes. I think it's a wonderful idea. It is exactly what I'd like to do."

"Are you sure you feel up to it?"

"I feel fine. It's been three weeks since I had Joseph. And having a baby doesn't exactly make you an invalid."

"No, but...what about the baby? You can't just leave him here while you run off to Austin. That's at least a six- or seven-hour round-trip."

Beth made a face. "Of course I'm not leaving him. I'll take him with me."

"You're going to cart the baby around with you while you track down a celebrity?" he asked skeptically.

"Fine. You come with me if you think I'm so incapable of managing on my own. Cory, too. You all can take Joseph back to your house while I locate Jackson Prescott."

"Beth..."

"What? Are you coming or not?"

Cater sighed. "Of course I'm coming."

Cory jumped up. "Me too." He grinned. "I wouldn't miss this for the world."

They left the ranch by the back road, then drove the three hours to Austin, going first to Cater's house in a quiet old section of Austin, where Beth fed the baby, then left him with Cory and Cater, adamantly refusing to take either one of them with her. "I am *not* taking one of my brothers with me, as if I can't handle it on my own."

She took Cater's car and drove to the Four Seasons hotel. She suspected that Cater had hoped that her anger would cool off on the drive over and that she would give up on her idea to confront Jackson Prescott, but it had not. She had spent the whole time fuming over what he had done, stoking her fury with memories of his kindness toward her and his apparent affection for Joseph, which made his betrayal all the worse.

She marched into the elegant hotel and asked at the desk for Jackson Prescott. Predictably she was told he was not available. Beth had expected this, and she found a comfortable chair in the lobby from which she had a clear view of the front doors and sat down to wait for him.

She had been there almost two hours when Jackson walked through the front doors with two men and a woman, all of them dressed in typically casual Austin summer wear. Beth jumped to her feet, a ball of anger and anxiety swelling in her chest. She strode over to the group purposefully. They turned, sensing her approach. One of the men took a step forward, putting himself between her and Jackson.

"Hold it right there. We got a restraining order against you reporters. Remember?" he said flatly.

"Jackson." Beth stopped, her voice even but carrying. "Are you going to talk to me, or are you going to have your goon toss me out?"

It had taken Prescott a moment to recognize the tall, attractive redhead striding toward him. She was slender, and now that her features were no longer pale and drawn with pain, all the promise of her strong facial bones had come blazingly to life. Her hair curled riotously around her face, full of life and color. For an instant he had thought she was an actress or model hoping to talk her way into a part in his movie.

Despite the anger he had been harboring toward her since the *Scandal* article came out, he could not suppress the leap of instinctive physical appreciation inside him. Nor could he keep his lips from twitching with amusement at her words.

"He's not a goon, Beth. He's my assistant director. It's okay, Sam. I'll take care of this."

He moved around his AD, reminding himself why he was angry with her. Beth, looking at his cold, set face, wondered why she had ever thought this man was warm and kind.

"I found out how much your word is worth," she began, pulling out the card he had given her and ripping it in two. " 'Just call me if you need anything,' " she mimicked savagely.

"Sorry," he replied in a voice that made it clear he did not mean the word. "I figured you had already gotten plenty out of me."

His words slammed into her like a fist, hurting more than she would have thought possible. Beth blinked back the tears that started in her eyes. "Excuse me for taking up any of your precious time just because I was in labor."

He snorted. "Don't try to turn the tables here. I'm not talking about taking you to the hospital, and you know it. I am talking about your turning me ov—"

But Beth paid no attention to his words, sweeping on in her rage, "How could you do this to me? How could you be this low? To take my life and turn it into some sideshow so you could get a little extra publicity! Quinn tried to tell me, but I thought I knew you. I told him you

would never be that cold or calculating, that you weren't
the sort to sell someone out—''

"What in hell are you talking about!'' Jackson snapped
back. He had been disappointed and unexpectedly hurt
when the story came out, but he had lived too long in
Hollywood to be surprised or enraged that Beth had
turned his helping her to her profit. But now, facing her
and her anger, he found his own fury springing to life.
"If you want to talk about selling someone out, what
about what you did to me? Did you honestly expect me
to take your calls after what you'd done? Were you hoping to find out a few more juicy tidbits to feed the press?''

"Uh, Jackson...'' The AD sidled closer, glancing ap-
prehensively around the lobby, where faces were turning
to stare at Jackson and Beth, drawn by the loud, angry
voices. "This is a little public....''

"What do you care?'' Beth shot at him. "I figure the
more public, the better for you guys. After all, it will
mean more precious publicity for your movie.''

Jackson, however, heeded the other man's warning. He
clamped his hand around Beth's upper arm and started
toward the elevators. "We'll finish this upstairs.''

"I don't want to go upstairs with you!'' Beth retorted.

"I realize that you prefer to make a public spectacle
of yourself.'' Jackson jabbed the Up button of the elevator
furiously. "But you are not going to use me to do it. If
you want to talk, we will do it in private. If not, get out
of the hotel.''

Beth faced his level gaze and knew that he meant what
he said. No doubt he would call security if she refused to
go with him, and they would toss her out ignominiously.
That would give those nasty tabloids a real field day.

In response, she jerked her arm out of his grasp and
turned to face the elevator doors in silence. The silence
continued between them after the doors opened and they

got on. Upstairs, at his luxury suite, Jackson stuck his key card in the door and stepped back for Beth to pass into the room before him. He followed, snapping the door closed.

Beth marched across the spacious sitting room to the windows at the far end. She stood for a moment, staring out at the view of Town Lake. Jackson, who had struggled to bring his fury under control on the ride up, walked halfway across the room and stopped, arms folded across his chest.

"All right," he began tightly. "What are you here for? If you expect me to pay you to stop the stories, you're dead wrong. I don't bow to extortion."

"Extortion!" Beth gaped at him, his words startling her out of her anger momentarily. "You're accusing me of extortion?" The idea was so absurd that she almost laughed. "Are you nuts?"

"No. And you can stop the histrionics, too. They're not going to convince me to pay you, either."

Her fury came flooding back at his words, so much so that she trembled under the force of it. Her hands itched to slap him. "How dare you! How dare you accuse me of asking you for money? After what you've done to me and my family? Do you honestly think you can scare me off with this talk of extortion?"

"I am not trying to scare you, Miss Sutton." Prescott struggled to keep his voice under control. He disliked this woman intensely, all the more so because he had liked her a great deal when he met her. It made him even angrier that seeing her now—her eyes bright and her cheeks flushed with rage, her body fairly vibrating—his body was responding to her in an unmistakable and very masculine way. He wanted to shake her, and at the same time, he wanted to kiss her, and that fact made him boil.

"I'm merely telling you the truth," he said carefully.

"The money you got from the tabloids is all you're going to get."

"What are you talking about?" Beth took an involuntary step toward him. It required all her self-control not to rush at him, screaming and scratching. "What money? All I've gotten from the tabloids is grief, and you know it!"

"You mean you were foolish enough to talk to them without getting paid?" Prescott quirked an eyebrow in an infuriating way. "No wonder you're coming to me now."

"I am not here for money!" Beth shrieked. "What is your problem? Don't you understand English? I *do not want* any of your filthy money. I wouldn't take it if you offered it to me. You are a lying, treacherous, backstabbing son of a bitch, and I hope you choke on your money."

"Then why did you come here?" Jackson moved forward, his eyes bright with anger. His brain was filled with pictures of grabbing her by the shoulders and shaking her until she stopped her crazy, circuitous, infuriating talk— and immediately after that, kissing her until she melted against him, weak and repentant. Jackson pushed down the primitive need and asked curtly, "Did you expect me to welcome you with open arms?"

"I don't expect anything of you. Not anymore. I just wanted you to know what I think of you. I wanted to tell you what a snake you are."

Beth hated him. She hated his smug, handsome face, hated his calm control in the face of her own livid anger. She wanted to sink her hand into that thick dark hair and pull. And as she pictured that with great delight, she pictured him jerking her up hard against his body and bending down to kiss her. The rush of pure, unadulterated lust shocked her into silence.

"Dammit!" Jackson slammed his fist down on the long

table beside him, making the lamp shake. "What the hell are you talking about? You went to the tabloids and told them that—that *dreck,* and now you're accusing *me* of being a snake? You have a lot of nerve. Or are you just insane?"

For a moment Beth could not speak. She stared at him, dumbfounded, as his words sank in. Finally she croaked, "Are you serious?"

Now it was his turn to stare. "What? Yes, of course I'm serious."

"You think—you honestly think that *I* went to the tabloids?"

"Well, of course. Who else? *I* certainly didn't run to them saying that I was the father of an illegitimate child by a woman I had kept secret in a little town in Texas!"

Beth pressed the palms of her hands against her temples. She wondered if she were in a madhouse. Jackson, watching her, felt his anger draining away. It occurred to him that perhaps she really *was* mentally unstable. Wasn't there some woman who had claimed postpartum insanity as a defense for killing someone?

"I did not tell the tabloids anything," Beth growled. "It had to have been *you.* You did it for the publicity."

Jackson let out a noise of disbelief. "After all the time I've spent avoiding those vultures, you're saying that I voluntarily told them this libelous stuff?"

"Well, *I* didn't!"

"Don't try to pull that on me," Jackson said in disgust. "*Scandal* called my publicist for verification of your story. That's the first I heard of it. My publicist denied it, of course. Then he called me and asked who the hell in Texas would have given *Scandal* a story about my having a baby in some backwater town there. He said they told him they had bought it from a woman in Texas, and that she had backed it up with pictures."

"It wasn't *me!*" Beth had a sick feeling in her stomach that she had been terribly wrong.

"That very first story quoted you as saying you met me when I was touring for *Pursuit.*"

"I didn't say that!" Beth protested. "That Julie Whatever called me and started asking questions. I didn't know who she was. She asked me how I met you, and I said, 'on the road.' She surprised me so much that I just answered automatically. But that's all I said. I didn't even know about your touring for *Pursuit.* Then she offered to pay me $10,000 for my story, and I hung up on her. The next thing I knew, there was this story about my giving birth to your son splashed all over the front page. Quinn said you had probably given them the story for the publicity, but I said, no, you wouldn't do that. Then that Carrigan guy—"

"Who?"

"The man from that other magazine, *The Insider,* the one who's been hounding me for the past three or four days! He told me that he had talked to you and wouldn't I like to give my side of the story? But I still thought they were lying, that you wouldn't do that to me. Then today Cater brought home another one of those tabloids, and it had an article about your fight with my brothers at the hospital. It had a picture of you with the bruise on your cheek, and it made it sound like they all jumped on you and beat you up. Well, it was pretty clear where they had gotten such a slanted story. But I still didn't want to believe it, so I called you to ask you about it, and I found out you hadn't put me on a list for my calls to be accepted, like you said you would. Naturally you wouldn't want to hear from me after you had done this to me."

Jackson stood for a long moment, looking at her. "I did nothing to you."

"It didn't look that way!" Beth snapped. "It looked

like you had casually ruined my life—told the world I had an illegitimate child, held me up to public ridicule, sicced all those newspapers and magazines on me. How you could have believed that I would do that to myself! To my family!'' She turned away, then swung back as a new thought hit her. ''How could you have thought I would do that to you? After the way you helped me, if I had sold some tabloid that lie, I would have had to be the lowest, most despicable person ever! How could you think that of me?''

''Over the years, I have discovered that people are capable of almost anything, especially where money and fame are involved.''

Beth shook her head. ''I would hate to see the world the way you do.''

She walked past him toward the door. Jackson turned, watching her, and as she opened the door, he said, ''No, wait. Don't go.''

Beth hesitated, then let the door close and turned back to him. He crossed the room until he stood directly in front of her, gazing down into her eyes. ''I'm sorry. I— I didn't want to think badly of you. When David told me, my immediate reaction was that it couldn't have been you. I didn't want it to be you. But, you see, I knew it wasn't me or my people, and it made sense that it was you. And when they said they'd bought it from a woman in Texas...well, it seemed pretty obvious. I wasn't surprised. Nothing that anyone could do anymore would surprise me. A few years ago a woman claimed that I had fathered her child when I had never met her in my life. She was trying to get money from me, figuring I would buy her off rather than go to court. I had a business partner I trusted—he was a friend, as well—who embezzled money from our business for months. One of my friends was stalked by some guy for almost two years. He said that my friend had stolen a movie idea from him. He also thought that Nazis were hiding out in his attic. People are crazy. They're greedy. They seem to be willing to do almost anything just to get themselves in the news. I'm sorry, but it is easy for me to believe that someone would sell me out to a tabloid, even someone I liked.''

He paused, then added, ''And I did like you. But I've learned that trusting someone just because you like them is a good way to get burned.''

''I understand. I guess it's easier not to be rich and famous.'' Still, she could not completely get rid of the little pang of hurt that came from realizing how despicable a person he had believed her to be.

He must have seen it in her eyes, for he reached out and took one of her hands between both of his own and said quietly, ''I'm sorry.''

''Then do you believe me now?''

''I suppose you could have made this whole thing up.'' Looking into her eyes, he knew he didn't believe that at all. ''But I don't think so. I believe you.''

He had not let go of her hand, and he raised it to his lips now and kissed her knuckles softly. Beth felt a quiver dart through her. Her hormones, she thought, were absolutely, utterly out of control. A few minutes earlier she had been consumed by rage; now she was getting all weak in the knees over the merest kiss.

''I apologize for doubting you,'' he went on. ''And I apologize for blocking your call.'' He smiled.

Beth pulled her hand away from his. This man's smile had entirely too much effect on her.

''How about you?'' he asked. ''Still think I'm the one who gave the story to the tabloids?''

''No.'' She paused. ''But how did they get the story? I mean, if neither of us told—and I'm positive that no one in my family would have—then who did?''

He shrugged. "Someone who saw me at the hospital and recognized me, I guess."

"But how did they come up with all that other stuff? About Joseph being yours?"

"Maybe the rag just made that up. Or they could have interviewed someone at the hospital...the nurses there thought I was the father. After all, that's where they must have gotten the story about the fight. No doubt gossip had amplified it, and the tabloid probably sensationalized it, too. Their version was wilder and more interesting than the truth—which, unfortunately, is why they print things like that instead of bothering to get the facts."

Beth stood for a moment. She didn't know what else to say, and there was really no reason to stay any longer. Yet she did not want to leave. "Well..." She glanced toward the door. "I better go now. Cater and Cory will be waiting to hear whether they have to bail me out of jail for attacking you."

Jackson smiled slightly and reached out a hand, taking her arm. "Don't go. Why don't you stay and have dinner with me?"

"I'd like to, but I have to be back to feed Joey in two hours." She smiled ruefully, realizing how very far away her world was from this man's. "I'm sorry. I'm afraid I don't live a very glamorous and exciting life."

"You would be surprised at how unglamorous and unexciting my life is," he responded. "We could eat now, if it's not too early for you. I didn't have any lunch, so I'm starving."

"Me either." She had been too consumed with getting to Austin and confronting Jackson to stop and eat. "That'd be great, if you want to." She hesitated. "Will there be a picture of us eating in the papers this week?"

"Surely that wouldn't rate high enough on the excitement scale. But if you want to, we can have it here in the

suite. That's what I usually do." He smiled. "You can
see exactly how exciting my life is."

"Mmm. Sounds like you're almost as much of a shut-
in as I am. Today is the first time I've been off the ranch
since Joey was born."

In the end, they decided to go downstairs and eat. Jackson's earlier companions were eating at another table in
the hotel restaurant, and they cast surprised glances at
Jackson when he walked in with Beth. He grinned at them
and held Beth's chair for her.

"They'll be eaten up with curiosity," he told Beth, a
mischievous glint in his eye. "I suspect that by now
they've copped to who you are. Now they're wondering
whether the story about Joseph is true, after all."

"You going to tell them?"

"I don't know. I may let them stew for a while. It will
be interesting to watch them maneuvering to find out."

They spent most of the time talking about Joseph. Jackson wanted to hear the details of his progress in the past
three weeks, and Beth was more than happy to supply
them. She reflected that she would never have believed
that she would be sitting here with a world-famous producer and director, telling him about her baby's smiles
and weight gains. But it did not feel odd; Jackson was
perhaps the easiest person to talk to that she had ever
met—or, at least, easy for her. She felt, in a way, as if
she had known him for years. On the other hand, she was
also aware of a little sizzle of excitement in her gut that
reminded her that she didn't know him at all, that he was
drop-dead sexy, and the first man that she had felt the
slightest interest in in eight months.

"What about you?" she said after a time, smiling
sheepishly. "Here I've been going on and on talking
about the baby. You haven't had a chance to get a word
in edgewise."

"I like hearing about Joseph. And what about me? I have nothing exciting to relate. Just days of setting things up for filming, of looking at locations and talking to people, hiring people, signing contracts. It's the part I like least about a film. When we actually start shooting is when I begin to enjoy it." He did not add that he had not intended to stay in Austin this long, that he had lingered, overseeing things that his assistants usually handled, just because he had been restless and reluctant to return to L.A. Sitting here now, looking at Beth, he wondered if he hadn't been subconsciously hoping that she would show up.

"And when will that be?"

"I go to L.A. the day after tomorrow. Then we'll be back in Austin in six weeks to begin shooting. After a couple of weeks here, we move out close to you for the barren land scenes. That's to accommodate one of the actor's schedules. After that, we return to Austin for another month or so."

"Close to us? Really?" Beth could not stop the pleased smile that spread across her face.

"Yeah. The location I was scouting the day I met you." Another thing that Jackson had chosen not to examine too closely were his reasons for deciding that the locations thirty and forty miles from Angel Eye were much better than the ones Sam had found two hours away from the town.

"That will be nice. Will you come by and see us? Maybe *The Insider* won't be camped on our doorstep by then."

"Yeah. I'll come see you. I'll even brave *The Insider* to do it."

"Wow. I *am* impressed."

When dinner was over, Jackson walked her out to her car. He found that he did not want to say goodbye to Beth in the full public view of the restaurant or the hotel lobby. She unlocked the door of her car, and they stood for an uncomfortable moment. He felt like a high school kid again, he thought, not wanting to say goodbye to his date and not knowing how to keep her there. He could not deny the sexual feelings that had been stirring in him the whole afternoon with her. Yet he felt odd feeling that way about Joseph's mother, as if he were breaking some sort of taboo. She was, after all, a new *mother;* doubtless the last thing on her mind was sex, and she would probably be appalled if she knew that the whole time they had been arguing this afternoon, he had been thinking about kissing her.

"Well, goodbye," she said, opening the car door.

"Goodbye." He held the door open for her as she stepped into the wedge between the car and door.

They stood for an awkward moment, neither of them willing to take the last step away. He bent, meaning to kiss her on the cheek, but at the last instant, his lips went to her lips instead. Their mouths touched as soft as velvet, and clung. Jackson braced his hands on the car door on one side of her and the roof of the car on the other, holding back from touching her. Beth felt enveloped by his warmth and scent, but she ached for more. She wanted to feel his arms around her, wanted to step into him, to wrap her arms around him and hold on for dear life. Yet she could not let herself do that, as if it would make the moment too real, too scary and fraught with problems. So only their mouths touched, tasting and exploring. Her hands dug into the material of her dress; his clenched upon the metal of the car.

When at last Jackson pulled back, both of them were breathing heavily. He gazed down at her flushed face, her eyes glittering like stars, and he wanted to jerk her against him and kiss her again. Instead he drew a deep breath and stepped back. Beth swallowed and managed a trembling smile, then quickly ducked into the car.

He walked away, not looking back. Beth went limp, crossing her forearms on the steering wheel and leaning against them, waiting for the trembling in her limbs to stop and her breathing to return to normal. *What was going on here?* She had come here breathing fire, furious with him and wanting only to slice him to ribbons. Now all she wanted was to be in his arms again—preferably naked and in a bed.

It was just the aftermath of pregnancy, she told herself—a flood of hormones that pulled her in strange directions. It was something she should have expected. It was no portent of the future. It had nothing to do with Jackson Prescott himself, other than that he was there—and quite handsome, of course—and potently male.

She drew a shaky breath. Who was she kidding? It had everything to do with Jackson Prescott and that sexy smile of his, those luscious blue eyes, the sharp angles of cheekbones and jaw. He was, in fact, devastating to her senses and, she was honest enough to admit, devastating to her emotions, as well. If she was smart, Beth thought, she would stay far away from him. He would not fit into the simple and uncomplicated life she had envisioned for herself and her baby, a life free of things like reporters hounding her and having her name splashed all over the tabloids—or having her heart broken again by another man far more worldly than she.

But then, Beth had never been one for playing it safe. And she knew that if Jackson Prescott did show up in Angel Eye two months from now, she would gladly open the door and let him in.

Chapter 5

The furor in the tabloids gradually died down. After a few more fruitless days, the reporter from *The Insider* disappeared. There was another article or two, but they were mere rehashings of old stories, and after another week, Beth was pleased to find that she had slipped quietly back into anonymity. The reporters stopped calling, as did curious acquaintances. Beth's life returned to normal—or as normal as life could be with a new baby.

But even that was settling into an easier routine. Joseph began to sleep through the night, supplemented with a short nap in the morning and a long one in the afternoon. All the redness and discolorations of birth had faded, and he was turning into a beautiful plump baby with a mop of dark hair.

Cater had returned to his house in Austin, so it was just Beth, Cory and her father at the ranch, and even Cory would be returning to college in Austin soon. But Beth was now able to manage both the baby and the house without feeling as if she had been run over by a truck. Sometimes, when the baby was asleep, she even tried sketching again. She did not yet start to work again in oils, but she was beginning to feel restless and a little eager to get back to her work—something she had wondered about ever happening again when she was in the heavy lassitude of her pregnancy.

She drew pencil and pen-and-ink sketches of her father or Cory or scenes around the house. She even found herself a few times trying to draw a picture of Jackson Prescott from memory, though she never could seem to get it right. She was not, she thought, familiar enough with his face—though it seemed to her that she thought about him so often that she should be.

He called her a few times from L.A.—short unimportant conversations that were mostly about Joseph and his new accomplishments or the business that was keeping Jackson occupied in Los Angeles. But Beth always got a knot of excitement in her stomach whenever she picked up the phone and heard his voice on the other end of the line.

He was returning to Austin soon, and only two weeks after that he would start shooting near Angel Eye. Beth would have been aware of that fact even if Jackson had not told her, for the entire town of Hammond was gearing up for the coming of the movie crew. They were staying in a motel in Hammond, which had the closest motel to the desolate area where they would be filming. Hammond had not had this much excitement for years. The weekly newspaper kept up a "movie watch," and locals were excited about being extras in the film.

Still, Beth was astonished when the doorbell rang late one afternoon, and she opened the door to find Jackson Prescott standing on her doorstep. "Jackson!" she cried, before she could stop herself.

Her hand flew up to her chest, and she felt suddenly

hot, then cold. Her stomach started to dance. "What are you doing here?"

"Filming a movie, hadn't you heard?" He smiled, taking off his sunglasses. "You going to let me in?"

"Of course. I—I'm just so surprised to see you." Beth stepped back to let him enter the foyer, resisting an impulse to check her hair. She was sinkingly aware of the fact that she was wearing much-worn denim shorts and an old tank top, rather too stretched by her larger breasts. "Uh, I, how did you find our house?"

"Everyone in Angel Eye knows where you live. Didn't you know that? I stopped at a convenience store and asked, and they were quite happy to tell me. Guess you don't worry much about security here."

Beth chuckled. "Not really."

"I took the road the kid told me, checked the mailboxes, and voilà! Here I am. I was afraid you might have a gate or something. What *was* that thing I drove across when I turned into your road? It felt like I was driving on a washboard."

"That's a cattle guard, city boy." Beth smiled. His casual way had allowed her nerves to vanish, and now she led him to the den, where Joseph was lying on his back in his playpen, moving his arms and legs and batting at the activity toys dangling from the webbed strap strung across the top of the playpen. "You want to see Joseph?"

"Of course." Jackson's eyes went to the backs of Beth's legs as she bent over the playpen and picked up the baby. She had certainly gotten her figure back, he noticed. Her legs were shapely and looked a mile long, and she filled out the skimpy top admirably.

Beth turned, baby in arms, and Jackson pulled his gaze back to her face. "Look at that!" he exclaimed, staring at the baby in wonder. "He's so big!"

Beth beamed. "Well, you have to remember, he's almost three months old now. You want to hold him?"

"Sure." He took him with the exaggerated care of one not used to infants and held him, looking down at Joseph long and carefully. "He's beautiful. Or shouldn't one say that about a baby boy?"

"Why not? He is."

Jackson caressed the baby's cheek and traced one eyebrow. The baby stared back at him gravely, pacifier firmly in place, and arms and legs pumping. Suddenly Joseph grinned hugely around his pacifier, as if he and Prescott shared some secret and hilarious joke. Jackson let out a delighted chuckle.

"Did you see that! He smiled at me."

"Uh-huh. Maybe he recognizes you."

"After three months?"

"You were one of the first people who ever held him. That's got to make an impression."

Jackson put his finger against the baby's hand, and Joseph curled his little hand around it firmly. Jackson bent his head closer, staring into his face and talking, trying to win more smiles. He was rewarded with a coo and a frenzy of kicks.

Beth, watching the two of them, felt a lump rising in her throat. She realized that this was the way she would like to draw Jackson, him standing there holding the baby, so large in comparison, bent over in awe and affection, held captive by the little creature.

They spent the evening in the den, playing with the baby and talking. Beth's father came in and joined them, and they wound up watching an old movie on television. Beth was rather amazed. The last thing she would have expected of a hotshot Hollywood director was to spend a family evening playing with a baby and looking at the tube with her dad.

He did not stay late. "Have to get up in the morning early to start filming," he explained as Beth walked with him to the door.

"How early?"

"Five or so."

"Five?" she repeated, stunned.

"Yeah. Glamorous, huh? People always think movie people stay up late partying and then sleep till noon. Well, usually I do stay up late, watching the dailies. But I never sleep late. We have to get everything set up, take advantage of the light. Every day is money gone, so you have to make the most of each one."

They had reached the front door. He laced his fingers through hers and led her outside. They strolled over to his car. "It's hectic. I probably won't be able to get over here much."

"I understand." Her heart began to beat a little faster. His words must mean that he wanted to see her more. *Or was it just the baby that brought him here?*

He turned to face her, leaning against his car. "Would you come visit the set?"

"Really?" Beth smiled. "Would it be okay?"

"Sure. I'll put your name on the list. They'll let you in and tell you where to go."

"When?"

"Tomorrow. Or whenever you'd like. I'll approve you for every day. That way you can come whenever you get the chance."

"That's very nice of you."

He grinned. "Nothing's too good for the mother of my 'secret love child.'"

Beth grimaced. *"Puhleeze."*

"They've stopped, haven't they?"

"Yeah."

"Bigger fish to fry." He took her hand and laid it flat

against one of his. With his other hand, he traced each of her fingers, slowly, almost meditatively, watching the movement of his finger. "I'm sorry you were put in that mess because of me."

"It wasn't your fault. All you did was be a Good Samaritan."

"Yeah, but it certainly wasn't your fault, either. I'm even sorrier that I doubted you." He looked back into her face in the dim light cast by the moon and stars. "I'm too cynical."

"It's easy to understand, if you have to deal with that kind of stuff all the time."

"The tabloids usually aren't that bad about me. I'm not a real celebrity, a star. I think they jumped on it because they've never been able to pin any sort of scandal on me before. When they got the chance, they went at it full blast."

"So you've always been a good boy?" Beth could hear the hint of flirtation in her voice, and it surprised her a little.

He grinned. "More like a dull one." There was an undercurrent of seduction in *his* voice, as well, a certain husky quality that did strange things to Beth's insides.

"I doubt that." She swayed forward slightly.

He did the same. "Trust me. I'm Old Reliable."

"And what should I rely on you for?" she asked lightly.

Jackson's only answer was to bring his hands up to cup her face. He gazed at her for a long moment, and his hands slid down her neck and onto her shoulders. The touch of his skin on her bare flesh sent a shiver through her, and Beth was reminded suddenly of how long it had been since she had been with a man.

She told herself that Jackson was slick and sophisticated, and that in any situation with him she would probably be in over her head. Joseph's father had been like that—wealthy, worldly—and look what had happened with him. She had to be more careful this time.

But then Jackson's mouth was on hers, and Beth stopped thinking at all.

She wrapped her arms around his neck and gave in to the sweet pleasure of his kiss. His arms went around her, and he pulled her in tightly against him. They kissed for a long time, oblivious to the world around them. Finally Jackson raised his head. His eyes glittered, and his face was flushed and slack with desire.

Beth drew a shaky breath. "Well..." she said. "I...uh..."

"Yeah." Reluctantly his arms fell away from her. "This is probably not a very good thing to start."

Beth shook her head. "Yeah." She realized that her verbal and physical signals were confused, which, when she thought about it, pretty much reflected what she felt inside—confusion. This was not what she needed at the moment. All her energies should be concentrated on the baby and on getting back to work. She did not need romantic feelings mixing up her insides.

"I better get back inside," she murmured.

"Okay. Will you come to the set?"

She nodded. "Tomorrow, if I can get someone to baby-sit Joey."

Baby-sitting, of course, was the least of her problems. There was always someone around who was happy to take care of the baby. It had, after all, been sixteen years since there had been a baby in the family. She had said it only to have an excuse for not showing up.

However, after a night of tossing and turning, going over all the reasons why a man was the last thing she needed in her life right now, Beth did not even think of using her ready-made excuse. Instead she called Daniel's son, James, who quickly agreed to come over and take care of Joseph for two or three hours—provided that Beth would introduce him to Jackson Prescott.

"I'm the only one who hasn't met him," he said plaintively. "And I'm the only one who would like to."

Beth chuckled. "Well, he said he would come over again, and when—if—he does, I'll introduce you."

So the next morning, at ten, she drove to the spot where they were filming. A guard stopped Beth long before she reached the trailers and the huddle of people in the distance. He checked his list, talked to someone on a walkie-talkie and a moment later a young woman showed up, looking harried, and escorted Beth along the dirt road to the center of the activity.

The trailers stood to one side. Stretching in front of them was a barren patch of ground, then a battered car in front of the facade of a wooden shack. There was a small truck on a set of tracks leading away from the car, and atop the truck were a seat and a camera. There was various other equipment scattered around, none of which Beth could identify except for banks of lights and a long boom with a dangling microphone. Several people stood or sat under a canopy, protected from the blazing August sun. A number of other people scurried around moving equipment and measuring things, talking into headsets. It looked like utter chaos.

Off to one side, apparently oblivious to the hubbub around him, stood Jackson, dressed in shorts and a T-shirt, with an old ball cap on his head to ward off some of the sun. He was talking to an older man with a long, graying ponytail and a backward-turned hat. Jackson was talking and gesturing, and the older man was nodding. The girl who had escorted Beth edged toward the men and caught Jackson's attention. He asked her a question, and she answered, pointing toward Beth.

Jackson turned and saw Beth, and a smile broke across his face. "Beth!"

He left the other two and came over to her. "Hi. You came. I wasn't sure."

"Yeah. Here I am."

He stopped just short of her and stood a little awkwardly. "I told Jackie to get you a chair in the shade. It's the most comfortable seat in the house. I have to work." He nodded toward where the other man stood waiting for him.

"Sure. I understand."

She didn't talk to him again until they broke for lunch, but she found it interesting to watch the filming. After a long time the chaos died down into stillness. An actress came out of one trailer, and an actor out of another, and two more people came forward from under the canopy. They took up their positions on the porch of the "shack" and beside the car, and then there was another round of waiting while more things were checked and people hurried out to fix the actors' hair and makeup for a final time.

There were a few minutes of filming, then several more takes, involving more checking of hair and makeup, and finally everyone broke away. The actors returned to their trailers and the canopy, and the chaos began all over again. Beth noticed that throughout the morning, which included several apparent crises, including an argument with the head cameraman and a tantrum by one of the actors, Jackson retained his calm. It was no wonder, she thought, that she had instinctively realized that he could handle a race to the hospital and a frantic birth. He was used to handling problems every day of his life.

Lunch was a catered buffet under the canopy, and Beth ate it with Jackson, sitting at a table in one corner of the little pavilion. Everyone left them alone, but Beth could feel the curious glances from the cast and crew.

"Don't you have one of the trailers?" Beth asked curiously.

Jackson grinned. "No. Just the two stars. The other trailer's the makeup and costume rooms. One corner of it is a little office, which my assistant works out of. Directors always seem to be in the middle of the fray. It's the way I like it. I want to keep my eye on everything. The last thing I need is to be shut away from it in a trailer."

"At least you would be out of the heat," Beth commented, sitting back and fanning herself with an empty paper plate.

He looked concerned. "Are you too hot? You want to go into the makeup trailer for a while?"

Beth laughed. "No. I'm fine. You forget, I grew up in this heat."

"I'm glad you came out."

"Me too."

"You want to have dinner tonight?"

"I thought you were going to be too busy."

"I have to eat. We could meet in Hammond. What do you say?"

"Okay." She knew it was foolish. She had given herself a thorough talking-to last night. There was no future in an affair with a director from L.A. To begin with, they lived thousands of miles apart, or at least they would once he returned to Los Angeles after the filming. With a new baby, there was no room in her life for a man, period, much less for one who would breeze into it for a few weeks and then breeze right back out, leaving her no doubt sadder, but probably not a whit wiser.

Besides, they lived such utterly different lives. Though she lived in a city, she was used to a quiet, serene life. She spent most of her days alone in her studio, painting. She didn't go to glittering parties. She didn't spend her days under the high pressure of deadlines. She worked and lived at her own pace, answering to no one, and that was the way she liked it. She was no more likely to give up her life than Jackson was to dump his career among the movers and shakers of Hollywood.

It was, obviously, a romance that was doomed from the start. Yet Beth could not bring herself to administer the deathblow cleanly and early. She liked being with him too much. So she agreed to have supper with him that evening. And when they found that everyone stared and whispered when they went into a restaurant in Hammond, Beth smiled and suggested that perhaps it would be easier if the next time they had dinner at her house.

She saw him frequently after that, despite his earlier statement that he would have little time on location. Somehow he seemed to make time, coming out almost every day to the ranch for an hour or two before he went back to watch the dailies. Beth noticed her family was getting used to having him around. James, who had been overawed to meet him, soon was chatting away with him about old films as if they had known each other all their lives, and even Daniel and her father allowed that he was "all right."

The baby, it was clear, soon recognized Jackson, who could always make Joey gurgle and coo and smile. Beth began sketching scenes of the two of them together, and when she found the pose that she liked the best, she decided to start an oil portrait, her first since she'd moved back to the ranch. If it turned out well, she thought, she would give it to him. Jackson had admired the large portrait of her mother that she had done a few years ago for her father and which hung over the mantel in the living room.

Jackson spent most of Saturday evening with her at the ranch house, and after she had put Joseph down to bed for the night, with the monitor beside her father's chair as Marshall watched an exhibition game in the den, she took Jackson outside, promising to show him the delights of an evening out in West Texas.

"We going dancing?" he asked in some amusement. "I better go back and put on my boots."

"Nope. Nearest dance hall's an hour away. I was thinking of someplace closer. Here, take this." She shoved a cooler at him and grabbed some quilts, waving him out the door. They put the quilts and cooler in the back of her father's pickup and climbed in the front.

Beth set out from the house, driving a way Jackson had never gone before, following a track that led deeper onto the land instead of out to the road. After a while the track disappeared, and Jackson realized that they were simply driving cross-country, dodging mesquite bushes and sagebrush and cows.

"Where are we going?" he asked as they bounced and rattled along. "By the way, can you bruise a spleen?"

Beth chuckled. "We are going to look at something I'll bet you've never seen, city slicker."

"Coyotes?" he hedged.

She smiled. "This looks like a good spot."

Beth pulled to a stop. Jackson glanced around. He couldn't see anything about this place that was different from any of the rest of the land. It was all dark, with darker lumps of bushes here and there.

"Come on." Beth jumped out and walked around to open the gate of the pickup. Jackson obediently followed.

Beth hopped up into the bed of the truck and laid out the blankets, then gestured for Jackson to join her. She opened the cooler and pulled out two beers, handing one of them to him. Then she lay down on the truck bed, patting the blanket beside her. Jackson lay down where she'd indicated.

"Is this it?" he asked.

Beth chuckled. "Yep. This is it. Lying out looking at the stars." She pointed straight up. "But look at them! You never see anything like that in the city. I know."

He had to agree. The night sky was enormous and velvet black, darker than it ever was in any city, and it was filled with a multitude of coldly glittering stars, the moon a silver-white crescent among them. It was relaxing, soothing, to lie out here in the cooling evening, surrounded by utter quiet and the vast reach of the empty land below and the starry sky above. Jackson could feel the strains of the last few stressful days oozing out of him.

He took another swig of his beer and set it beside him, then crossed his arms behind his head and gave himself up to contemplating the vastness of the universe for a while. Beth, who had seen the same view thousands of times, still gazed at it in admiration. In her career, she dealt with beauty—recreated it, brought it out in rich textures and glowing colors, struggled to add it where it was not. But nothing she could ever do could compare to the beauty of nature, the perfect blend of color, texture and space. It was a fact that she had realized anew time after time, always with a pang that was part ache and part joy.

They started to talk, first about how the filming had been going and when he and the others would be returning to Austin to finish filming there, then drifting to her work and her house in Dallas, and finally to what it had been like growing up in Angel Eye, Texas.

"I always wanted to get out," Beth remembered with a smile. "Now I find it rather peaceful and beautiful in its own stark way. But back then, all I could see was the dullness and the gossip and the never-ending emptiness. I felt like if I stayed here I would smother to death."

"Me too. Where I grew up was a little bigger, different

landscape—magnolias instead of mesquite—but stagnant. Choking. I couldn't wait to get out.''

"Course it didn't help having three older brothers who were the biggest guys in town. I hardly ever went out the first two years I was in high school because all the boys were so scared of Quinn. Thank God he graduated and went off to college, so at least I managed to have a few dates my junior and senior years.''

"You have an interesting family—an artist, a rancher, a novelist, a cop—that's a mixed bag.''

"Well, we never believed in being ordinary." Beth smiled. "And the boys aren't as different as it sounds. Quinn's a cop, and Cater writes mysteries. When they were young, all three of the boys had the biggest collection of *Hardy Boys* mysteries you've ever seen. That's what I read, too. I'm probably the only girl in the world who didn't read Nancy Drew. Probably the only reason Daniel didn't do something similar was because he got married right out of high school, and they had Jimmy pretty quickly. So he stayed here and got work in Hammond, and Dad gave them some land. And ranching's in all the boys' blood. Whenever Dad or Daniel needs extra workers, Quinn and Cater come to help.''

"Which way do you suppose Cory is going to go?''

"I'm not sure. He's still at that stage where he's interested in half a dozen things. But I think at heart he's a rancher. Now, Jimmy, Daniel's son—''

Jackson laughed. "I don't think that boy's interested in working the land." Jimmy had bent Jackson's ear about movies and directing every time he had found Jackson at the house, and he had been ecstatic when Jackson had told him he was welcome to watch the filming. Jimmy had been on location every day since and was quite annoyed that school was starting next week, so he wouldn't be able to see the last few days of filming.

"Mama was artistic," Beth went on. "I guess that's where we get it. She drew and painted when she had the time, which wasn't often. And she used to tell the most wonderful stories. I remember she always said that when we kids were older, she wanted to write and illustrate children's books. But then, about the time the rest of us were getting big enough we didn't need so much seeing after, along came Cory. Then she died."

"That must have been hard for you. How old were you?"

"Thirteen. Yeah, it was hard. She was my friend and ally, as well as my mother. You know, us girls against the guys. And being a teenager, too—there are just some things a father and brothers can't help you with. My friend Sylvie and her mother always went shopping together, and sometimes they fought over what Sylvie could buy, but they had *fun.* Her mom would stay up when Sylvie was on a date, and when Sylvie came in, they would talk about it. Sometimes, when I went on a date, I would go over to Sylvie's to dress and do my makeup and hair so that when I said, 'How do I look?' I'd get a response like, 'Oh, I like that color eye shadow,' or 'Hey, your hair is different,' instead of 'Fine, honey.' Dad wouldn't have noticed my hair unless I dyed it green."

Jackson chuckled. "Your dad's great. We walked around the yard the other night—looked in the barn, looked in the corral, checked out the row of trees he planted. I'll bet he didn't say more than two sentences—and both those times were when I asked him a question. Then, when we came in, he nodded at me and said, 'You're good company, son.'"

"That's Dad. The less you talk, the better company you are. He said he got used to not talking, being out on the land by himself so much, you know. But he was a good father. He tried really hard to make up to Cory and me for Mama dying. He went to all our school plays and parent-teacher conferences. He was in the stands at all the boys' games. He even went to my dance recitals." Beth giggled. "I can still remember looking out in the audience and seeing him sitting there with this look of grim resignation on his face. Poor man. I think he felt guilty because he never remarried after Mama died. He told me once that he thought he should have given us another mother, but he couldn't bring himself to put some other woman in Mama's place. He loved her so much."

They were silent for a moment, then Jackson asked softly, "What about Joseph's father?"

He could feel Beth's body go rigid beside him. "What about him?"

"Well, he seems conspicuously absent," he said cautiously.

"He *is* conspicuously absent. And he is going to remain so."

"Does he even know that Joseph was born?"

"No. He doesn't even know about the *possibility* of his being born."

"You didn't tell him you were pregnant?"

"No."

"Don't you think he at least has the right to know he has a son?"

"He has *no* rights." Beth sat up, her jaw clenched. Why did Jackson have to bring *him* up?

"I'm sorry." Jackson laid a hand on her back.

She flinched, but when his hand remained, warm and undemanding, she relaxed a little. "No. *I'm* sorry." She let out a long sigh and lay back down. "I get a little...antagonistic on that subject."

"So I see. I didn't mean to upset you. I was just thinking about it from the male perspective. I would think he would want to know, to be a father to Joey." He turned on his side and lay propped up on his elbow, looking down at her.

"You don't know Robert. I don't think he would give a flip about knowing about Joey. It's my guess that he would tell me that he already has two sons and, besides, how does he know that Joseph is really his? That's the sort of man Robert Waring is."

"I see."

"He's cold, calculating, deceitful—" Beth drew a breath and forced herself to relax. "Oh, I'm not being fair to him. He's also charming—extremely charming *and* handsome, *and* sophisticated, *and* intelligent. I met him at a party at a bank opening. I had painted the portrait of the chairman of the board that hung in the lobby, so I got an invitation to the grand opening. Robert did business with them. He was urbane and witty, and after the opening, he asked if he could take me out to a late supper. Well, it went on from there. I would see him every few weeks. He lived in Chicago, and he came to Dallas often on business. I suppose that's why it took me so long to figure it out. I didn't know that back in Chicago, he lived with his wife and two teenage boys."

"Ah."

"Yeah. Ah." Beth grimaced. "I was hopelessly naive. It never even struck me as odd that the only numbers I had for him were business numbers—his office phone, his pager, his cellular phone. He frequently worked late, and usually if we talked in the evenings, he was at his office. I assumed he was a bachelor who wasn't home much— if I thought at all. Looking back on it, I'm not sure I did."

"No need to kick yourself about it. People don't expect someone to lie to them at every turn, particularly someone they're close to. If a person sets out to fool you, they will—unless they're really *bad* at it."

"He wasn't bad at it. Not at all. I found out by accident. I was doing a portrait of the bank president's wife—a very nice and very chatty woman. We talked a lot while she was sitting for me, and sometime in there, I mentioned Robert and having met him at the opening of their new building. She said, 'Oh, yes, Robert, I've met him several times. Such a charming man, and his wife is so elegant.' You can imagine how I reacted."

"Mmm-hmm."

"I'm sure I turned completely white, but I hid behind my easel and managed to say, 'Oh? I didn't realize he was married.' She told me that he very much was and had two sons. Then she said that I mustn't get mixed up with him, of course not knowing it was a trifle late for that. He was, she said, a terrible ladies' man. So after she left, I called him up and asked him if it was true, and he told me yes and not to be hysterical. He made it quite clear where I ranked on his list of priorities, which was somewhere down below his golf game, I think."

"I'm sorry. I know that's terribly inadequate, but..."

"Well, live and learn, Dad always says."

"Some lessons are harder than others, though."

"Yeah. About a month after that, I figured out that I was pregnant." Beth smiled a little to herself. "It was hard at the time. But I can't really say I regret it. Otherwise I wouldn't have Joey."

"That's true. He is worth a lot of pain."

"Yeah."

Jackson gazed down at her for a long moment. He brushed his knuckles down her cheek. "I am not married," he said. "Never have been."

Beth looked back at him, wondering where this was going. She could not read his expression, for his head was backlit by the light of the stars and moon. "What are you telling me?"

He smiled. "I'm not sure. I guess…that I'm not the same sort of man as Robert Waring."

He paused. It was on the tip of his tongue to blurt out that he loved her, that he wanted to have much more than a few evenings with her. But he stopped himself. *That was crazy.* He barely knew Beth Sutton. He was an adult, not some crazy teenager who fell in love on the basis of an intense meeting and a few hours spent in her company. He had a movie to shoot. In a few more days he would return to Austin to resume filming there, and after that he would go back to Los Angeles.

Jackson wanted to kiss her. He wanted to make love to her out here under the stars. But something held him back. Making love did not necessarily mean making promises for the future. But, somehow, he felt that with this woman, for him, it would be a promise.

He bent down and kissed her lightly on the lips. "We had better be getting back."

"Right now?" Beth asked, her eyebrows rising. She had seen the hesitation on his face, the desire that had flickered in his eyes and been squelched. "But you haven't gotten to the best part of one of these Angel Eye evenings."

"Oh? And what is that?"

"This," she replied, hooking her hand behind his neck and pulling him down for a kiss.

Chapter 6

Her lips were soft and melting, and Jackson could not keep from responding to them. A kiss, after all, was not making love, and he would stop long before they reached that point.

Their lips clung, their tongues twining around one another, seeking, exploring. It seemed to Jackson that the more he tasted her, the more he wanted. They kissed again and again, their desire escalating.

Beth shivered and pressed up against him, her arms wrapping around him. It had been so long since she had felt this kind of passion, this roaring, rushing ocean of desire that swept her along almost mindlessly. *Had she ever felt it?* She couldn't remember it—not like this. She had meant only to kiss him as she had the other night. She had, she admitted, felt a trifle annoyed at his ability to turn away from her so easily, and she had wanted to prove that she could make him desire her. But now she found herself at the mercy of her own passion, her body, its desires dormant for so many months, reawakening to its own needs.

His mouth was urgent and hungry, every kiss a demand and a delight all in one. His hand moved down her body, setting up a wild tingling wherever it touched. He cupped her breast, his thumb circling her nipple through her blouse. Beth let out a little moan, and she felt a tremor run through Jackson's body in response.

They broke off their kiss, and Jackson rained kisses down her throat and onto her chest. Completely forgotten were his plans for restraint and control. His fingers went to her blouse, unbuttoning it and delving beneath her lacy brassiere to touch the soft orb of her breast. His touch felt so right, so good, that Beth unconsciously moved her hips. She realized that she had been wanting this for days—maybe even weeks. She just had not acknowledged it, had not wanted to accept the fact that she could again be this hungry for a man…if, indeed, she ever had been. She could not remember feeling such a volatile storm of sensations and emotions before. It was, frankly, a little frightening.

"No, wait." Beth edged away, putting her hands up to his chest.

Jackson stopped, his breath rasping in his throat. For a long moment he struggled for control. Then, with a groan, he rolled away onto his back and flung one arm across his eyes.

"I'm sorry," Beth said, sitting up. "I know I'm the one who started that, but…I don't know, it was all moving too fast. I'm not ready for—" *For what? Commitment? Sex? Loss of control?* "I don't know. I don't want to make another mistake."

He nodded. "You're right. This probably isn't the time or place." He had known that before they kissed—*now if he could just convince his raging libido of that fact.*

"No. You were the one who was right. We should have

gone home when you suggested it.'' Beth began to scoot toward the gate of the truck.

Jackson reached out a hand and grabbed her arm, stopping her. She glanced at him. He smiled. ''Maybe so. But I'm glad we didn't.''

Heat rose in Beth's cheeks, but she flashed back a grin. ''Me, too.''

The next day, Beth was standing in line at the grocery store in Angel Eye, a basketful of diapers, baby food and food in front of her, when she glanced over at the magazine rack. There, on the front of the tabloid, right next to a picture of a car trunk lid on which an image of Jesus had supposedly formed, was a picture of her and Jackson walking out of some door. They were talking, their heads turned toward each other, and they were holding hands. Across the top of the photograph, the headline blazoned: Prescott's Secret Love Nest!

Beth groaned, then glanced quickly around to see if anyone had heard. She wondered if anyone else had seen it, if they had recognized her. After another furtive look around, she snatched the top issue of *Scandal* off the rack and looked at the picture up close. The door they were exiting, she decided, was the front door of the ranch house. She couldn't stop a little smile at the thought of how her father would react to having his home labeled a ''secret love nest.''

How had they gotten this shot? She decided that it must have been taken with a telephoto lens, with the photographer sitting somewhere out of sight. She certainly hadn't caught a glimpse of anyone taking their picture at any point. *But how had they known to send a photographer out to take it?* It boggled her mind the way the tabloids were able to jump so quickly on a story. She supposed that someone on the movie crew had tipped them off—or any of the townspeople of Hammond or Angel Eye who had happened to see them together. She and Jackson hadn't been very secretive about their relationship.

Beth read through the story, a mishmash of truth, speculation and downright lies. But it sounded convincing, even to her. They even mentioned in the story that her child was named after Jackson's father. Beth shook her head. She had never thought that *that* decision would come back to haunt her.

For a brief moment, she thought about calling Julie McCall at *Scandal* and setting the record straight. But even a moment's immediate reflection made her change her mind. For one thing, it would be hard to convince the woman that there had been nothing between her and Jackson, not when they had a picture of the two of them holding hands. For another thing, she rather doubted that the tabloid cared about publishing the truth. They just wanted a good story, and no doubt a "secret love child" and "secret love nest" were more appealing. What was it about secret love that was so intriguing to people, anyway?

Maybe no one would notice, she thought desperately, but that hope was dashed when the cashier looked up and saw her. "Why, hi, Beth! How are you? See you got your picture in the papers."

Beth smiled weakly. "Yeah. Hi, Maggie Lee."

"What will your daddy say about all that?" the checker went on, snapping her gum and dragging Beth's groceries over the scanner.

"He won't like it. I imagine you can guess that."

Maggie Lee chuckled. "Sure can. Marshall never was one who liked attention." She paused for a moment, then asked, "So what's going on with you and that movie fella? You all going to tie the knot or what?"

"We're just friends. You can't believe all that stuff in the tabloids."

"Aren't they a hoot? I just love those things. But, you know, I figure some of that stuff has got to be true. They couldn't just publish those things if they were bald-faced lies. There has to be some kernel of truth there, that's what I always say."

Beth suppressed a sigh. She wondered how many people reasoned as Maggie Lee did. Probably a lot, she decided in despair. She endured the rest of Maggie Lee's conversation, paid her bill and got out of the grocery store as fast as she could.

"Don't let it bother you," Jackson counseled when he came over that evening and she showed him the copy of *Scandal,* which Peg Richards from up the road had thoughtfully dropped by. "Just shrug it off."

"Doesn't it bother you?"

"Some. But there are worse things. At least they aren't accusing us of killing somebody or being unfaithful to our spouses or something. They've done worse than this to people before."

"I suppose." Beth leaned over his chair, looking down at the cover again. "It's just—oh, I hate having people know stuff about me. Even worse, having them think they know stuff that isn't true. I even thought about calling the magazine and telling them what really happened."

"Uh-uh," Jackson said quickly, shaking his head. "Trust me. You do *not* want to talk to them. I've known people who have made that mistake. They would turn your words around, and you would come out looking like a fool or someone wicked. Remember how they ran with that one thing you said to them last time?"

"Yeah, I know." Beth sighed and went to pick up the baby, who was beginning to make fussy noises in his playpen. He wriggled his arms and legs, fighting to go to Jackson, and she obligingly plopped him down in Jackson's lap.

"Don't worry," he reassured her. "You get used to it."

"I'm not sure I would." Beth sat down beside him, distracted from her irritation with the article by the sight of Jackson with the baby.

She had been working on the portrait of him with Joey off and on for several days. She had gotten to where she worked on it every day during the baby's nap and often in the evenings after Jackson left and she put Joey to bed. At the moment she was suffering from her usual midwork doubts and was afraid that the finished product would turn out all wrong. Well, she consoled herself, if it did, she didn't have to show it to Jackson.

She continued to look at him, wondering how a man playing with a baby could be so sweet and so sexy all at the same time. She hadn't been able to stop thinking about the other night in the bed of the pickup truck. There were times when she wished that she hadn't stopped. She looked at Jackson's fingers, long and thin, big-knuckled, with a light sprinkling of hair across the backs of his hands. He had beautiful hands, she thought, and remembered them roaming her body through her clothes. She found herself wishing that she could feel them against her bare skin.

"We're going back to Austin in a couple of days," Jackson said and shot her a sideways glance.

Beth's heart dropped. She wondered if he had seen the disappointment in her face. "Oh. Well..."

"It's not that far to Austin," he went on. "I was thinking that I could take a weekend off soon and come to visit...if you'd like."

"Sure."

"Or maybe you could come to see me there." He was still looking at her in that cautious way, and Beth realized that he was feeling his way along, unsure of how she would react.

It made her smile to think that this world-famous director was not entirely confident of her interest in him. "I'd like that," she told him honestly. "But I can't leave the baby."

"Bring him with you. I rented a house for the time we're in Austin. You could both stay there. I could rent a crib. And I can set my assistant to finding a nanny to take care of him for a while if you wanted to go out and do anything. You could stay a few days...if you'd like, of course."

"Yeah," she answered, smiling. "I'd like. Very much."

Beth was excited the whole drive up to Austin. She told herself that it was because it was the first time she had taken off with the baby on her own for any length of time. But she knew that was not the reason for the quivery anticipation in her stomach—or at least not for most of it. She was excited about seeing Jackson again. It had been over a week since he'd left Angel Eye. She wondered if he had missed her, if he had thought about her every day as she had been thinking about him. She wondered if his nerves, too, were jangling with anticipation. *Would he be happy to see her? Or would he think that she wasn't as pretty, as funny—as anything—as he remembered her?*

Many of her questions were answered when she pulled into the driveway of the house to which he had directed her and, before she had even gotten out of her car, the front door of the house opened and Jackson came out, grinning. An answering smile broke across Beth's face, and she quickly opened the door and jumped out. Jackson was down the steps and across to the circular driveway in about three steps, and he pulled her into his arms, lifting her off her feet.

"It feels like it's been forever," he said and kissed her thoroughly. Beth was rosy and laughing by the time they stepped apart. "Has it only been a week?"

She nodded. "And a few days."

"Every day seemed about thirty-six hours long." He pulled her into his arms again for another hug. Behind them, the baby set up a wail.

"Oops. I'd better get Joey out of his car seat." Beth slipped out of Jackson's arms and got into the back seat to unstrap the baby. Jackson was already reaching to take him when she turned around.

"Wow, look at this fella!" Jackson exclaimed. "Hey, slugger, you've grown since I saw you last. Same baby blues, though." He kissed the baby on the forehead, then cuddled him against his shoulder. "Do you think he remembers me?" he asked with a tinge of anxiety.

Beth had to chuckle. "I'm sure he does. He's crazy about you. In fact, I think he missed you. He was a little cranky at the beginning of the week."

He shot her a look. "Oh, right. I'm not *that* gullible about him."

"I'm serious! I really think he was wondering where you were."

Jackson gave the baby another pat and handed him back to Beth so that he could carry their bags into the house. "I thought we would have dinner here tonight," he said. "I guessed that you might be tired from traveling. We can go out tomorrow, if you want."

"You cooked?" Beth asked, surprised, as she followed him into the Mediterranean-style stucco house.

"Do I detect a note of chauvinism in your voice?" he

responded tartly, then grinned. "Actually I had it catered. Believe me, you'll like it better."

He carried her bags through a spacious entryway and down a hall. On one side of the hall were rooms. On the other side were rows of windows, looking out at a spectacular view of Town Lake.

"Wow!" Beth stopped and looked down. Right below them was a sparkling aqua swimming pool with a miniature waterfall, and beyond it the bluff dropped straight down to a small inlet. In the distance the lake shimmered in the late-afternoon sun, the sails of boats bright triangles of color against the dark water.

"Yeah. Beautiful, isn't it? The family that lives here is on vacation in Europe. Fortunately they were willing to extend it for an extra month." He turned into the next door. "Here's your room."

It was a modernistic room with stark white furniture, accentuated by a neon bright bedcover and drapes. Beth stepped into the room behind him, relaxing at his words.

Jackson saw her expression. "What? Did you think I was going to plop your things down in the master bedroom? I told you—no strings attached."

"I know." She smiled. "It's just nice to have my opinion of you confirmed."

He opened a door and stepped through into a small sitting room. "I put the crib in here. I thought this would be a nice place for him."

"It's great," Beth answered honestly. "We might just move in with you."

"Is that a promise?" He smiled, then turned serious, pulling her into his arms loosely, the baby between them. "I'll tell you the truth—I've been lonely as hell this week. Every evening when we stopped, for an instant I would feel this anticipation, but then I would remember that I wouldn't be going out to the ranch to see you and Joey.

I would have given a lot to have come home and heard just one little gurgle or coo—or that crazy wind-up swing that plays faster the tighter you wind it.''

Beth laughed. ''Maybe I should have brought the swing with me.''

Jackson left to set out their dinner, giving Beth a chance to change and feed the baby. When she came out, Jackson had the table set in the breakfast room, where they could look out over the water as they ate. Beth put Joseph down on a blanket in the middle of the wide, empty floor, accompanied by a few of his toys. Replete and dry, he amused himself while they ate a leisurely dinner and talked.

They stayed up late, long after Beth had put Joseph down in his bed, enjoying being together too much to go to bed. Beth knew she would regret it the next morning, but she did not retire until she was yawning so hugely that Jackson pulled her to her feet and turned her in the direction of her bedroom. She gave in, and he walked her to her door. There he kissed her good-night, and though the kiss turned into several kisses, at last he pulled away and went back down the hall and up the stairs to the aerie of a master bedroom on the floor above.

They spent a lazy Saturday, lounging by the pool or playing with the baby. That evening a smiling gray-haired woman, whom Jackson characterized as ''bonded and certified and thoroughly checked-out,'' came to sit with the baby while Jackson and Beth went out to eat. Beth went a little reluctantly; it was the first time she had left Joseph with anyone but a member of the family. However, with a mental squaring of her shoulders, she walked out the door. And only twice during the evening did she give in to the urge to phone the sitter to see how Joseph was doing.

However, she could not bring herself to stay out after midnight, and the first thing she did when they got back to Jackson's house was to go to the baby's room and peer over the side of the crib at him. Joey was sound asleep, of course, his chubby-cheeked face a study in relaxation. Beth smiled down at him, swallowing the lump in her throat.

She heard a noise and turned her head. Jackson had walked quietly into the room, and he came up now to stand behind her. He encircled her waist with his arms and leaned his head against hers, and for a long moment they simply stood, watching the baby sleep.

Then, softly, they slipped out of the room and back down the hall to the modernistic living room. The large sectional sofa was a buttery soft dark green leather, a lovely contrast to the immaculate white carpet, which Beth shuddered to even think of keeping clean. They sat down together on the sofa and stretched their legs out in front of them. He slid his arm around her shoulders, and Beth leaned against him, letting her head rest on his shoulder. It was a natural and very pleasant feeling, being with him this way, almost as if they were an old married couple relaxing together with the baby asleep down the hall.

They talked desultorily as they sat. After a moment's silence, Jackson said, "I wanted to tell you why I asked you about Joey's father."

"It's all right. You don't need to explain. It was a natural question. I just overreacted."

"I don't know about that. But I don't think it was really an idle question on my part. You see, I found out last year that I have an eighteen-year-old daughter that I never knew about."

"What?" Beth sat up, jolted, and turned to look into his face. "Are you serious?"

"Very," he replied grimly. "When I was sixteen, I was very much in love with a girl. Jessica Walls. She was a year younger than I was. We had all these plans, how we were going to go to college together and get married when we were juniors and—well, you know how kids are. We were serious and intense. The summer before my senior year, right about the time I turned seventeen, she moved away. It took me completely by surprise. She came over one evening and told me she and her mother were going to Atlanta for the summer. The summer turned into my whole senior year. She wrote me the next August, after we'd been exchanging letters all summer, and told me she wouldn't be coming back at all. I was heartbroken and furious. I felt that she had betrayed me. I didn't do well in school. I dropped out of sports. It was a bad year. Anyway, when I graduated, I had no desire to go to college, and I hadn't exactly been a stellar student anyway, so I decided to go far away. The West Coast seemed as far as I could get. I wound up in L.A. and sort of lucked into that first movie. I got interested in directing and, well, after a while, I forgot all about Jessica."

He sighed and stood up, beginning to pace in front of the couch. "Until last year, that is. She wrote me a letter, and in it she told me that the reason she had left town all those years ago was because she was pregnant. Her family was very religious, and she said it broke her parents' hearts. She felt guilty and bad, and when her parents insisted that I know nothing about it, she agreed, to please them. She and her mother went to live with her aunt in Atlanta. Her aunt was several years younger than her mother, and she had never been able to have children. So she took the baby and raised it as her own. It was a little girl. The aunt named her Amy."

"Why did she tell you after all this time?"

"Because Amy needed money. Her aunt has been very

sick for the last few years, and they've had big medical bills. They don't have enough money to send Amy to college. So Jessica decided to break her vow to her parents in the hopes that I would give her the money for Amy to go to school. She sent me a picture of her, I guess to convince me that Amy really was mine. It's pretty obvious that she's a Prescott.''

''So what did you do?''

''Gave her the money, of course, and I paid off the medical bills, as well. I would do more, except that it would make Amy wonder. She thinks the college thing is some kind of scholarship that Jessica got for her from her employer, and she doesn't know about the medical bills. But if I gave them more money to live on, she would have to wonder.''

''She still doesn't know that you're her father?''

He shook his head and sat back down beside Beth. ''No. I wanted to see her, but Jessica was dead set against it. She says Amy has no reason to believe that she's anything but the aunt's daughter. She doesn't have any of those yearnings that adopted children have to know their real parents, and they don't want her to be disturbed.'' He shrugged. ''Hell, I can hardly insist on it, knowing how it would shatter her life. I mean, Jessica has been living there close to her all those years, and she never let on.''

''Oh, Jackson...'' Beth reached out and put her hand on his arm. ''I'm so sorry. It must be hard for you.''

''Yeah. It's weird. I mean, I never even knew she existed, and now, even though she's really a stranger to me, I feel a connection, a *longing* to know her. My life would probably have been completely different if Jessica had told me. Hell, Jessie and I might have gotten married, and I'd be back home in Alabama being a roofer or something.''

"A loss for the movie world."

"I guess. I suspect her parents were right and it would have been a bad decision. Both of us would probably have wound up miserable. Still, it's hard knowing you have a child and you've never even seen her. That you've missed all those special times, that if she saw me, she would look right past me and not have a clue who I was."

"It's her loss, too," Beth told him, putting her arms around him and leaning her head against his shoulder. "You would have been a great dad. I can see it with Joey. You're wonderful with him."

"I love him," he said simply. He smiled sheepishly. "Does that sound silly?"

"No, not at all. I think it's wonderful." Beth could feel her throat swelling with emotion.

He stroked his hand across her hair. "I'm glad you think so." He hooked his forefinger beneath her chin and tilted it so that she was looking into his face. He looked at her for a moment, then said softly, "Because, you know, I think I love the little guy's mother, too."

Chapter 7

Beth stared at him in shock. Jackson chuckled. "Caught you off guard, huh?"

"But—but you couldn't."

"Why not?"

"I mean—well, it's too soon. You're probably mistaking your feelings because of our sharing Joey's birth and—"

"Elizabeth Sutton, are you trying to tell me that I don't know my own mind—or my own heart? I am thirty-six years old, you know, and have been functioning on my own for some time." His eyes twinkled with amusement.

Beth had the grace to blush. "Of course I don't mean that you don't know what you think or feel. It's just—well—" She faltered to a halt as she realized that, of course, that was exactly what she *had* meant.

Jackson was a grown man and obviously not the sort to fall in love every few weeks with a new woman. After all, he had gone this long without getting married even once, which in Hollywood was no mean feat. Warmth spread throughout Beth as she accepted that he *did* know what he meant; he *did* love her.

Jackson smiled. "I'm not asking you to reciprocate. I know it's sudden. But I wanted to tell you how I feel."

"Jackson, I…"

He shook his head, placing his forefinger against her lips. "You don't need to say anything. I don't expect it."

He bent and kissed her lips lightly, tenderly, then raised his head and gazed down into her eyes. Whatever he saw there must have pleased him, for his face softened with feeling, and he bent to kiss her again, this time more deeply. Beth let out a sigh of pleasure, and her arms went around his neck.

Their lips moved against each other with ever-increasing passion, until Beth's blood was racing hotly through her veins. Desire pooled between her legs, setting up a throbbing ache. She moved her legs, unable to keep still, and delighted in the immediate and unmistakable response of his body. They had shifted and moved as they kissed, until now they were lying pressed together full-length on the sofa. Their arms were tight around each other, and their legs intertwined. His hand roamed down Beth's back and onto her hips, cupping and caressing, then finally down onto her legs.

She had taken off her hose and shoes earlier, when she had gone to check on Joseph, so his hand slid over bare flesh. He moved upward, beneath her dress, caressing her thigh. His fingertips reached the lacy edge of her panties, and he hesitated, then edged beneath the lace. Beth shivered at the intimate touch.

She was on fire, aching for him. She didn't want to think about the future or the consequences. She wanted only to feel, to give herself up to the fire roaring through her. His mouth left hers and trailed hot kisses down her throat while his hand roamed over her buttocks, squeezing and caressing. Beth murmured his name, and Jackson groaned in response.

"You're beautiful," he whispered. "So beautiful."

He rose up on his elbow and looked down at her. "I want you."

For answer, Beth merely smiled. It seemed to be enough, for he stood up, reaching down to pull her up, too. They started up the circular stairs to the master bedroom, pausing every few feet along the way to kiss and caress each other again, all the while peeling off various articles of clothing. Their progress was slow, and by the time they reached the bed, they were naked, with a trail of clothes behind them.

They fell on the bed and rolled across it, kissing and touching each other in a frenzy of desire. Finally, when they could stand the teasing no longer, he moved between her legs. She opened to him, arching up to meet his thrust. He went deep inside her, and Beth let out a long sigh of satisfaction as he filled her. He moved slowly, afraid that he might hurt her in this, her first lovemaking since the baby, but after the first brief twinge of pain, Beth felt only pleasure. She wrapped her legs around him, urging him on, and he began to move faster, pounding into her with all the force of his passion.

He let out a hoarse cry as his seed poured into her, and Beth clung to him tightly, her own tidal wave of pleasure rushing through her.

Afterward, lying awake in the darkness, Jackson's arm around Beth, he said softly, "Don't go tomorrow."

"What?" Beth murmured sleepily, floating on a hazy wave of contentment.

"I don't want you to go back to Angel Eye tomorrow. Stay for a few more days. You could do that, couldn't you?"

"Sure." Beth smiled. "I could do that."

She wound up staying for the rest of the week. She hadn't intended to. She was afraid that they would grow tired of each other, that their budding relationship would start to bend under the stresses of togetherness. She worried that Jackson would press her to reveal her feelings for him, now that he had told her that he loved her, and she wasn't prepared for that. She wasn't even sure how she felt about his loving her, let alone how she felt about him.

But, to her amazement, none of her forebodings materialized. He did not mention again that he loved her. She could feel it in his caresses and see it in the way he looked at her sometimes, but those moments only created a feeling a warmth inside her, not anxiety or pressure. Nor did he ask how she felt about him or even try to work the conversation in that direction.

They did not grow tired of each other. Jackson was gone most of every day, working, leaving Beth to putter around the house, taking care of the baby and doing whatever she wished. She visited Cory and Cater a few times. Cater lived in a restored turn-of-the-century house, and he let Cory have the garage apartment out back while he was going to U.T. Cater, who was plotting his newest book, was stuck and was happy to avoid the problem for a few hours of talking or playing with the baby or going to a movie. Of all her brothers, Cater's personality was the most suited to Beth's, and though he was not the closest to her in age, they got along the best. Cory, as always, was thrilled to have an opportunity to see Joseph. It had surprised everyone the way he had fallen for Joey, for Cory had been the most sports-oriented of the boys, the most likely to return to the ranch, not someone interested in children. Now he was talking about changing his major to elementary education.

Beth told herself that this week was not a real indicator of what life with Jackson would be like, that it did not show that he was the perfect man for her. After all, she wasn't working and had nothing to do but take care of the baby in a beautiful home and putter around doing whatever she felt like. When she and Jackson were together, it was special, not something that was going to continue to happen for the rest of their lives. It was fun because it was temporary, and at the end of the week they would return to their lives.

Beth drove home on Sunday. Jackson asked her to stay a few extra days. He had to return to L.A. Thursday, he told her, so they wouldn't be able to see each other on the weekend. But much as Beth did not want to leave, her mind kept telling her that she should. She was with Jackson too much, she thought; it was coloring her thinking. She was drifting into thinking that she was in love with him, that they might have a life together, and she told herself that such thinking was dangerous. They were very different; they led different lives and expected different things. She needed to be by herself, she thought, to see things from another perspective.

The other perspective, she quickly found, was loneliness. She had hardly driven out of Austin before she began to miss Jackson. She told herself that it was silly, that it was only temporary.

Unfortunately the temporary condition went on far too long. Beth found herself wanting to turn and say something to him. She stored up little anecdotes about the baby or Angel Eye or her father to tell him. She missed his laugh. She missed his smile. She missed his warm arms around her. At night in bed, she woke up and reached for him, then realized with a dropping heart that he was not there. Sometimes she cried, even as she told herself that she was being ridiculous.

To occupy herself, she worked on her portrait of Jackson and Joey with renewed zeal. It was coming to life beneath her hands, and there were moments when she was sure it was going to turn out to be one of the best things she had ever done. She thought about Jackson's face when she gave it to him, and the thought made her smile.

Jackson called her every night, even during the time when he was in Los Angeles. He sounded tired, and Beth was aware of an urge to be with him, to make him smile with a quip or a story, to smooth the frown from his brow and massage the knots of tension out of his neck and shoulders. He told her that he missed her, too, and they made plans for her to drive up to Austin again as soon as he returned.

Then Joseph got a cold. It was the first time he had ever been sick, and Beth nearly panicked. His nose started running, and he had the sniffles. His skin was hot to her touch. He got worse as the evening went by, and her father's assertion that it was only a cold did nothing to ease her fears. The doctor's office was closed when she called, but one of the other pediatricians in the practice soon returned her call. He, too, did not seem overly impressed by Joseph's symptoms, and he suggested that she bring him into the office the next morning, meanwhile giving him liquid acetaminophen to reduce the fever. But Joseph was cranky and wouldn't go to sleep. He continued to cry, no matter how much she rocked him or patted him. He would fall asleep for a few minutes, then wake up and cry again.

About nine o'clock she called Jackson. "Joey's sick."

"What's the matter with him?" Jackson sounded alarmed.

"It's a cold. The doctor says it's not an emergency, and so does Dad, but he sounds so awful and chuggy, and he won't sleep." To her surprise, her voice hovered near tears. "I'm sorry to bother you."

"No. Don't be sorry. Listen, I'll drive down there."

That did make tears start in her eyes. "No, that's okay. It's not anything, really. I know I'm being a worrywart. I'm sure the doctor's right."

"But you shouldn't be worrying alone."

He made it to the ranch in less than three hours, setting a speed record for time from Austin, Beth was sure. When he rang the doorbell and Beth opened the door, her heart lifted. Joey was just the same, but suddenly she *felt* better. Jackson enfolded her and the baby in his arms, and Beth leaned her head against his shoulder, feeling comforted.

Insisting that Beth go to bed and get some rest, Jackson stayed up with the baby, rocking and walking with him. Finally he lay down on the bed with Beth, the baby between them, and the three of them slept.

About five o'clock, the baby woke up, crying, and Beth fed him. Jackson sat up, sleepy-eyed, and rubbed his head, looking around him vaguely. "How's he doing?"

"Okay, I think." Beth grinned sheepishly. "I feel like an idiot for getting you down here. Kids have colds all the time."

"Yeah. But it's a first for this one. And for you," Jackson replied, smiling. "I better get back to Austin. Why don't you and Joey come with me? We could take him to a pediatrician there."

She shook her head. "No. I'm sure he'll be fine. I probably ought to take him to his regular doctor. They have his records."

"Okay. Will you come up when he's feeling better?"

Beth nodded. "This weekend, probably."

"And you'll call me if he gets worse—or you'll come to Austin?"

"I promise."

He reached out and cupped her cheek tenderly. "I love you."

"I love you, too," Beth replied automatically.

Jackson froze, staring at her intently. "Really?"

Beth smiled self-consciously. She hadn't even known she was going to say it until she did, but she knew that it was the truth. "Yes. Really."

He grinned. "Beth…" He reached out and took her hand. "When you come to Austin this time, stay with me. I mean, for longer than a week or even two. I—I want you stay with me forever."

Beth stared at him, astonished. "What are you saying?"

He paused, considering, looking a little amazed himself. "I think I'm asking you to marry me."

"What!" Beth jumped to her feet, fear clutching her stomach. "But, Jackson…this is so—"

"So sudden?" he ventured, his eyes lighting with amusement. "So unexpected? Isn't that what they say in old novels?"

Beth giggled. "I guess so. But I'm serious. I don't think you've taken the time to think about this."

"I don't have to think. What matters is how I feel. I know that I love you. I know that I've been miserable for a week without you. I know that I was happier that week when you and the baby were with me than I have been at any other time in my life."

"But, Jackson…"

"But what? You just said that you loved me."

"Yes, I do. But that's a big step—from loving someone to marrying them. People do fall out of love."

"I'm not going to fall out of love with you. And I won't stop loving Joey, either. We're a family, Beth, and we have been since the day Joey was born. I knew it then, but I was too embarrassed and disbelieving to say so. From the day I met you, I haven't been happy apart from you."

Pleasure flushed Beth's cheeks, but she stepped back, shaking her head. "I don't know. I—I'd have to think about it. There are things to consider. I mean, you have to live in Los Angeles. And I live in Dallas."

"You could do what you do anywhere in the country. There are just as many—no, I'm sure there are *more* people in L.A. who want to have portraits painted than there are in Dallas. If nothing else, it's bigger—and think of the egos. I have a room in my house that would be perfect for a studio—great sun, a beautiful view. But we don't have to live in Los Angeles, either. We could live wherever we wanted. There are lots of movie people who don't reside there. Between computers and faxes and phones and planes, you can communicate all you want with the studios. Hell, you can't get away from those people anywhere in the world. I know—I've tried."

Beth smiled faintly. "It's not just that. It's the idea of Joey having to grow up the child of a famous person, of his always being thrust into the spotlight. Those tabloids messing in our lives. Having people intrude on me and my family like that—following us and taking pictures of us and popping up everywhere, printing wild stories all the time."

"They *are* a fact of life. But you'll learn to deal with them. I promise. I have. And, really, this is the most exposure I've had in them except for when I dated Melanie Hanson. Even then, it was because they wanted stuff on her, not me. Once this blows over, they'll hardly ever have stories about us. Directors and producers just aren't the fodder that actors and singers and models are. And I promise you that I will put everything I've got into making sure that you and Joseph are shielded from them. It's possible. Other people have kept their kids out of the limelight."

Looking at him, Beth wanted to say yes. Her love for

him welled up in her, but still she held back. She had to be practical, she thought. She had to think for both herself and Joseph. She could not afford to make a wrong decision again just because she was in love with a man. She had to make sure that there was a solid basis for their relationship, that they could make it work.

Seeing her hesitation, Jackson reached out and took her arms reassuringly. "Hey. You don't have to give me an answer right now. I'm not trying to rush you. I love you, and I'm willing to live with your decision. If you don't want to marry me, I'll accept it. If you want to wait for a while, that's fine, too. This isn't a now or never proposition. I told you—I plan on loving you for the rest of your life."

Beth smiled gratefully at him. "Thank you. I do need time to think about it. I just don't...want to make a mistake."

"Sure." He bent and kissed her on the forehead, then stepped back. "You're coming up this weekend, if Joey's feeling better?"

She nodded, and he left. Beth followed him to the door and stood watching until his car disappeared in a cloud of dust down their road. *What was she going to do?*

Beth spent the rest of the week nursing Joey through his first cold. As her father and the doctor had indicated, it was a rather minor ailment, and he was feeling better by the end of the day, his fever gone. Within two days, his runny nose was drying up, and he could breathe more easily.

Beth found that her own problem, however, was not as easy to deal with. She kept thinking about Jackson and his proposal, in a quandary about what to do. She thought of how much she loved him and how happy they had been together. But she reminded herself that she had to be logical, that one week of getting along beautifully did not mean that their whole lifetime would follow the same pattern. *What would their life be like when they had to deal with problems? How would they get along when things were rocky instead of smooth?* And no matter how much she loved him, she just was not sure that she could handle the fame. She had hated the way the tabloids had intruded on her life. *Wouldn't it be much worse once they were married?*

When she wasn't worrying over her decision to marry or not marry Jackson, she thought about Robert Waring. Ever since Jackson had told Beth about his daughter, she had been wondering if she had been wrong not to tell her former lover that she was pregnant. Maybe his reaction wouldn't have been what she expected. Even if he was a creep, maybe he would have been interested in Joseph; maybe Joseph would benefit from having a father.

Wouldn't Joey wonder about his father when he grew up? And what was Beth to say about the man? That she had decided without even asking Robert that he would not be interested in knowing whether he had a son? That she had decided for both of them that Joseph should have no father? Perhaps things *had* turned out better because Jackson's girlfriend had not told him that she was pregnant. But perhaps they hadn't. At least Jessica had had the excuse of being a teenage girl who had listened to her parents' advice. Beth had made the decision all on her own, as a grown woman. *What if she had just been punitive toward the man because he had hurt her?*

That thought cut Beth like a knife. She couldn't bear to think that she might have made a decision that was unfair or even harmful to her child simply because she wanted to get back at the man who had deceived her. And how could she ever really be free of the man if she knew that she had deceived him in turn?

Finally, on the morning when she was to drive to Austin again, still debating what she was going to tell Jackson, Beth decided to end one of her worries. She picked up the phone and dialed a Chicago number, a little surprised to find that it took her a moment to recall it. Once it had been indelibly etched on her brain. It was Robert's private line, and his secretary did not pick it up.

After three rings, Robert's familiar low voice answered, crisp and efficient. For an instant, Beth's throat closed and she could not answer.

She cleared her throat. "Hello, Robert."

There was a stunned silence on the other end of the line.

"This is Beth Sutton," she went on.

"Yes. I recognized your voice," he replied coolly. "I just could not believe that you had had the nerve to call."

"What?" Anger bubbled inside Beth. *He* was upset with *her?*

"After that righteous indignation of yours, now I find out that you were seeing that Hollywood director all the time. My secretary showed me a copy of that tabloid and said, 'Elizabeth Sutton? Isn't that the name of the woman in Texas who used to call you?' Of course, she just thought it was a curiosity. She didn't realize you had been telling me you were in love with me all the while you were having an affair with him."

"I can't believe this. *You* are accusing *me* of infidelity? After what you did? To begin with, those stories are untrue, and even if they were, at least I wasn't married with two children. I wasn't cheating on my spouse!"

"You were lying," he retorted evenly. "I find it hypocritical of you to berate me because I lied to you."

"I didn't lie to you. Honestly, Robert, I wouldn't have thought you naive enough to believe the tabloids. Or is it just a convenient excuse for you? Makes you feel less in the wrong?''

''My God, Beth, I saw the picture of you with him on the front of one of them.'' For the first time there was the faintest thread of emotion in his cool voice.

Beth had to smother a giggle at the thought of Robert, handsome and dignified in his Italian suit, picking up a tabloid and devouring it. ''Well, believe what you want, Robert. I called you because over the months I have realized that I—acted unfairly.''

''Stop right there.'' There was an irritating smugness in his voice. ''Please don't humiliate yourself, Beth. I can assure you that there is no chance of our resuming our affair.''

Beth let out an inelegant snort. ''That is *not* why I called. What I *am* trying to tell you is that when I found out that I was pregnant, I made a unilateral decision to keep the baby and raise it as a single parent. I decided not to even tell you. I've thought about it a lot recently, and I realize that I may have been unfair. You probably had the right to know that I was pregnant with your child. I shouldn't have kept it from you.''

There was another long silence. Then Robert's glacial voice said, ''If you think that you are going to get a dime out of me for that baby, you are dead wrong. The whole world knows that it's Prescott's.''

''It is *not* Jackson's child,'' Beth snapped back, fury rising in her. ''How dare you accuse me of something like that!''

''Don't be absurd. It's obvious that you're hoping to get money out of me in return for not bringing a paternity suit. And I'm telling you right now that you won't win. That child is not mine, and I will not let you extort me into paying child support.''

For the first time in her life, Beth was so furious that

she literally saw red. It took her a moment before she was in control of herself enough to speak evenly. She thought of this man, who would not even acknowledge Joseph, and she thought of Jackson, driving three hours to see Joey when he caught a cold. "You are absolutely right, Robert. You are not his father and you never could be. Jackson Prescott is his father."

She hung up the phone with a sharp click. Then she threw her things into the car, wrapped up the portrait of Jackson and the baby and stuck it in, too. At last, after strapping the baby in his car seat, she set out for Austin.

Her confrontation with Robert Waring had left her feeling free, not only of him, but of the fears that her relationship with him had engendered in her. She wanted to race to Jackson, to tell him that suddenly, from an unexpected source, she had been shown the path she should take. Maybe her heart had played her false with Robert. She had fallen impetuously in love with him without really knowing him. But her affair with Robert Waring was a far different thing from the love that had developed between her and Jackson, just as Jackson was a far different man than Robert.

Even though she had spent only a brief time with Jackson, as she had with Robert, she knew Jackson as she had never known Robert. She had seen him in a crisis; she had felt his support and strength. They had weathered some bad times; she had just been fooled by the fact that they had done so with laughter and warmth. The race to the hospital, childbirth, even the ridiculous confrontation between Jackson and her brothers, had all been problems, as had the stories splashed all over the tabloids. It was simply because they had gotten through them so well that she had thought they had never faced anything but happy times.

She had seen Robert for only brief stretches of time,

moments that had been consumed with the physical fire
between them. But she and Jackson had been together day
and night. They had been together making love and
changing Joey's diaper. She knew him—knew how he
acted, what he thought, how he handled things. Perhaps
she did not know every detail about him, but she knew
the essentials, the things that really mattered, as she had
never known with Robert Waring. It didn't take a lifetime
to figure out that she loved Jackson or that he was the
right man for her. It only took letting go of her fears and
listening to her heart.

She zipped along the roads leading to Austin, listening
to music and singing along. She hoped Jackson would be
home when she got there, as he had been the last time.

He was. But this time when he came out to greet her,
there was an oddly wary look in his eyes. Beth hopped
out of the car, smiling, and ran to leap into his arms and
hug him fiercely. She began to rain kisses all over his
face, and he laughed with delight, finally seizing her face
between his hands and holding her still long enough for
a thorough welcome kiss.

They got the baby out of the car and carried the bags
inside. Jackson carried the baby, talking to him and
checking him out for any lingering signs of his illness.
Beth walked into the open living area and whirled around
to face him. She beamed across the room at Jackson.

"I've got something to tell you."

"Wait." Jackson sighed. "You'd probably better see
this first. You're going to come across it sooner or later.
We might as well get it over with."

Beth frowned, his grim expression sending tendrils of
fear creeping through her. "See what?" She had the awful feeling that all her plans and hopes had just come to
naught.

He crossed to the coffee table in front of the sofa and

picked up a thin magazine. Beth let out a groan, recognizing a tabloid even at that distance. "Not another article."

Jackson nodded. "It's a beaut."

He handed it to her. Across the top, above the name *Scandal,* ran a headline about the mummy of an alien baby, thousands of years old, that had been found in Egypt. The rest of the paper was filled with a picture of Jackson with his arm around a beautiful blond woman. Both of them were smiling broadly and obviously happy. The caption read: Prescott Dumps Texas Cutie, Returns to His First Love. The woman was Melanie Hanson, one of the most beautiful and popular actresses in Hollywood.

Beth's heart felt as if it had dropped to her toes. For a moment she couldn't speak. She simply stared at the picture as though, if she looked long enough, it would somehow change into something more acceptable. She looked up bleakly. "Jackson?"

"God, Beth, don't look at me like that. It's not true. I swear to you that it isn't."

"But that's you. That's her. It doesn't look spliced."

"It's not. That is us. We had dinner together when I was in Los Angeles last weekend. And we were happy to see each other. But it isn't what they say. Melanie and I are friends. That's it. We are very good friends. It doesn't mean any more than a picture of you and one of your brothers with your arms around each other."

"But you said the other day that you and she were once an item. Didn't you?"

"Yes. And we were. We dated some when she first starred in one of my movies. But we quickly realized that we weren't interested in each other romantically. We liked each other, but as friends. We've been good friends ever since. She and I have gone out like this a hundred times, and they've never made a big deal of it before. It's just because of the stories about you and Joseph. They're trying to keep the story going. To sell papers."

"Oh." Beth had been watching his face, and now she looked back down at the paper in her hand. It seemed bizarre that any man would not be madly in love with a woman as beautiful as this one.

"It's you I love, Beth. You are the only one." He looked at her anxiously, his muscles so taut with tension that the baby picked up on it and began to whimper in his arms.

"Okay. I believe you."

Jackson let out an enormous sigh of relief. "Thank God." He started toward her. "I was afraid that I was going to lose you."

"No. I've learned to have faith in you. Not the tabloids." She grinned. "Besides, I'm making a vow. I am going to learn to deal with them."

"I promise you, I will put a stop to these stories somehow. I won't let it happen again."

"That's going to be a pretty tall order. You know how the tabloids are about Hollywood weddings."

He stopped again, staring. "What? Are you saying that—"

"I mean, when we get married, they'll be flying over with helicopters and trying to sneak into the church and all that, won't they?"

Jackson's face lit up. "Yes, they will. And you know what, at this moment I don't really care."

He crossed the remaining stretch of floor in two long steps and pulled her against him with his free arm. The baby, in his other arm, cooed, watching them intently, as Jackson bent and kissed Beth.

Jackson raised his head, grinning. "Hell, we just might invite them to the wedding."

* * * * *

CULLEN'S CHILD
Dallas Schulze

A Note from Dallas Schulze

"Write an anecdote to go with your short story," my editor said casually. I tried to muffle my whimper of dread. Give me a choice between writing about myself and walking barefoot over hot coals, and the coals win out every time.

It's just so hard to know what to say. I haven't lived in exotic places or done exotic things. I've lived in California for over twenty years now, most of them spent married to a really terrific guy who makes my life complete.

I have more hobbies than you can shake a stick at. I like to cook, especially to bake. If there's a needlecraft I haven't tried, it's only because I haven't heard of it yet. My current passion is quilting, but I also cross-stitch and knit. I collect dolls and dress them—the fancier and the more intricate the garment, the better. I love to garden, though I don't have as much time for it as I'd like. My reigning passion is writing, of course. Give me a notebook and a pen and I can occupy myself for hours.

When I was asked to contribute to a Mother's Day collection, my first response was, "Me?" After all, I'm not anybody's mother, unless you count my very spoiled calico cat, and I think she considers me more slave than parent.

Then my editor told me the theme for the book was babies, and I thought, Who can resist a baby? Who'd want to? So I thought up a story about a woman who thinks she has a very good reason for resisting a particular baby, and I put a baby smack-dab in the middle of her life. I hope you enjoy reading the end result as much as I enjoyed writing it.

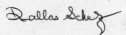

Chapter 1

A baby had never been part of the bargain.

Darcy Logan's expression was grim as she stared out the car window at the rain-washed scenery. The weather matched her mood, bleak and gray. She'd never been to Washington before and she hadn't seen anything yet to make her regret that lack. Oh, it was green and lush all right, but in the week since she and Cullen had arrived, she hadn't gotten more than a glimpse of the sun. It had been raining when they'd landed at the airport. It had been raining when they'd attended Susan Roberts's funeral and it had continued to rain in the five days since then. She was starting to think it never did anything else.

Of course, the weather was appropriate, considering the event that had brought them here. Cullen's sister had been two years short of her fortieth birthday when she died from cancer, leaving behind a six-month-old baby girl.

Darcy shivered. She'd never met Susan but her heart ached for what the other woman must have gone through. How terrible to be facing your own death when you should have been dealing with 2:00 a.m. feedings and diaper rash.

Cullen had taken his sister's death hard, she thought, glancing at him. Grief had carved lines that bracketed his mouth and had left a dulled sheen in his eyes. He hadn't been sleeping. She knew that because she hadn't been, either. Especially not the last couple of days since Cullen had told her that Susan had left her baby in his care.

Darcy's first reaction had been disbelief. And when Cullen had made it clear that he had every intention of fulfilling his sister's request, panic had taken over, closing her throat and making her heart pound.

"I owe it to her," he'd said before she could get out any of the words of denial.

"Don't make any quick decisions." She was amazed by how level her voice was. You'd never know that she felt like screaming her denial to the world.

"There's no decision to make. Susan made me the baby's guardian. She trusted me to do what's right for her."

"That doesn't necessarily mean that *you* have to raise her yourself," Darcy had protested reasonably. "Susan trusted you to make the right decision for her baby, but that could mean that somebody else—"

"There is no one else."

The flat statement had made her feel like an animal in a trap.

"What about your parents? Susan lived with them. She must have trusted them. They're the baby's grandparents. They might welcome a chance to raise her."

"No." Cullen had turned away from the window of their hotel room and looked at her, his eyes bleak. "The last thing she would have wanted was for my parents to raise her baby. That's why Susan made me her guardian, because she knew I'd never let that happen."

Darcy had stared at him, bewilderment and panic churning inside her. "But you said she lived with them."

"Because they made sure she was incapable of doing anything else," Cullen had said bitterly.

"I don't understand."

"You will when you meet my parents. I don't think I can explain it to you before then." He'd picked his denim jacket up off the bed. "Let's get some lunch."

And Darcy, too shaken to pursue the discussion, had followed him from the room and eaten a meal that could have been sawdust for all the attention she'd paid to it.

That had been yesterday and now, here they were, about to pick up Cullen's niece. About to destroy the happiness she'd found these past few months.

"This is it." Cullen's flat announcement dragged her out of her thoughts. He pulled the car over next to the curb.

Darcy glanced at the house, seeing a neat, two-story brick building bracketed by tidy flower beds. The white trim extended to the perfectly centered wooden porch, which housed a metal glider covered in pastel floral cushions. All in all a pleasant, if not particularly inspired, picture. Certainly nothing to cause the bleak expression in Cullen's eyes. He couldn't have looked more grim if the view had been a bombed-out inner city block rather than a plainly affluent suburban neighborhood.

She struggled with the urge to reach out and smooth the lines from beside his mouth. Despite the fact that they'd been lovers for eight months and had lived together for the last five of those months, she wasn't sure she had a right to try to soothe his pain.

They'd met at a party given by a mutual friend. By the end of the evening Cullen had persuaded her to go out with him, despite the fact that she'd avoided even the most shallow of entanglements for the past six years. But she'd been alone so long and he'd refused to take no for an answer. He'd made her laugh, something she'd done precious little of lately. So she'd agreed to go out with him, telling herself that her agreement had nothing to do with the fact that he made her heart beat a little too fast.

A week later she'd found herself in bed with him. Three months after that, when he'd found out that her apartment building was about to be turned into condos, Cullen had suggested that she move in with him. She'd refused, feeling that odd little flutter of panic that came with the thought of getting close to someone again. But he'd pointed out that she'd spent every weekend at his place, not to mention two or three nights a week. She was practically living there, anyway. Besides, everyone knew that two could live cheaper than one. Think of the money they'd save.

It was a silly argument. Neither one of them had any real financial worries. Cullen and his partner ran a very successful construction firm in Santa Barbara. Darcy's salary as loan officer in a small bank might not put her in the *Fortune 500* but she made enough to be comfortable. Living together had nothing to do with saving money and they both knew it.

Still, she'd let herself be persuaded. The truth was, Cullen filled up some of the empty spaces in her heart. He was like a fire on a cold, snowy night and she couldn't resist the urge to draw closer to him, to warm herself on his heat.

Five months later her heart was still turning over in her chest every time she looked at him. Not that it came as any surprise. Cullen Roberts had probably been stirring heart palpitations in women since he'd reached puberty.

Darcy looked at him, trying to define what it was about him that made him so impossibly attractive. His dark brown hair was worn just long enough and shaggy enough to make a woman want to run her fingers through it. His eyes were a clear, vivid blue and always seemed to be laughing, even when his mouth was solemn. And when he did smile... Well, a smart woman would run for cover, Darcy thought. She'd always considered herself a smart woman but she hadn't run far enough or fast enough.

But he wasn't smiling now. He was staring out the windshield, his hands still gripping the wheel, his mouth tight, his eyes bleak. Darcy noticed that he still hadn't looked at his parents' house, the house where he'd grown up.

"It's a very pretty house," she said when the silence had stretched to uncomfortable lengths. "Looks like a nice neighborhood to grow up in."

Looks like a great place for a motherless baby, she wanted to say, but didn't.

"I haven't been back here in seventeen years," he said, finally turning to look at the house. "When I left, I swore I'd never come back."

The uncharacteristic bitterness in his voice startled her. Since he'd never mentioned them, she'd assumed he wasn't close to his parents. And the fact that they hadn't exchanged so much as a word at his sister's funeral had confirmed the accuracy of that assumption. But the old anger that roughened his voice still caught her off guard.

"I guessed there were...problems between you and your parents," she said hesitantly. "But seventeen years is a long time."

"Not long enough. I wouldn't have stayed as long as I did if it hadn't been for Susan." The name cracked in the middle, his mouth twisting with pain as he thought of his dead sister.

Darcy touched the back of his hand where it was clenched on the steering wheel. This was the first time either of them had faced any sort of personal crisis and she was uncertain about offering him comfort. She'd barely known he had a sister until the early-morning call last week that had told him of her death.

"I should have come back for her," he said abruptly. "I shouldn't have let her stay here."

"She wasn't a child, Cullen. She was four years older than you are. If she chose to stay, there was nothing you could do about it."

"You don't know Susan. She isn't—wasn't," he corrected painfully, "strong the way you are. She didn't have the ability to stand up for herself. She'd stand up for me but never for herself."

Strong like her? God, did he really believe she was strong? She must be a better actress than she'd realized, Darcy thought bitterly, if she'd kept him from seeing just how weak she really was.

"Still, she was thirty-eight years old, Cullen. And she had a job at a day-care center. She didn't have to live with your parents. She could have moved out."

Cullen was already shaking his head. He shot her a look that said she didn't understand.

"You don't know my parents." Without another word, he pushed open his car door and got out.

Darcy fumbled with her seat belt, aware that her fingers were trembling. She had to talk to him before he saw his parents. Ever since he'd told her what was in Susan's will, she'd been trying to find the words to say what needed to be said. But they needed to be the right words, just the right tone of voice.

She finally mastered the unfamiliar latch just as Cullen pulled open her car door. It was more misting than raining, just damp enough to be annoying but not enough to warrant an umbrella. Darcy could feel the moisture settling on her hair as she slid out of the rental car. Cullen's hand came under her elbow, steadying her. Just as he'd been doing since they'd met—steadying her, taking care of her. God, she couldn't lose that now. And she would if she couldn't talk him out of this. She put her hand on his arm and tilted her head back to look up at him, ignoring the dampness.

"You know, Cullen, I've been thinking about this situation." Yes, that was good. She sounded calm, no trace of the screaming panic she felt inside showed in her voice. "I know you want to honor Susan's wishes, but have you considered the possibility that your niece might be better off staying with your parents?" She saw denial flicker in his eyes and hurried on before he could interrupt. "After all, even if *you* had problems with them, this is the only home she's known. Maybe it wouldn't be such a good idea to take her away from all that's familiar. The lawyer said that your parents want to raise her and this is a beautiful neighborhood. The schools are probably terrific and—"

He put his finger against her mouth, stilling the tumble of words. "I know we haven't really discussed any of this, Darcy, and I'm probably not being fair to you to make decisions like this without your input. But Susan made me Angie's guardian and I'm not leaving without her."

"I'm just trying to think of what's best for the baby," she said. She felt her cheeks heat with shame. *Liar. You're thinking of what's best for you. You know what's going to happen if he brings this baby home. You're going to lose him.* "Are you sure she wouldn't be better off with her grandparents?"

"You haven't met my parents," he said again, and there was something in his tone that told her it would be a waste of breath to continue the argument.

"What about the baby's father?" She was clutching at straws, but when you were drowning, it was worth grabbing at any possibility.

"The lawyer said he wants nothing to do with the baby."

"He might feel that way now. But that doesn't mean he won't change—"

"He's married and has three kids, Darcy. In the letter Susan left me, she said not to contact him, that he knew about the baby and had offered her money but he wanted no actual involvement."

"Oh." Darcy spared a moment of sympathy for Cullen's sister, for the hurt she must have felt. But she couldn't help but feel a wave of panic on her own behalf. Cullen wouldn't leave the baby with his parents and the baby's father wanted no part of her. That didn't leave very many options.

"Don't look so upset, honey." Cullen smiled down at her.

"I'm not upset," she lied.

Darcy didn't know what he read in her eyes, surely not the fear she felt. She'd spent years learning to control her expression, learning to reveal only what she chose. But whatever Cullen saw, it made his face soften, one side of his mouth kicking up in a lopsided version of the smile that had persuaded her to go to bed with him barely a week after they'd met.

He smoothed one finger over the curve of her cheekbone. "We'll work everything out, Darcy. I promise. Once the three of us get back to Santa Barbara, we'll take time to sort it all out."

The three of us. Words right out of a nightmare.

Darcy couldn't force a smile but she managed to nod. Apparently it was enough to satisfy Cullen because he bent to drop a quick kiss on her cold mouth.

"Thanks, sweetheart."

Linking his hand with hers, he led the way up the cement walkway. Darcy felt like a prisoner walking to her doom. These past eight months with Cullen had been the happiest of her life. And unless he changed his mind about letting his parents raise his sister's child, it was all going to come to an end.

Cullen could feel Darcy's tension in the hand he held. He knew she was upset, knew that he was probably being unfair in making a unilateral decision on such a major issue. They should discuss the impact a baby would have on their lives, talk about what kind of changes it would mean, how they would deal with those changes. He should ask her how she felt about bringing a baby into the life they'd built together.

He *should* do all those things, but at the moment he couldn't get past the basic facts: Susan was dead and she'd left her baby to him. She'd trusted him with the most precious thing in her life. And nothing—not even Darcy—was going to keep him from fulfilling that trust.

Darcy would understand, he told himself. Once she'd met his parents, she'd understand why there had been no choices to be made about this, why he hadn't consulted her, asked her what she thought.

There was a knot in his chest as he stepped onto the porch. He'd been a scared, angry seventeen-year-old when he'd left home. That was half a lifetime ago. At thirty-four, he was a successful businessman, with money in the bank. He owned his own home, two cars and half a boat. And since meeting Darcy, his personal life was on track. He was, by any standards you cared to apply, successful.

So why was he standing in front of his parents' door with a knot in his stomach and the feeling that he'd failed in some indefinable but significant way? It was a feeling that had been all too familiar when he was growing up, a feeling he'd thought he'd left behind him when he'd left home.

Darcy tugged on the hand he was holding, making him realize that he was crushing her fingers.

"Sorry." He released her. "I'm a little uptight, I guess."

"It's been a rough week." She reached up to touch the lines of strain that bracketed his mouth. Cullen was momentarily soothed by the concern in her eyes.

He brushed his fingers across her cheek. Even after all these months, he sometimes found it hard to believe that she was really his. He'd wanted her from the moment he'd seen her. He'd gone to his friend's barbecue only because he had nothing better to do, thinking he could always leave early if he wanted. Darcy had been standing in a patch of sunlight, her hair so pure a gold it almost hurt to look at it. He'd wangled an introduction, taken one look at the smile in her pale, almost crystalline gray eyes and fallen like a ton of bricks.

Darcy's light shiver brought him back to the present, back to the task at hand, which was getting Susan's baby out of his parents' house. He gave Darcy a quick, strained smile that didn't quite reach his eyes.

"This shouldn't take long."

Cullen ignored the doorbell and rapped his knuckles against the smooth oak of the door. He was aware of Darcy glancing at him, her eyes curious, and knew that she must have a lot of questions. He'd never talked about his family with her, so she could have no idea how he felt about this homecoming. But then, he didn't know much about her family, either. Maybe he should ask—

The sound of footsteps on the other side of the door made him break off the thought. The sharp tap of high heels on polished oak floors. His mother. The only woman he'd ever known who wore high heels at home. And then the door was opening and, for the first time in seventeen years, he and his mother stood face-to-face.

She hadn't changed much. There was more gray threaded through her medium-brown hair, a few more lines on her forehead. But her eyes were the same—looking at him, measuring him, finding him wanting. Just as she had when he was a boy.

"Cullen." Maeve Roberts's greeting was flat and emotionless.

"Mother." He was so tense that his neck ached.

"Come in." Her eyes, the same deep blue as her son's, flickered over Darcy. "Both of you."

Darcy felt the tension in Cullen as they stepped across the threshold. Not exactly a fatted calf kind of welcome, she thought.

The interior of the house was as neat as the exterior. Light oak wood floors, creamy white walls, a few delicately shaded watercolors on the walls—all very pale and restful. Not the kind of decor one associated with children. She felt her hopes of Cullen leaving the baby here slip a little more.

"Nothing's changed," Cullen said, half to himself. "This is just the way it looked when I was a kid."

"Your father and I enjoy our home," Maeve said over her shoulder. "We've seen no reason to change it."

She led the way into the living room, which was decorated with the same lack of color as the entryway. In here, the floor was covered with a plush carpet in a pale fawn color. Guaranteed to show every bit of dirt, Darcy thought. She resisted the urge to glance behind herself to make sure she wasn't leaving footprints.

"Cullen is here, William." Maeve made the announcement in the same flat tone of voice with which she'd greeted her son.

There was a strong resemblance between William Roberts and his son, Darcy saw as the older man set aside the paper he'd been reading and rose from his chair. It was there in the shape of his face, in the tobacco brown of his hair, still visible through the liberal sprinkling of gray. His eyes were blue, also, though a paler shade than his wife's and son's.

But where Cullen's eyes usually sparkled with life and his mouth always seemed to hover on the edge of a smile, there was a stillness about his father's face, a tightness about his mouth that made it difficult to imagine him smiling at all.

"Cullen." He nodded as if greeting an acquaintance he hadn't seen for some time.

"Dad." Cullen's greeting was just as cool. "This is Darcy Logan. Darcy, my parents."

Darcy murmured an acknowledgment, aware of William's cool eyes skimming over her and dismissing her.

"Are you my son's mistress?" Maeve asked in the same tone she might have used to ask if Darcy liked jam on her toast.

Darcy's mouth gaped in shock. She was at a loss for an answer. *His mistress?* Did anyone actually think in those terms anymore? Cullen's hand squeezed hers. In warning? In support?

"Darcy and I have been living together for the last five months," Cullen said. "Not that it's any of your business."

"I think we have a right to know what kind of moral atmosphere you're taking our grandchild into," Maeve said, pressing her lips together.

"No, actually, you don't." Cullen's tone was almost pleasant. "Susan's will gave me sole custody of her daughter."

"If she'd lived longer, Susan would have changed her mind," William said heavily. "She'd begun to realize the sin she'd committed, bearing a child out of wedlock as she had."

"I'm sure you helped her see that. I'm sure you made sure she knew every minute of every day just what a crime she'd committed."

"Unlike you, Susan had some understanding of the importance of strong moral behavior." William didn't so much as glance in Darcy's direction, but she knew the words were a reference to her presence. Clearly, as far as Cullen's parents were concerned, the fact that he had a mistress—good Lord, had they really used that term?—made it clear that Cullen didn't share his sister's understanding.

"Where's the baby?" Though she could feel the anger in him, Cullen's tone was level.

"She's upstairs." Maeve glanced at her husband. "We feel it would be better if she stayed with us. Clearly, you're in no position to be taking on the rearing of a child."

"Bring her down."

"Though your father and I didn't ask for this burden, we feel it's our duty to—"

"Are you going to bring her down or should I go up and get her?"

The steel in Cullen's voice cut through his mother's words. Glancing at his face, Darcy suppressed a shiver. She hoped never to see that look turned in her direction.

"Don't speak to your mother in that tone," William said sternly. "We've decided the child would be better off under our care. If you—"

"I don't give a damn what you've decided." Cullen's eyes blazed with an emotion perilously close to hate. "Susan made me the baby's guardian. If you want to argue with that, then you can do it in court."

"I see you haven't changed since you were a boy," William said, and the words were not intended as a compliment. "You're still overly emotional and thoughtless to a fault."

"You mean, I'm not a block of morally unimpeachable ice like the two of you. I'll take that as a compliment."

"You're thinking only of yourself here. You're not giving a thought to what's best for the child. If she stays with us, she'll have stability. She'll grow up with a firm understanding of right and wrong, with—"

"Without love, with no sense of self-worth," Cullen interrupted. "You'll break her spirit the same way you broke Susan's, the way you tried to break mine. Only I was lucky enough to have Susan to love me, to push me out before you could destroy me the way you did her." He took a short step forward, using the advantage of an extra two inches of height to loom over the older man. "Now, are you going to bring her baby down here or am I going to have to tear the goddamned house apart to find her?"

Cullen didn't raise his voice. He didn't have to. The cold rage in his eyes was threat enough. Darcy put her hand on his arm, half-afraid he might actually strike his father. His muscles were rigid as iron beneath her fingers. The silence stretched.

William looked away first, his pale eyes shifting to his wife. He nodded abruptly. "Get her."

Maeve's lips compressed. She glanced at Cullen and for an instant, Darcy saw some emotion flash through her eyes, something that could have been hatred. It was gone immediately, but the memory of it stayed in Darcy's mind, chilling her.

What kind of people were they that they could look at their son with such hatred, that they could talk about their recently deceased daughter having committed a terrible moral sin? Where was the grief they should have been feeling over Susan's death? The regret that their relationship with their only remaining child was such a shambles? Darcy shivered and drew her jade green jacket shut over the matching dress. It seemed colder in here than it did outside.

Maeve left the room at a measured pace, the skirt of her neat, powder-blue dress barely shifting as she moved. She was as tidy and soulless as the house, Darcy thought. No wonder Cullen was so determined to take charge of his niece. What must it have been like growing up in such a sterile, judgmental household? She'd spent less than ten minutes here and already felt chilled to the bone.

No one spoke while they waited. The tension that stretched between the two men was at odds with the pristine, colorless room. From the little she'd seen of them, Darcy suspected that Cullen's parents were strangers to strong emotions of any sort. Unless you considered feeling morally superior an emotion.

She heard the click of Maeve's heels in the hall and then the older woman walked into the room carrying a blanket-wrapped bundle. There was suddenly a hard knot in Darcy's chest, making it hard to breathe. She let her hand drop from Cullen's arm as he stepped forward to meet his mother.

Maeve hesitated a moment, her eyes meeting her son's. Whatever she read there apparently convinced her that further argument would be a waste of time. With a look of unconcealed dislike, she allowed him to take the baby from her arms.

Cullen showed none of the hesitancy Darcy might have expected from a man who had little or no experience with babies. His hold was secure, if a little awkward. She noticed that his hand was not quite steady as he eased the blanket back from the baby's face.

Uncle and niece stared at each other with identically colored blue eyes. The baby managed to work one hand free of the soft white blanket, waving it aimlessly in the air. She gurgled a greeting.

"Hello, little one." Cullen's facial expression was nothing short of captivated.

Baby Angie, with a wisdom far beyond her six months, solidified her position by rewarding him with a grin that crinkled her small face and revealed two tiny teeth. Cullen returned the grin and Darcy watched helplessly as his heart fell firmly into the infant's tiny hands.

Chapter 2

"Are you sure she's warm enough?" It was the second time Cullen had asked the question in the twenty minutes since they'd left his parents' house.

"She's wrapped in a blanket and the heater is on. Besides, it's damp but it's not that cold outside. This is Seattle not Siberia."

"Sorry." Cullen's smile was self-deprecating. "It's just that she's so little."

"Most babies are." Darcy flicked on a turn signal preparatory to making the turn into a supermarket parking lot. Baby Angie had come with a limited supply of basic necessities like diapers and formula. Clothes could wait until they got back to Santa Barbara, but the rest of it couldn't.

Once inside, they found the baby-food aisle easily enough, but the array of choices made Cullen's eyes glaze with fear. Taking pity on him, Darcy made a few quick choices, tossing items into a cart and trying to ignore the bundle in Cullen's arms, a feat considerably more difficult than she would have liked.

At the checkout counter, Cullen tried to hand Darcy the baby so he could get out his checkbook.

"No!" The refusal was automatic and held a panic-stricken note that made his eyebrows go up. She forced a smile. "I'll pay for it. I've already got my checkbook out." She waved it for emphasis.

"Okay."

She thought he gave her a questioning look, but the clerk chose that moment to admire Angie, who was peering over the edge of her blanket to offer that irresistible two-toothed smile. The clerk smiled fatuously. Cullen looked proud. Darcy kept her eyes resolutely turned away.

By the time they reached the hotel, the knot in her stomach had grown to roughly the size of a basketball and all she wanted was to lock herself in the bathroom with a full tub of hot water and not come out until her skin looked like a topographical map of the Sierras.

But when she mentioned the idea to Cullen, he looked as if she'd just threatened to abandon him in the middle of a jungle without so much as a can of bug repellent. He ran a construction company, for heaven's sake, she reminded herself. So how was it possible for him to look so utterly helpless holding a baby?

"I think she's wet," he said, sounding every bit as helpless as he looked.

"Babies do that. We bought plenty of disposable diapers." She pulled the box from one of the grocery sacks and set it on the bed.

To his credit, Cullen didn't ask her to do the job for him. He carried Angie over to the bed and laid her down, unwrapping her from her blanket with methodical care. Darcy told herself that she should get started filling the tub, but she didn't move. Cullen's hands looked huge as he fumbled with the series of tiny snaps that ran down each leg of Angie's pink romper.

The minute her legs were freed, Angie began kicking

and waving her arms in the air. She opened her perfect rosebud mouth and squealed loud enough to wake the dead. Cullen jerked back as if she were a rattlesnake coiled to strike.

"What's wrong? Did I hurt her?"

"There's nothing wrong. She's just letting you know she's here."

"As if I hadn't noticed," he muttered, warily approaching his niece once more.

It took some effort, but he managed to remove both plastic pants and wet diaper. Angie kicked harder, apparently delighted to find herself bare bottomed. Cullen disposed of the wet diaper and pulled a new one from the box Darcy had helpfully opened.

Diaper in hand, he leaned over Angie.

Both her tiny legs churned like pistons.

He gave Darcy a questioning look as if she might know the trick for getting a six-month-old baby to hold still.

Darcy shrugged.

Looking grimly determined, Cullen turned back to his niece.

Ten minutes and three ruined diapers later, lines of defeat had appeared beside his mouth. His fingers were locked around diaper number four, the knuckles white with tension as he eyed his opponent. She grinned up at him, and babbled something that sounded suspiciously like "I win."

Darcy was torn between laughter and sympathy. A heavy lock of dark hair tumbled onto his forehead. His eyes held a wild look generally only seen in trapped animals. There were damp patches on the underarms of his shirt, though the temperature in the room couldn't have been more than seventy degrees.

Darcy took pity on him. No matter how much she wanted to keep her distance, she couldn't stand by and watch him suffer. Not to mention that, at the rate he was going, they were going to run out of diapers long before they boarded their plane tomorrow morning.

"Let me try." She came forward and held out her hand for the diaper.

"I don't think she wants to wear a diaper," Cullen said as he handed it to her.

"She's just testing you to see who's the boss." She opened the diaper and set it on the bed next to the wiggling baby.

"*She* is," Cullen conceded immediately.

"Are you going to let yourself be bullied by a baby who probably doesn't even weigh as much as fifteen pounds?"

"Yes."

"Coward." She looked down at Angie, who waved her arms and babbled happily. Darcy couldn't help but grin back at her. She felt something loosen in her chest, like a key sliding into a lock that hadn't been turned in a very long time. But she didn't want to open that particular lock, she reminded herself. Not ever again.

"Your uncle is a coward," she told the baby. "Imagine a grown man like him letting a little thing like you bully him."

Angie babbled and cooed as Darcy caught both her ankles in one hand and lifted her far enough to slide the diaper under her bottom. A minute later, the baby was diapered, and a clean romper tugged on over her wiggling body.

"How did you do that?" Cullen demanded suspiciously, as if he hadn't watched the entire operation.

"You just have to be firm and remember that you're bigger than she is."

"I was afraid I'd hurt her," he muttered, staring down at his niece.

"Not likely. Babies are tougher than—" The words

caught in her throat, painful, as if she'd swallowed a fishhook.

"Than I think," Cullen finished for her, apparently seeing nothing odd in her abruptly ended sentence. "I guess they'd have to be or else the whole human race would be out of business. It's just that she's so little." He leaned down to touch Angie's hand and she promptly grabbed hold of his finger. "Look at how tiny her fingers are. And did you see her toes?"

"Yes." Darcy was pleased to hear how steady her voice was.

"It's incredible, isn't it?"

"Incredible," she said dully. Cullen glanced at her and she forced a quick smile as she turned toward the phone. "She'll probably be hungry soon. I'll call room service and see how we go about getting her formula heated up."

"And I wanted to call Sara and see if she'd be willing to do some shopping for us tomorrow morning."

"Shopping?" Sara Randall was Cullen's secretary. Darcy had met her a few times and liked her.

"For baby stuff. You know, cribs and strollers and whatever babies need. She's got three grandchildren. She's bound to know what to buy."

Darcy nodded and picked up the phone. "Good idea." Shopping for baby furniture was right up there on her list of favorite things, right next to having a root canal or getting her hair died purple.

"I don't know what I'd have done without Susan." Cullen's voice was low, in deference to the baby sleeping in a crib provided by the hotel. "She was the only thing that made life bearable when I was a kid."

The two of them were lying in bed. Darcy was exhausted, physically and emotionally, yet sleep had never seemed less likely. It was obvious that Cullen felt the same.

"The two of you must have been close." She looked over at his profile. He'd drawn only the sheer inner drapes earlier and the light of a full moon shone through them, illuminating the room with pale clarity.

"We were. I would have run away from home long before I was seventeen if it hadn't been for Susan. I didn't want to leave her and I knew she wouldn't come with me."

"Why? If things were so terrible, why did she stay?"

"It sounds melodramatic but I think they'd broken her spirit." Darcy heard the rustle as he shrugged. "I don't ever remember hearing a word of praise from either of my parents. From the time I was little, I was told what a failure I was, how I had to try harder to be worthy of the Lord's love. I remember thinking that I could do without His love if only *they'd* love me."

"They must have loved you." Darcy's protest was weak as she remembered the icy dislike with which they'd looked at him earlier.

"I don't think so. I'm not sure they even love each other. They're cold, soulless people, Darcy." There was no anger in his voice, only the flatness of someone stating a fact. "They never hugged us or told us we'd done a good job. If you got bad grades, you were sent to your room to contemplate your sins—their exact words—and they didn't speak to you for a week. If you got good grades, they never said a word. I think it would have been easier to deal with out and out anger. If they'd hit me, at least it would have been a reaction of some kind, an acknowledgment that they felt *something* for me."

"It sounds like a lonely way to grow up," Darcy said softly, her heart aching for the small boy he'd been.

"It would have been if it hadn't been for Susan. She was four when I was born and I think she was so desperate for someone to love and to love her that she practically adopted me as her own. She was always there for me, proud of me if I did something good, telling me I'd do better next time if things went wrong.''

"She sounds wonderful.''

"She was the best,'' he said simply. "I kept in touch after I left. As soon as I was scraping out a living, I asked her to come live with me. She always put me off and I let her.'' There was bitter self-condemnation in his words.

"You couldn't make her leave, Cullen,'' Darcy said. She reached out hesitantly and touched his shoulder, feeling the knotted muscles there. "She made her own choices.''

"I think she was afraid to leave them. Or maybe she was afraid she'd be intruding on my life.''

"Maybe. But she still had to make her own choices. You can't beat yourself up because she didn't take you up on your offer to help her leave.''

There was a long silence and she hoped Cullen was thinking about what she'd said. He couldn't hold himself responsible for the choices his sister had made. No one could force someone else to do what was best for them.

"She didn't tell me she was sick.'' There was a lost sound to the words that made Darcy's heart twist.

"She probably didn't want you to worry.''

"If she'd told me she was sick, I would have been here for her.''

"I know you would have.'' Darcy eased over, closing the gap between them.

"I talked to her a month ago and when I asked if she was all right, she said she was a little tired but that was all. I was in a hurry and I forgot to tell her I loved her.'' His voice was suspiciously thick.

"She knew, Cullen. I'm sure she knew.'' She could hardly get the words out past the lump in her throat.

Acting on instinct, she slid her arm under his neck and pulled him toward her. He was stiff for a moment, rejecting the comfort she was offering. The stiffness left him abruptly and his arms came around her in a convulsive movement.

"I didn't get to tell her goodbye."

His hold on her was painfully tight, but Darcy didn't protest. She stroked her hand over his thick, dark hair, offering him wordless comfort. There was little else she could do for him. Only time could heal his wounds.

And sometimes a wound was so deep that not even time could reach it. Her eyes were bleak as she stared over Cullen's head at the crib and the sleeping baby it held.

Any uneasiness that either of them might have felt the next morning over the intensely emotional scene of the night before was swallowed up by the hustle and bustle of getting ready to go to the airport. Angie was not a morning person and she announced this fact most emphatically.

Unfortunately there wasn't much that could be done about it, so the ride to the airport was made to the accompaniment of her protests. By the time they boarded the plane, she'd begun to regain the sunny nature she'd displayed the day before. At Darcy's suggestion, Cullen gave her a bottle to suck on as they took off and it seemed to do the trick because there were no more tears between Seattle and Santa Barbara.

In fact, she cooed her pleasure as she arrived at her new home. The adults, on the other hand, were more than a little the worse for the wear. After a week of emotional ups and down, the condo looked like paradise. As soon as Darcy got out of the car, she turned her face up to the sun, letting its warmth beat down on her.

But not even the California sun could warm her all the way through, she thought as Cullen got out of the car behind her with Angie cradled in his arms. His eyes met hers and she forced a smile. He had enough to deal with,

what with his sister's death and suddenly finding himself
with an infant to care for. He didn't need the additional
pressure of her own personal demons.

Sara Randall had proved herself more than worth her
weight in gold. She'd not only gone shopping for everything a baby could need, but she'd arranged to have everything delivered. Cullen's partner, Kiel Jackson, had
provided a key to the condo and the two of them had set
up the spare bedroom as a temporary nursery.

Tired as she was, Darcy welcomed their presence, especially Sara's. The older woman was more than happy
to hold Angie and exclaim over what an extraordinary
baby she was. In the fervor of her welcome, Darcy hoped
her own lack of enthusiasm would be more easily over-
looked. Not that she didn't agree that Angie was a re-
markably beautiful and good-natured baby. It was just that
she really didn't want to get close enough to notice such
things.

She only had to get through tonight, she told herself,
listening with half an ear as Kiel filled Cullen in on the
business of the past week. Tomorrow she'd be going back
to work and she wouldn't have to deal with the painful
ache that twisted her heart every time she looked at Angie.

A little time and distance, that was all she needed to
get things into perspective, to settle everything in her
head. A few days and she'd find a way to deal with the
situation. Not that there was much "dealing" to be done.
She could either adjust to Angie's presence in her life—
in *their* lives—or she could give Cullen up. And since
she was unwilling to do the latter, then she'd have to find
some way to cope with the former.

Darcy woke suddenly, her heart pounding, her skin
chilled and damp. Bits of nightmare chased her from
sleep, images too thin to catch yet that left her trembling

with remembered fear. It had been a long time since she'd had this particular nightmare, but the aftermath was still familiar. She'd never been able to remember much about it except for the sound of a baby crying.

A shallow wail brought her upright in bed, her breath catching in her throat. Still foggy with sleep, for an instant it seemed that the nightmare had followed her into the waking world, just as she'd always been afraid it would. But when the wail came again, Darcy realized what it was. Angie.

It was a real flesh-and-blood baby crying, not the wraith of her nightmares. Darcy sagged, her breath gusting out of her on a half sob of relief. Angie cried again and she felt Cullen stir. She started to sink back down against the pillows. He'd take care of the baby, just as he'd been doing since they'd brought her home.

Another wail, this one with a lost, inquiring sound that had Darcy on her feet before the sound died down. She could no more ignore that cry than she could walk on water. It called out some deep maternal response that couldn't be denied.

The addition of a crib had turned the condo's spare bedroom into a nursery. A heavy oak dresser served both to store Angie's small wardrobe and act as a changing table. The double bed had been shoved into a corner to make room for the crib, a stroller, a car seat, and a box of toys. Angie hadn't brought much with her by way of material possessions, but Cullen had made up for that lack.

Angie wailed again as Darcy entered the room, the sound dying down to a series of sad little whimpers. Ignoring the clutter illuminated by the night-light, Darcy walked across the room and stopped beside the crib. Angie was lying on her back, her face crumpled with tears.

"What's the matter?" Darcy asked softly.

At the sound of her voice, the baby's eyes flew open.

She stared up at Darcy for a moment as if pondering her presence. In the week since they'd brought Angie home, Darcy had managed to keep her distance for the most part. After considerable thought, she'd decided that that was her only option.

It was a ridiculously simple strategy but it had worked fairly well so far. She simply did her best to be elsewhere when Angie needed attention. There were times when it hadn't worked out that way, of course. If Cullen was showering or on the phone and the baby needed something, Darcy didn't ignore her. Not only would that have been unfair to the baby but it would have made her aversion to his niece obvious to Cullen. The last thing she wanted was him questioning her feelings about Angie and babies in general.

Making up her mind, Angie lifted her arms in a clear demand to be picked up, babbling something that could probably be interpreted as "What took you so long?" Darcy wondered if Angie thought she was her mother. Or did she remember Susan, wonder at her abrupt disappearance?

Angie babbled again, jerking her arms impatiently, but Darcy hesitated. She'd done her best to avoid holding the baby if she could. It hurt too much. It was stupid really. It wasn't as if she hadn't held other babies in the past few years.

Last year, there had been a mini baby boom at the bank and it seemed as if someone was bringing in a new infant every other week. She'd held each of them, admired them and had managed to hold the memories at bay. But Angie was different. Angie wasn't just in her life for a moment. Angie was here to stay and it would be so easy to let herself forget, to let herself get too close. That wouldn't be fair to either of them.

Cullen had been so busy adapting to his abrupt introduction to fatherhood that he hadn't had time to notice anything else. He'd even been letting his partner, Kiel Jackson, run their construction company so he could devote himself completely to easing Angie's transition to her new life. But eventually things would slow down a little and he'd realize that she treated his adorable niece much as she would a python, interesting enough to look at but something from which to keep her distance. And then he'd want to know why she was so careful to keep Angie at arm's length.

And just what was she going to say? "Sorry, I just don't like babies?" Or did she tell him the truth and risk seeing the look in his eyes change to contempt? The thought caused a stabbing pain in her chest.

Angie's smile faded at the delay and she whimpered, her lower lip quivering pathetically. Darcy moved automatically to stop the howl that was sure to follow that look. Cullen hadn't had a decent night's sleep since they'd got home from Seattle. If she could help him sleep a little longer by changing a wet diaper and settling the baby back in her crib, she'd do it.

She'd held Angie before. So the solid weight of her wasn't the shock it had been the first time. Still, Darcy's heart jerked a little as she felt Angie's small body settle into her arms. She closed her eyes a moment, her breath catching on the sharp pain in her chest.

Swallowing hard, she opened her eyes and drew a deep breath, forcing her thoughts to the here and now. She carried Angie to the dresser and laid her down. She could do this. She could change a diaper and get one six-month-old child back to bed without falling apart. After all, you didn't have to become emotionally involved to change a diaper. A couple of minutes and she could crawl back into bed, cuddle up next to Cullen and hope that the warmth of his body would drive away her own inner chill. How long could it take to diaper one baby?

Longer than she'd anticipated. Especially when that

baby was more interested in kicking and squirming than in getting a dry diaper. When Darcy started trying to pull off the plastic pants, Angie drew her knees up and waved her arms. A brief but vehement struggle later, Darcy was the proud possessor of both plastic pants and soggy diaper. Angie grinned at her and babbled happily.

"Don't tell me you were trying to help," Darcy muttered.

She dropped the diaper in the diaper pail and pulled a fresh one from the stack nearby. Angie kicked both legs, delighted to find herself bare bottomed, pleased to find herself with an audience at one o'clock in the morning. Or maybe just delighted with life in general.

Darcy smiled despite herself. It must be nice to be six months old and have nothing to worry about except growing up. Not that Angie's life had been picture-book perfect so far. Finding herself an orphan at six months was not exactly part of a fairy tale. But Angie had had Cullen to come to her rescue. Darcy folded a diaper and managed to get it under the baby.

Cullen had come to her rescue, too, though he probably didn't realize it. Before she'd met him, her life had been painted in shades of gray. Largely by her own choice, Darcy admitted to herself. She'd spent years building fences around herself, making sure she didn't get too close to anyone, that she didn't open herself to that kind of hurt.

And then she'd met Cullen and he didn't seem to notice the fences or, if he did, he'd chosen to cut through them. And she'd suddenly found herself living in a world of color again. Did he have any idea what he'd done? Did he know he'd dragged her out of her shell, made her feel again? Made her vulnerable again?

"You're a very lucky little girl," she told Angie. "Your uncle Cullen is a very special man and you're lucky to have him. *I'm* lucky to have him."

But would she have him much longer?

She pushed the question away as she finished diapering the wiggling baby and picked her up. Despite the tiredness revealed by her heavy-lidded eyes, Angie didn't seem to have any immediate plans to go back to sleep. Darcy couldn't help but smile at the infant's determination.

"You're a stubborn little thing, aren't you?"

Angie muttered, her eyelids drooping a little before being forced upward. Darcy rocked her gently, keeping her voice to a singsong rhythm.

"Afraid you'll miss something important if you go to sleep? It'll all still be there in the morning."

She continued to talk to the baby, nonsensical words, their meaning less important than the sound of her voice. As she spoke, she forgot about keeping her distance, about holding herself aloof. The soft weight in her arms felt sweetly familiar and right.

The dimly lit room was a pleasant haven, safe and secure. Darcy began to sing quietly to the baby, momentarily forgetting all the reasons she couldn't let herself get close to this small scrap of humanity, and allowing herself to simply enjoy the feel of having her arms full again after being empty for so long.

Chapter 3

The man standing in the doorway thought he'd never seen anything more beautiful in his life than the picture the woman and child made. Darcy was wearing a plain white T-shirt, size extralarge, that came halfway down her thighs. Cullen had never understood how something as basic as a T-shirt could look so sexy, but one thing he'd learned in the past six months was that Darcy Logan could probably make a trash bag look sexy.

But it wasn't sex he was thinking of at the moment. Or at least, that wasn't *all* he was thinking of, he amended, looking at the smooth length of leg beneath the hem of the T-shirt. Until this moment he hadn't realized just how beautiful a woman could look holding a baby. The tenderness in Darcy's expression as she looked down at Angie sparked a warmth somewhere deep inside Cullen.

She looked so utterly natural holding the baby, so right. The very picture of mother and child. For a moment he felt a piercing grief at the thought of his sister, who would never again hold her baby and sing to her. But a part of

Susan remained behind in little Angie. He couldn't bring his sister back but he could do his best to live up to the faith she'd had in him. He'd raise her child for her. With Darcy's help, he hoped.

She'd been so uncomfortable around the baby that he'd begun to wonder if Darcy was afraid of her. God knew, he could sympathize with the feeling, he thought ruefully. Angie scared the life out of him. There was no reason Darcy wouldn't feel the same.

As far as he knew, she didn't have much experience with babies. Though she'd certainly known enough to guide him through his first fumbling attempts at some of the basics like diapering and bathing and feeding. At the time he'd been too grateful for her knowledge to question its source. Vaguely, he'd thought it must be some inborn instinct that women had, but he doubted that knowing how to put on a diaper was part of the genetic code.

Now here she was holding Angie as easily as if she'd been doing it since the child was born. He envied her that look of easy competence even as he wondered how she'd come by it. It occurred to him that, despite the months they'd lived together, there was a great deal he didn't know about her. The present had been so absorbing that there hadn't seemed to be much reason to discuss past histories. Maybe it was time to think about changing that.

"You're very good with her," Cullen said quietly.

Darcy jumped and turned toward him, careful not to disturb the now-sleeping baby. The light was dim, but for an instant he thought she looked guilty, as if she'd been caught doing something she shouldn't. The guilt—if that's what it had been—disappeared immediately, replaced by the carefully neutral expression he was coming to associate with anything to do with the baby.

"It doesn't take any talent to change a diaper," she said lightly.

"I don't know about that." Cullen's smile was rueful as he came into the room. "It took me quite a few tries to master the skill, and I wouldn't have managed at all if you hadn't shown me how."

"You'd have figured it out. A man who can build a house isn't likely to be permanently stumped by a diaper." Darcy's tone was quiet but matter-of-fact.

"Houses don't wiggle while you're trying to nail up the next stud," he pointed out. "The first time I tried to change her, I'd have been willing to swear she had six legs and all of them moving at once. If you hadn't come to my rescue, I'd still be in that hotel room in Seattle trying to get her to hold still long enough for me to sort everything out."

"If you'd waited for her to hold still, you would still be waiting. Babies don't do still very well." She carried Angie over to the crib and Cullen followed, watching as she eased the infant down onto the mattress.

"So I've learned. Where did you learn so much about babies?" It was a casual question but he felt Darcy stiffen and there was a tiny pause before she answered.

"Baby-sitting," she said. "I did a lot of baby-sitting when I was a teenager."

"I didn't know that."

"No reason you should," she said, lifting one shoulder in a half shrug.

Her tone was so completely normal that Cullen wondered if he'd imagined that brief moment of tension. He reached down to tug a pink cotton blanket up over Angie.

"She'll just kick it off," Darcy pointed out.

"I know." Cullen brushed the back of one finger over Angie's cheek, marveling at the softness of her skin. "She's so small and helpless," he murmured. "It's kind of scary when you think about how dependent she is. Makes you a little nervous, you know."

"I know." Something in her tone brought his head up, but she turned away before he could see her expression. "Since she's settled, I'm going back to bed."

"I'll be in in a minute." But he was speaking to her back.

As Darcy left the room, Cullen turned back to the sleeping baby. Resting his hands on the top rail of the crib, he looked down at her, but for the first time in a week, he wasn't really seeing her. He was seeing Darcy the way she'd looked when he'd first come in, her face soft and practically glowing with tenderness. As soon as she'd realized he was there, that expression had disappeared, wiped from her face as if it had never been. As if there was something wrong with her showing affection toward Angie.

In the short time they'd lived together, he'd learned that Darcy was a very private woman. She reminded him of an iceberg, concealing so much more than she ever revealed. He had the feeling that she kept an important part of herself hidden away from him. Sometimes he wondered if he knew her at all.

Angie shifted in her sleep and the little blanket slipped halfway off. With a half smile, Cullen tugged it back over her tiny form. Brushing the tip of one finger over her cheek, he turned and left the room.

Darcy was in bed when Cullen entered their bedroom. Her eyes had had time to adjust to the darkness and she watched as he pushed the door partially shut behind him and crossed to the bed. His chest was bare and she let her gaze drift over the mat of dark hair that covered muscles hardened by physical labor. Cullen was as likely to be found swinging a hammer as he was reading blueprints.

Though she couldn't see it in this light, she knew his

skin was tanned from working in the sun without a shirt. The hair on his chest tapered to a dark line that arrowed across the flat plane of his stomach before disappearing into the low-slung waist of the black, cotton pajama bottoms he wore.

Despite her emotional turmoil, she felt desire stir in the pit of her stomach. Though they'd slept together every night, they hadn't made love since he'd gotten word about his sister's death, nearly two weeks past.

He stopped beside the bed. There wasn't enough light for her to read his expression but she could see the glitter of his eyes and knew he was looking at her. Perhaps it was the darkness or the lateness of the hour or the stress of the past couple of weeks, but it seemed to Darcy that he was suddenly almost overwhelmingly male.

He seemed to loom over the bed and when he lowered his hands to shove the pajama bottoms off his narrow hips, the hunger that tightened her belly was mixed with a touch of purely feminine uneasiness. She wasn't afraid of him but she was abruptly aware of the very definite differences between a man and a woman. He was so much stronger than she. There was comfort in that knowledge but a part of her acknowledged the potential danger inherent in that strength.

Her breath caught in her throat as the black cotton slid off his hips, revealing the strength of his arousal. Cullen must have heard the revealing sound because he grinned with pure masculine arrogance. If she hadn't been melting inside, Darcy would have been tempted to sock him in the ribs as punishment for that look. The throbbing ache in the pit of her stomach urged her to pull him down to her, to let him soothe that ache as only he could do.

She might have done just that if he hadn't grinned again and set his hands on his hips, bending one knee in a classic masculine pose, flaunting himself with infuriat-

ing impudence, daring her to resist him. She couldn't and
he knew it, damn his blue eyes. But that didn't mean she
had to give in without a fight.

Darcy eased out from under the covers and stood up.
Without a glance in Cullen's direction, she grasped the
hem of the plain white T-shirt and eased it slowly upward,
baring her body an inch at a time.

Cullen felt his mouth go dry as she drew the shirt up
over her hips, exposing the triangle of soft blond curls at
the top of her thighs. The slender curve of her waist and
the inviting hollow of her belly button were next and then
she paused. She gave him a sidelong glance that he felt
all the way to his toes.

She inched the shirt a little higher, baring her midriff
and the beginning swell of her breasts. His fingers curled
into his palms as he fought the urge to grab her and rip
the shirt from her before tumbling her back onto the bed.
She looked at him again, as if measuring his desire. Apparently satisfied with what she saw, she drew the T-shirt
the rest of the way off.

Cullen stopped breathing. It didn't matter how many
times he saw her like this, he was never prepared for the
impact she had on his senses. Her full breasts swayed as
she tossed the T-shirt away. She lifted her hands and ran
them through her hair, turning slightly so that he had a
perfect view of the inviting thrust of her breasts as her
arms lifted.

It was a game they'd played before, teasing each other
with pretended indifference, driving each other crazy by
looking but not touching. The game had only one ending,
but there was pleasure in drawing it out, in building the
fires slowly, letting the heat climb.

Tonight, Cullen wasn't in the mood to draw things out.
It seemed as if it had been months since he'd touched her,
forever since he'd touched that smooth, golden skin.

Darcy gasped when his hands closed over her hips, his fingers curving into her soft bottom as he pulled her up against his hard body with almost violent force. She threw her head back, her urgency rising to meet his. His mouth came down on hers, his tongue plunging into her mouth with no preliminaries, only a stark, driving hunger that added to the ache in her.

Her fingers dug into the rock-hard muscles of his upper arms. She twisted herself closer. His arousal was hot and hard against the softness of her belly, making her whimper with hunger. It seemed as if it had been so long since he'd held her like this, loved her like this.

Cullen lowered her to the bed, bracing his arm against the mattress as he followed her down. His knee slid between hers, and Darcy opened her legs to him, the tension inside coiling almost painfully tight.

"I don't want to wait." His voice was husky as the tip of his erection brushed against the dampness of her most sensitive flesh.

"Who asked you to?" she got out breathlessly. The arch of her hips was an irresistible invitation.

Cullen's first thrust took him deep within her, filling the emptiness. Darcy sucked in her breath and arched her body to take him deeper still. She needed to feel him all the way to her soul, needed to know that he was hers and hers alone.

Cullen groaned as he felt the heated dampness of her surround him. He felt completed, made whole in a way only she could do. He caught her hands in his, pinning them flat to the bed as he withdrew and thrust again.

Darcy dug her heels into the bed and arched to meet him. He lowered his body to hers, the muscular width of his chest crushing her breasts, the crisp mat of hair abrading her tender nipples. There was a tightly coiled spring low inside her belly and every thrust, every brush of his body against hers drew the coils tighter still until it seemed as if the pressure of it was more than she could bear.

And then Cullen's hands slid under her, his fingers digging into the soft flesh of her bottom, pulling her up to meet his solid penetration of her, deepening an embrace that couldn't possibly get any deeper, making her his all the way to her soul.

And the tension inside her shattered into tiny fragments of sensation. If she'd had the breath to do so, Darcy might have screamed. But he'd stolen her breath, her soul, her heart. She dug her fingers into the damp muscles of his shoulders, sobbing with the force of her pleasure.

Cullen groaned as he felt her climax take her. She shuddered beneath him as tiny muscles rippled and contracted around him, dragging him headlong into his own satisfaction. He pulled her higher on his invading flesh, feeling Darcy's nails bite into his shoulders as the movement prolonged her own pleasure.

And then he gave himself up and let the heavy pulse of release take him.

Through eyes blurred with tears of pleasure, Darcy saw Cullen's face above her, the skin tight across his cheekbones, his lips drawn back from his teeth, a guttural groan bursting from him. She lifted her legs and locked her ankles across his lower back, arching her body into his. He shuddered against her as the movement deepened their already impossibly deep embrace. The pleasure seemed to go on and on, long rolling waves of sensation.

It was a long time before Darcy gathered the strength to open her eyes. She felt heavy with exhaustion yet so light that it seemed possible she might float up from the bed without Cullen's weight to hold her down. There was a pleasant tingly feeling to her skin.

Cullen shifted, easing his weight onto his elbows and

looking down at her. It was too dark for her to read his expression but she caught the white gleam of his teeth as he smiled.

"That'll teach you to tease, Ms. Logan."

"I've certainly learned my lesson, Mr. Roberts." Her voice was almost as steady as his.

"See that you don't forget." The last word ended on a groan as she tightened certain muscles, demonstrating an admirable grasp of the situation.

"I certainly wouldn't want to tease," she said, widening her eyes in a show of innocence at odds with the far from innocent movement of her body.

"I can see that you wouldn't." Cullen flexed his hips, letting her feel his growing arousal.

"I wouldn't want to disturb you." It took considerable effort to keep her voice steady.

"I like being disturbed." Cullen wrapped his hands in her hair, using the hold to tilt her head back. Darcy shivered as she felt his teeth against the taut line of her throat.

It wasn't as urgent this time. Arousal built slowly, drugging her senses, melting her body into his until it was hard to tell where one stopped and the other began. Her response to Cullen never failed to surprise her. She'd always thought of herself as a rather cold person. But Cullen brought out a fire in her that sometimes threatened to consume her.

She moaned, her fingers clinging to his shoulders as the world rocked around them once more.

And for a little while Darcy could push aside her fears that she was going to lose him.

Chapter 4

"I can't believe that one baby requires all this stuff just to go out to dinner. A small army could march across the Gobi with less."

Darcy grinned as she watched Cullen struggle with the car seat and a bulging diaper bag. It was the first time they'd ventured out of the house with Angie in the two weeks since they'd picked her up in Seattle.

"An army doesn't have to cater to the needs of a baby," she told him.

"Well, if this is what it takes, there'd be a lot fewer wars if they did. Three months in boot camp couldn't prepare a man for carting all this stuff around," he groused. "Not to mention they'd be too tired to fight because they'd never manage to get a decent night's sleep."

The last was a mutter as he walked out the door to put his burdens in the car. Darcy was left alone with the baby. She looked at Angie, who was lying on the sofa with pillows mounded around her to keep her from rolling off. Having pulled one sock off, Angie was doing her best to bite her toes.

Darcy's hands twitched with the urge to pick her up but she resisted. She'd had plenty of time to think about the situation. Since coming back from Seattle, she'd thought of little else. The situation seemed impossible: she wanted nothing to do with having a baby in her life but Cullen now came with a baby attached.

And the one thing she was absolutely sure of was that she *did* want Cullen in her life. The realization of just how much was rather frightening to someone who'd spent the past six years carefully wanting nothing and most especially wanting no one. She'd lived with Cullen almost six months, but it had taken Angie's arrival to make her realize how much she'd come to depend on him, how much she needed him.

Her first reaction to the baby had been denial. If she told herself he didn't matter so much, then he wouldn't. But she'd never been much good at lying to herself. The truth was that she couldn't bear the thought of going back to the sterile, empty, *safe* existence she'd led before Cullen had come into her life. The happiness she'd found with him might be fragile—he'd surely hate her if he ever learned the full truth about her. But fragile or not, she didn't want to give it up, didn't want to give up the man who'd given it to her.

And since she couldn't ask Cullen to give up his sister's child, she was going to have to find a way to come to terms with Angie's presence in her life. Not so complex really, she told herself as she watched the baby contentedly playing with her own toes. Cullen hadn't noticed anything odd about her behavior toward his niece so far. And if he did, she'd just tell him she wasn't the maternal type. Then all she had to do was keep a little emotional and physical distance between herself and Angie.

How hard could that be?

Losing interest in her toes, Angie looked around for a

new distraction. Her flailing hand found the stuffed cloth block she'd been playing with before discovering the delights of toe chewing. She lifted it and studied it with a seriousness worthy of an entomologist examining a new species of beetle. Her eyes were exactly the color of her uncle's, that same clear, heart-melting blue. Darcy found herself smiling at Angie's serious expression.

"Ready?" Cullen's question preceded him. Darcy's head jerked toward the door as he entered.

"Yes." *There was nothing to feel guilty about,* she scolded herself.

"How are my two best girls?" At the sound of Cullen's voice, Angie abruptly lost interest in the block. Her head turned until she found him. Immediately her small face creased into a two-toothed grin and she began to kick both her feet in excitement.

Cullen's answering grin was nothing short of enthralled, Darcy thought as she watched him walk over to the sofa. Despite the lack of sleep he'd complained about, he looked devastatingly handsome. A shock of dark hair fell onto his forehead, emphasizing the blue of his eyes. He was wearing black jeans and a blue shirt almost the exact shade of his eyes. She'd bought him that shirt for Christmas. Now she almost wished she hadn't. He didn't need anything to make him look more attractive. The man practically qualified as a lethal weapon as it was.

"How's my girl?" he asked Angie as he leaned down to pick her up. His hands looked huge against her small body but he held her easily, with none of the uncertainty he'd shown at first. Held in midair, Angie babbled happily, both legs churning with the excitement of having Cullen's attention.

I know just how you feel, Darcy thought wryly.

The restaurant was new to both of them, a family kind of place with a menu that ran more toward hot roast beef sandwiches with mashed potatoes than filet mignon with tiny vegetables.

"I didn't think Angie was ready for Chez Bev," Cullen said, mentioning a restaurant they'd been to several times.

"I doubt they're ready for her, either." Darcy's tone was dry, but she didn't look particularly disappointed by his choice of restaurants, Cullen thought, glancing at her as he settled Angie into a high chair.

"You could be right. Imagine the waiter's expression if she spit a mouthful of baby carrots at him." He latched the tray in place before sliding into the red vinyl booth.

"It would cause a major crisis," Darcy agreed. "The chef would probably come out to ask her what it was about his special recipe that didn't appeal to her."

"I'm not sure her French is up to task," Cullen said seriously.

Angie babbled something and slapped both hands against the metal tray of the high chair as if demanding to know where dinner was.

"I don't know. I think she could get her message across in most languages," Darcy said dryly.

"You could be right." Cullen found a toy in the bulging diaper bag and handed it to his niece to distract her from the delay with mealtime. Angie promptly began to gnaw on the plastic ring.

Seeing that she was occupied, at least momentarily, he turned his attention to Darcy. One thing he'd learned about babies was the truly amazing amount of time they required. It seemed as if he hadn't had time to draw a breath. He'd been telling himself that he and Darcy would talk, that they'd discuss the changes Angie had made in their lives. But it had been two weeks and they'd yet to talk.

He'd never realized just how big a job it was to take

care of a baby, especially since he'd been thrown in at the deep end without the slightest preparation for the task. Without his secretary, who'd been willing to extend her job description to include shopping, and Darcy to show him the fine points of diapering, among other things, he doubted if either he or Angie would have made it to the end of the first week.

He thought he was starting to get the hang of it now, but it still seemed as if most of his waking hours were spent dealing with the minutiae of life with a baby. And the brief bits of time he had for anything else were spent trying to keep up with his business. Kiel hadn't complained about dealing with his partner's work as well as his own but Cullen didn't expect him to keep doing it. Besides, there were decisions that took the two of them to make. Add Darcy's job to the mix and the end result was that the two of them hadn't had a moment to themselves.

Except in bed. They communicated just fine there. But when he was in bed with Darcy, his urges ran to something more elemental than discussing life changes.

But now, here they were, alone, unless you counted Angie and the couple of hundred other patrons in the restaurant. It wasn't exactly intimate and he hadn't planned on starting a serious discussion tonight but maybe they could talk without too many interruptions.

"Darcy, I—"

"What can I get for you?" Their waitress looked about eighteen. She wore the same nondescript brown and white uniform the other waitresses wore but she'd accessorized hers with black ankle socks, combat boots and a small gold stud through one nostril.

Cullen managed to keep his expression under control until the girl had taken their order and left. Once she was gone, he leaned across the table.

"Who do you think does her makeup?" he asked, keeping his voice low.

"Lon Chaney. I'm sure I saw that same look in the original *Phantom of the Opera.* It's the hair I'm not sure about."

"You mean that spiky thing on top of her head is her hair?" Cullen widened his eyes in mock disbelief. "How does she get it to stand up like that?"

"Years of practice and a can of mousse."

The girl returned with their drinks. Once she was gone, Cullen's eyes met Darcy's and she dissolved in giggles. His rich chuckle joined her laughter. Angie chortled happily, unconcerned with the cause of the adults' good humor.

"We haven't laughed much lately, have we?" he said as their laughter faded.

"Things have been a little hectic." Darcy reached for the pottery cream pitcher and added a generous dollop to her coffee.

"That's an understatement." Angie threw the purple plastic ring onto the table and Cullen automatically returned it to her.

"I'm a banker. We're supposed to understate things." Darcy reached for her spoon. The plastic ring landed right next it and Darcy picked it up and set it on the high chair's tray.

"I know I said we'd talk—about the baby and everything. We need—" This time Angie threw the ring on the floor and then leaned over to look at the results of her effort. Cullen bent and scooped it up and started to hand it to her.

"She'll put it in her mouth," Darcy commented.

"What?" His thoughts on other things, he stared at her blankly.

"She'll put that in her mouth." Darcy nodded to the ring. "It's been on the floor."

"Oh. Right." He turned and stuffed the ring back into the diaper bag and came up with a cloth ball. Angie took it from him with a squeal of delight.

"Not that it really matters."

"Not that what matters?" he asked, feeling as if he'd lost the thread of the conversation.

"Whether or not she put that in her mouth after it had been on the floor. If she can survive chewing on her own feet, I suspect she's tough enough to survive the little bit of dirt it might have picked up."

"Then why did you stop me from giving it to her?"

"Because there's a grandmotherly looking type at the counter who's keeping an eye on us, and I was afraid she'd slap your hand if you did something she disapproved of."

Cullen looked in the direction she'd indicated, his glance colliding with that of an older woman who was sitting at the lunch counter. She beamed at him. He smiled in return and then turned back to Darcy, who was watching him over the rim of her coffee cup, her gray eyes bright with humor.

"Why is she looking at me like that?" he asked sotto voce, as if the woman might actually be able to hear him from fifteen feet away.

"She's impressed by how good you are with the baby."

"I haven't done anything." He returned the cloth ball to Angie, who'd flung it into the middle of the table. She promptly threw it again. Fetch was one of her favorite games, as long as someone else was doing the fetching.

His patience with Angie was so effortless that he wasn't even aware of it, Darcy thought. He'd turned his entire life upside down without a second thought to give his niece a home. And he didn't even see anything extraordinary about what he'd done. Watching him with the baby, it occurred to her that he was born to be a father. The role fit him like a well-tailored suit.

The realization seemed to open a gaping chasm between them, with her on one side and Cullen and the baby on the other. The bright lights suddenly seemed a little blurred and there was a constriction in her throat. She lowered her head and pretended to search for something in her purse while she got her emotions under control.

"Are you all right?"

Cullen leaned across the table and Darcy didn't have to look at him to know that he was looking concerned. Why couldn't he do things the way men were traditionally supposed to do them? Why couldn't he be an insensitive lout, oblivious to her feelings?

"I'm fine," she said, dragging a crumpled tissue from the bottom of her purse and dabbing it against one eye. "I just had something in my eye. It's out now."

She lifted her head and gave him a bright smile to show that everything was peachy keen. Cullen looked doubtful and she had the feeling that he might have pursued the issue if the waitress hadn't chosen that moment to return with their order.

"Here you go."

If Darcy had been starving to death, she couldn't have been any more grateful to see a waitress. Spiky hair, nose stud, combat boots and all, the girl couldn't have looked better if she'd been wearing white wings.

"Here's our food," she said cheerfully, just in case Cullen hadn't noticed the plates being set in front of them. She knew, even if Cullen hadn't yet figured it out, that there wasn't much chance of having an intelligent conversation while feeding a six-month-old baby.

He might want to talk about the changes in their situation, but she didn't. She didn't want to have to try to find a way to tell him that she'd continue to live with him but that she wanted to have as little as possible to do with the baby. He was sure to want to know why and she didn't have the words to give him. Unless she told him the truth and that was out of the question.

Apparently, Cullen realized that serious conversation and feeding a baby were not compatible activities. Darcy gradually relaxed as the conversation stayed on relatively neutral ground. She told him what had been going on at her job. He mentioned a new construction project that he and Kiel were going to bid on.

It was so much the kind of conversation they'd always had that if she closed her eyes, Darcy could almost have believed that it was B.B.—Before Baby.

She watched with admiration as he managed to eat his meal while feeding Angie. She'd never been half so good with— She cut the thought off, turning her thoughts from that particular path. It wasn't difficult, she'd had years of practice.

They were nearly finished with their dinner when the older woman who'd smiled at Cullen earlier approached the table.

"I hope you don't mind, but I just had to get a closer look at your baby."

"Not at all," Cullen said, casting a quick look in Darcy's direction. She shrugged. He'd learn that babies had a way of starting conversations between total strangers, whether you wished it or not.

"I couldn't help but notice her when you brought her in." She leaned over to peer at Angie, who gave her a cheerful smile. "Not a shy bone in her body," the woman said delightedly. "She's the spitting image of my Wanda. Not now, of course, because she turned forty-eight this last March. She says she's only forty-one but that's not something a mother's likely to forget, now is it?''

She fixed Darcy with bright blue eyes and Darcy nodded obediently. "I can't imagine how."

"Exactly what I told Wanda. Besides, I have her birth certificate," Wanda's mother said triumphantly.

"I doubt these folks want to hear about that, Millie." Millie's husband had been standing behind her, looking mildly embarrassed by his wife's chatter.

"I suppose not, but it's just so exasperating. I mean, she can have all the nips and tucks she wants and dress up like a teenager and I don't say a word about it, but it seems to me she's going a bit far when she starts lying to her own mother about her age."

Silence seemed the only safe response. Darcy saw a suspicious tuck in Cullen's cheek and knew he was struggling to hold back a laugh. Obviously he was in no hurry to leap into the conversation.

"Millie." Mr. Millie was starting to look as if he wished he were somewhere else.

"All right. I'll stop nattering on." Millie smiled down at Angie again. "I just had to tell you two what a beautiful little girl you have here. Not that I can't see that you already know that," she added. "She's lucky to have parents who care for her the way you two obviously do."

"Oh, but—"

"Thank you." Cullen's voice cut across Darcy's automatic attempt to correct the woman's assumption that they were Angie's parents.

With a last smile at the baby, Millie departed. At another time Darcy would have been amused to see that Mr. Millie had his hand firmly around his wife's upper arm as if to prevent her from dashing back to talk some more.

But there was a funny ache in her chest that made it difficult to see the humor in the scene. It was silly to let something so small cause her pain. What did it matter that Millie-Wanda's mother thought Angie was her child?

It didn't matter at all except that, for a moment, she'd have given almost anything for it to be true.

"I didn't see any reason to get into explanations," Cullen said.

"No, of course not." Darcy forced a smile as she looked at him. "She was quite a character, wasn't she?"

"I think her husband was about ready to gag her."

"I have a sneaking sympathy with poor Wanda." Darcy wondered if it was her imagination that made Cullen's humor seem a little forced. "All that nipping and tucking and then betrayed by your own mother."

"Must be rough."

They finished their meal, though Darcy could barely remember what she was eating. She refused dessert with a smile. The tightness in her stomach made her wonder if she'd be able to keep down what she'd already eaten.

Angie was asleep almost as soon as Cullen strapped her into her car seat. The drive home was silent, with Darcy pretending an intense interest in the scene outside her window. She knew, with an instinct she didn't question, that Cullen had every intention of having that long-delayed talk tonight. The one that would inevitably involve some discussion of the future, of Darcy's place in the future he and Angie were bound to share.

Logically, she supposed such a discussion couldn't be postponed forever, not when it involved Angie's future. But surely it could be delayed just one more night.

Cullen turned the car into the slot in front of the condo and it had barely stopped moving before she reached for the door handle.

"I'll get the diaper bag," she said, snatching it up and making her escape.

It took time to get a baby out of a car seat. Maybe she

could be in the shower by the time Cullen reached the condo. She might have succeeded in doing just that if it hadn't taken even more time than usual to dig her keys out of the bottom of her cavernous purse. She was going to get a smaller purse, she promised herself as Cullen joined her on the porch, the baby asleep in his arms. Or a bigger key chain.

"I'm going to hop in the shower," she said without looking at him.

"Darcy." Cullen's voice halted her flight across the living room. "I'd like to talk to you."

"Could it wait?" she asked without turning.

"I think it's waited long enough."

"I was just—"

"Please."

The single word was more effective than if he'd shouted. She stopped and turned to look at him, trying to keep the uneasiness from her voice.

"It's getting late—"

"It's not even nine o'clock."

"I have to get up in the morning."

"It's Saturday. You can sleep in."

He wasn't going to give up. Darcy sighed.

"Why don't you put Angie to bed?" She ran her fingers through her hair, letting it tumble back to her shoulders like a pale gold curtain. "I'll put some coffee on."

"Thanks." They both knew he wasn't thanking her for making coffee.

Chapter 5

Cullen stopped in the kitchen doorway and indulged himself by simply looking at Darcy. The warm scent of coffee filled the air. She was getting mugs from the cupboard. Their position on the second shelf meant she had to reach to get them and her T-shirt rode up, baring a swatch of pale skin above the waist of her jeans.

He knew the taste of that skin, knew that if he dragged his tongue along the length of her spine, she'd tremble with need. He knew the way the soft flesh of her bottom yielded beneath his fingers. Knew that kissing the back of her knee made her giggle. He knew every inch of her, every muscle, every nerve, just where to touch her to have her dissolve in his arms.

She was his. He hadn't been her first lover but he'd been the first to satisfy her, the first to show her the potential of her own body. He'd never asked about her past lovers, any more than she'd asked about his. Never questioned her shocked surprise the first time she'd come apart in his bed.

Whoever the man was—and he had the feeling there'd

only been one—he'd been a fool. But Cullen admitted to a sneaking feeling of gratitude toward the unknown fool. He liked it that he'd been the one to introduce Darcy to passion. He didn't care if he was first but he damn well wanted to be last.

As if sensing his gaze, Darcy turned suddenly to face him, her fingers tight around the cups she held.

"I didn't hear you," she said, her voice a little sharp with surprise.

"Sorry. I'll try to learn to stomp." Cullen pushed himself away from the door and came farther into the kitchen. "Coffee smells good. Thanks for making it."

"You're welcome. It's decaf. I didn't think either one of us needed caffeine at this time of night."

"You're probably right." He certainly didn't need anything to keep him awake and she looked tense enough to shatter at any moment.

She set the mugs on the counter and poured coffee in them while Cullen got a carton of half-and-half from the refrigerator.

"Did you get Angie to bed all right?"

"Out like a light."

Cullen poured a dollop of half-and-half into the mug decorated with a lavender and white carousel horse. The other mug displayed a folk-art-style painting of a cat. The mugs were among Darcy's contributions to their living arrangements. Before she'd moved in with him, he'd had two plates, two forks, two knives, two of everything. And the only coffee cup he'd owned had been a chipped white cup that looked as if it had been recovered from the wreck of the *Titanic*. Darcy's collection of colorful mugs was only one of the many ways she'd brightened his life.

Without discussing it, they took their coffee into the living room. Darcy curled up on the sofa. Cullen chose the big leather chair that sat at an angle nearby. He took a sip of his coffee and then stared down into it. Darcy took a sip of hers and then studied a piece of lint on the arm of the sofa.

The silence was deafening.

"I wanted—"

"You said—"

They both broke off and looked at each other. Cullen nodded. "You first."

"I was just going to mention that you'd said you wanted to talk to me."

"Funny. I was just going to mention the same thing." His smile was rueful. Darcy's was uncertain. But the tension that had been threatening to suffocate both of them was broken.

Cullen set his cup down on the thick sheet of glass that formed the top of the coffee table. It was supported by a gnarled piece of driftwood. He was going to have to get a new coffee table, he thought absently, noting the sharp corners of glass. Either that or find a way to pad the edges of this one. Angie was already standing up with a bit of support. According to what he'd read, it wouldn't be long until she was trying to walk and he didn't want her to crack her head open on the coffee table.

He said as much. Darcy looked surprised but she glanced at the table and nodded.

"The edges could probably be padded, maybe tape some old towels to the glass." She shook her head, her mouth curving in a half smile. "Early American Baby decor."

"Not likely to start any new trends."

"Well, it might not attract the designer crowd," she agreed.

"Do you mind?" he asked abruptly.

"That *House & Garden* isn't beating a path to our door?" She raised her brows.

"That there've been so many...changes because of the baby." He saw her fingers tighten around the mug and her eyes shifted away from his.

"I think it goes with the territory," she said lightly.

"Yes. But I couldn't blame you if you resented it." He set down his barely touched coffee and stood up. There was too much churning inside him for him to sit still. "You didn't ask for any of this."

"You didn't, either."

"No. But Susan was *my* sister, not yours." He turned and paced to the sliding-glass door that led out onto the patio. Twitching aside the curtain, he stared out into the darkness, half wishing he hadn't brought the subject up. They'd been rubbing along together all right. Why rock the boat?

Because you don't want it capsizing under you when you least expect it. Because you don't want to lose the best damn thing that's ever happened to you.

He turned back to her with an abruptness that made Darcy jump. "Look, I know I didn't give you any choice about this. And I know I should have. I had no right to throw your life into turmoil without even discussing it with you."

"What was there to discuss?" She leaned forward to set her cup down, the faint tremor in her hand belying the calm reason of her voice. "You couldn't leave Angie where she was and there was no one else who could take her."

"Yes." They were the same arguments he'd used on himself and the logic of them sounded just as inescapable as it had then. But that didn't soothe his conscience. "I should have—"

"You did exactly what you should have," Darcy interrupted. She stood up and walked over to where he stood, setting one slim hand on his arm and looking up at him. "I'm not upset or angry that you didn't discuss this with me, Cullen. The decision was only yours to make and you couldn't have made any other."

He stared down at her, an uncharacteristic brooding look in his blue eyes. She was so good at hiding what she was thinking, what she was feeling. It could have been a natural part of her makeup but he'd always suspected that it was something she'd learned through hard experience.

From the first moment he'd met her, he'd seen the shadows in her eyes. Someone or something had hurt her in the past. Hurt her badly enough to put those shadows there. They'd begun to fade over the past few months, as if she were—very slowly—starting to forget whatever it was that had marked her. Or if not forgetting, then at least putting it behind her.

But just lately the shadows were back, turning her clear gray eyes smoky, muting the sparkle he'd come to love. He was afraid she was slipping away from him and if he lost her, he'd lose the best part of his life.

"You're not happy."

The flat statement hit Darcy with the force of a blow. She let her hand drop from his arm as she took a quick step back, grateful that the light from the single lamp wouldn't be enough to reveal the way the color had drained from her cheeks.

"I don't know what you mean." It was a weak response, but it was the best she could do. She'd been so sure that she'd concealed her feelings from him, so careful not to allow even the smallest crack in the facade.

"I mean, you're...uncomfortable around Angie." Cullen hesitated over the choice of words. The feeling he got from Darcy wasn't discomfort. It was more like fear, but that sounded too ridiculous to say out loud.

"I haven't spent a lot of time around babies, that's all."

"You said you'd done some baby-sitting," he reminded her.

"Baby-sitting is a little different from having one around full time," she said lightly.

"True."

But he continued to look at her, those clear blue eyes asking questions she couldn't—wouldn't—answer. If he knew the real reason...

"I—I guess I'm not really the maternal type," Darcy said, lifting one shoulder in a half shrug. "I mean, I think Angie's adorable and all that, but she doesn't *do* a whole lot, if you know what I mean. You can't talk to her or anything."

She shrugged again, keeping her face turned from the light to hide the color burning in her cheeks. She hadn't realized she had it in her to sound so completely shallow and inane. *You can't talk to her.* As if she expected to be able to discuss Dostoyevski with a six-month-old baby. If Cullen hadn't despised her before, he probably would now.

"I guess that sounds pretty stupid," she muttered when he didn't say anything.

"No. I think I understand what you're saying." What he didn't understand was why she was telling him such a barefaced lie. He didn't doubt that there were a good many people who felt that way. He could even understand it to a certain extent. But he'd have bet any amount of money that that wasn't how Darcy felt.

"I used to think I wanted to be a mother," Darcy said, almost choking on the words. "But I guess maybe I don't have the requisite genes. I know that's not what you want to hear. Obviously you'd like me to say that I'll be a terrific mother to Angie, but I don't think I'm cut out for the job. I know that's a real problem.''

She stopped and swallowed hard. It required every bit of self-control to keep her voice level while she said what had to be said. "If you want me to move out—"

"No!" Cullen's response was reassuringly quick and emphatic. "That's the last thing I want.''

He reached out and caught her hand in his as if afraid she might dash out the door that instant. Darcy drew a deep breath and closed her eyes for a moment, relief so powerful inside her that her knees actually felt weak.

"I don't want you to go,'' Cullen said firmly. He pulled her into his arms and Darcy went willingly, resting her head against his chest and feeling the strong beat of his heart beneath her cheek.

"I don't want to go,'' she said, and Cullen knew the admission didn't come easily.

She guarded herself so carefully, he thought, bending to rest his cheek against the top of her head, inhaling the soft scents of shampoo and soap. Darcy rarely wore perfume and he'd decided that the natural smell of a woman was far more erotic than the most expensive perfume could ever be.

"We'll work things out,'' he told her.

"But Angie has to come first. I wouldn't want to hurt her.''

"We'll work everything out. If the fact that you can't talk to her really bothers you, just wait a year or so. According to Sara Randall, she'll be talking like a magpie by then.''

Darcy's laugh was choked and she closed her eyes to hold back tears. What had she ever done to deserve a man like Cullen Roberts? But there was something to what he said. If she could hold on until Angie was a little older, until she wasn't quite so afraid of—

She blocked the thought, focusing instead on the feel of Cullen's arms around her. She always felt safe when he held her.

"We'll work everything out," he said again.

If she'd just tell him what was really bothering her, maybe he'd be able to do something about it, Cullen thought. He felt as if he was shadowboxing. He could get glimpses of the enemy but there was nothing to catch hold of, nothing to tell him what he was fighting.

But he wasn't giving up. He was going to find out what was behind those shadows in Darcy's eyes and he was going to banish them forever.

Cullen rearranged his work schedule, bringing most of his paperwork home with him so that he could take care of Angie. When he had to be out on a site, he left her with Sara Randall's youngest daughter. Divorced, with two children of her own, Marie welcomed the extra money and Cullen knew Angie would be well cared for.

Though it had been less than a month, it was already impossible for him to imagine his life without Angie in it. Until his sister's death, he hadn't given much thought to fatherhood. He'd had a vague idea in the back of his head that he might like to have a child someday but, at thirty-four, he hadn't felt that there was any rush to make plans.

Now, abruptly, he found himself plunged into the deep end of parenthood and enjoying it more than he'd ever have imagined. Every day was a new discovery, for himself as well as for Angie. She'd filled a gap in his life he hadn't even realized was there.

With her and Darcy, his life was complete. All he had to do was figure out a way to prove to Darcy how right the three of them were together.

*   *   *

Darcy had mixed feelings about seeing the ties grow
ever stronger between Cullen and his niece. She couldn't
wish anything less for either of them, but with each day
that passed, it seemed clearer that she didn't—couldn't—
fit into the tidy picture before her.

Still, things were better than they had been. Talking
with Cullen had helped. She hadn't told him the truth—
at least not all of it—but she'd made it clear that he'd
better not count on her to round out the happy family
picture. And it seemed as if he'd accepted that. He certainly didn't thrust Angie into her arms in an attempt to
encourage some kind of bonding between them.

Without the pressure of expectations—even if they had
been strictly her own—Darcy found herself, paradoxically, more comfortable around the baby than she had
been. She relaxed enough to allow herself to enjoy the
innocent pleasure Angie took in everything that happened
into her field of vision.

She'd almost forgotten the sheer fun to be had in
watching those moments of discovery that came so often
for an infant. Angie was fascinated by everything she saw
and innocently confident that the world was her personal
oyster.

It would have taken a much harder heart than Darcy's
not to be touched by the baby's pleasure in life. There
was a certain pain in watching Angie, but it wasn't as
sharp as she'd expected it to be. Apparently, time really
did, if not heal, then at least numb all pain.

As long as Cullen didn't expect her to be responsible
for Angie, she could almost let herself believe that things
might work out, after all.

The early-summer days slipped by in a not unpleasant
pattern. An evening in early June found Darcy and Cullen
both at home. Darcy had fixed dinner and afterward
they'd settled in the living room. Cullen was reading a

list of recent changes in the building code that could affect projects he and Kiel had coming up. Darcy had a new mystery open in her lap, but her attention kept wandering from the book.

After twenty minutes on the same page, with not a word of it sticking in her head, she gave up. She looked up, wondering if Cullen's building codes were as boring as her novel. If they were, maybe he'd be interested in watching an old movie on cable. He was sound asleep, which answered her question about how boring the building codes were, she supposed.

Darcy's features softened as she looked at him. He probably needed the sleep. Between running J&R Construction and taking care of Angie, he was handling two full-time jobs. It was no wonder he was dozing off at seven o'clock.

She caught a movement out the corner of her eye and turned to see Angie crawling in her direction. Well, "crawl" wasn't an entirely accurate description. It was more a series of belly flops, but what she lacked in coordination, Angie made up for in determination. Since discovering this new method of locomotion a few days before, she'd become an inde-fatigable explorer, which had required some hasty re-decorating to get every possible danger out of her reach.

Now Angie was making her way toward Darcy with solemn perseverance, her blue eyes fixed on Darcy's bright purple socks. Smiling, Darcy wiggled her toes a little. With a grunt of effort, Angie heaved herself the last few inches and flopped onto her belly in front of her goal. Her tiny fingers closed over Darcy's toes, her grip surprisingly strong.

Darcy wiggled her toes again, enjoying the little girl's intent frown as she studied this new toy. Having examined with sight and touch, there was only one choice left, which was taste.

"Hey." Darcy laughed softly as she leaned forward to scoop the baby up. "It's one thing to chew on your own toes but you can't go around munching on other people's. It's just not done in polite society."

Angie was willing to give up the purple sock in exchange for being held. Besides, her new position put her in reach of other interesting objects. Chubby fingers closed around the gold chain Darcy wore around her neck. The chain had been a birthday gift from Cullen not long after she'd moved in with him and she rarely took it off.

"That was a present from your uncle," she told the baby. Angie didn't lift her eyes but continued to study the chain very seriously. After a moment she leaned forward to taste it. Laughing, Darcy pulled her back. "You're going to have to get over this tendency to put everything in your mouth, punkin."

Deprived of the chain, Angie reached for Darcy's nose. Darcy shook her head free and caught one little hand in hers. Bringing it to her mouth, she nibbled on the tiny fingers, drawing a rich baby chuckle. For a few moments she completely forgot all the reasons she needed to keep her distance, for Angie's sake as well as her own, and she let herself simply enjoy the small person in her arms.

From his position on the sofa, Cullen watched the two of them through slitted eyes. He knew that the instant Darcy realized he was awake, she'd get that oddly guilty look on her face and hand the baby to him.

No maternal feelings, his Aunt Fanny. In the rare moments like this, when she forgot whatever it was that haunted her, she was as natural a mother as it was possible to imagine. Her quiet laughter mixed with Angie's fat chuckles and he thought he'd never heard a sweeter sound in his life.

She loved Angie, whether she knew it or not. And though she'd never said the words, he knew Darcy loved him. And God knew, he loved her more than he'd ever dreamed possible. He'd cajoled her into moving in with him, then he'd waited for her to open her eyes and see that what they had was too special to give up. His becoming Angie's guardian had thrown a monkey wrench in the works, but only for a little while. Surely Darcy was starting to see that they could work things out.

Smiling, she buried her nose in Angie's neck, eliciting squeals of delighted laughter as Angie's chubby hands caught fistfuls of Darcy's pale gold hair. Cullen felt his heart swell with love for them both and he was unashamed of the sharp sting of tears at the backs of his eyes.

He was willing to admit to a few doubts, but now he knew that it was going to be all right, after all.

Chapter 6

"What have you got planned for today?" Cullen asked. He was sitting at the table, feeding Angie her breakfast when Darcy walked into the kitchen.

"Shopping. And I wanted to catch up on some paperwork I brought home with me yesterday. Everyone and their dog wants a loan. There aren't enough hours in the day to get everything done."

She opened the refrigerator and peered inside, hoping for inspiration. The sight of last night's leftover pizza made her stomach churn sluggishly and she shut the door. Maybe she'd just have a cup of coffee this morning.

She'd awakened in the middle of the night again last night and had been unable to resist the need to go into the nursery and stand next to the crib, watching the steady rise and fall of the baby's breathing. Reassured, she'd gone back to bed, only to wake an hour later, trembling in the aftermath of a nightmare. It was the third night this week that her sleep had been chopped up and the strain was starting to tell. She felt gray and worn.

"You look tired," Cullen commented as she poured

herself a cup of coffee and sat down across the table from him.

"Thanks," she said dryly. "Nice to know I'm looking my best."

"I didn't say you looked bad. I said you looked tired." He fed the baby a spoonful of carrots, deftly scraping the excess off her chin.

"There's a difference?" She took a sip of coffee, hoping the caffeine would jump start her sluggish brain.

"I heard you get up last night."

"I had a little trouble sleeping. Too much going on at work, I guess." She shrugged. To her relief, Cullen accepted the explanation for her insomnia without question.

"You need a day off."

"This *is* my day off."

"Not if you've brought home paperwork." He managed to sneak another bite of carrots into Angie's mouth. She pursed her lips as if to spit them out, saw Cullen watching her and grinned instead. He shuddered.

"You have disgusting table manners," he told her firmly. She banged her spoon on the metal tray of her high chair and squealed her delight at this description.

"I don't think she believes you," Darcy commented.

Hearing her voice, Angie turned and favored Darcy with the same carrot-smeared grin. Darcy smiled back, feeling that odd little twist in her chest that had become so familiar in the weeks since Angie had come to live with them. She was such a beautiful little girl. It would be so easy to love her. If only she dared take that risk.

"Can your paperwork wait?"

Cullen's question drew her attention back to him. He'd dampened a cloth and was busy wiping carrot off of Angie's face and hands.

"I suppose it could. Why?"

"Because we're going on a picnic."

"A picnic?"

"You know, one of those meals where you sit on the cold, hard ground, fending off wasps and ants and getting sunburned. A picnic."

She wrinkled her nose at him. "You make it sound so appealing."

"The challenge is half the fun," he said briskly. He stood up and lifted Angie out of her high chair. She kicked madly. "I've arranged for Marie to take Angie for the day."

Darcy hesitated over the refusal she'd been about to give him. "Just the two of us?"

"I thought it might be nice for a change."

"I don't mind if Angie comes along," she said quickly. "She's a good baby."

"She's a pest." Since he was tickling Angie's toes at the time, it was clear that "pest" was not the pejorative it might have been. Settling the baby in one arm, he looked at Darcy, his azure eyes holding an expression that made Darcy's heart beat a little faster.

"I want some time without distractions. And being a distraction ranks high on Angie's best talents."

"I really should do some of that paperwork," she said slowly.

"The paperwork won't go anywhere. Come on, Darcy. Play hooky with me."

The coaxing tone was more than she could resist, as was the thought of having him to herself for a whole afternoon. She didn't resent Angie's demands on his time but she wouldn't have been human if she didn't miss the times when it had been just the two of them.

"Okay. A picnic sounds like fun, ants and all." Besides, who knew if there would be another time.

Darcy leaned her head back against the seat and let the wind from the open car window blow through her hair.

It would look like a haystack by the time they got to whatever spot Cullen had chosen for their picnic, but she didn't care. She'd made up her mind that she wasn't going to worry about anything today. Not the future, not the past, not even the present that was all tangled up in both of them. Today, she was simply going to enjoy the moment.

She'd been mildly surprised when Cullen headed the car north out of Santa Barbara, but when she asked him where they were going, he shook his head and said it was a surprise. The idea of a mysterious destination fit right in with her mood so she simply leaned back to enjoy the trip.

They were driving up the coast highway and the Pacific sparkled on their left. A few miles above Santa Barbara, Cullen turned inland, driving between rolling hills that still showed green from the winter rains. Live oaks dotted the land, their heavy trunks and twisted branches revealing their age. He turned onto a gravel road, drove a couple of miles and stopped the car in a tiny valley that nestled between two hills. As soon as he shut the engine off, silence washed over them.

"What do you think?" There was a certain tension in his voice as if her answer was important to him.

Darcy looked from him to the emptiness around them. "I think it's beautiful," she said truthfully. "But it seems like a long drive for a picnic."

"I'm going to build a house here." He pushed open his car door and got out. Darcy followed suit. She looked at the site again, visualizing a house cradled against one of the hills, the little valley stretching out from the front door.

"It's a wonderful place for a home."

"I don't want to disturb the site any more than necessary, so it may take a little longer than usual because we won't be bringing in as much heavy equipment.''

Darcy came around the car to help him unload the picnic things from the trunk. Cullen continued to talk about his plans for the house as they headed for the shade of an ancient sycamore, laid out a blanket and spread their picnic items along one edge of it.

By the time they'd eaten the sandwiches they'd bought in town, Darcy felt as if she could see the house he'd described. Redwood and glass, a style somewhere between traditional and modern, with plenty of light filling the rooms and a big deck carefully fitted around the existing oak trees. The house wouldn't blend in with its surroundings right away, but in a few years when the sun had weathered the redwood to a soft, faded gray, you'd probably have to look twice to know there was a house there.

''It sounds beautiful,'' she said wistfully. She drew her knees up to her chest and narrowed her eyes as she pictured how the house would look. ''I envy the people you're building it for.''

''Don't.''

''Don't what?'' she asked, still looking out at the imaginary house.

''Don't envy them.''

''Why not?'' Now she turned to look at him, her brows raised in surprise.

''Because it's us. Or maybe, we're them.''

''We're who?''

''We're the people who are going to live in that house.'' Cullen had been leaning back on his elbows but now he sat up, close enough that his shoulder almost brushed hers. ''It's my lot, Darcy, and it's our house I was describing. If you like it, that is.''

''If I like it?'' She stared at him.

"If you don't, I'll come up with another design."

"No. No, the design sounds perfect." She turned and looked back at the spot where he'd planned to build. The house was still there in her mind's eye, only now it was her house—her's and Cullen's.

And the baby's.

She shivered a little, the image blurring around the edges. He was asking for a bigger commitment than they had now. He hadn't said it yet but the question was there.

"I don't know, Cullen." She shook her head. "It's a beautiful place and the house sounds wonderful but I— Oh."

Her words ended on a squeak of shock as she turned back toward him and saw what he was holding out to her. It was a small black box. A jeweler's box. Just the size box to hold a ring. Darcy stared at it in shock, her mind spinning. When she didn't reach to take it from him, Cullen brought up his other hand to open it. Nestled on a bed of black velvet was a diamond solitaire, utterly simple, utterly beautiful. Utterly terrifying.

"Marry me, Darcy."

"Oh, God." She lifted one hand to her mouth, still staring at the ring like a rabbit mesmerized by the glare of headlights on a country road. Realizing that "Oh, God" was not exactly an intelligent response to a proposal, she tried again. "Why?"

"Because I love you."

It was the first time either of them had spoken the words out loud and the simple beauty of them made tears well in Darcy's eyes.

"Oh, Cullen. I love you, too."

"Good." His grin was a little crooked around the edges. "That makes the feeling mutual. Say yes and everything will be perfect."

The word trembled on the tip of her tongue. *Yes, she*

loved him. Yes, she would marry him. It seemed such an obvious progression.

But it wasn't simple at all.

Darcy scrambled to her feet and turned away from him. She pressed her forearms against her diaphragm, trying to still the flutter of panic there.

"I can't marry you."

"Why not?" Cullen asked calmly as he stood up behind her. "You love me. I love you. What could be simpler?"

"I wish it was that simple but there are things you don't know about me."

"There are things you don't know about me. That's one of the things marriage is for, so you can get to know everything about the person you love."

"No. There are bad things you don't know," Darcy said, her voice so low he had to strain to hear it over the whisper of the breeze in the grass.

"Like what?" Maybe, finally, she'd tell him what it was that tortured her so. He closed his hands around her upper arms, trying to reassure her without words that he was there for her. "Tell me, Darcy."

"I was married before."

Cullen's fingers tightened momentarily in surprise. He hadn't been expecting that. A part of him instantly rejected the idea that she'd ever belonged to anyone else, bound by ties of man and God tighter than any he'd yet claimed.

"That's not a crime," he managed to say calmly. "Are you divorced?"

"Yes," she said indignantly. She pulled out of his hold and turned to look at him. "Do you think I'd be living with you if I were still married?"

"I don't know. You said there were things I didn't know. Being divorced isn't a crime, either." His eyes searched her face, searching for something he didn't want to find. "Are you still in love with him?"

"No! God, no." It was her turn to take hold of him. "I don't love anyone but you, Cullen. I don't think I ever loved him. I was lonely and he seemed kind and...we got married. But I didn't feel anything for him that was even close to what I feel for you."

"I believe you." He felt the knot in his stomach uncoil a little as he drew her close and stroked his hand over her pale gold hair. "You haven't told me anything to make me regret proposing, Darcy. Is that all there is?"

It wasn't her marriage she'd been afraid to confess to, Darcy thought as she pressed her face against the soft cotton of his shirt and felt the reassuring thud of his heart. Her marriage was the least of the secrets she was keeping.

"You can tell me, Darcy."

Maybe she could. If she could tell anyone, it would be Cullen. But what if she told him and then he looked at her the same way Mark had? Mark had promised to love, honor and cherish her, but in the end he'd hated her, blamed her for what had happened. Maybe he'd been right to blame her. She'd managed to survive it when Mark looked at her that way. But if she ever saw the same look in Cullen's eyes, she knew something vital would shrivel and die inside her.

"Darcy? Is there something else?"

"No." She closed her eyes as she whispered the denial. She couldn't take the chance.

"Then there's no reason why you can't wear this," Cullen said, his voice husky as he slid the ring on her finger.

She curled her fingers as if to stop him, but it was too late. Opening her eyes, she stared at her hand where it rested on his chest. The diamond glittered back at her, warm with promise, glittering with hope.

"What about Angie?" she whispered, still staring at the ring.

"We've managed so far, haven't we?"

"Yes, but—"

"Then we'll keep managing."

He made it sound so simple. Darcy moved her finger, hypnotized by the rainbow lights that danced from the ring. Was it possible it really was that simple? And she was simply complicating things unnecessarily?

"Stop trying to complicate things, honey." Cullen's words matched her own thoughts so closely that Darcy wondered if he could actually read her mind. "We can make this work if we want it bad enough."

"I don't know."

"I know." He slid his fingers under her chin and tilted her face up to his. His eyes were so bright and clear that it seemed as if the sunlight was caught in them. "I love you, Darcy."

"I love you, too," she said, her tone more despairing than happy.

"You're going to have to work on that," he chided. "You're not supposed to sound so gloomy about it."

"I'm sorry." She summoned up a smile. "I do love you, Cullen."

"That's better. Not perfect, but better. You'll have years to practice after we're married."

"I haven't said I'll marry you," she protested in a panic.

"You haven't said you won't, either."

Her eyes searched his, wondering how it was possible that she was the only one with doubts. But there was no trace of doubt in his eyes. He looked as if he knew exactly what he was doing. She only wished she felt the same.

"I think it's traditional to kiss right about now," he said lightly.

But there was nothing light about his kiss. The kiss was pure hunger and need. Darcy could have resisted the hunger, but she wasn't proof against the need. Her head was still spinning with doubt as her hands slid into the thick, dark hair at the nape of his neck.

Cullen groaned and crushed her closer still, deepening the kiss to passion. Darcy answered with a passion of her own, her mouth opening to his, welcoming the invading presence of his tongue. The kiss went on and on until she felt almost light-headed from lack of oxygen. They broke apart at last, stepping back to stare at each other.

"Darcy?" He made her name a question. For answer, she reached for the buttons on his shirt.

She didn't notice the roughness of the blanket against her back. All that mattered was the solid weight of Cullen's body above her, the feel of him within.

Lying there in the open with no witnesses but the sun and the wind and a hawk tracing lazy circles in the sky, they confirmed their love in the most elemental of ways. In the final moment, as her body arched taut as a bowstring against his, the sun caught on the ring he'd given her and the resultant rainbow seemed dazzling with the promise of dreams fulfilled. If only she dared to reach for them.

The trip back to Santa Barbara passed in almost complete silence. Darcy alternated staring at the ring on her finger and staring out the window, between elation and terror.

Angie greeted them both with her usual good cheer, clearly holding no grudge for having been abandoned for the better part of a day. Darcy hung back, as usual, watching as Cullen picked Angie up and swung her over his head. There was a familiar ache in her chest, but for the first time she recognized it for what it was. It wasn't a longing for the past, it was a hunger for the present, a need to be part of the picture, a yearning to come in out of the cold.

Though the day's heat lingered on the evening air, Darcy shivered, frightened by the depth of her need. Inside her, a little voice was saying that she didn't deserve to step into the warmth, that she could never make up for her terrible failure.

She was careful to keep her left hand hidden while they chatted with Marie. She wasn't at all sure about her engagement. The last thing she wanted to do was accept congratulations. She was grateful when Cullen didn't say anything to the other woman, but then on the way home she wondered if that had been out of consideration for her or because he was having second thoughts.

But when they went to bed, he turned and drew her into his arms, and he certainly didn't feel like a man having second thoughts. Having burned away some of the urgency earlier in the day, this time around their lovemaking was full of tenderness. Soft sighs, gliding touches, a slow build to a shivering completion that left them both replete.

"I love you," Cullen whispered against her hair.

"I love you, too."

Darcy lay awake long after he'd gone to sleep. Staring into the darkness, she realized that she couldn't marry him without telling him the truth. The thought sent a chill through her but she knew it had to be done. She couldn't keep a secret like that for the rest of her life and it was better that it come out now, before the ties between them were woven any tighter.

She tried to tell herself that it would be all right. He wasn't anything like Mark. If anyone could understand, it would be Cullen. Tears burned her eyes and wet her cheeks as she stared into the darkness, the weight of old guilt so heavy on her chest that it actually hurt to breathe.

God help her, how could she expect anyone to understand that she'd been responsible for her own baby's death?

It seemed as if she'd barely dropped off to sleep when the nightmare grabbed her. There was the crib, all draped in black ribbons. Somewhere a baby cried—her baby—but she couldn't get to him. Something held her feet in place. The cries went on and on and she tried to lift her hands to cover her ears, but the same force kept her hands captive. She could only stand there, listening to the crying, struggling to break free.

And then Mark was standing in front of her, his pleasant face twisted with grief and hatred, his mouth an ugly slash, the words spilling out like venom-tipped darts. *What kind of mother are you? This was your fault. Your fault...your fault...your fault...* And then he was gone and the crying stopped and there was only silence. She was free to move at last, but it was too late. She crumpled to the ground, sobbing. She was alone. Alone. Just as she'd always be, just as she deserved to be.

"Darcy! Wake up!" Cullen's voice was mixed with the sound of her own sobs as Darcy swam up out of the depths of the dream. Her fingers dug into the muscles in his arms as she pressed herself against him, drawing strength from his solid warmth.

"It's okay. I've got you safe," he murmured, stroking her hair, holding her until the tremors eased. "That must have been one hell of a nightmare."

Darcy said nothing. She felt the weight of his ring on her finger and opened her eyes to stare at it in the darkness. It might have been her imagination but she thought she could almost see a flicker of light in the heart of the stone. But it was gone in an instant, as if it hadn't been there at all.

Her thinking, which had been muddled from the moment Cullen had said he was building a house for the two of them, was suddenly crystal clear. The dream had been a reminder, a warning. She'd almost let herself forget, almost let herself believe that she could leave the past behind. But it couldn't be done. Some things just couldn't be forgotten. Or forgiven.

"You want to tell me what it was about?" Cullen asked, his hand stroking her back.

"I can't marry you."

His hand froze for an instant. "You mean, you dreamed you couldn't marry me?"

"No. I mean, I can't marry you." Darcy pulled away from him and he let her go without a struggle. She could feel his eyes on her as she slid off the bed and groped for the robe she'd draped over the foot of the bed. She slid it on just as he turned on the lamp next to the bed.

"Why can't you marry me?" He sounded more curious than hurt, but Darcy knew it was because he didn't believe she meant it. But she meant it. She knew what she had to do and this time she wasn't going to persuade herself otherwise.

"I just can't. It would be a mistake." She belted the robe around her narrow waist and ran her fingers through her hair to comb it into a rough sort of order.

"Does this have something to do with your nightmare?" Cullen slid off the bed and she averted her eyes from his naked form, not looking at him again until she heard the whisper of jeans being pulled on and the rasp of a zipper.

"It's not the nightmare." A partial truth, anyway. "I just realized that it would be a terrible mistake if we got married. It wouldn't be fair to you."

"Let me be the judge of what's fair to me," he snapped.

"And it wouldn't be fair to the baby," she continued as if he hadn't spoken.

"I thought we'd settled that issue."

"No. We just postponed it. I know you think we could work things out, but the truth is that I can't be what you want, Cullen."

"You *are* what I want, dammit! Why would I ask you to marry me if I wanted something else?"

"You want a mother for Angie and you think I'll become that if you just give it a little time."

The color that stained his cheeks confirmed the accuracy of her words.

"I'll admit that I've got my fantasies of the three of us as one big happy family," he admitted gruffly, "but if that doesn't work out, that's okay. What's important is that we love each other. Or have you changed your mind about that, too?"

"No. I love you." She bent her head to stare at the ring she'd twisted off her finger. "It's because I love you that I can't marry you. And I can't live with you anymore, either."

"Oh, for chrissake! Don't give me a bunch of psychobabble. You don't *not* marry someone because you love them."

"That's exactly what I'm doing." She tossed the ring onto the bed, where it lay between them. All the life seemed gone from it. It was suddenly just a band of gold with a lifeless rock in it.

Cullen lifted his gaze from the ring to Darcy's face. He was chilled by what he read there. She meant it. She really intended to leave. He drew a slow, steady breath. She was upset. He'd rushed her this afternoon, just what he'd promised himself he wouldn't do. Whatever her demons were, he'd known they couldn't be conquered easily. Obviously the nightmare had shaken her badly. In the morning, when she'd calmed down, they'd be able to talk about this. He'd give her more time, if that's what she needed. But he wasn't going to lose her. Not without a fight.

He bent to scoop the ring off the bed, closing his fingers so tightly around it that the setting dug into his palm.

"It's late. We're both tired. Why don't we go back to bed. I'll sleep on the sofa," he added quickly, seeing the objection in her eyes. "You can't move out in the middle of the night, anyway," he added, striving for a reasonable tone and finding it with considerable effort.

Darcy nodded slowly. "I should be the one to take the sofa, though. It's not big enough for you."

Cullen wondered if it struck her as ironic that she'd just driven an emotional stake through his heart and now she was worried about the sofa being too short. But it probably made perfect sense to her since in her mind she was doing this for his sake, anyway.

"I'll take the sofa." At least that way he knew she couldn't sneak out in the middle of the night because he'd be between her and the front door.

He walked past her but stopped in the doorway and turned to look at her. She stood beside the bed, her arms at her sides, her head bent so that a curtain of pale hair fell forward to conceal her profile. He was hurt and angry and there was a part of him that would have liked to shake some sense into her. But she looked so lost and alone standing there.

Ridiculous as it was, he knew she really believed she was doing this for his own good. In a bizarre way, he supposed this was proof that she loved him. And he didn't doubt that she was hurting every bit as much as he was.

He ran his fingers through his hair, aware that they were not quite steady. When he spoke, his voice reflected the weariness he felt. "Look, I know I rushed you this afternoon. I'm sorry."

"You don't need to apologize." Her voice was so low, he had to strain to hear it. "This afternoon was wonderful."

If it had been so wonderful, then why was she leaving him tonight?

"I thought so, too," he said mildly. "What I'm getting at here is, don't make any hasty decisions. It's late. You're tired. It was an emotional day. You just had one hell of a nightmare. It's not a good time to be making life-altering decisions. Let's sleep on it and we'll talk in the morning."

He waited, but there was no response, unless he counted a faint movement of her head that could have been either a nod yes or a shake no. He chose to interpret it as the former. Not that it really mattered because they were going to talk in the morning, if he had to tie her to a chair to get her to listen.

He sighed. "I'll see you in the morning, then." He turned and left without waiting for a response.

Cullen didn't bother turning on any lights in the living room. Sinking onto the sofa, he set his elbows on his knees and let his head drop forward into the support of his hands. He sat there for a long time, listening to the rhythm of his own breathing and the soft sound of Darcy's muffled weeping from the bedroom.

Chapter 7

Cullen hadn't expected to sleep at all, but he dozed off sometime around six in the morning, only to be awakened at seven by Angie's announcement that she was ready to get up. Bleary-eyed, he rolled off the sofa, groaning at the stiffness in his back, and stumbled into the nursery. Angie stopped crying as soon as she saw him, giving him that cheery, two-toothed grin that never failed to melt his heart.

"Good morning, imp." She babbled happily in reply, lifting her arms to be picked up.

Cullen changed her and dressed her in a pair of cotton rompers. He carried her out to the kitchen, eyeing the bedroom door as he went by. There was no sign of life behind it. Maybe Darcy was still sleeping. Maybe some sleep would make her see how ridiculous the whole idea of her leaving was.

He fed Angie her breakfast, his attention a little more absentminded than usual. He was just wiping traces of cereal off her hands and face when the doorbell rang.

"Who do you suppose that is?" he muttered as he

hoisted Angie out of her seat. Eight o'clock on a Sunday morning wasn't exactly a normal time for drop-in visitors.

"Kiel. What are you doing here?"

"Good morning to you, too." Kiel raised one dark eyebrow as he walked past his partner into the living room. Cullen shut the door and followed him. "You look like hell," Kiel said bluntly.

"Thanks." Cullen thrust his fingers through his hair and ran a hand over his unshaven jaw. "What are you doing here?"

"Darcy called me." Kiel seemed surprised that Cullen didn't know. "She said you had some things you needed moved. Said it was urgent."

"She called you?" Cullen repeated, feeling as if he'd just been kicked in the gut.

"Yes, I did."

He looked past Kiel to see Darcy standing in the archway that led from the living room to the rear of the condo. She was wearing a pair of jeans and a white T-shirt—one of his T-shirts. Her hair was pulled back from her face in a ponytail, and he was uncharitably pleased to see that she looked every bit as lousy as he felt.

"Why did you call Kiel?" he demanded.

"Because my things won't fit in my car," she answered reasonably.

"Your things?" That was Kiel, looking startled. "Are you leaving?"

"Yes."

"No." Cullen's answer overrode hers. "I thought we were going to talk this morning."

"There's nothing to talk about." Her voice was steadier than he would have liked. She sounded so damned sure.

"There's plenty to talk about." Angie wiggled impatiently, tired of being held when no one was paying any attention to her. Cullen bent to set her on the floor, reaching to hand her a cloth ball to play with. "You can't just leave like this," he said to Darcy as she straightened.

"It's for the best."

"Best for *who?* You? It sure as hell isn't best for me."

"Maybe I should come back later," Kiel said, looking as if he'd like nothing more than to disappear in a puff of smoke. Neither of them heard him.

"You don't understand. I tried to explain."

"Explain? You didn't explain anything. Dammit, Darcy, you can't do this."

"I am doing it." Her voice shook with suppressed emotion. "Someday you'll—"

"If you say I'll thank you for this, I swear to God I won't be responsible for my actions," he snarled.

"Look, it really does sound like you two have things to discuss." Kiel edged toward the door, stepping over Angie, who'd abandoned the ball in favor of exploration.

"Don't go." Darcy took a quick step forward, her hand lifting as if she were a shipwreck victim and Kiel was her last hope of rescue.

"Do go," Cullen said, stepping back to clear a path to the door.

Kiel looked from one to the other, clearly torn. Before anyone could say or do anything, there was an odd sound from Angie, who was sitting on the floor next to the sofa. All three adults looked at her. She looked...odd, Cullen thought. Suddenly afraid, he started toward her.

"What's wrong?"

"She's choking!" Darcy was across the room in a heartbeat and had Angie up and facedown across her lap. Using the flat of her hand, she struck the baby four quick blows across the back. When there was no response, she repeated the maneuver.

Afterward, Cullen could have sworn that he actually

heard the pop as the object she'd inhaled popped loose. It dropped from her open mouth and fell to the carpet. There was a moment of utter stillness and then Angie drew a ragged breath. She drew a second and expelled it with a frightened wail.

Cullen sank to his knees, shaking with reaction.

Darcy pulled Angie up and into her arms, rocking her, murmuring soothingly to her as Angie cried out her fright. Kiel bent to pick up the near fatal object and Cullen wasn't surprised to see that his friend's fingers were unsteady.

"It's a button," Kiel murmured, sinking into a chair. "Just a button." He held it out to Cullen.

"I noticed one was missing off one of my shirts a couple of days ago," Cullen said. He closed his fist over the button as if he would crush it. "I thought it had probably come off in the washer."

"A button," Kiel said again, sounding dazed.

Angie's sobs didn't last long. She'd had a fright, but she wasn't hurt and, with no real concept of death or dying, the memory of her fear faded quickly from her mind.

"Here. You should hold her." Darcy's voice sounded thin and her face was almost as white as the T-shirt she wore.

Cullen took the baby from her, closing his eyes for a moment as he felt the wonderful *alive* weight of her. When he opened his eyes, he saw Darcy halfway to the bedroom, her uncertain stride evidence that her knees were no steadier than his. The door closed behind her with a quiet click.

"Maybe you should go after her. She looks pretty shook up," Kiel said.

"Yeah." Angie wiggled to tell him that he was holding her too tight and Cullen loosened his hold. He looked down at her, confirming that she was really and truly all right. Her thick dark lashes were still spiky with tears, but she smiled at him as if she hadn't a care in the world. Which, he supposed, she didn't. He only wished he could forget the terror of the last few minutes as easily as she had.

He stood up and Kiel did the same. "Here. Look after her for a few minutes."

"Me?" Kiel automatically closed his hands around Angie as Cullen thrust her against his chest. "I don't know anything about babies."

"Neither did I," Cullen said over his shoulder.

"But..."

The bedroom door cut off the rest of Kiel's protest. Cullen wasn't worried. He knew his partner would manage. What concerned him now was Darcy.

She was sitting on the edge of the bed, her arms wrapped around herself, rocking back and forth while slow tears seeped down her white cheeks.

"Are you all right?"

She shook her head without speaking, her face twisted with pain. Moving slowly, Cullen crossed the room and knelt down in front of her.

"You did an incredible job, Darcy. I wouldn't have known what to do for her."

"It was my fault," she said, the words choked.

"Your fault? How do you figure that? It was a button off my shirt."

"All my fault," she moaned, unhearing. "Mark said it was and he was right."

"Mark? Your ex-husband?" It was a stab in the dark but it was obvious that the close call with Angie had triggered some old memories.

"He said it was my fault," she said again, her eyes staring at something he couldn't see. Whatever it was, it was obvious it was tearing her to pieces. Taking a chance, Cullen reached for her hands, prying them loose from where they gripped her elbows and closing his fingers around them, trying to tell her without words that she wasn't alone.

"What did he think was your fault, Darcy?" he asked quietly, wondering if he was finally going to get an answer to the demons that preyed on her.

She blinked and suddenly seemed to see him. He expected to see the shutters come up in her eyes, blocking him out again, but there was nothing but pain and a kind of weary acceptance in her eyes, as if she'd run as far and as long as she could.

"It was my fault our baby died."

Cullen's fingers tightened over hers, his eyes going momentarily blank. A baby? She'd had a baby? He felt as if he'd just received a kick over the heart. He struggled to keep the shock and hurt from showing in his face, but he must not have succeeded.

"I'm sorry, Cullen. I should have told you."

"You're telling me now," he said, his voice steadier than he'd expected. "Tell me what happened."

"We... I guess it never was a very happy marriage," she said in a voice drained of emotion. "We got along okay but there was never really any spark between us. I think we both knew it was a mistake, but then we found out I was pregnant. Things seemed to get better between us and we were happy for a while. Even after the baby was born. Mark was so thrilled that it was a boy."

"What was his name?" His voice was raspy but she didn't seem to notice.

"Aaron. We named him Aaron. He was a beautiful baby. Quiet but happy." She smiled dreamily, lost in memory.

"What happened?" Cullen asked, knowing that if there

was any chance of healing, it could only come after the wound was completely exposed.

Darcy's smile faded and her eyes darkened from smoky gray to almost black. "He died. I put him in his crib one night and in the morning he was...gone. Sudden Infant Death Syndrome, the doctor said. He said it just... happens sometimes. Nobody knows why for sure." She sounded almost clinical now, but Cullen could feel her nails digging into his hands where she held him.

"Did the doctor say it was something you'd done?"

"No. But I knew it was. And Mark knew it, too. 'Babies don't just die,' he said."

"But didn't the doctor say that that was exactly what did happen sometimes?" he asked gently.

"Yes."

"Then why don't you believe him? Because Mark said it was your fault?"

"There had to have been some reason," she said fiercely.

"Do you think the doctor was lying to you?"

"N-no," she admitted hesitantly.

"Is this why you don't want anything to do with Angie?" Her hands jerked convulsively in his, but he refused to release them, just as he refused to let her look away from him. "Is it?"

"Yes!" The word exploded from her. "What if it happens again? What if it *was* something I did? And even if it wasn't, what if something else happened? I couldn't go through that again. I couldn't."

She began to cry, not the silent tears she'd shed before but deep, gut-wrenching tears. Cleansing tears. Or at least, that's what Cullen hoped. Standing, he scooped her into his arms and settled down with his back against the headboard and Darcy cradled in his lap.

He let her cry, holding her and murmuring softly to her

but not trying to stem the flood of tears. When they'd finally subsided into hiccuping sobs, he handed her a fistful of tissues and waited until she'd mopped her eyes and blown her nose.

"What happened to Aaron wasn't your fault."

"You don't know that," she muttered thickly.

"Yes, I do. The doctor told you it wasn't your fault. If Mark said differently, he was speaking out of pain." It took a considerable effort to speak calmly about her exhusband when what he really wanted to do was demand his address so he could go and beat him to a pulp. "Sometimes things happen and there's no reason for them. That doesn't mean you stop living."

"What if it happened again?" She sounded like a child, afraid of the dark.

"Are you sorry you had Aaron? Do you wish he'd never been born?"

"No! He was the most wonderful thing that had ever happened to me."

"But you could have saved yourself a lot of pain by not having him," he pointed out.

"But I'd have missed out on so much." Her voice trailed off as the shock of her own words went through her. "I'd have missed out on so much," she whispered again.

"If you try to protect yourself completely, you're not living," he said quietly.

"I don't think I could bear it if it happened again," she said, and they both knew she was talking about Angie.

"It won't. But if something, God forbid, were to happen to her, we'd get through it. Together."

Together. When he held her like this, it was possible to believe that they could get through anything together. She closed her eyes and pressed her face closer against the bare skin of his chest. She felt Cullen shifting but she didn't open her eyes until she felt him lift the hand that lay against his chest.

"Will you wear this?" The ring looked small in his hand, a fragile circle signifying commitment and promise. "We don't have to get married right away. You can take as long as you want to think about it. And if...if you really feel you have to move out, I'll help you." She could hear how much the words cost him. "But as long as you're wearing this, I'll know that you're still mine."

For answer, Darcy spread her fingers so that he could slip the ring in place. She knew it was her imagination, but it seemed as if the sparkle was back. Hope and promise in rainbow sparks. They lay there without speaking, savoring the feeling of being together—really together this time.

A muffled thud from the living room broke the quiet moment. "I suppose I should go rescue Kiel from Angie," Cullen said. "He looked as if I'd handed him a live bomb."

Darcy followed him from the room, smoothing her tangled hair back. It must be obvious that she'd been crying but Kiel was a good friend. And she wasn't quite ready to let Cullen out of her sight. When he was with her, she believed in the future he saw so clearly, but she wasn't sure the magic would linger away from him.

The look of gratitude on Kiel's face when he saw them was comical. His dark hair looked as if it had been combed with a hand mixer and there was a wildness in his eyes, as if his sanity was starting to crack. He was on his hands and knees behind the arm of the sofa and Darcy assumed he'd been playing peekaboo with Angie.

"She never stops moving," he said, climbing to his feet as Cullen bent to scoop Angie off the sofa. "And she can just about outrun me."

"She can't even crawl decently, yet," Cullen said, giving his partner an unsympathetic look.

"She's still fast," Kiel said darkly. He glanced from Cullen to Darcy. "You two work things out?"

She held up her left hand by way of answer and he broke into a grin. "I take it you don't need any help moving?"

She caught Cullen's questioning look and shook her head. She wasn't moving out. He was right, a life without taking chances was no life at all. Drawing a deep breath, she came forward and held out her arms.

"Let me hold her, please." With a look that combined both pleased surprise and concern, Cullen handed Angie over to her.

Darcy cuddled the baby against her heart. It felt so right to be holding her like this, to let herself feel the love she'd been trying to keep locked in her heart all these weeks.

"Do you think she's old enough to be a flower girl?" she asked, lifting her head to look at Cullen, letting all her love shine in her eyes.

"I think we could set a trend for flower girls in strollers," he said, his voice shaky with emotion.

He put his arm around her, pulling her against his side. The shadows were gone. All that was left was love.

*   *   *   *   *

THE BABY MACHINE
Ann Major

To Tara Gavin—
Again! And again! And again!
All my books should be dedicated to her.

A Note from Ann Major

Because I was deeply in love with my husband when he asked me to marry him, I said yes in the next breath.

Then he said he wanted five children, and I said, "I don't want any."

Not that I didn't like babies. I just felt too young and immature to assume such responsibility.

After we'd been married a year Ted pressured me to get on with producing the longed-for brood. To convince me that having a baby was easy, he insisted that I watch one of his patients in the delivery room. Since the woman had already had eight children, he figured the delivery would be a snap.

What men don't know about women could fill volumes of romance novels. The poor woman couldn't have screamed louder if you'd thrown her naked to a starving group of grizzly bears. Needless to say, another year passed before I would even allow him to whisper the word *pregnancy*.

When I finally did give birth to our first son, I felt as proud as a queen who'd produced a long-awaited, royal heir. I instantly felt committed to Ted in a new and profound way.

Romance for me has never had much to do with candle-lit dinners and champagne, but everything to do with the connection of two people on emotional, spiritual and physical planes. So, for me, watching a football game with my husband can be a very romantic kind of thing. Just driving up to the high school to pick up one of our kids—together—

seems sexy and romantic. Thus, I don't feel our children have interfered with our romance as much as they have enhanced it because of the deeper emotional texture they have brought to our relationship.

Of course, as a young mother I always insisted that my children take naps every afternoon from two until five. Not that they always slept, mind you, but the little dears did dutifully stay in their rooms and were silent—even Kimberly, even when she was a terrible two.

Everyone thought I selfishly wanted that time to write, and I did...weekday afternoons.

But on the weekends when Ted was home... Guess again.

Ann Major

Chapter 1

Anger and grief burned through Jim Keith Jones like acid as he set the chain saw down and picked up the ax. In six days, that rich vulture, Kate Karlington, would repossess what to her was probably just another motley collection of real estate, but what to him was a lifetime of dreams and hard work.

He'd built his little empire from scratch—vacant lot by lot, house by house, building by building. He'd painted and hammered and mowed and hauled trash—there hadn't been a job he'd been too good to do to keep his properties up for his tenants.

Next Friday, Karlington would smilingly pick his bones clean and leave him for dead. Only, he wouldn't be dead; he'd be groveling in the gutter where he'd started, alive with the bitter reality that he had failed again.

Karlington wasn't the only reason his mood was so foul. It was May, a month that could be oppressive in Houston because so many days were as white and humid and smotheringly hot as this one. But today was especially dreadful because three years ago to the day he'd buried Mary on a muggy afternoon like this.

Jim Keith's filthy sleeveless sweatshirt was drenched with perspiration. His curly black hair was glued to his tanned brow. His dark eyes were bloodshot from the ravages of the binge he'd gone on the night before. His damp ragged jeans clung so tightly to his hard thighs, the navy denim looked as if it was painted on.

Slowly, carefully, his powerful brown arms lifted the ax and then sank it into the rotten trunk with all the savage vengeance his lean muscular body was capable of. When the blade crunched into soft wood, his perfectly sculpted mouth grimaced as if razor-edged steel had sliced through his skull. No wonder. He had a six-star hangover. He had celebrated the anniversary of Mary's funeral by tying one on.

He had gone home last night and drunk his dinner and watched home videos of Mary until he'd passed out. He did that every time her birthday and their wedding anniversary rolled around, too.

This morning he'd awakened to a fuzzy white television screen, crawled to his refrigerator, drunk a single beer, brewed a pot of black coffee and scrambled a mountain of eggs. Then he'd showered and driven to his sister Maggie's house and dutifully picked up his nine-year-old son, Bobby Lee, who had tearfully begged him to let him sleep in or watch cartoons instead of taking him to some apartment complex to work. Not that Bobby Lee ever did much.

Father and son were now hard at work cleaning up Jim Keith's worst apartment project, which was located just off the Eastex Freeway in a crime-ridden neighborhood populated with low-income families. Or rather, Jim Keith was working. Bobby Lee never really did much.

But even after a morning of mowing and chopping and weed pulling, Jim Keith still felt like death warmed over.

On her deathbed, Mary had begged him to be strong.

Dear God, he'd tried.

He swung the ax again, and wood chips flew as the blade bit into the trunk. For three long years he'd tried. But every night when he finished work, the demons of loneliness and dark grief still haunted him. It was all he could do to get through the days and nights, all he could do to go through the motions of being a father, of being a businessman.

Of being a human.

But he was losing it.

In those last months before her death, he hadn't cared about anything except saving Mary. He hadn't thought of his future or his son's, and because he hadn't, he'd borrowed money and taken Mary to Germany in the hopes of finding a miracle cure that his insurance wouldn't pay for. That was why he was badly overextended. That was why, despite his economizing over the past three years, despite his working seven days a week, come Friday he was really going to lose everything, even the roof over his head, to Karlington.

While oil revenues, property values, and job opportunities had plummeted, utility bills and property taxes had soared. Thus, the Houston real estate situation had deteriorated dramatically. Entire office buildings were fenced off and vacant. Thousands of apartment buildings had been bulldozed and the land sold for next to nothing. Entire neighborhoods of foreclosed houses sat empty. Banks had failed. Things were turning around now, but it was too late for him.

The economic situation would have been precarious for any man, but it had proved too much for a heavily indebted man devastated by the death of his beautiful young wife. Karlington had swooped down like a scavenger and bought his notes at a humiliatingly low, deeply discounted price. Nothing could save him from her—nothing short of a miracle.

And he'd lost faith in miracles when Mary died.

He wouldn't have bothered to clean up the project today, since it was as good as Karlington's, except wielding the ax was therapy.

The blade sliced one final time into the soggy trunk, and the rotten pecan tree groaned, toppling with a violent thud to the spongy, overgrown lawn.

He pitched the ax into the weed-choked flower bed beside his wheelbarrow and scanned the empty grounds for Bobby Lee. Jim Keith frowned when he saw the abandoned trash can and the door to number 20 sagging open. He'd ordered Bobby Lee to pick up everything inside and out of that apartment two hours ago. It was a thirty-minute job at best even for Bobby Lee, who moved as slow as molasses, but it looked as if Bobby Lee hadn't even spent five doing it.

Since Bobby Lee liked cars, Jim Keith headed toward the parking lot. Jim Keith's frown deepened as he considered Bobby Lee's laziness. The kid took after the Whits, Mary's easygoing bunch, most of whom were lazy as hell and hadn't amounted to much. Not that they cared. They got through life on charm. Maybe he shouldn't worry. When they found life too tough, most of them married well.

Mary herself had been no fireball. But she'd more than made up for it by being so pretty and sweet and fun-loving—and so damned good in the sack. She'd loved him since they'd been kids. His friends had teased him about the way she'd chased after him down the halls in high school.

"Oh, hi there, Jimmy," she'd purred from behind him, acting as if she was surprised to see him even though she was breathless from her breakneck run. When he'd turned around, she'd tossed her nose in the air so that her gold straight hair danced on her shoulders. Then she'd casually smiled up at him as if she wasn't especially anxious to see him after all. So then, of course, he'd had to prove himself and chase her. She'd known how to set the hook, let him nibble just a bite or two to get a delicious taste, before she snapped the line good and tight.

They'd been petting one night, and he'd wanted her so badly he couldn't wait. And she'd said, "Jimmy, you can't have me unless you marry me."

"Is that a proposal, baby?"

She'd giggled. "Now that you mention it—"

He'd started the car and driven hell-bent for Mexico. The old car had died at the border. They'd had to walk across the bridge and look for an official to marry them. Neither of them was even eighteen. They'd sold the car for scrap and hitchhiked back to Houston. He'd paid the first month's rent with the money from the car and dropped out of high school and started working harder than he'd ever worked.

Mary had always praised everything he'd done. Somehow he hadn't cared that she was so disorganized and never got much done. He'd loved her. God, how he'd loved her. They'd had tough times, but they'd made it. Until she'd gotten sick. Until he'd failed to save her.

Never again would he let himself fall in love. Because bright as the years with her had been even when they'd been poor as dirt, her illness and death had taught him about the dark and terrible price of love.

He scowled when he reached the parking lot and saw it was empty. Now where the hell was Bobby Lee?

Jim Keith was about to turn around when he saw the gleaming perfection of a dark green Jaguar gliding smoothly beneath the towering pine trees.

Then he stopped dead in his tracks when he recognized the woman behind the wheel—Kate Karlington.

Not that she'd recognize a lowlife like him. But he knew what she looked like, from seeing the society columns in the newspaper.

Fighting the murderous rage building inside him, he shrank behind the wall of his building as she stealthily parked her car under a towering cottonwood. High on her own success—her inherited success—she thought she knew everything and was always writing columns in the Houston papers about how to succeed in a recession. If she was so smart, how come she drove a car like that to this neighborhood and risked it being stolen or stripped?

She had her nerve, too. He'd had her served with a peace bond to stop her from snooping around his projects and harassing his managers. If he called the cops now, they'd haul her to jail. The thought of the elegant know-it-all Kate Karlington handcuffed and on her way to the clinker brought out the wicked white grin that had captured Mary's heart.

When the regal-looking young woman coolly unfolded her long, slim body from the car, holding a briefcase, his wolfish grin deepened. Then his eyes skimmed over her angrily—top to bottom.

Why did she have to be so damned beautiful?

His heart began to pound like a sledgehammer, and no longer solely from anger. The hot day seemed to press in on him harder than ever. It wasn't even noon, but he felt an odd, unwanted hunger.

Which only made him hate her all the more.

Black-and-white pictures didn't do her justice.

Mary had been soft and gentle and golden. This witch's beauty was so strong and bold and opulently charismatic, it struck him like a body blow even at this great distance. Her hair was shiny coils of vivid flame caught in a green silk scarf at her nape. She had the kind of figure a man who didn't despise her would die to get his hands on— lush breasts, a narrow waist, curving hips and long legs. She had a brisk walk that told him she was a woman of immense energy.

In the bedroom he imagined she would be volcanic.

Why the hell had his mind wandered to the bedroom?

Kate wore a green silk blouse and green linen slacks. He noticed the crisp, starched look of those slacks. They had obviously been ironed within seconds of being put on. Precisely applied and dramatic makeup darkened her eyes and made her lips brighter.

He found he couldn't take his eyes off her till she disappeared around the back of his building. But that was only because the sneaky bitch was his enemy.

No way was he calling the cops.

No way would he forgo the pleasure of teasing and torturing her himself.

Chapter 2

Kate Karlington, who was reputed to have inherited her father's cold but very shrewd business mind, was fastidious to a fault. Above all she appeared *in control.* Her curly red hair was tightly pulled back; her linen slacks crisply pressed. Every business document in her briefcase was tidily filed by subject and date. Every square in her calendar was carefully marked with her plans for that day.

Her teachers and her strict father had severely punished her for inefficiency, sloppiness and neglect, and she had learned their lessons well. Thus, when she stumbled in one of Jones's potholes in his poorly paved parking lot and got a run in one of her expensive stockings, she frowned impatiently. She paused to study the ruinous neglect of Jones's forlorn-looking buildings. Pink bricks were blackened from mildew. Several broken windows were taped.

Neglect ate into profits. She deplored greedy, short-sighted landlords like Keith Jones who milked their properties for all they were worth, thereby depriving tenants of the basic amenities they were paying their good money for. Did Jones realize how foolish he'd been? Dissatisfied tenants always moved. Couldn't he see that his neglect had lowered his rents and caused his high vacancy rate?

Fools like him deserved to go bankrupt. Not that they ever blamed themselves. No doubt Jones saw her as the villain in this foreclosure.

Her heart hardened as she viewed the sagging gutters at the roofline and the many huge potholes in the asphalt parking lot. Paint peeled from wooden facings. This project was in even worse shape than his other properties. She wished Jones hadn't fallen behind on his notes, so she wouldn't have to foreclose next week and sink her good money after his bad or, worse, bulldoze the buildings. Not that his properties weren't prime locations.

How she pitied poor people who had to live in buildings like these. Her green eyes narrowed on a crack that ran from the top of one building, all the way down to a scraggly bush and to—

To two filthy, unlaced athletic shoes sticking out from the dense foliage. The toes were glued together in a raptly tense, pigeon-toed position. The ragged cuffs of a pair of equally filthy jeans were all that was visible of the slim little boy.

Kate softened inwardly. She wanted people to believe she was a cool, controlled, brilliant businesswoman who gloried in her independence and glamorous single life, who gloried in the local fame she had achieved through her weekly column. She wanted them to think that she was just like her controlled, highly disciplined father who had never loved another human being in his life, that her sole passion was enlarging the Karlington empire, just as his had been. In truth, she wished she *was* like that. She wanted to be as invulnerable to hurt as he had been, but there had always been in her that secret weakness, that craven, instinctive yearning for any scrap of tenderness and love.

When she was growing up, her father had never allowed her to have a pet or friends. Later, after she'd run away to her aunt Mathilde's, he'd coldly refused to take Kate back. Instead, he'd sent her to schools as far away as possible, rarely allowing her to come home for holidays. So she had grown up lonely. Feeling isolated and rejected even after she'd obtained several degrees, she had fallen for the first man who had pretended he loved her. Not that the illusion had lasted long, for her father had ruthlessly exposed all of Edwin's failings and his true motivations in marrying her. Edwin had had other women all along. He had married her for the Karlington money; he had never loved her.

After he'd left her, she'd discovered she was pregnant. When she told him, he'd been coldly indifferent. During those brief first months of her pregnancy, she'd imagined that at last she would have someone she could love and who would love her. Then, at the end of her fifth month, she had miscarried.

The baby's memorial service had seemed the end of everything. It had taken her a long time to recover. Outwardly she seemed fine. Inwardly the wounds sometimes felt as raw as ever.

Her failed marriage had made Kate wary of men, but even though the loss of her baby had hurt far more, even though she didn't trust herself with men, she secretly longed to try to have another child. And it seemed that the closer she got to her thirtieth birthday, the stronger the instinctive urge to be a mother became. She couldn't walk through Neiman's or Saks without staring at the children's clothes in frustration and wishing she had a little girl or a little boy of her own to buy something cute for. She would remember the months of joy when she had planned for the birth of her baby, and all the darling things she had bought. Only to have to pack them away.

Was she really doomed to spend her whole life alone?

The ragtag boy was so quiet and still, for a second she was terrified he'd been hit by a car and crawled out of the street to die. Then she heard a page flip and an awe-struck exclamation.

"Golly-damn-bongo!"

She sank down beside him, sighing in relief and in shock at his language, for never having had them, she idealized children. "Hello there," she said softly.

He started guiltily, scrambling out from under the bush, intending to run.

Until she grabbed him gently but firmly by the collar.

Despite his filthy T-shirt and ragged jeans, he was beautiful. He had dark curly hair and dark flashing eyes. "I didn't mean to scare you," she said, again in her gentlest tone.

"I wasn't scared. I ain't some sissy," he said in a rough, put-on, big-boy voice.

"Am not," she corrected. "Of course you're not. But what were you doing under there?"

He thrust back his chin and glued his dark rebellious eyes to a distant spot behind her. "Just readin'," he mumbled, reddening.

"Must be good. Can I see—"

"No!"

Her brows arched.

"I mean it's nothing you'd be interested in—ma'am," he said more politely.

When she reached down for the magazine, he lunged to grab it.

Then the wind caught the sexy centerfold, and it fluttered like a flag. The boy cried out in acute dismay, springing for the slick, greasily thumbed thing.

But she was quicker.

"Oh, my," she gasped, shocked as she got an eyeful of bulging bosom and pink fanny.

The little scamp would have run, but she clung to his collar.

The young woman who adorned the centerfold was amazingly proportioned. *Golly-damn-bongo is right,* Kate thought with a smile, and then was horrified that she could be amused. Boy and woman blushed as they studied the centerfold with equal fascination until she remembered herself and snapped it out of his line of vision.

Kate found the picture deeply degrading to all women on principle. No wonder little boys grew into men seeing women as nothing more than sex objects. No wonder rich men thought women could be bought. Not just rich men. She remembered the way Edwin had used the Karlington money to attract younger women.

"Where did you get this, young man?"

"Found it."

"Where?"

"Dunno."

"You do, too!" She shook him slightly.

"Under a bed. I was cleaning out an apartment for my father...picking up trash...."

"Where is your mother?"

"Dead."

The word wrenched her because of her own lonely, motherless childhood and her hard, rejecting father.

"She died three years ago when I was only six." He lowered his head.

Kate had been about the same age when her own mother died. If this beautiful child were hers, Kate would never have set him to clean some trashy apartment.

"Where's your father?"

"Doing the yard."

Kate frowned. So his father was the yardman. It surprised her that Jones, who was so close with his money when it came to paint, lumber and asphalt, would spend a cent on grass. She guessed that even he had some standards—low as they were.

"Don't tell on me," the boy pleaded in a pitiful voice. "Dad's not feeling too good and he gets mad when I slack off."

She'd always been terrified of her father, too. "Is he sick?"

"Hung over."

Kate's eyes narrowed. There was ice suddenly, on her forehead, icy indignant rage spreading from the nape of her neck down her spine. Why had this wonderful little angel been given to some alcoholic brutish laborer who would neglect him, a man who was obviously lousy at his job...when she—

"I won't let him hurt you," she said protectively as she led the child into the courtyard.

She saw the ax and the chain saw first; and then the wheelbarrow and the mower and the tangled mountain of clippings the dark giant had piled beside him.

When she walked briskly up to him, he ignored her and continued to rip weeds from the flower bed.

He wasn't lazy.

Kate admired energy in people, especially when they applied it to something constructive. She didn't have a single employee who worked so ferociously as this brute.

She saw him well for the first time.

Rivulets of steamy sweat raced down the man's neck and his arms. She licked her lips. Just for a second before she caught herself, she felt a funny feeling start in thepit of her stomach at the sight of so much hard male muscle. She, who had schooled herself never to look at men, couldn't be fascinated by this man's flexing, bronze biceps.

She tried to swallow but couldn't. She looked away instead. "Hello," she said, intending her firmest, no-nonsense tone, only to be furious when her voice sounded vulnerable and shaky—almost sexy.

She didn't want to like him.

Her experiences with men had taught her they came in two categories. Rich men of her own class were too often like her father—selfish to the core. When they wanted to get rid of a child, they paid someone to take care of it. When they wanted a woman's body, they found her price. Such men didn't have to give emotionally of themselves. All her father had ever given her were things. When she was a teenager and had asked him to take her places, he'd had a fancy convertible delivered to her school.

Poorer men worshiped money as ardently as rich ones because they believed it was magic. She had learned that from Edwin, her ex-husband, who had pretended he'd loved her when all he'd ever wanted was her money.

"I—I said hello," Kate repeated, forcing herself to look at the man again. Dear God. Her voice came out even huskier than before.

He went still, as if the raspy sound had electrified him.

Her gaze fixed on his rigid brown arms. She felt her own muscles go as tense as his. It was as if she were in tune with this scowling brute. Which was ridiculous.

Slowly he brushed the dirt from his fingers and rose angrily to his full height.

Clearly he didn't want to be interrupted.

He was very, very tall. Well over six feet.

She liked tall.

No, she didn't!

He was a sleek-muscled, black-haired, deplorably handsome Adonis, who was so disgustingly male and virile that her womb ached with sudden awareness of the profound loneliness of her life. Despite the differences she imagined between herself and him—class, education, ambition, the zillion cultural refinements she possessed and he could not possibly—his hot, faintly insolent gaze lit that spark of deep feminine yearning.

He was as set on disliking her as she was on him. But for an infinitesimal moment as his smoldering black eyes slid from her face down her body, she knew that on some primitive level she wanted to devour him in the same hideous, stripping way his gaze was so hatefully devouring her.

No... She—she, cool, collected Kate Karlington, who had schooled herself to turn up her nose at the advances of far more eligible bachelors, wouldn't allow herself to have the hots for this sulky, muscle-bound Neanderthal.

Her blood burned through her like fire anyway. Suddenly she felt so dizzy, she was afraid she might actually faint.

"What's the matter?" he demanded in a harsh baritone that was absolutely beautiful.

"I—I'm fine...."

"You're shaking like a leaf."

"Allergies," she lied.

"Right," he muttered in that velvety, deeply unsettling tone.

He was smarter than she'd thought. She had to make her point and escape him. "I—I found your son in the parking lot—reading...."

The brute's dazzling smile made her whole body tighten. Why did his rugged masculine face have to be carved in such appealingly tough lines? He had a strong jaw, a straight nose. Spiked black lashes set off his bold angry eyes. She noticed the tiny lines at the corners of those dark eyes that seemed so intelligent—silent testimony that when he wasn't sulking, he had a sense of humor.

"Bobby Lee reading?" His wicked smile broadened. "That's a new one."

She caught the smell of his beery breath, and some stronger, sweaty male scent that was not altogether displeasing as he ruffled his son's black hair with brutish pride. When the beast's gaze raked her with scathing intent, she took a hesitant step backward before she reminded herself of her mission.

"Don't you even care what he was reading?" she demanded.

Her high-and-mighty tone brought a swift scowl.

"I care," he said with soft menace. "Show me."

"Here!" She thrust the magazine forward.

Roughly he yanked it from her and studied the nude centerfold with an embarrassing avidity.

Kate colored when his black eyes flicked back from the lush splendor of the naked girl to trail down her own body.

As if to compare her to—

His look shamed her to the core.

She wanted to run, to die.

He rolled the magazine up and stuffed it into the back pocket of his jeans. Then he knelt to his son's level and said, "We'll take this up again tonight when we're alone...and have a man-to-man talk. For now, get back to number 20 and clean it up—on the double. Or I'll give you an extra hour of pulling weeds."

The kid bolted like a streak of lightning.

"The threat of weed pulling always gets him going," the Neanderthal muttered with a grim smile, his gaze following the running child and his flapping shoestrings.

She was furious. "Is that all you intend to do?" She curled her long nails into her palms. "What kind of father are you? You find your son reading filth, and...and you don't even care.''

The man's eyes returned to her slowly. ''He's my kid—not yours! And I'm a helluva lot more concerned about his habit of shirking work than the fact that he has a boy's natural interest in sex.''

''A boy's natural interest? Is that what you call it? Why am I surprised that someone like you would be more concerned with driving a child, too young to work, to do your job than with his morals? You probably don't even know what morals are. You probably don't care that he cusses, either.''

The man's hard features went tighter. ''Hey—you're way out of line, lady. Who the hell do you think you are, coming here, criticizing the way I raise my child? All boys do some cussing and looking at pictures like that when they get the chance.''

As he moved toward her, she shrank from him. To her horror, her shoulders hit cool pink bricks, and she realized he had her cornered against a cracked, mildewed wall. He leaned into her, his huge body cutting her off from freedom.

''Where were you raised—a convent?''

She whitened. He was closer to the truth than he knew.

''It's plain as day you have problems you can't deal with, lady. You're probably so damn rich, you never worked an honest day in your life. You just go out and buy what you want or use your money to take what you want. You probably think you're too good to get dirty and sweaty. Well, I started working younger than him. Work won't hurt him. Neither will that magazine.''

''Why did I ever think I could talk to you?'' She started to push past him, but he brought his arms up beside her, blocking her escape.

''And another thing, lady—the fact that I'm not horrified by Bobby Lee's interest in sex has nothing to do with my morals, which I probably have way more of than you do.

"I let you butt your long, uptight nose into my life just for the fun of it. But you got me all stirred up and curious. Why the hell is a beautiful woman like yourself so scared of sex when it's the best thing this life has to offer?"

"A man…like you…would think that."

"Most of the women I've known would agree."

"Only the worst kind of woman would consort with someone as low as you."

"I should break your snotty little neck for that."

"Violence…from a man like you wouldn't surprise me, either."

He took a deep calming breath. "I don't know why I give a damn what you think, but, for the record, I'm not some kind of savage where women are concerned. I married my high school sweetheart. And I would have been faithful to her till I died if she hadn't died first." His voice broke, and he looked away, his shattered face darker and angrier than ever as if he despised himself for revealing anything so personal to her.

She saw the wild grief in his ravaged eyes and forgot her terror of him.

There was a long awkward moment. She felt drawn to him because she instinctively knew that his grief and loneliness were every bit as terrible as her own.

On some crazy, overwrought impulse, she gently touched his arm, her soft fingertips sliding comfortingly along his hard, hot muscles. Flesh to flesh. Heart to heart. Woman to man.

The touch of him compelled her. For one long instant, she felt the most powerful, uncanny connection to him she had ever felt to anyone.

Then he jerked his arm away. "Don't touch me! Don't

you ever put your lily-white hands on me again,'' he
roared.

''I—I didn't mean to! I must have been crazy to! It...it
was an accident!''

''Good!''

''Just get out of my way, and I'll go,'' she said primly.

''Not till you tell me what you're doing on Jones property. My, er, boss gave me instructions about a certain
woman—Karlington. He told me to call the cops if she
came around.''

''I'm not her!''

''She's got red hair.''

Her eyes widened, and he laughed at her fear.

''If you don't let me go, I'll scream.''

''Would you really?''

She tried to nod, but the muscles in her neck felt frozen.

''I could stop you from that, you know.''

But instead of pressing his physical advantage, he lifted
his arms, and she moved away from the wall, away from
him, only to trip over his wheelbarrow and cry out furiously.

When he started toward her, she held up her hands.
''No— Don't come near me! I can get up by myself.''
She brushed frantically at the loose dirt and grass on her
linen slacks.

''You didn't tell me what you're doing here,'' he demanded.

''I—I was looking for an apartment.''

''Like hell.'' His words were harsh. ''This isn't exactly
your kind of neighborhood.''

''N-not for myself,'' she improvised wildly. ''For
someone who...who works for me.''

''Oh, right. Some lowlife like me. Lady Bountiful
apartment hunting for her...her yardman, maybe? Why is

that such a hard one to swallow?'' He flashed that cynical smile of his again and dug in his pocket.

He knew she was lying, and for some idiotic reason she felt ashamed that he thought she was a snob.

While his fingers moved beneath the denim, her gaze flicked to his powerful body.

The bronzed muscular perfection of his lean frame drew her. For no reason at all, she thought of her big double bed and how empty and cold it felt every night.

She looked breathlessly away, but not before his dark gaze swung to her, and she felt the leap of some wild charge between them. He was as turned on by her as she was by him.

She shuddered, and he scowled. She realized a man like him might have taken her touching his arm as an invitation to do anything; he was so strong, she couldn't have stopped him. She was lucky he disliked her and had jerked away from her.

She didn't feel lucky. She felt lonely.

So lonely.

Dear God. She wanted to run, to forget Keith Jones and his deplorable properties and his even more deplorable employee.

But the brown hand had closed over the object it had been digging for. Carelessly, the yardman pulled his hand from his pocket and tossed her a shiny key.

His toss was on. But she was so upset, her catch was off. As she leaned down to pick it up, she was aware of his bold eyes on her.

''Number 15 is empty and ready to rent,'' he said casually in that harsh, but oh-so-compelling voice. ''I cleaned it and repaired the appliances myself, and I could give you a personal tour. I'm good with my hands.'' He paused. Maybe to let that last sentence sink in and torment her. ''Good at fixing things, I mean. There's a kitchen, a

living room, a bath. And, of course, a bedroom." He
drawled that last word ever so suggestively. "Or you can
look it over yourself."

She gasped in relief. "I—I'll look it over on my own."

"Independent lady…"

"Bingo."

"You can leave the key in the door. I'll be here…if
you need me…. For anything."

She felt hot and weak. He was horrible. He seemed to
hate her, and yet he seemed to find some savage delight
in tormenting her, too. Why did some terrible wanton
weakness make her want to ask him to show her the apartment after all?

No….

When she whirled away from him, she thought she
heard him chuckle darkly.

But when she turned back, he scowled at her obligingly.

Damn the man.

Chapter 3

Kate stood frozen in the doorway of number 15, wanting to leave but not wanting to risk more attention from the insolent yardman, who was now mowing the courtyard.

So she lingered in that shadowy entrance—trapped by her ridiculous fear of a man who was so far beneath her, she should never have noticed him in the first place. Nevertheless, she had to admit to a grudging admiration for him, at least for his work. Menial though some might believe it, he obviously took pride in it.

The apartment was immaculate. Not only did all the ancient appliances sparkle, they worked. Maybe his boss wasn't so bad after all. Maybe Jones did try to offer decent housing. Maybe he just couldn't afford to paint the outside.

Since her gaze was glued to the man's broad back, she saw the splash from the swimming pool only out of the corner of her eye. But she panicked when she realized that Bobby Lee, who had been playing by the pool only a few seconds before, had vanished.

As she raced for the pool, she had no way of knowing

whether or not he could swim. Then she saw a sickening dark shape with flailing legs on the bottom of the deep end.

Rushing through the chain-link gate, she sprang toward the pool, but as she dove, the slim heel of her Italian sandal snagged in a crack in the cement. She pitched wildly off balance, her head striking the hard tile edge of the pool. Her body slid into the water just as the kid's curly black head broke the aqua surface.

When Kate woke up, her throat and nasal passages burned with every breath. She groaned as she felt large hands gently probing her damp hair. Then the brutal fingertips dug too deeply into the gash in her scalp, and her eyes snapped open.

"Ouch!"

For an instant she didn't recognize the swarthy hard face so close to hers. Then the dark eyes flashed, and the man smiled sardonically as if he didn't respect her much.

And she knew who he was.

Confused, she glanced wildly past him and saw scuffed black work boots tossed in a corner, a masculine tie looped carelessly over a doorknob and a denim work shirt draped over a dresser that was littered with magazines and newspapers and a tattered paperback copy of *The Fatal Skin* by Honoré de Balzac.

He wasn't neat. Which didn't surprise her.

But he read. Which did.

"Where am I?" she demanded even as she saw that the insolent brute had taken advantage of the situation and maneuvered her into his bedroom.

"My bed," he replied, his husky voice low and somehow dangerous.

She pushed his hands away furiously.

"As if I couldn't figure that out! I meant why am I

here? How did I get here?'' she squeaked shrilly, struggling to sit up.

"I wouldn't sit up if I were you," he advised. "Take it easy. You've had a blow to the head. Not that it seems to have improved your disposition. On the contrary—"

"It'll take more than a blow to my head to keep me in your bed!"

But as she spoke, the crisp cotton sheet and heavy blankets sliding downward against her cool skin almost exposed a bare breast. Blushing, she grabbed at the sheet, conscious of a new horror and an excellent reason for staying right where she was.

Beneath his sheets and blankets, she was stark naked.

She froze, her hands groping wildly over her body just to make sure while his gleaming dark eyes told her he was enjoying her discomfiture immensely.

"You...you stripped me," she whispered, yanking his sheet to her chin and holding it there primly.

His loathsome smile broadened. "Doctor's orders."

A dozen hot nerves were quivering in her temple. "I'll bet!" She was about to explode. Instead she stopped herself and sucked in her breath.

"You were soaking wet. Doc said the first thing to do was make sure you were dry and warm. You see, you hit your head on the pool edge and fell in—unconscious."

"And you saved me?"

"You got it, baby. I'm your hero. I pulled you out of the pool and called a doctor. Which makes me your Sir Lance in shining armor."

He smiled as if he was loving every minute of this!

She felt a killing rage and an unendurable shame. "Not in a million lifetimes." Just the thought that he was gloating over having seen her without a stitch on made her cheeks burn.

"And where are my clothes?"

His black eyes went cold. "I bet Bobby Lee you'd act high and mighty and refuse to thank us."

She clamped her lips together in a stubborn line. Gratitude was the last thing she felt. Still, he did have her trapped...and in his bed. "Thank you—for saving me," she muttered grudgingly. "Now...if...if you would...please...please...just get my clothes, I'll dress and go."

"Relax." His avid attention focused on her hot face. "You're not leaving till the doctor gets here and says you can."

"I—I'm sure...I've caused you enough trouble."

"Don't worry about it," he murmured ruthlessly. "I knew you were trouble the minute I set eyes on you. Besides I've enjoyed...getting to know you better."

Inwardly she was seething—and he knew it. His gorgeous mouth was twitching, which meant he loved it. Outwardly she struggled to act calm and dignified. "Look, you may be used to situations like this—"

"Why do I have the feeling you're about to hurt my feelings by attacking my morals again?" he taunted softly.

"Well, a man like you probably has strange naked women in his bed all the time—"

"Right! A man like me.... So, we're back to me being a lowlife, are we? No one has been in my bed...since my wife died. And you, my holier-than-thou Karlington witch, are no stranger to me. If I did want a woman, you're the very last I'd choose—to have naked in my bed." He had drawled her name very softly, very nastily.

She bristled even as his frigid tone sent a chill down her spine. "How do you know my name?"

"When you were out cold, I told Bobby Lee to look in your purse for your driver's license."

He was lying. She could feel it.

"Bobby Lee's okay, then?" she asked weakly.

"He was diving for a toy car. He's fine."

"You should have been watching him."

The man's features were half in shadow, the hard angular planes revealing little. "Hey, you're the last person I'd let tell me what I should and shouldn't do. You're the fool who would have drowned if I hadn't saved you."

"Well, if you'll just get my clothes, I'll cause you no further trouble."

"No way do I believe that.... Not that I'll give you your clothes...."

Her pulse began to throb unevenly.

"Don't worry—I have no designs on your body, charming though it is," he said bluntly. "But you're staying till the doctor says you can go. You see, Miss Karlington, my boss told me you were repossessing everything he owns. He ordered me not to allow you to set foot on his property till you got title. He'll fire me for sure if he finds out I let you snoop around here and then you nearly drowned in his pool—because of my kid."

"I hope you do get fired. I hope you starve."

Low, harsh laughter came from his throat. "Because you've always been so rich, you've never had it tough," he murmured tightly. "You wouldn't mind Bobby Lee losing his home."

"I—I don't want to hurt Bobby Lee. Only you—because—"

"Because I didn't pussyfoot around someone as high and mighty as you think you are," he ground out. "Because I was afraid you'd go into shock and I had the audacity to undress you when you were shivering and unconscious. Honey, you were out cold, and your skin was like ice."

She was still stuck on the word *honey,* savoring it, hating him for saying it in that cynical and yet deeply caressing tone that made her feel very feminine and cherished even as it turned her blood to molten fire.

"If you get me fired, Bobby Lee'll pay, too. What happens to me, happens to him. The question is, are you as cold and ruthless as Jones says you are?"

"Oh, all right. I'll see your doctor," she snapped, not answering his question because for some reason she didn't want to admit she was probably worse than Jones said she was.

His eyebrows arched nastily.

"I'm staying for Bobby Lee's sake! Not yours. And I won't say a thing to Jones to get you in trouble even though you're insolent...and...arrogant. Even though you don't know your...your place."

"Which is light years socially beneath your brightly shining star?" he added shortly.

"You said it, buster. I'll even pay for the doctor. There's a fifty in my purse—"

"I'll pay," he growled.

"Oh, don't be so proud! You can't possibly afford—"

"Jones'll reimburse me. The last thing he'd want is *your* money."

"You make it sound as if he hates me." It irritated her that Jones went around running her down to her future employees.

"Yeah. Do you blame him?" Flushing darkly, the brute leaned closer, and a shiver of alarm darted through her. "But then, Jones hasn't had the pleasure of getting to know you personally—on the intimate level that I have."

Kate tried to tell herself that he was crude and uneducated and insolent, that she hated the idea of such a man's dark callused hands on her skin, of his bold eyes burning now with memories of her naked body. But as his gaze devoured her lips, and his mouth came nearer, a

violent quiver went hotly through her, and without fully
realizing what she did, she closed her eyes and pursed
her lips almost expectantly.

If he'd been as tempted to kiss her as she'd been to let
him, he mastered the impulse. Instead of his warm mouth
on hers, she felt a draft of cool air and heard his raspy
chuckle as the door swung open.

When her eyes flew open again, the Balzac novel was
gone and a tanned hand was pulling the door shut.

Monday morning, Kate's temple still ached as she
flicked on the lights of her darkened office and walked
briskly to her desk with her heavy briefcase. She opened
her crisp beige drapes, and hazy sunlight flooded her opulent, immaculate office.

She wore a starched white cotton blouse and a perfectly
pressed denim skirt. Her hair was pulled straight back
from her face and secured tightly in a big white clip.

For a long moment she stared out the ceiling-to-floor
windows at the bustling city wrapped in smog. She felt
strangely restless and lonelier than ever before, cut off
from that world of ordinary people who had families and
lovers and children.

Her father had warned her she would be alone at the
top, that her money would set her apart, that she could
trust in nothing and in no one except herself; that men
would want her only for her power or for her fortune, that
she would have to learn to make men her tools, her serfs,
and not become theirs.

Own or be owned. Control or be controlled. Those
were her father's rules. He said there was no such thing
as a power vacuum. Either you were in charge or you
were exploited.

Once she had not wanted to believe that, and she had
been naively loving. But Edwin's cruel betrayal had

taught her that her father was right. Never had she felt more exploited than when she'd lain in the hospital after her miscarriage and her father had coldly informed her by phone how much he'd paid in the divorce settlement to be rid of Edwin.

She had asked her father, "Did you tell him I lost the baby?"

"You little fool... Yes."

And when Edwin had not bothered to come to the baby's memorial service, her heart had hardened. Not only toward him, but toward all men.

Kate came back to the present.

She turned her back on the window and sat down, a tiny solitary figure dwarfed by her immense office. With a shaking hand she withdrew the thick, perfectly organized Jones file from her briefcase and thumbed through the neat pages.

Involuntarily her thoughts turned to her accident Saturday and to that humiliating encounter with Jones's insolent yardman and to his friend, the helpful Dr. Sager. When she took over the Jones properties, she would have that rude, impossible handyman fired. Then she remembered Bobby Lee and realized that much as she hated helping the father, she would have to arrange for one of her friends to hire him for the sake of his child. She had seen the man's work and could personally recommend him. Even though she knew that, professionally, she was an idiot to let go of someone so good, she was too afraid of seeing him again.

Because she had dreamed of him.

Because she had longed for him even though she knew he hated her, and she hated him.

She had puttered about her apartment Sunday, going through the motions of neatening and straightening drawers and closets that had already been perfect. She had felt edgy and restless and lonely, which she, independent Kate Karlington, resented because she believed she didn't need a man for anything.

Not true. Men had one use for which there was no good substitute. She thought of how warm the yardman's hard arm had felt beneath her fingers before he had jerked away from her.

Her thoughts strayed beyond sex. More than anything in the world, Kate wanted a child. She wanted someone to love, someone who would love her. But she was old enough to have come to terms with some other facts about herself and her beliefs. Her cruel experiences had taught her to distrust herself with men; she didn't want to risk another failed marriage.

She remembered how joyous, how filled with hope she'd felt when she'd been pregnant. The motherhood angle seemed a more enduring love bond.

There should be some sort of painless baby machine a mature woman such as herself could use to get pregnant.

A baby machine....

In spite of herself, Kate smiled faintly and closed her eyes, trying to imagine one. It should be a robot with steel arms and bright lights for eyes. The procedure to get pregnant would have to be painless and, of course, it wouldn't be fraught with emotional complications. But neither the vision nor the procedure would take shape in her mind. Instead she imagined an angry man whose powerful body seemed made of melted bronze, whose raven-black hair was glossily curled, whose cruel white smile made her shiver as he pulled her naked body beneath his onto a soft bed of tangled white sheets.

Softly she touched her breasts through her starched cotton shirt, and unbidden came the forbidden memory of the yardman's insolent black eyes moving lingeringly over her body, of the molten electricity that had raced through her every time he'd looked at her even when she'd known he disliked her. She remembered his breath, warm and beery smelling, and yet earthily pleasant; she remembered his desperate pain when he'd mentioned the death of his wife. And she remembered his dear, motherless little boy. For all their differences, she sensed the man was as lonely as she was. More than anything she wanted to see the man and his beautiful little boy again.

She tried to imagine the man, dressed in a three-piece suit, with an education as fancy as hers. Fortunately, Kate's ridiculous daydreams were shattered when her large polished mahogany door was pushed open by her secretary. Esther Ayers rushed in clutching her baby daughter, Hannah, in one arm and a bottle of juice and a stack of legal papers in the other.

"Sorry, Kate, but Mom had to go to the dentist, so I had to bring Hannah in for an hour or so. You see, yesterday we took Mother to a restaurant for Mother's Day after church. Mother shattered a molar when she bit into an oyster."

Mother's Day—Kate ignored her own pain as she remembered going to her own mother's grave and then to the grave of her baby with a bouquet of daisies. She had never gotten to celebrate a single Mother's Day with her mother. She herself would probably never really be a mother.

She got up slowly and held out her arms to the golden two-year-old. With a giggle, Hannah sprang into them.

Esther set the papers on her desk. "These have to be signed so they can go out—today."

"You know I love for you to bring Hannah," Kate said softly. She touched her forehead to the child's and then caressed her golden ringlets. "Hello, there, my beautiful darling. Now how many piggies—"

"Fingas, Kate! Toes! Not piggies!" Hannah squealed, hiding her eyes bashfully.

"Your Mr. Jones has been calling all morning demanding to see you," Esther said.

"My lawyers have advised against such a meeting till the day of the foreclosure."

"You should try telling him that."

The phone rang again.

"That's probably him," Esther said.

Esther was about to pick up the phone, but Kate lifted the receiver herself, knowing Esther really wasn't tough enough to handle certain macho, overbearing types. Kate knelt so Hannah could get down to explore.

"Karlington Enterprises. Miss Karlington's office," Kate said smoothly, pretending to be her secretary.

"Honey, put the dragon lady through, and I swear I'll take you to the fanciest lunch Houston can offer."

Bribery. Kate frowned, even though she knew Esther was too loyal to ever go out with him.

"I'm so sorry. Miss Karlington has someone in her office at the moment, sir," Kate said frostily. Which wasn't exactly a lie.

"Good! She's there! I'll be right over."

"No, I don't want—! I mean *her* lawyers have advised her not to see—"

"Honey, the trouble with this damned country is the lawyers are running it."

"She's too busy to see you. Besides, you're the last man she wants to see."

"Then why did she come snooping around my property Saturday? You tell her that one of my people says she took off her clothes, hopped in his bed and sexually harassed him. Those are some pretty serious charges. I try to run a moral establishment."

"He what? I tell you Ms. Karlington did no such thing! He stripped her—"

Kate broke off, her skin flaming as Esther's curious gaze rose to hers.

"She tried to seduce him into kissing—"

Frantically Kate waved her curious secretary out of the room.

"She most certainly did not!"

"I'm surprised Miss Karlington would keep her secretary so well-informed about such activities—"

Kate's voice was steel. "This is Kate Karlington, Mr. Jones."

"I knew it all the time."

"And I don't want to see you."

"Oh, but you do," he said very softly. "Every bit as much as I want to see you. Women have chased me all my life. From my yardman's description of you, I doubt you'll be any exception. I'm looking forward to meeting you—in the flesh."

"You are as impossible as that horrible man who works for you."

"He and I have a great deal in common."

"I wouldn't brag about it if I were you."

"Funny, but he told me that under different circumstances, you two could have hit it off."

"He what?" she screamed.

When he didn't answer, she realized he'd hung up.

Dear God! He was probably on his way over.

Chapter 4

"I-cream! I-cream!" Hannah leaned forward and pointed to the giant poster of a pink cow licking the top of a huge double-dip parfait coated in chocolate syrup and peanuts. Then Hannah turned her attention back to the man behind the black-and-white-tiled counter who was digging in a huge ice-cream carton for a ball of vanilla.

"I want my *big* i-cream!"

"He's making it, Hannah darling. Just as fast as he can," Kate said soothingly.

"Zakly like the picture?"

"Exactly, precious."

As soon as Kate had hung up from speaking to Jim Keith Jones, Hannah had insisted on being taken downstairs to the ice-cream parlor, which was on the street level. Such trips had become ritual affairs whenever Esther brought her daughter to the office, and today Kate had been only too happy to leave Esther to deal with the troublesome Mr. Jones.

The glass door of the shop suddenly swung open, and a familiar-looking black-haired little boy burst inside and

dashed to the counter. "Dad, can I have one of those—"
He pointed to the same poster that had caught Hannah's
attention.

Hannah put her thumb in her mouth and chewed on it,
regarding the interloper curiously while the door was
opened slowly and closed again.

"Sure, son. Whatever you want," came the deep velvet
tones of an unforgettable, masculine baritone. Kate turned
around wildly. The bold blaze of devil-black eyes stared
holes through her.

Her heart began to hammer in a painful rush.

"Why, if it isn't the beautiful witch Karlington," came
the smooth whisper of the yardman Kate would have
given anything to avoid. He didn't look the least bit surprised to see her. Nor the least bit flustered.

Kate clutched the counter for support as the man behind it placed a cherry on top of Hannah's magnificent,
double-dip parfait. "There you go, miss—"

"It's not as big as the picture," Hannah cried in dismay.

The yardman smiled grimly. "Most things men do
don't live up to a woman's expectations. Not that I've
had many complaints from women."

Kate ignored the plastic cup and the towering parfait
in the outstretched hand and whirled angrily to stare at
the tall man now striding toward her.

He had talked to his boss.

She was about to tell him he was the most conceited
blabbermouth she had ever met, but she stopped short. He
no longer looked at all like a yardman. Someone with
impeccable taste had put him in an ele-gant black three-
piece suit, and he looked even better in it than she'd imagined he would.

No longer did he seem such a lesser being—a ghetto-
toughened, uneducated hunk fit only to do menial work.

No, this man could fit as easily into her elegant world as he could a darker, more dangerous one. Despite his rough edges, there was the unmistakable aura of keen-minded power about him, as if he was as ruthlessly used to commanding others as she.

Why did the image of that tattered novel by Balzac flash in her mind?

"What a coincidence," he purred raspily, "our meeting again." He was smiling in that grim, bold way that so unnerved Kate because she sensed that their meeting here was no coincidence. He had deliberately hunted her down for some purpose of his own.

She flashed him a tight smile of dismissal and picked up Hannah's parfait.

"Thanks for telling your boss what happened! Did he send you over to do his dirty work?" she whispered.

"Oh, this was my brainchild," he replied while his son ordered a parfait.

"Why?"

"Would you believe I was worried about you and wanted to make sure you were okay?"

"No!"

"Right." His voice was both soft and deep, but he didn't smile. "And you probably intend to hold what happened Saturday against me forever."

"You and I are hardly going to have a forever."

"I'm truly glad you're better."

She couldn't believe it when he touched her injured temple very gently, smoothing her red hair away from her face. "We may be more involved than you think."

"I-cream! I-cream!" Hannah cried impatiently. "Melting!"

"Sorry, darling." Kate turned her back on the yardman and carried Hannah to the nearest booth, placing the mountain of ice cream in front of her, and sitting opposite the child so she could help her.

The yardman handed his son a five-dollar bill, and, without asking if he could join Kate, pulled up a tiny pink stool that was much too small for him and thrust his long legs on either side of it. Hannah had eaten only one bite, but ice cream was already dripping over the plastic sides of her cup and down her chin. Nevertheless, she smiled flirtatiously at the handsome man she took to be her new admirer.

The elegant yardman smiled back at her, picked up a napkin and wiped her small face with a fatherly, well-practiced expertise.

The ogre's roughly carved features were almost sweet as he dealt with Hannah.

"You have a beautiful little girl, Mrs. Karlington—underneath the chocolate syrup," he said.

"It's Miss—"

"Right. I think my boss read somewhere that your husband ran off with a younger woman."

"And I divorced him and took my maiden name back. And Hannah's—not my daughter, either."

The yardman's hard black eyes met Kate's, and she realized he'd caught the pain in her voice.

"But you wish she was," he said quietly.

"Yes," Kate admitted, unnerved that he seemed to understand her on a soul-deep level.

"Maybe you wouldn't like a kid any more than a husband if you were stuck cleaning up chocolate twenty-four hours a day."

"You're wrong. Very, very wrong." Kate frowned.

Bobby Lee joined them, sitting on a stool across from Hannah.

"Why did you really come here?" Kate asked the yardman.

"I told you—to make sure you're okay."

"I'm okay. So you can go. Unless you have some other reason—"

"As a matter of fact I do."

"I'm all ears."

"Since you're going to buy the Jones properties, and I...I work for Jones, I thought maybe I should ask what you intend to do about his people. I mean the little guys...like me."

"I intend to keep most of his people," she hedged, not wanting to admit that she had decided to terminate him.

"That's a relief."

She flushed guiltily.

His face grew hard. "And what about me? Are you going to toss me out into the cold?"

Again he seemed to have read her mind.

Something inside her froze. "Each case will be judged individually," she whispered, turning pale.

"I'm afraid I made a very bad impression."

"Yes."

"I did so deliberately."

"Why did you have to tell your boss everything that happened?"

"He and I are very close."

He took her hand, and the shock of his touch was electric. She tried to draw back, but he held on to her slim fingers tightly.

"W-what do you think you're doing?" she managed to ask.

"Now, this isn't an apology. It's an explanation. I don't like people who walk over other people. Who use their money to buy lawyers and steal legally. I see them as bullies." His hard voice softened. "Even when they are very beautiful."

The warmth in his eyes made her shiver. "I can see

Jones has been talking to you out of hand. If your boss has problems, it has nothing to do with me. It's due to his own ineptness."

His fingers tightened on hers. His hard mouth thinned, but he did not defend his boss. "Has your own life gone perfectly? Have you never made a mistake that you deeply regret?"

She stared at him in silence, too aware of her small hand locked in his larger one. Too aware of his heat, his power, his charisma. His immense frame seemed to shrink the size of the booth, to overwhelm her.

"You can work for me—for double what Jones paid you," she said on a desperate note.

His mouth twisted. "You're more generous than you know. But I won't hold you to that."

Hannah looked up and declared proudly, "I'm tru." She lifted her golden head out of the ice-cream dish, her chin and nose dripping with chocolate syrup and vanilla ice cream.

And one glance at her brought the adult conversation to an abrupt end.

Ten minutes later, when Jim Keith strode into Kate's outer office and lavish waiting room, Hannah giggled flirtatiously at him. He smiled back at her on his way past Esther, who was talking on the phone at her desk.

"Wait for me here, Bobby Lee," Jim Keith commanded, pointing to a chair near Hannah.

Bobby Lee ran over to play with the little girl. Jim Keith was about to push open the massive mahogany door that led to Kate's office, when Esther called to him frantically.

"Sir? Sir, do you have an appointment?"

"Your boss is expecting me."

Esther studied her appointment book. "I don't see a ten forty-five."

Jim Keith moved swiftly to her desk, leaned down, and scribbled his name. When he finished, huge, bold black scrawl filled the entire page. "Now you do. We've talked on the phone."

"Jones?" Esther squeaked, deciphering the scribble. Then her big eyes traveled slowly from her book up the vast length of the man to his smiling face. When his masculine beauty struck her full force, her mouth sagged open.

"You're much better looking in person, too," he said with a gentle, arrogant smile. Then he moved away—toward Kate's door.

As he pushed it open, he heard Esther buzzing Kate frantically. "I'm sorry, Kate. I—I couldn't stop him! Keith Jones is on his way in."

"Call security," Kate ordered brusquely just as Jim Keith walked up to her desk, seized the phone, and replaced it in its cradle.

"Why, it's...it's you," she gasped, her horrified eyes trailing up the long length of him just as Esther's had. Kate turned purple. "You're...that awful yardman."

He forced a smile. "Not awful—surely. Think of me as your gallant rescuer."

"You should have told me who you were Saturday!"

"It was more fun not to."

"I don't like being made a fool of. You'll pay for that little joke, Mr. Jones. Do you hear me?"

"With what? You're already set to take over everything I own," he countered pleasantly.

"A snake with your vile sense of humor deserves to go under."

"Just like a rich witch like yourself deserves to trample

everyone in her path. You've taken a lot of other men's properties. Did they all deserve to go under, too?''

"Oooooo!''

"Baby, I learned a long time ago there's no justice in this world.''

He leaned over and grabbed the file she had on him and his properties. When she got up, he waved her down and snapped the manila folder open and thumbed through it, quickly scanning the bleak numbers.

He whistled. ''You damn sure have the goods on me!''

"I know everything about you, Mr. Jones.''

"Everything about my financial predicament,'' he clarified. Looking up, his dark face was weary with defeat. "But not everything. Still, you're thorough,'' he admitted grimly.

For some reason she didn't feel like gloating. Her mouth felt too tight to smile. "I try to be businesslike, Mr. Jones.''

"Ruthless! You certainly have me by the—''

"Which is right where I want you.''

"Indeed?'' His brazen gaze swept below his belt and then back to her with a derisive grin.

Her swift blush of humiliation was not nearly so satisfying as he'd anticipated. Instead he was moved by her wide vulnerable eyes. She was scared. Fortunately, before he said anything mushy or stupidly comforting, two burly security guards rushed in.

"Take him,'' Kate ordered coldly, recovering herself.

"I could have turned you over to the cops Saturday,'' Jim Keith whispered as the men moved toward him. "I knew who you were. Or I could have let you drown at the bottom of my pool. Instead I saved your life.''

She didn't answer. She refused to look at him.

Her men grabbed his shoulders. "Let's go, mister.''

Jim Keith shrugged them away. "Kate, for God's sake,

you've won," he whispered. "I just came over here because I'd really like to talk to you."

She continued to stare down at her desk. She clenched her hands, and he saw that her knuckles were white. He was almost surprised when she uttered a strangled whisper to her two men. "You can go for now. I'll buzz you— if I need you."

When they were alone again, she got up and went to the window and, turning her back, stared down at the city. The sunlight backlighted the sexy shape of her body, and he remembered just how good she'd looked naked in his bed. His loins tightened.

Suddenly her vast office seemed airless. His suit felt like a straitjacket, and he was tugging at his tie.

"So—what could we possibly have to talk about?" she asked in a quiet, businesslike tone.

"I need more time," he rasped. "Six months."

"I am afraid not."

"You were born rich," he began.

She breathed deeply. Which made her breasts rise and fall. Which made him feel hotter. He yanked the knot of his tie loose.

"A harder fate than you can possibly imagine," she whispered. "My mother died, and my father... I ran away when I was five and lived with an older, childless aunt for a year. Then my father took me away from her and put me in boarding schools. I hardly saw him—until I was grown."

"The finest schools, I'm sure. And after that you languished at Harvard and Cornell."

Languished... "Yes...." She nodded.

Jim Keith tried not to see the tears in her eyes. He forced a hard note into his voice. "Well, I was born poor, which might be a tougher fate than you could imagine, honey. I would have given anything to have the time or the money to get even one college degree—here locally. You have three eastern degrees.''

"Lucky me.'' She caught herself. "Look—I thought you wanted to talk business. I've got more to do than listen to your poor-boy jealousies.''

He got up slowly. "I'm not jealous of you, damn it. I wouldn't be you for anything in the world. Is your work only money, numbers...''

"What else should it be?''

"I spent years building up everything you're going to take Friday.''

"I know.''

He moved nearer. "But do you know how that feels? I know my stuff doesn't equal a fraction of your net worth, but I put myself into buying it. Into running it. I don't sit around in some fancy skyscraper with dozens of employees and handmaidens bringing me coffee. I know every tenant and every man who works for me. Every manager. I've overseen every repair. I've done a lot of them myself.''

"Then you've spread yourself too thin. Mr. Jones, you borrowed a great deal of money three and a half years ago, and yet your properties are terribly neglected. What did you do, party it all away?''

"Party it away?'' he asked, thunderstruck. He thought of Mary—sick and thin, dying even, and the money he'd borrowed to save her. Maybe he'd been a fool not to listen to the American doctors who'd warned him the German doctors would fail, but this witch's contempt made something explode inside him.

"You're in way over your head, too, honey,'' he growled. "What I did with the money is none of your business.''

"If I could see where you'd spent a dime on your property—''

"You push. You want more, more, but nothing you get will ever be enough without—"

Later he would never know what drove him to do what he did. Later he would hate himself. But he didn't think. The rage inside him had been building for months, for years, from that first terrible moment when Mary had been diagnosed, and suddenly Kate was here—sexy Kate, his destroyer.

Kate, cruelly beautiful, magnificently beautiful with her healthily flushed cheeks and flaming hair; Kate, more wondrously beautiful and far more desirable even than his gentle Mary. Kate, who made his blood pulse with angry blazing needs he would have given anything to deny if only he hadn't been too furious and too aroused to think straight.

She looked so cool and imperious—untouched by the real world and real feelings, so untouched by the kind of unfair fate he had endured. Had she ever known the bitter taste of failure? He could not go down without making her suffer just a little, too.

So he grabbed her, his fingers sinking into her soft flesh with a crushing grip as he caught her to his hard body. Then his angry lips were devouring hers with more hunger than he'd ever felt. His tongue filled her mouth, tasting her, exploring her. Claiming her. His hands slid down her back and buttocks, arching her into his body.

And she felt good, so good that his hunger was suddenly stronger than his anger. Maybe she was hard and ruthless when it came to business, but in his arms, she became the softest and most pliant creature. She made not the slightest effort to resist him.

At first she went rigidly still, but when his mouth touched hers, she made a soft, endearing little moan that tugged at his heart. She opened her lips to his tongue. Her need seemed delicious and sweet. She seemed somehow so untouched and innocent. And suddenly he craved more of her.

Her trembling hands came around his neck, her fingers gently clutching at first and then raking through his inky hair as if she could no more deny her own feelings for him than he.

"I'm supposed to hate you," she whispered raggedly even as she clung, breathing hard, pressing her slim, trembling body into his.

"Likewise," he muttered as he lowered his mouth to hers again. This time her tongue came inside his lips, and her response aroused him to do more, to want more, until he felt himself swept near some fatal edge on a burning tide of desire.

She was his enemy, and surely God had the cruelest, the most warped sense of humor to make Kate Karlington the one woman whose look and touch could make him want to get past his grief over Mary.

But he did. He wanted to strip her and devour her slim pale body. All day Sunday, visions of her naked loveliness had haunted him.

He wanted to plunge deep inside her and stay encased in her warm velvet flesh, joined—until he made her know that she could never belong to anyone but him.

He cursed God that she who thought him a fool for his failures was the one woman he wanted. Suddenly he knew how ridiculous she must find him. How she must despise him. This realization made her sweet-tasting, eager mouth and warm voluptuous body a torture.

He forced himself to let her go, and the instant he did, she slapped him.

Then she gasped at the livid white mark on his tanned cheek and stumbled backward. The intense emotion in her eyes was more desperately sad than angry. "Get out," she whispered. "Get out."

Her half-open, cotton blouse hung limp and wrinkled. Her lovely face was tear-streaked and swollen from his kisses. Her eyes were ravaged and pain-filled. Her hair had come out of its clip and fell in wild tangles about her shoulders.

She looked young and vulnerable, more fragile than he could ever have imagined Kate Karlington being. But more than anything, she was desirable.

"I'm sorry," he whispered hoarsely. "I shouldn't have kissed you. I just wanted to make you know that I was more than just a bunch of debits and credits in one of your files. More than a failure. I'm a man. A human being. I guess I won't blame you for cutting me to ribbons now."

He expected her to lash back at him. Instead her face softened. Her vulnerable green eyes widened, and he felt uncomfortably aware of some powerful unwanted bond with her. Her hands shook as she tried to rebutton her blouse.

Maybe she wasn't an ice-cold witch after all. Maybe the fiery softness he'd sensed in her when she'd yielded to his kisses was real. Maybe she was as lonely and as deeply hurt by life as he.

"You're wrong about me," she said, pulling her hair back nervously into her clip. "And...I'm sorry I slapped you." She reached up to stroke his rough cheek where she'd hurt him.

Her fingers were unbearably cool and light against his burning skin.

His hand closed over her delicate wrist. When he felt her pulse racing beneath his thumb, his own heart began to pound. He wanted to take her in his arms, to kiss her again.

Was he crazy?

"Mr. Jones, I don't really want to take over your properties right now. I—I would have let you have the time, but the fact is, time won't help you.''

Every nerve in his hard body tightened warily.

''You need capital, Mr. Jones, and you don't have it. I do.'' Her voice was sweet; she almost sounded as if she really cared.

He *was* crazy. *She was his enemy.*

He cast her slim hand aside and stepped back, rejecting the comfort of her touch and her voice because he wanted them too much. ''Right. You're all heart,'' he ground out.

''Then I'll see you Friday,'' she whispered as he rushed past her toward the door. ''Then we'll be done with each other once and for all.''

''Till that happy day,'' he muttered bitterly, ignoring the shimmering pain in her eyes as he stalked out.

Chapter 5

Jim Keith signed away everything he owned with an angry flourish of scrawling black ink. Then he threw his pen down in disgust and rose from the desk to his full height.

Although he didn't look at Kate, he was too aware of her sleek, long-limbed body in that exquisitely tailored, navy linen suit, and the cool perfection of her professional presence somehow magnified his masculine feelings of failure. He had spent the past week alternately hating her and hungering for her and then despising himself for the insane war going on inside him.

He glanced toward her and was struck again by how pale and exhausted she appeared this morning, as if she, too, was suffering. There were dark circles beneath her lovely eyes. She looked thinner—hardly a worthy foe. The stark truth was he'd been bested by a spoiled woman who was so fragile, he could easily have torn her apart with his bare hands. Not that he had ever physically hurt a woman, not that he even wanted to hurt her—not in that way. No, what he wanted—

Just for a second his gaze slid from her white face to

the prim starched collar of her creamy blouse, which she had buttoned all the way to the top as if to conceal as much flesh as possible. He remembered another blouse, a white cotton blouse—torn open nearly to her waist, the thick cotton wrinkled from his rough lovemaking. He remembered how wantonly beautiful she'd looked, flushed from his kisses—not so perfect but somehow so human— and he wanted to be alone with her. To loosen those buttons, to touch the skin beneath the creamy cotton, to show her that although she had taken everything he owned, he could conquer her just as easily.

He squared his broad shoulders in a gesture of denial. What he had to do was get away from her, to forget her. To start over.

He grabbed his bulging briefcase and was almost out the door when she called out to him, the honey of her phonily sweet voice making his stomach claw.

"Mr. Jones, before you go, I'd like to talk to you— alone."

Although gently spoken, it was a command.

His mouth tightened as he fought against the violence he felt. Somehow he managed an indifferent shrug. "What could you and I possibly have to talk about now?"

"I have a proposition that might interest you."

Her tone was softer, beguilingly softer—it tore him apart.

Jim Keith's black gaze swept from her blazing green eyes downward, noting her curves hungrily, and thinking that despite her pallor and her prim suit, despite her extreme nervousness, she had never looked more beautiful.

"Sorry, not interested," he muttered brutally, shoving the door open with his thick briefcase.

She went white, those huge eyes of hers flickering with pain at his insulting tone. He realized suddenly that she wasn't gloating, that she hadn't really wanted to hurt him—that this foreclosure was strictly business as far as she was concerned.

Too bad he couldn't write it off as just another business deal gone sour.

The craziest thing of all was that *he* actually felt an odd pang of remorse at having hurt her.

"I really would like to talk to you," she said, her voice tighter, but nicer than he deserved.

Nicer than he wanted.

"All right. But make it fast." He yanked the heavy chair away from the desk and sat down again while the others paraded dutifully out of the room.

"Does everyone always do what you want them to?" he spat contemptuously.

She paled at some unhappy memory, but she ignored Jim Keith's thrust. "Last week, you asked me what I intended to do about the people who worked for you. About you. And I said—"

"I remember what you said. Every damned word. You don't have to repeat it. I know you're as eager to be rid of me as I am to be rid of you. I won't hold you to what you said."

"I really would like to offer you a job."

"No way."

"You haven't even heard what I have in mind."

"Look, you've now got everything I ever owned. Isn't that enough? Are you determined to gobble me alive, too?"

"No—"

"Yes. You are. Look, I've been on my own since I was sixteen. Paper route. All sorts of things. I haven't worked for anyone in years. And never for a woman. Much less for the one woman who repossessed everything I once owned. I wouldn't know how to be one of your obedient lackeys."

"I wouldn't expect you to be," she said in that thick, velvety voice.

"How could I work for you—managing properties that were once mine?"

"Lots of people have done it."

"Not me. Besides, why would you want to hire a failure?"

"I don't see you that way."

Although her kind words warmed him, he laughed mirthlessly, more determined than ever that what he really wanted was to rid himself of her forever.

"Except for that one loan three and a half years ago, your management has been superb. I have taken on a lot of properties besides yours, and I'm overextended. I—I don't mean financially... I really do need some managerial help." She wrote down a figure on a piece of paper and handed it to him. "This is the annual salary I'm prepared to offer you. I wish I could pay you more, but as you know, the real-estate market is precarious. I wouldn't want to make a promise I couldn't afford to keep."

He glared at the huge number and then at her, even more furious than before—because he needed the money so desperately, and she was being so generous.

No! She wasn't generous! When she wanted something, she bought it.

But the offer tempted him. So did the woman.

"Is there anything you've ever wanted and never been able to buy?" he demanded in a hard whisper.

"You might be surprised."

Working for himself, he'd never taken home nearly as much as she was offering him—which she knew. He'd plowed most of his profit back into the properties. "What makes you think I'd be worth that amount?"

"I'm sure you'll earn every penny."

He wondered what she wanted him to do to earn so

much money. He sucked in a deep breath and decided it would be stupid to insult her by asking.

If he went to work for her, he'd be selling out.

If he didn't, he'd be a fool. He was dead broke. Hell, he needed the job. He would make enough so he could save, so he could eventually reinvest and begin again on his own. It wasn't as if she'd own him forever.

"I know you don't like me very much," she said softly, "but we won't have to see that much of each other."

"Is that a promise?"

"Yes." The pain in her voice tugged at some tender emotion in him he didn't want to acknowledge. "I'm sorry. About today. I—I really don't want you to hate me."

He wished he did hate her, but he remembered how cute he'd thought she was when she'd gamely taken him on about Bobby Lee's lurid reading material. He remembered her diving into that pool to save his kid. He remembered the wild terror he'd felt when he'd pulled her limp body from the pool, when he'd struggled to force air into her lungs. He remembered as well his thrill of joy when she'd spit out water and gasped that first tortured breath. Most of all he remembered how awed he'd been by the perfection of her naked body, how hungry he'd been for the taste of her mouth, how hungry he still was—and for so much more than kisses. Even though he wanted to hate her, he was powerfully drawn by her.

He wanted to work for her...and not just for the salary, and not just to find some way to exact revenge. He wanted to figure her out.

"How could I possibly like you?" he asked cruelly in response to her earlier statement. "You're a Karlington. You've bought me—like you've bought everything else you ever wanted."

"Must you always be so rude...and—and so insolent to me?"

"Why not? You have it coming. Besides, when you get to know me better, you'll find out I have a lot more flaws."

"When I get to know—"

"Yes. You see, I've decided I have no choice but to take the job. And whatever it is, I'll do my best to satisfy you, honey. At the price you've named, I am yours." As her shimmering green gaze fearfully met his, he could feel his own heart surging very hard and very fast. "And I promise you, Kate—you'll get a helluva lot more than your money's worth."

Kate Karlington had frequently remembered his promise in the three months that had followed, for never had any employee worked harder and made himself more invaluable to her than Keith, as she called him now. It was as if he was determined to prove his worth both to himself and to her.

Not that she saw much of him. He deliberately kept out of her way. And the fact that he did, only made her perversely crave to be near him. She sought him out on a thousand pretexts, and it hurt her that although he was unfailingly courteous, he remained tightly guarded around her, while with everyone else, he was genial and easygoing. With Esther he was almost flirtatious, and Kate could always tell when he was in her outer office by Esther's warm laughter. Occasionally he took Esther to lunch. And because he did, a tight, jealous coolness had come into her own relationship with her secretary.

Keith welcomed input from both tenants and managers and, to Kate's surprise, from her. He was not threatened by other people's good ideas. On those rare occasions when she chose to override him, he usually gave in gracefully. She'd known he'd be good, but not nearly as invaluable as he was. While she was steady, he was more innovative and more willing to take risks. Although they didn't think alike, their talents balanced each other. They worked well together.

He was very protective of her and wouldn't allow her to go out to troubleshoot at the tougher projects, especially at night. He handled all the difficult clients and hostile tenants himself. Thus, she was working shorter hours while her properties were better run, better maintained, safer and more profitable than they'd ever been before. There was only one thing he could be awful about: he'd repeatedly and quite arrogantly refused to help her buy discounted notes or negotiate repossessions.

Once when she'd needed to go out of town and had asked for his help with a foreclosure, she'd lost her patience and pressed him too hard.

"No," he had thundered, his control breaking. "You may think you own me body and soul, but you don't, Kate. Not quite. I won't steal for you—no matter how much I need the damned money you pay me."

"You leave me no choice—"

"Why don't you fire me, then?" he asked, his eyes blazing as he strode toward her. He was so furious, he had forgotten what she suspected was his unwritten code—to keep to the opposite side of any room he was forced to share with her.

Kate glanced fearfully up at him. Physically he was so huge and powerfully built, he could have done anything to her.

Not that he raised either of his large, tightly clenched, brown fists. Still, she backed away just a little, licking her dry mouth.

"Why don't you put us both out of our misery? Fire

me. Then we'll finally be rid of each other." His eyes met hers and then ran down her body burningly.

"D-don't look at me like that."

"Like what, honey?"

"Like you want to eat me alive."

His face tensed; so did his whole body, as he sought to curb his fierce emotion. "Maybe that's not so easy sometimes. Especially when I think you really want me to."

"I don't!" she denied swiftly.

"You're lying. We both know it."

"No—"

He laughed. "If you don't like it, go on then, fire me. Do it, honey, and I'm outta here."

She knew he would go; she'd never see him again. Some part of her wanted that as much as he did. And yet some other part only felt alive knowing he was near.

Kate glared at him. "I—I can't."

"Then do your own dirty work," he snarled softly. "But, honey, I'm available to you—personally—anytime after hours."

"What?"

"You bought me, remember? You can have my body. Just not my soul."

His insolent macho remark cracked like a bullet. Surely he didn't think her so, low, so desperate—"Dear God," she whispered.

His feverish gaze made her all too aware that he had meant every chilling word. He smiled wolfishly as a telltale tide of hot color crept into her cheeks.

"You are awful," she gasped. "Simply awful."

He just smiled.

She was silent.

"If you change your mind, honey, you'll have to chase

me. Because I damn sure don't intend to throw myself at you again and beg you for it," he taunted.

"You're crazy if you think I'd ever, ever do that!"

His black eyes cut her like impaling shards of razor-sharp glass. "Maybe..." His dazzling smile was equally ruthless. "But I think not."

"You coldhearted, conceited bast—"

She uttered a wild, strangled cry, but when he reached for her, she was too agitated to note that his hard face had softened with remorse and concern for her. Not wanting his pity, she pushed him away, and he stiffened as she ran blindly past him.

She had rushed home to pack and then canceled her business trip because she was too overwrought to go, and the next morning she had convinced herself that she really would have to fire him. But the first thing she saw when she walked into her office was a single red rose and a crisp white note covered in his bold black scrawl. *Forgive me. I was very angry and very rude. And I'm sorry.* That was all. There was no signature. But she sank down in her chair, clutching his note and the rose to her heart.

After that terrible confrontation, Keith was more careful than ever to avoid her. But when Keith's sister, Maggie, who often baby-sat Bobby Lee, brought the little boy to see his father at the office, Bobby Lee always left his aunt and father and rushed in to say hi to Kate. The boy seemed to sense the natural affinity she felt for children, and the two of them grew closer. The child was so open and friendly with Kate that she could easily bestow on him all the warmth and affection that his father would have coldly rejected. Maggie and she had become friends, too.

Once when Kate had been embracing Bobby Lee in a proud, motherly hug after he showed her a blue ribbon he'd won in a swim meet, she'd looked up to see Keith standing silently in the door. His expression had been dark, almost...almost jealous. No. She was wrong. The last thing Keith wanted was kindness or warmth for himself from her. He probably just resented his son developing a close attachment to her.

Something Maggie had said about Bobby Lee's mother had made Kate increasingly curious about Keith and about that ill-advised loan that had caused him to lose his holdings. Since Keith always cut her off every time she got near any subject that was remotely personal, Kate did what she'd always done—she bought the information she wanted by hiring a private investigator. And after she found out that he'd come from a big, poor but loving family, that he'd married his high school sweetheart whom he'd apparently loved so deeply, he'd mortgaged himself to the hilt to try to save her when she'd become ill, Kate had burst into tears, regretting that she'd foreclosed on his properties.

Kate remembered how he'd come to her and begged her to extend his loans for six months. If she'd only known why he'd borrowed the money, she might not have been so tough, and now he might not be so determined to keep their relationship so cool and professional. She longed for a way to make amends, to establish some middle ground that would lead to a warmer, friendlier relationship, but he was so fiercely proud and so determined to avoid her, she was baffled as to how to approach him. When Esther, who had become his friend, told her he'd begun to date again, Kate felt more desolate than ever.

She was losing him.

She had never had him. So, he was the father of the most darling little boy, a child she could have easily adopted for her own.

So, Keith had stripped her and teased her. So, he had kissed her once and made her feel more wantonly alive than she'd ever known she could feel. So, he was fabulous at running her business. So, he was the most handsome hunk she'd ever known and was right about her wanting him—desperately.

To him she was merely the woman who'd foreclosed on him, and his boss, a woman he would brutally humiliate the first chance he got. She knew that he was saving his money, planning for the day when he could quit her.

Why did she care anyway? Hadn't she learned anything from Edwin? The wrong kind of relationship with Keith could prove far more devastating.

But Kate couldn't quit wanting him. One summer evening she was leaving her office late when she saw a ribbon of light beneath Keith's door. She was surprised since he usually stayed away from his office—to avoid her, she suspected. Then she remembered Esther gaily having told her he'd been forced to make a late appointment with Mr. Stewart, a difficult owner from out of town for whom they managed two thousand rental units and three strip shopping centers, all of which needed an infusion of cash.

She should have gone home; instead she knocked hesitantly on Keith's door.

He opened it himself, and as always, just the nearness of his darkly handsome face and his broad-shouldered frame in that crisp white shirt made her blood pressure rise.

"Kate," he drawled coolly, frowning, his black gaze meeting hers and darkening briefly before he forced a wary smile.

She hardly noticed Mr. Stewart's short, rotund figure rising clumsily from his chair. She was shivering from the feel of Keith's fingers at her slim back, guiding her inside, as if their relationship was an easy, harmonious one.

"I'm sorry to interrupt," she began.

"On the contrary, I'm glad you did," Mr. Stewart said.

Keith led her to the chair beside his own. "Since you're here, maybe you can convince Mr. Stewart he's going to continue to lose money if he doesn't put some real money into his properties."

Then she and Keith worked together, as though they were equal partners, smoothly presenting their arguments, backing each other up, and an hour and a half later Mr. Stewart handed Keith a large check and promised more.

Then Mr. Stewart was gone, and Kate was alone with Keith for the first time since that last terrible encounter.

"You were good," he said quietly, his dark eyes fastened on her face in that intense way that made her pulse race.

"So were you," she whispered, unused to praise from him and feeling too hot suddenly.

She wished she could forget that awful taunt of his, but it haunted her. *If you change your mind, honey, you'll have to chase me. Because I damn sure don't intend to throw myself at you again and beg you for it.*

Unaware of her thoughts, he stood up and pulled his suit jacket off the back of his chair. She got up, too, and went nervously to the window.

If you change your mind...

Behind her he snapped the chain on his desk lamp, and the tiny room melted into soft darkness. She became aware of the sparkling stars and the spread of city lights and of the brilliant silver moon. It was Friday night, a night lovers spent together. As usual, she was set to spend it alone.

Her stomach growled unromantically.

He laughed huskily, almost easily—something he hadn't ever done around her. "Sounds like someone besides me worked up an appetite."

"I *am* hungry," she admitted, shyly meeting his eyes

again and feeling drawn to him as never before. He looked away.

If you change your mind, honey, you'll have to chase me....

Suddenly she realized she was starving, and not just for food. For companionship. For Keith's companionship. For much much more than that.

He rammed his hands deep into his pockets, spoiling the fit of his suit. "We'd better get the hell out of here."

"It's such a pretty night," she whispered, stalling, not following him as he headed toward the door.

"Hot and humid," he said a little impatiently as he thrust the door open.

"But pretty from here," she said, lingering still. "What do you do most Friday nights?"

"Not much," he said grimly.

"Do you have a date tonight?"

"Do you?"

"Not yet," she said.

"What's that supposed to mean?"

"I—I could buy you dinner?" *Was that chasing?*

"I don't think that's such a good idea," he countered.

Rejection. Her father had never wanted to spend time with her. She had never known how to make friends.

Why had she bothered to ask him? She felt hollow now. She should shut up and thereby salvage what was left of her wounded pride. She should leave and pretend she felt nothing. But she had no pride where he was concerned, and even to her ears, her low voice sounded too pleading.

"Look, I know you probably still resent what I did three months ago when I foreclosed—"

"Don't," he said almost sharply.

"But I'm sorry," she went on desperately in a rush. "I—I didn't know about your wife then."

"How did you find— The last thing I want to discuss with you is Mary." But his tone was softer, gentler, as if he sensed her pain.

"I—I don't blame you for hating me."

"Damn."

When she approached the door, she felt him tense as if her nearness bothered him, too, but he just stood there stiffly, waiting for her, holding the door, not looking at her.

"I know you didn't want to work for me, and still you've been wonderful—"

She walked on past him, passing so close to his body that her arm brushed his. Fleetingly she felt the warmth of him like a small electric shock.

She stopped. "Keith, you may not believe this, but I know what it feels like to lose...everything. To...fail."

"You're right. I don't believe it."

She heard his key click in the lock. She would have given anything to know what he was thinking, what he was feeling. She wondered if he had any idea how truly sorry she was.

She had always wanted love and affection and warmth, but she'd never known how to get it. Her shoulders hunched.

Then from behind her came his low voice, slower and warmer than she'd ever heard him speak to anyone. "Kate, how do you feel about barbecue?"

She whirled around, feeling a sudden overwhelming eagerness, her eyes shining. "What?"

He took her trembling hand in his and smiled. "It's yes to supper, if you'll come eat barbecue with me."

"I never do. You'll have to pick the restaurant."

"No problem. And another thing, Kate—tonight, I pay."

"You don't have to." She grinned impishly. *"I'm chasing you."*

His swift hot glance told her he knew exactly what she meant. "Are you sure?"

"Very."

For a moment he hesitated. Then his arm touched her back possessively, and he led her toward the elevator.

Chapter 6

Jim Keith was coldly furious with himself as he took a pull from his long neck and watched Kate across the crowded restaurant. She was saying hi to some tony acquaintances of hers, and from the way Kate's glamorous, blond girlfriends were eyeing him and Kate was blushing, he figured they must be teasing her about him. Since they looked like society types, they probably disapproved of her going out with a guy who wasn't part of their rich crowd. The beer was icy, which was good, because he suddenly felt so hot.

Why the hell had he let that vulnerable, pleading look of Kate's get to him and make him agree to come out with her? Why hadn't he made some excuse and said he planned to spend the evening with Bobby Lee? Why did sharing a simple dinner with Kate have to seem so dangerous?

Because she had said, "I'm chasing you," in that sweetly beguiling way that had made his flesh feel tight and wild. That made him know how much he wanted her.

Because just finding himself alone with her in the vel-

vet darkness of his car had made him forget they came
from two different worlds, made him forget that she was
rich and he was a failure. More than anything, he had
hungered fiercely to pull the car over and put his hands
all over her.

Not that she had come on to him again during the short
drive to the restaurant. She'd seemed as tense and shyly
nervous as he—as if she'd regretted asking him.

He took another pull from the bottle as he remembered
that drive. While he'd turned on the air-conditioning full
blast, she'd flipped his radio to a booming rock station.
But the jungle beat had only fired his blood. When he'd
finally stopped at the restaurant, her fingers had been so
shaky, she hadn't been able to unfasten her seat belt.
She'd cried out in frustration, and he'd turned off the
radio and helped her, saying hoarsely and yet gently,
"Look, we can forget you said it. You can still back
out—"

"So can you," she had whispered.

And maybe he would have if she hadn't reached across
the darkness almost reluctantly and touched his rough
cheek with those tender, trembling fingertips, if she hadn't
then buried her face gently in the hollow of his neck for
a long moment, drawing a deep, shaking breath. If he
hadn't taken her in his arms and held her comfortingly.
If she hadn't felt so small and warm, so utterly defense-
less and yet so deliciously feminine—so damnably right.

Just when he'd figured she'd never have the guts, she'd
picked up the gauntlet he'd so cruelly thrown down. If
she'd capitulated earlier, she wouldn't have been half so
dangerous. But now he no longer saw her as some cruel,
avaricious vulture who'd mercilessly stripped him. Even
if she was too rich and too elegant, too well educated and
too hung up for someone of his more common background, he also saw that she was vulnerably human. He

was beginning to see that her cold rejecting father had made her feel worthless and unlovable.

Keith had also grudgingly come to admire certain aspects of her character. Despite her money, she didn't behave condescendingly to him. She didn't shirk work, and she seemed to appreciate his. They both had high energy levels. She genuinely loved kids. Indeed, she was always so sweet to Hannah and Bobby Lee that at times Keith was almost jealous of his own son.

Nor could Jim Keith deny that she was the cause of his starting to get over Mary. Whenever Kate came within five feet of him, every muscle in his body got so tense and hard, it was all he could do not to seize her and show her how much he wanted her. That was why he'd been so awful to her and tried to force her to fire him when she'd pushed him about helping her with that repo. He hadn't known how he could go on working for her, wanting her and pretending he didn't.

But she hadn't fired him even when he'd hurt her. And he'd realized he would have been even more miserable if she had. So he'd played this waiting game, his pride demanding that she, who was so far above him socially and monetarily, she who was his boss, humble herself and come to him.

He didn't like her being richer and probably smarter than he was, but he had found more to like about her every day. He had always been confident about his appeal to women, but the opposite was true of her. She had no idea how attractive she was. He hadn't ever seen her flirt with another man. He felt sorry for her, and yet at the same time he was glad she lacked confidence with other men. That made the fact that she found him attractive and was brave enough to show it all the more special.

Thus, what he felt now was much more powerful than a mere physical attraction or that initial vengeful desire to get even. If she was confused, so was he. He knew she was afraid of him, afraid of all men, and yet hellishly compelled anyway. Just as he was.

He'd taken Esther to lunch to learn about Kate. Esther had described Kate's motherless childhood, her cold, rejecting father, the lonely boarding schools, and Edwin's marrying her for her money and then breaking her heart by leaving her, forcing her to deal with the unexpected pregnancy alone. But the thing that had hit him the hardest was what Esther had said about Kate's miscarriage.

"She was like a ghost when she came out of that hospital," Esther had said. "When Edwin didn't come to the memorial service, Kate wouldn't let anyone else comfort her. We were afraid that she might do something desperate, but slowly she got better."

Jim Keith's heart had gone out to Kate for her lonely life. Since he'd always had to work so hard for every dime, since she was rich and he was broke, she probably saw him as a money-grubbing bastard who could never be interested in her without ulterior motives. She'd probably think he was after her money or revenge. Then he'd played on her fears and made things worse by saying he'd sold her his body.

Damn—he regretted that.

From across the room, Kate smiled shyly at him again, and the vulnerable warmth in her eyes lit every part of him. A long shuddering wave of desire racked him as he studied the lush curve of her mouth and remembered her sweet taste. His hand froze on the long neck. Then slowly he raised the bottle to his lips and tried to quench his hot thirst for her with another icy swig.

But Kate couldn't seem to quit looking at him, and as he drained the bottle, he knew nothing but the taste of her lips could ever satisfy him. He set the empty bottle down and shoved it away, easing his long body slowly off the wooden bench.

As if in a dream, she moved toward him, too. Behind her the red-and-white-checkered tablecloths and blinking neon beer sign that hung on the wall blurred hazily.

They met halfway across that smoky, crowded room— on the edge of the dance floor, standing so close, they could have touched, and yet not touching as the silence between them grew as hot and taut as his nerves. Someone put a quarter in the jukebox, and the throbbing rhythm and the singer's melancholy crooning only magnified the tense longing he felt for her.

"Dance with me," she whispered.

His breath caught as she came into his arms. She stretched onto her tiptoes; one of her slender hands reached up and clutched his wide shoulder, and just that feather-light touch against his crisp cotton shirt brought a sudden flare of heat to every male cell in his body.

"Kate..." he said hoarsely, warningly.

Her light fingertips moved across his shoulder to his throat. "Please, Keith. Hold me."

When her warm breath whispered across his skin, he knew he was lost.

"Why the hell not?" he muttered thickly as his hard arms circled her closely.

When she pressed her slim body into his, his blood began to pound with a furious rush. He crushed her so tightly against his chest that he could feel her nipples grow erect beneath her thin silk blouse. Instinctively her slim body swayed so perfectly with his that it seemed they'd been dancing together all their lives. And yet, it wasn't that way at all. For she was thrillingly, wondrously new to him.

He lowered his dark head and saw that her inky lashes were trustingly closed against cheeks that were rapturously aglow. His hand stole slowly up and down her back, beneath the thick waves of her silky hair, molding her to him even more tightly until his every breath was hot and raspy. Until his heart thundered, until his blood coursed through his arteries like fire. Until the music and the beer and the soft perfumed essence of her voluptuous body worked together to destroy what was left of his iron control.

They were only halfway through the song when he felt too wretchedly turned on to take another step. Sweat was beading his dark brow when he broke away from her abruptly.

In the dimly lit restaurant, she looked at him with wide, unafraid eyes, her red hair curling against her pale face. And he thought never had any woman seemed more beautiful.

"What's wrong?" she asked innocently.

"Either we get the hell out of here and I take you to bed—now, or we sit down and order," was all he could manage.

She almost sprinted to their table. He followed at a slower pace. They ordered ribs and sausage and more beer.

Maybe it was the beer that got him talking. Maybe it was just Kate—looking at him with those adoring green eyes as if she hung on his every word. Whatever it was, he forgot how rich and socially wrong she was for him and broke every damned rule he'd ever made about how he'd behave around her.

He'd sworn he'd never get personal. To his horror he found himself telling her about Mary, how he'd loved her, how happy they'd always been even when they'd been poor, how he'd wanted to die when she'd died, how he'd felt so guilty about failing to save her that he hadn't cared much about real estate for a long time, how he'd gone on living only because of Bobby Lee. But how lately he'd been glad he had—because of Kate.

Most women didn't want to hear about another woman, but Kate seemed so genuinely interested in him that he couldn't stop talking. At several points, her hand had closed over his, and it was as if he gave her his pain and she willingly took it.

He told her about his habit of drinking on Mary's birthday and on their anniversary, about how he'd been doing that the night before he'd met her and that was why he'd deliberately goaded her that first day. He told Kate that even when he'd thought he'd hated her, from the minute he'd seen her sneaking onto his property, he'd stopped grieving so much for Mary.

Not that he told Kate everything. Not that he admitted the reason he'd worked so hard for her was to please her, to win her admiration, her respect. Not that Kate confided in him. But she listened, and he felt a deeper closeness to her.

The evening would have been ordinary, had his feelings for Kate not been so dazzling that even the ordinary became wonderful. After they ate, he called Maggie and made sure she didn't mind Bobby Lee's sleeping over. Then he drove Kate down to Galveston, and they walked along the beach, talking still. Later he took her to a nightclub to dance. And all too soon he found himself inside her elegant sky-rise apartment, sipping Scotch from her expensive crystal as he held her in his arms and looked out upon her magnificent view of the sprawling city and the Galleria. Then he was kissing her, and her body was melting into his, her mouth and skin sweeter and more intoxicating than the smoothest, hottest liquor.

He had no idea how he negotiated the dark halls and

circular stairway as he carried her up to her bed, nor how he got her undressed and into that bed. All he knew was that when he fitted her naked body to his, when her legs wrapped around his waist and her voluptuous lips caressed his mouth and throat, this was what he'd craved from the first moment he'd set eyes on this lush, vibrant, passionate creature.

Her careful control was gone. She was writhing and twisting; and her warm flesh stirring against his thighs set him aflame. He caught her to him and held her tightly as she impatiently urged him into that final, most intimate embrace. He kept trying to go slow, and she kept passionately urging for more. Only in that last moment, when he was ready to plunge deeply inside her, did he remember that he had to protect her.

"Just a minute, honey," he murmured, his heart thudding violently as he released her.

Leaning across her trembling body, he fumbled for his wallet on the floor. He had the thing out of the wrapper and was pulling it on when her velvet-soft voice stopped him.

"No," she whispered in that same beguiling tone that had tempted him to come out with her tonight, gently trying to push his hand away. "You don't have to put that on."

Her soft, warm, soothing lips moved along his neck while her seeking hands explored his body, tempting him from his purpose, and for an instant he did forget everything except the exquisite torture of those slim hands circling his manhood.

Then he was on fire to enter her. But he had always taken responsibility for any woman he'd ever made love to, and not even passion could make him set aside his fierce principles. He had to protect her from the consequences of tonight's lovemaking.

You don't have to put that on, she had said.

Why the hell not? he wondered.

Her fingertips lightly stroked his silken male flesh in delicate circular motions until he shivered, tightening, until he felt he'd burst in her hand if he didn't get inside her.

He was panting hard—dying for her. Every nerve cell in his body urged him to take her.

She opened her body so that he could slide inside her. "Are you on the Pill?" he demanded.

He felt her tense before she reluctantly whispered, "No. But it doesn't matter, darling." She reached for him with trembling hands and tried to coax him forward into the velvety warm, satin softness he was aching for.

But he couldn't. Not till he knew why she didn't want him to protect her.

He saw her radiantly tender face when she was with his son, and stronger than Keith's passion to have her was the sudden, coldly intelligent realization that she wanted far more from him tonight than mere sex.

Very gently his hard hands wrapped hers and wrenched them from his waist. She gasped as if in pain. His own loins cramped as he bolted out of the bed and strode angrily toward her window.

"What's wrong?" she called to him.

"You tell me."

"I don't know."

"Don't lie to me, damn it. This is some sort of setup. I want to know what's going on. Why did you ask me out? Ask me here? To your bed? What do you want?"

"You."

The husky torment in that raspy sound tore his heart,

but he laughed harshly, bitterly. "Are you so desperate for a husband that you'd try to manipulate me into getting you pregnant, so I'd marry you?"

Silent tears leaked from the corners of her eyes as she turned her face away. "No."

"Honey, that's a lousy way to trap a man."

"I—I never wanted to trap you. I just wouldn't mind having a—" She stopped herself as if she realized it would be stupid of her to admit anything.

And suddenly he knew, and the truth chilled him more than the thought she might want to marry him.

She wasn't after him. She had never wanted him. Why should she? On that first day she'd seen him as some immoral, oversexed, low-class stud. As some failure. Despite his work to win her respect, that's probably how she still saw him.

Hell, she'd bought him, hadn't she? How could he respect him? Especially when he'd even taunted her that he'd throw his body into the bargain if she chased him hard enough? Maybe that gibe put him partly at fault, but he was furious at her anyway. Furious and hurt because all her heated passion tonight had been a lie...to trick him, to use him.

"You just wanted a baby? So—that's what tonight was about?"

She was sobbing.

"My baby?" he demanded cruelly. "Or just any dumb stud's baby?"

"I—I didn't think it out."

"Like hell." He didn't flatter her or himself by giving her the benefit of the doubt. "If you'd gotten pregnant, you wouldn't have even thought I deserved to know. You wouldn't have told me, would you?"

As she continued to weep soundlessly, he scooped up

his slacks and shirt and stalked furiously out of her bedroom.

He would never have thought that a woman who'd been so softly willing could have made him feel so lousy and hurt and cheap—so bruised to his very soul.

Maybe he deserved this. Every intelligent instinct had warned him to stay the hell away from Kate Karlington.

And in the future he damn sure would.

Chapter 7

The week since Keith had stormed out of her apartment had been busy and very confusing for Kate. Keith's fury, which she considered unreasonable, had persisted. He hadn't come to work for three days, and when he finally did, he worked with a cold, silent efficiency that terrified her.

Not once did he so much as look at her, nor voluntarily speak to her, or refer to that night, but she knew that the injury she had done him had made him as miserable as she was. She wanted to go to him—to apologize, to beg his forgiveness. At the same time she didn't quite know what to say or how to say it.

What had happened had made her realize how desperately she wanted him, and how much she really did want a baby—before it was too late. And somehow when he'd been making love to her, these two longings had forged themselves into one. It wasn't as if she'd deliberately seduced him to get pregnant. It was just that after they'd ended up in her bed, and he'd made her aware of that possibility, she'd hadn't wanted to do anything to prevent it.

Which had started her thinking.

Was it really so terrible that she'd wanted his baby? It wasn't as if she'd intended to hold him responsible. She had thought he would be happy to have sex with no strings attached. What other man had ever wanted a deep involvement with her?

Her father had never wanted a real relationship. Nor had Edwin, who had married her only for her money. When she had been in the hospital after miscarrying their child, never once had either of them come to see her. She had felt so lonely then she had wanted to die.

Was Keith a different breed?

Every time she looked at Keith, she remembered how wild and dark his flushed face had been right before he'd sprung away from her. He'd wanted her badly, as badly as she wanted him. And even now, when he was so cold and sullen, she knew he avoided her because he still wanted her. So they stayed apart, each a tightly coiled bundle of nerves, each lashing out at everybody else until the entire office staff was as cross and irritable as a spring forest full of grumpy bears.

Thus, when Esther walked into Kate's office frowning late on that rainy Friday afternoon, to tell her that a female tenant had been robbed of her rent money and then pistol-whipped while using a pay phone outside the project to call the police, Kate had lashed out at her secretary unfairly.

"Well, what are you telling me about it for? Isn't this the sort of thing that gives you the excuse to go running into Keith's office for a long private chat behind closed doors?"

"For your information, I have tried to reach him. Not that I'm the one who's so interested in him. Only I can't get him on his car phone. He's supposed to be in Spring at Mr. Stewart's shopping center, but Mr. Stewart says he never showed up.''

"Then I'll go," Kate said, jumping up restlessly.

"Keith'll be furious. You know he doesn't want any of the women on that property—especially this late in the afternoon." It was the project where Kate had first met Keith.

"Good! I hope he does get mad! I'm sick and tired of his chauvinism.''

"Honey, you've had him mad night and day ever since last Friday.''

"Oh—so you noticed!''

"Yes, and it's time you two started snapping at each other instead of at me!''

"You're so right!''

Kate wasn't so eager for a fight by the time she reached the project. In the dark the shabby project looked more ominous than it had the day she'd met Keith. When she saw several shadowy figures lurking in the dark alley behind the apartments, smoking under the eaves, she shivered.

A spray of sparks showered to the earth as the men flicked their cigarettes to the ground when she parked her Jaguar. They moved toward her, only to stop when a tall man yelled from the back of a building and yelled. "Yo!''

Keith stepped out of the shadows.

He had obviously beaten her here. He went over to them. When they finished talking, their lighters flashed as they lit fresh cigarettes and Keith rushed angrily through the misting rain toward her.

"What the hell are you doing here?" he demanded, yanking her out of her car.

"I heard about the robbery—"

His large possessive hand crushed down on her shoulder as he shoved her against her car. "I already took care of that. I gave the tenant two rent-free months and put her in an ambulance headed to the hospital. Which brings us back to why you're here when I told you to stay the hell away from this side of town.''

''You just manage this property. I own it, or have you forgotten—''

''Never for a minute.''

''And I'm the boss—your boss—or have you forgotten?''

''Maybe not for long. I don't want to work for anyone who makes stupid, self-destructive decisions.''

In a quieter tone, she said, ''I didn't think you'd care—now.''

His fingers ground into her upper arm. ''What the hell is that supposed to mean?''

''You know. After our date last Friday—''

With a longing that bordered on pain, her silent green eyes rose to his. His dark face was set in hard, unreadable lines.

''If you think I want you riding around in that flashy car in a neighborhood like this when it's getting dark and a woman was just assaulted for a lousy few hundred bucks, you're crazy.''

In spite of his anger, she felt a tiny thrill at his obvious concern.

''Get back in your car,'' he ordered. ''I'll drive you home.''

''What about your car?''

''I'll come back for it later.''

''I—I don't want to put you to that much trouble.''

''Honey, that's all you've ever done.'' But his deep voice no longer sounded quite so stern. In fact, it was almost gentle.

''I'm sorry for Friday, Keith,'' she whispered, gathering her courage.

"Yeah. So am I, honey." Lightly his hands touched her damp cheek, and the warmth of his fingers flooded her with rich bittersweet yearning. "I wish we'd met some other way. I wish you were some ordinary girl. Or I wish I was some rich guy...rich enough to date you on equal terms. But I'm not. As you just so sweetly reminded me, you repossessed everything I owned, and you're my boss now. And that's that." He opened her door. "Get in the car, Kate, before you get soaked."

"So, it's over," she whispered.

"You know as well as I do it wouldn't work. You're too damned rich, and I'm too damned proud."

She nodded reluctantly.

The windshield wipers slashed back and forth. He drove fast, even though it was pouring and the freeway was under construction—he drove as if he was very angry and wanted to be rid of her as soon as possible.

"But I—I can't forget what a wonderful time I had with you that night," she murmured.

"You will," he said grimly. "We have to, but it was good, too good. You know, Kate, Esther told me about Edwin and...the baby you lost. I'm sorry...."

"I—I didn't realize how much I still want a child...."

"I figured that one out, too, honey." Again his voice was curiously gentle.

"I was so happy when I was pregnant. It was like I already knew the baby and loved it. Maybe all new mothers feel that way, or maybe it was just that I've never had anybody all my own."

"Find a rich guy the next time. Have his damned baby."

"I didn't mean to use you. I—I didn't even think about getting pregnant till you stopped to get that thing—"

"Okay. Maybe I can buy that."

"But I thought you'd be getting something out of, er, the encounter, too."

"You don't just go to bed with some jerk and have his kid because you want a kid that day," he said tightly as he drove up the ramp into her parking garage and eased her car into its numbered space and cut the headlights.

"You're not some jerk, and I do want a child. Is that so wrong, Keith?"

"Yes! Think of the kid. You should get married first. Kids need fathers, too."

Not the kind of father she had had.

But as she looked at Keith, she felt an involuntary twist of tender longing. He cared a great deal about Bobby Lee. She had always known that not all fathers were like hers. She remembered how jealous she'd felt of school acquaintances who spoke adoringly of their fathers.

It was utterly dark, so all she could see of Keith was the shadowy outline of his carved profile. Maybe if she had been able to see him better, she would never have been so bold.

"*I should get married....* Is that a proposal?" she whispered.

"Hell, no."

"Then you're going to make me humble myself and beg you for it—again?"

"What?"

"I'm asking you to marry me, you big, beautiful, hunky, poor-boy Neanderthal," she said, shocked and embarrassed by her own forwardness even as she touched his cheek. Even as her mouth fused hotly with his.

A wave of shockingly intense desire pulsed through them both as he curved his hand around her neck and slanted her tantalizing lips against his.

From deep in his throat he groaned, "Oh, God... Kate, what are you doing to me?"

"I assure you my intentions are most honorable this go-round."

Her proposal of marriage tempted him even more than her generous salary had tempted him three months ago when she'd asked him to go to work for her.

"No!" Keith thundered ten minutes later when they were alone in her luxurious apartment and he'd downed his second Scotch. "No way! Kate, are you crazy? You don't love me. I don't love you. The last thing you want is to be stuck with me for life when all you really want is a baby."

"You were the one who informed me that babies need fathers and so honorably suggested marriage," she said primly, defending herself. "Not me. I was perfectly willing to forgo that sacred institution and just try to get pregnant on my own."

"That wouldn't be fair to the...to *our* baby."

"Okay. So, I'll concede that point—I believe you did tell me once that your morals were more old-fashioned than mine," she agreed sweetly, pouring him a third glass of Scotch. "I didn't believe you at the time. But I'm beginning to see that you're not the man I thought you were at all."

"If you're trying to get me drunk, I can hold my liquor," he growled, not trusting her. Not trusting himself.

"I know."

"How would it be fair to me or you if we married each other when neither of us really want marriage?"

"What if marriage gave us something we did want? And what if it was only for a year?"

"What?"

"Maybe less than that. And why wouldn't it be fair—

if we both got something we wanted? I know you're attracted to me, and I... Well, you know I feel the same way about—''

He felt a hot shiver of unwanted excitement go through him.

"You little fool, that's not enough to base a marriage on."

"Okay, but it would be a big perk...at least for me."

In spite of himself he smiled.

"And suppose I agreed to tear up the foreclosure papers on your properties and extend your loans with a very generous interest rate—say over the next five years—if you married me for that year...."

"You'd go that far—"

"I want a baby...more than anything. *Your baby.* The second I'm pregnant, you can pack your bags and I'll grant you a divorce. You'll have your property back. And I will retain all rights to the child."

All rights to his child! She wanted to have his child and then to be rid of him. Suddenly the smooth Scotch scalded his throat like acid. *Nothing had changed.*

"Why, you make it sound as simple as just another...foreclosure deal." His voice was so low, at first she didn't catch the soft menace in it. Then his hand jerked, and the crystal glass he'd been holding flew wildly against the wall where it exploded into millions of sparkling, razor-edged pieces. His deep voice exploded with the same violence. "Why am I surprised you think I'm that low? When that's what you've thought since the day you met me? You think because you took my properties so easily, you can take everything else just as easily... including my self-respect."

"Keith, I—I...I didn't mean..."

"Goodbye, Kate. I'd be willing to do a lot of things to

get my properties back, but I'd never sink so low as to sell my own child.''

Desperate to prevent his going, she raced in front of him and threw herself in front of the door. ''All right. All right. I hadn't thought of that—that you'd feel like that.''

''Why the hell not? Because you see me as some sub-human?''

If she hadn't looked so utterly desperate, he would have shoved her aside and walked out for good.

''Keith...I—I think I'm beginning to see that you're really nothing like any man I've ever known. Not my father...not Edwin.... They didn't care about women or relationships or children or...''

Words could never have stopped him, but that look of forlorn agony in her beautiful eyes made him hesitate a second longer. Then he tried to push her roughly aside.

But she clung to his arm.

''Save your strength for the next man on your list of contenders to be your...your baby machine,'' he roared because the mere thought of other men ever touching her stabbed him with jealous anger.

''I don't have a list,'' she said very softly. *''There's only you.''*

She felt the strong grip of his hands on her arms, pulling her against him.

''Why me?'' he demanded gruffly as she nestled in-stinctively against the hard comfort of his warm, muscled chest and listened to the thudding rhythm of his heart. ''Why me, you little fool?''

''I'm not sure. For one thing, I trust you. And I do respect you. You've earned every dollar I've ever paid you and more. You didn't sleep with me when you could have. You don't pretend you feel more than you do.''

''Maybe I just thought you were smart enough to see through me if I did.''

"Keith, all my life I've been so lonely and so terrified of loneliness," she whispered. "The other girls at my boarding school went home on the weekends, but I never could. I just want somebody of my own, somebody I can love who maybe someday will love me. I know most of the men I might marry would really be marrying me for my money, and I don't want that kind of marriage again...where I think I'm loved, and I'm not. I—I promise you I won't be the indifferent kind of parent my father was. And if you wanted the baby as much as I do, I would never take it away from you. You could see it, and love it as much as you wanted to. I would want you to. I just never imagined..."

And Keith, who understood loneliness and need, was lost.

"Kate. Oh, God, Kate." Maybe she'd had money, but she really hadn't ever had much else. Maybe there was something of real value that she needed from him.

The hot moistness of his breath comfortingly touched her nape. Slowly he squeezed her slim shaking body more tightly against his as his own emotions raged out of control.

She shivered as his lips moved burningly through her hair, across her cheek.

"I must be getting as crazy as you," he murmured. "The answer's yes."

Then his mouth claimed hers in a shattering kiss that brought something far deeper and more mysteriously profound than mere physical pleasure. It seemed to her that when his mouth touched hers, his soul touched hers. But, of course, such a thought was ridiculous. She didn't love him. And he certainly didn't love her. Hadn't he said she could have his body—but never his soul?

But after the kiss was over, her eyes remained blissfully closed, her body warmly aflame, her thoughts sweetly tumbled and hazy. As he held her, she could feel the steady hammering of his heart, the disturbed huskiness of his breathing. He was every bit as aroused as she.

"Kate?"

She opened her eyes drowsily when he shook her and stared at his smoldering gaze and darkly carved features. "You're so good-looking," she said dreamily. "So—so sexy."

"I'll marry you, honey—but on my terms. Not yours."

He really was the most impossible man. She licked her lips. *But he was terribly handsome. And he did kiss divinely.* She forgot everything when he kissed her. She pursed her lips expectantly.

"First," Keith began sternly, "Bobby Lee will move back in with Maggie. I will live with you during the week, but I will visit him every Saturday and Sunday during the daytime hours and come home to you after five."

"But I don't mind him living with us. In fact I would love having him around—"

"Kate—no! He hardly remembers Mary, and he already sees you as more of a mother figure than I like. I don't want him becoming too attached when you'll be so temporary in his life."

She felt oddly hurt. Left out.

"That's not all. You will give me control of my former properties as well as your company for the year we're married. And we stay married, not till you get pregnant but until the baby's three months old. And if you do get pregnant, when you're three or four months along, you'll stay home and take care of yourself while I work...."

"That's impossibly chauvinistic...."

"If you're determined on this crazy plan, I won't have the mother of my child or my child at risk, while you drive yourself at the office. I know how hard you work. I know what happened to you the first time, how terribly hurt you were. Honey, you would never have come up with this crazy scheme if you were over that miscarriage.''

That much was true.

"And," he continued, "when we do divorce, I'll pay child support, and I'll want generous visitation rights.''

"Is that all?''

He nodded.

Strangely enough she wasn't nearly as furious at his preposterous terms as another woman might have been. She remembered how tired she'd gotten in the fourth month, how indifferent Edwin had been about her health. She heard herself agree weakly, wantonly. "Oh, all right.'' She sighed. "But only if you kiss me again.''

"I think kissing has landed us both into enough trouble for one day.''

"But we're formally engaged now,'' she protested, her heart pounding.

Apparently he wanted her lips as much as she wanted his. And when that devastating kiss had turned into a dozen expertly placed all over her body and she found herself sprawled half undressed beneath him on her couch, again he refused to let her seduce him.

"Stay the night,'' she begged, loosening his tie.

"No, Kate.''

She pulled his tie through his collar and let it fall to the floor. "Why not? We're getting married.''

He got up and moved to another chair. "Because if you got pregnant first, you might welsh on me. Then I'd lose you, my property and all rights to my kid.''

"You're tough.''

"So are you, honey. This is probably not much more to you than just another foreclosure deal. But I'm risking everything I care about.''

After he left, she felt lonely and dissatisfied. But for

some reason as she crawled into bed, aching for the feel of his arms around her, his parting words brought more comfort than pain. Every time she remembered the way his eyes had seared her, a tremor went through her. Because in that last moment he had made her feel that she meant everything to him.

Chapter 8

"Well, it's about time you showed up," Kate said softly, fighting to conceal her ripple of excitement as she closed her desk drawer quickly. She didn't want Keith to see her mirror and comb and lipstick tube and realize she'd been anxiously primping because of him.

Keith's avid black gaze burned across her face and then down her body, but he said nothing.

"I left word with your secretary hours ago that all of the prenuptial documents were ready. I thought maybe you were going to change your mind and...jilt me," she said quietly.

"No way," he whispered but with such force that he startled her.

For an instant his eyes locked on hers again with that unnerving intensity. She wondered what he was thinking, what he was feeling when he moved toward her.

"Here are the papers...." she began, leaning down to pick them up.

"They'll wait," he murmured tightly, tossing them back down on her desk. They scattered messily, several white pages falling to the floor.

Before she could stoop to retrieve them, he gathered
her hands and pulled her to him, holding her so close, she
felt the dizzying heat of him deep inside her body. "You
look especially beautiful today. So beautiful, it's hard to
concentrate on the business aspects of our marriage."

She had dressed carefully to make him think that, and
yet the passion in his voice was so much more than she
had expected, and she was filled with a strange longing
that made her feel awkward and unsure.

"Keith, you don't have to woo me," she said in a
strangled tone.

"Maybe I want to," he muttered harshly.

A shadow of pain crossed her face and she turned away
from him. "But you don't have to. You know this is a
done deal."

"I bought you something," he said, his voice tighter
and harder as he slipped a tiny velvet box into her fingers
before he let her go.

She opened the box and could not quite suppress a gasp
of pleasure when she saw the small but very lovely diamond winking at her from the black satin interior.

Humbly she touched the stone and then jerked her hand
back. She was stunned by the thoughtful, romantic gesture. And happy. So happy, she was afraid.

"Do you like it?" he asked in a low, guarded tone,
taking the ring out and slipping it on her finger. "I know
it's not very big."

His ring on her finger felt far more binding than the fat
stack of documents her lawyers had compiled. And far
more wonderful.

"You...you shouldn't have. I mean you can't possibly
afford it," she whispered, striving for control. "You
didn't have to...." Then she blurted, "You know this
isn't a real marriage."

His hand tensed on her wrist and he yanked her nearer.

"I know, damn it. But maybe I could forget it—if you didn't constantly remind me."

Did he want to forget it? As much as she did?

Before she could ask or argue further, his hard mouth was on hers, kissing her angrily at first and then with surprising gentleness. When his warm lips played across hers and opened them, a moan of unadulterated pleasure escaped her.

He pulled back but continued to hold her so that her face was nestled against his throat.

"Kate, are you going to throw my poverty up to me for the rest of my life? Do you ever think of us as two human beings? As just a man and a woman?"

She turned pale and began to tremble. How could she ever explain that she was far too terrified of dreams of such happiness to ever hope they could feel that way about each other?

"I'm sorry," he muttered when she didn't answer. His dark face was grave. "I shouldn't have asked. I shouldn't push you. Like you said, this is a done deal. You spelled out the rules, and I agreed to them. You don't want me. Just a kid. Let's leave it at that."

He let her go and, ducking his dark head, charged through the door and slammed it.

After he was gone, she stared miserably down at her slim hand, turning his ring so that it flashed and hating herself for making him unhappy. She had stupidly spoiled a moment he had tried to make special.

She halfway expected him to back out of their "done deal." But five minutes later his secretary was at the door with a terse note from Keith demanding the legal documents.

Within minutes he had signed them, and they were back on Kate's desk.

As she stared at his bold black signature, she remembered the day he'd coldly signed over his properties to her. Suddenly she was more frightened than ever.

Not that he gave her time to be afraid for long. Keith rushed her to plan the wedding quickly.

So they could get it over with, he said brutally when she asked why he was in such a hurry.

And one week later they were married.

Still, in that limited time, Kate had made sure that her second wedding was far grander than her first. She made all the lavish arrangements to prove to her wealthy family that she was proud of her new husband and future marriage, never realizing that her groom might find the ceremony stilted and their elegant reception at the city's poshest country club pretentious and stuffy.

Keith, bored and weary from the much-rehearsed ceremony, from the long photographing session afterward and then from standing more than an hour in the receiving line, ignored several icy looks of disapproval from his new family and bride and excused himself, leaving a white-faced Kate behind while he wandered restlessly through the well-heeled throng.

His tux was rented, and his black tie felt itchy and tight around his neck. Maybe this was what a real wedding was supposed to be like, but it was beginning to feel as dreary as a funeral. Maybe that was because Kate's family didn't try to conceal that they thought he wasn't good enough for her.

He felt their eyes boring into his back as he made his way cynically to the tables piled with elegant food. He thanked the Lord for his uncle John, who was laughing too loudly from the champagne and drawing some of the stuffy Karlingtons' disapproval away from himself. Bobby Lee was taking his share of the heat, too. More

Karlingtons were frowning at the boy for chasing several of his Jones cousins at the far end of the ballroom.

At one point Keith had offered to corral the children, but Kate had smiled and said she wanted Bobby Lee to be happy at their wedding.

Keith was about to pick up a fancy fried chicken leg when he caught the disdainful sound of his own name drip like acid from a cultured, feminine tongue.

He whirled. But saw no one. For a second he thought the wedding was making him paranoid.

"Her father would roll over in his grave," drawled another haughty voice from behind a trellis laced with white roses.

"How could she marry so far beneath herself? Again? This one's even poorer than the first."

There was muffled laughter.

"I—I, uh, I think this one's rather more attractive than Edwin," a third woman's voice countered timidly. "And his little boy is absolutely adorable."

The others pounced.

"Of course, *you,* Mathilde…would notice that the scoundrel's attractive…in a vulgar, primitive sort of way! Gold diggers usually are—as *you* should have learned from your own disastrous marriages! And as for being adorable, his brat is a little savage!"

Keith downed a glass of champagne in one gulp. Then he seized a second glass and made his way to the other side of the trellis.

The stoutest of the three blue-haired biddies almost dropped her glass when she saw him. But he gallantly caught it. Managing a cynical little bow, he replaced it in her much-beringed fingers.

"Why, thank you, ever so," she said in a chilly tone.

"My pleasure—*ladies.*"

They blushed like girls.

Keith smiled boldly and lifted his goblet. "To the bride.... To her good fortune. And to her future happiness...with me." He clicked his glass to each of theirs. "Weren't you just saying that I, uh, was a lucky man?"

The stout one almost choked.

"Don't let me interrupt your conversation," he continued.

"It wasn't important," one of them snapped.

"Indeed," he purred, his steely voice softening only because Kate had come up and shyly taken his arm.

"We were saying we thought your wedding was lovely, dear," Mathilde said timidly.

"Be happy for me, Aunt Mathilde," Kate whispered, casting a radiant glance at him.

The ladies' faces froze. So did Keith's smile as he wondered why Kate's entire family believed that the only reason he could want her was for her money.

"I feel happy, too," he murmured very tenderly, very protectively, concentrating solely on his bride. His fingers tightened against the back of her satin gown as he crushed her closer. And as his lips brushed hers, he felt the primitive thrill of male possession.

She was his. And he was glad. Neither she nor the Karlingtons would have believed the truth—that neither her money nor the return of his properties had anything to do with his marrying her. She was a beautiful, desirable woman. He wanted her for herself alone. He had wanted her so much, he would have made a bargain with the Devil to have her.

And in a way that's what he had done.

Their honeymoon hideaway was an ultramodern, two-story beach house with high sloping roofs and skylights loaned to Kate by one of her wealthy relatives. Located on Bolivar Island and, therefore, vulnerable to the violence of hurricanes from the Gulf of Mexico, the mansion stood on high concrete pilings that had been sunk deep into the soft sand.

Standing on the wooden deck, Keith stared out at the silver rollers that swept the beach. The view was no better than that from his own rougher beach house on the same island. The same surf caressed the same sand with the same constant roar. The same salty breeze rushed around both houses. The same moonlight lit the night. And yet the two houses, his so shabby and this one so elegant, seemed worlds apart.

He wondered suddenly about the woman he'd married. She had played a CD of Ravel while they'd eaten lobster; he would have been just as happy with country-western music and hamburgers. She had served him the finest, driest French wine; he was so used to Texas beer, he was still thirsty.

Was there any way a man of his simple tastes and common background could ever understand a well-educated woman who'd been to every glamorous city in the world? All he knew was that he suddenly wanted to.

More than anything.

If he had acquired this sudden taste for an elegant woman, maybe he could just as easily learn to like very dry Chablis.

Who was he kidding? Why would it even matter?

Wasn't he only a male body she had bought to satisfy this need for a child she had not been able to satisfy in any other way? Wasn't she going to ditch him the second that was accomplished?

Not if he played this hand for all it was worth.

Slowly he turned his back on the dark water and walked across the deck to go inside where Kate was waiting for him.

Tonight was their wedding night. It was high time he

started finding out who she was and what she really wanted from him.

Kate was sitting up in bed scribbling enthusiastically. Her brows were drawn together, her mouth pressed into a tight line as if she was concentrating very hard. He smiled. Was she composing one of her know-it-all columns for the newspaper?

He would have liked to tell her that just because she and her snooty clan had been born rich and had had opportunities, maybe they weren't all that much smarter than he was. Maybe Kate was just lucky; maybe her money had shielded her from the hard knocks that would have taught her nobody knew as much as they thought they did.

His gaze was drawn to her dark curling lashes resting on her smooth pale cheeks like tiny fans.

He had expected fancy, impractical lingerie, but her shoulders were bare above the white sheets. In the dim golden light of the bedroom, she looked fragile and innocent, incredibly lovely and as pure and sweet as a virgin.

Even if she'd bought him, even if she thought that meant she owned him, even if he were no more than that body she had temporarily hired for stud services, it had become impossible for him to hate her.

She moved, and the sheet slipped and he saw the lush curve of her breasts. He felt a sudden raw eagerness. His heart surged with what he told himself was nothing more than the most natural and selfish male desire.

Besides, it had been a long time since he'd had a woman. Too long. If she was using him, he was using her.

He closed the door heavily, so she would look up at him. But when she did, her expression was so uncertain as she bit her lip that he wondered if she felt humiliated because she'd been the one to propose. He realized he was just as unsure of his feelings for her.

Nervously she set her tablet aside and turned the light off when he began to undress. As he ripped his trousers off, he tried not to think of all that was wrong in their relationship. This beautiful, assertive woman would be his till three months after she gave birth to his child. He had a year.

If she couldn't learn to love him, so what? He'd learned the hard way that this was no fairy-tale world. Maybe he wasn't ready for love, either.

She turned him on. By marrying her, he would get everything back that she'd taken from him. She'd get something she wanted, too.

Even if he couldn't win her, their marriage was a mutually profitable business deal. Even if their relationship didn't work out, this was a no-lose situation.

All this seemed so simple until he got into bed and caught the scent of her expensive perfume. Until he saw the tears in her shining eyes and the sudden quenching of her smile as her lips began to tremble. Until he felt the warmth of her body clinging to the sheets. Until he took her into his arms, and her slim body slid warmly against his own, arousing something deep and eternal in him that was so much more than simple desire.

His hands raced over her hot naked skin, pausing on the almost flat curve of her abdomen.

She wanted a child.

His child.

She wanted his child more than she wanted anything else in the world. Didn't she know that his child might tie her to him?

Her hands came around his neck and sifted through his thick black hair. He touched his lips to hers ever so softly, and was surprised by the sweet emotion that filled him.

Then his tenderness was followed by fiercer emotions and fiercer needs. His shaking hands tangled in her long, flowing hair as he dragged her nearer.

She moaned as he ran his mouth over her, kissing her throat, her breasts, kissing her everywhere until the tart taste of her womanly essence filled him. His pulses began to throb.

And suddenly she was writhing and moaning, and the whole thing spiraled out of control as is often the case in human relationships.

Mating and creating could form the deepest of human bonds.

Her satin-smooth skin was as sweet as warm honey.

God, he wanted her so much.

He had sworn to himself he would be able to keep his distance from her—even in bed. But the passionate melting together of their bodies carried their souls, as well, and what followed between them brought a bewildering tide of glorious new feelings and hungers. As he was caught up by the force of forbidden needs, he knew that all the boundaries in his life had suddenly been shattered forever.

He had been alone.

He was alone no more.

It was as if he were her first, and she were his. It was as if all their lives they had been looking for each other. Neither understood the wild rapture that possessed them the moment that they began to make love. But the incandescent emotion that thrilled every cell of their beings utterly overpowered them.

He took her a second time, so that he could savor the wonder of her more slowly, so he could savor the glowing emotion he felt when he was inside her. She did the same, running her hands with guiltless wonder over the muscular contours of his magnificent bronzed body, reveling in him like a wanton, kissing him everywhere as he had kissed her the first time, but again it wasn't long before that strange sensual rhythm of their bodies and minds became a vital power that drew them out of themselves and swept them away from all their previous realities and carried them to a new one that was theirs alone.

When it was over, Keith fell back into himself and was terrified. He wanted to crush her close, to beg her to forget their stupid bargain and to love him.

But she believed in buying and selling. She wanted his baby—not his love. So he got up without a word, pulled on jeans and a shirt and stormed barefooted out to the beach.

He meant only to get some space and then return to her.

But she pulled on a white robe and followed him, calling to him from the balcony, and suddenly the terrible need he felt for her was way too much. He knew he would break and confess his true feelings. If she even believed him, she would probably despise him. So, instead of returning, he started running, his feet digging desperately into the wet cool sand as he sprinted away to escape the opulent mansion and the lovely woman who called down to him.

He didn't know if he would ever be strong enough to go back. Suddenly he knew this marriage could turn out to be the biggest mistake of his life.

Chapter 9

*K*eith had left her. Maybe forever.

Kate had grown up in the South, but the modern South. Not being a southern belle, she had not simpered, played hard-to-get games or denied her true needs when she had been with Keith.

No, she had chased him by asking him out first, by proposing. Nor had she hidden her eagerness for him in bed.

And now he was gone.

Where was he?

Had he really found her so hopelessly undesirable that he never wanted to see her again? Had her desperate need for him driven him away? Was he going to disappear like everyone else she had tried to love?

Not even the thought that Keith had made love to her twice and might have given her a baby softened the blow of his leaving.

She'd watched him run down that beach until he'd become a fleck and dissolved into nothingness. Then she'd crept back to bed and lain in the dark, straining to hear the sound of his return above the roar of the surf, feeling even more desolate when he didn't come back than she had the night she had lost her baby.

The sun was blazing when she finally forced herself to rise lethargically from her bed. That single glance in her bathroom mirror at her hollow-eyed, soulless white face had been so terrible she had not dared look at herself again.

Their honeymoon was to have lasted a week. No way could she return to Houston and face the humiliation of everyone knowing that Keith had left her after one night.

So she stayed at the house, somehow living through the heavy hours. In the afternoon she went out on the deck and listlessly watched the endless roll of the surf as the sinking sun turned the tips of the waves and the clouds to flame.

She wished she could be numb inside. She wished that she could stop thinking, that she could stop feeling. That she could regain some control.

But it was no use. The sun disappeared, and the waters darkened quickly as the last of the pinkness vanished in the sky. And she stayed outside shivering in the lonely darkness.

The moon came up, and she thought its silver glow on the waves looked the same as it had in Keith's hair when they'd been in bed. She remembered the way he'd touched her nipples with his callused fingers. Her skin began to burn as she remembered how his mouth had roamed her body.

No!

Her anguish was suddenly so great, she wanted to scream. To die. She had to stop torturing herself by thinking of him.

She glanced away from the sparkling water to the beach

where she had last seen him. Suddenly she saw a tall figure running toward her from the beach.

It couldn't be Keith.

But her heart began to pound. Thinking herself crazy, she forced herself to look away. Then she turned back, unable to resist watching the man.

There really *was* something familiar about those broad shoulders.... About the way the moonlight glowed in his black hair.

Then the man turned from the beach and headed toward her.

And she knew.

"Oh, Keith," she moaned softly, thankfully, closing her eyes and leaning back against the house, willing herself not to act too eager. But when she felt the heavy tread of his footsteps on the stairs, her eyes flew open. Her pulse raced.

He came to an abrupt stop ten feet away from her.

Shyly she lifted her head and fought to manage a haughty, controlled Karlington look.

Across the darkness he whispered huskily, "Forgive me."

How could she do anything else?

"Why did you go?" she asked, her haughty air crumpling, her false voice shattering.

His face was as gray and lined with exhaustion as her own. His deep voice cracked in an equally betraying manner. "I...I didn't think that my leaving might hurt you."

"I—It didn't...." But her voice broke again.

"Okay." In his blazing eyes she saw the most powerful emotion. "I was so afraid you'd be gone," he said humbly, holding his arms out to her. "I wouldn't have blamed you. I behaved wretchedly. You deserved better."

How could she resist such sweetly sincere humility?

From a man as proud as Keith? And since she was no southern belle, she came flying into his arms.

He crushed her to him, shuddering as if just holding her aroused powerful, uncontrollable needs. Then he shoved her up against the wall of the house, and their bodies melted together.

His thrilling salty mouth was wet and hot and seeking as it covered hers. He hadn't shaved, and the rough new growth of his beard burned her skin and lips. But she was clinging, sighing, surrendering to the volcanic tide of emotion his hard lips and hands so magically aroused.

Within seconds they were both on fire.

Very gently she wrapped her legs around his waist, and he walked, carrying her like that, inside.

He ripped her clothes off and then his and made love to her in the moonlight on the thick carpet by the fireplace. He was wilder and more primitive than the night before, and he stirred her to new heights of passion that left her quivering and spent and utterly and completely his. And when it was over he didn't get up and leave her. Instead he picked her up in his arms and carried her to bed, pulling her to him beneath the sheets so that their bodies curled together like two perfectly matching spoons. They stayed that way for the rest of the night and long into the morning. And when they finally awoke, their arms and legs warmly entangled, the first thing he did was make love to her again.

He never told her where he had gone that first night nor why, and even though it worried her, she was too afraid of spoiling their new happiness to ask. And although she masked it, another dark, unspoken fear took root and grew in her heart.

If he could leave her once like that without a word—he could do it again.

But in spite of that dark, festering fear, she fought to savor every bright moment of happiness he was willing to give her, and even living with that doubt, she was happier than she'd ever imagined she could be with anyone. She grew to love everything about him, even his faults, and even his little annoying ways—like the way he always left her bathroom trashed every time he took a shower. Like the way he always tore the plastic wrapper off the newspaper and threw it absently onto the carpet.

She didn't mind that he was always grumpy until his first cup of coffee, that after work he needed thirty minutes of solitude to decompress. It didn't bother her that he couldn't hang a towel straight or that he couldn't seem to remember how to load the dishwasher right. He threw his clothes all over the living room furniture every night when he came home. But his presence was so dear, she couldn't scold him for such habits. Not when he loved to cook. Not when he sang to her as he cooked, and quite charmingly, especially since he couldn't carry a tune.

Their life together quickly fell into a pleasant routine. He followed her to work every morning, and at work he found a thousand excuses to seek her out. They threw themselves into every project with more enthusiasm and energy than ever before. He wanted her opinion and approval on every decision he made. His hands-on approach to management left her the freedom to do what she loved—juggle numbers.

But much as she loved working with him, she looked more forward to their workday ending.

They would come back to her apartment together. When she closed the front door, and Keith would begin ripping off his tie and jacket, she would feel a leap of excitement. *For the first time, she felt as if someone belonged to her.*

They would cook dinner together, eat together, and she

would usually do the dishes. They would talk, and before long—always when she had begun to monopolize their discussion or win their argument—he would start kissing her. Every day he gave her more pleasure than the day before. And it was only after he had fallen asleep in her arms that she would think of that awful first night when he had left her without a word. Then she would think of the future and the day he would walk out like that again—forever.

Besides that bleak future, what bothered her most about their life was that Keith stuck to his rule about Bobby Lee. Except for the times that Maggie brought Bobby Lee to the office, Kate didn't see much of the little boy. Some evenings after supper Keith would kiss Kate goodbye and go over to Maggie's to see his son. When Keith spent those first few Saturdays and Sundays away from her doing things with Bobby Lee, she missed them both unbearably.

She was feeling very depressed and lonely one Sunday when Keith came home early and found her. He saw her sad face and stunned her by asking her if they could have Bobby Lee over to eat supper and spend the night the next Friday night.

She was overjoyed and planned their supper down to the last detail. Then when Bobby Lee said what he really wanted was to go out for hamburgers, they went out instead. The evening went so wonderfully that Bobby Lee begged to stay the entire weekend with them. She begged, too, and Keith had reluctantly agreed.

After that weekend, Keith refused to let Bobby Lee spend another. Even so, Kate began to dream that Keith might really come to love her, that they might become a real family.

Keith teased her, he charmed her, he seduced her. But never once did he tell her he loved her. Sometimes when

she was feeling down, she wondered if he made love to
her so often because he wanted to get her pregnant so he
could be rid of her. She began to wish she wouldn't get
pregnant immediately, that their life would follow this
idyllic pattern long enough for him to fall in love with
her.

But one Monday morning she walked into the kitchen
as Keith was frying bacon, and the thick sickening smell
of bacon grease hit her like a heavy wave. For a second
or two, as she groped to open the window and turn on
the exhaust fan, she couldn't breathe.

As she gulped in fresh air, she thought she'd be okay.
Then a second later, a stronger bout of nausea hit her.
She swallowed and then dashed for the bathroom.

When the humiliating spasm had passed, Keith helped
her up. She felt even weaker and paler when she realized
he had seen everything.

His handsome face was ashen. "So—are we going to
have a baby?"

"I—I think so."

When she stared up at him forlornly, he pulled her into
his arms and held her for a long moment as if she and
the child were very precious to him. She clung, liking the
way his hard hands were so gentle as they stroked her
hair, wishing with all her heart that he would say he
wanted to stay with her forever.

Instead, he let her go, his dark face tense again. "Well,
it looks like things are working out the way you wanted."

"For you, too, I imagine."

"This was your idea—not mine, remember?" he said
bitterly.

"Yes."

And without another word, he turned and left her.

In spite of her joy over the baby, she felt doomed.

Chapter 10

Keith had changed toward her drastically as soon as he'd learned about the baby. A new silent darkness had crept into their relationship.

Not that Keith was ever deliberately unkind. Not that Keith didn't support her in every imaginable way. Not that he hadn't helped her select a doctor and driven her to her checkups. Not that he wasn't endlessly patient with her mood swings and morning sickness. Not that he wasn't endlessly helpful when she was too tired to shop or do housework.

But there was a brooding quality about him now, a profound lethargy that seemed to drag him down. And her, too. He didn't laugh as much, and he was guarded and less spontaneous than before. Keith didn't insist she had to quit working as he had vowed he would, but as the months passed, she gradually turned more and more of her business affairs over to Keith and spent more of her time preparing for their baby.

With every day, Keith seemed to withdraw from her more. He came home later. He never initiated a conversation with her, and when she entered a room, he no longer looked up and smiled in the old way that had made her feel special.

Only at night, when they were in bed, did he now seem to belong to her. And even then, when he took her in his arms, she thought he did so reluctantly, as if he were fighting some part of himself, as if he were willing himself not to want her. But always when her mouth sought his, when her body surrendered to his, he melted, too, and their lovemaking bound some deep part of him to her, if only for those few fleeting moments of ecstasy. But afterward, he withdrew again and became that courteous stranger, who said the right things and did the right things. She would lie in the darkness, knowing that she was losing him and wondering what she could have done differently to have made him love her, wondering what was so wrong with her that no one had ever wanted her for herself alone.

Edwin had married her for her money, and so had Keith. The only difference was that Keith had been more brutally honest. He had never bothered to lie and say he loved her.

Even worse than her sleepless nights were the lonely weekends when Keith visited Bobby Lee. As the months sped by, her misery grew. Every Saturday morning when Keith left, she felt more abandoned than the one before. But she said nothing until one fateful Saturday a week or so before her due date.

That morning she felt heavy and irritable and dangerously moody and sorry for herself as she followed Keith to the living room. As he put his hand on the door to go, the pressure of the last few unhappy months mushroomed inside her. Suddenly she rushed up to him and, putting her hand on his, begged him to take her with him.

"Look," Keith began patiently enough. "I hate leaving

you all day—especially now, but you have my number...."

His number! Because her pregnancy played havoc with her hormones, she could swing from mildly dependent and needy to wildly hysterical at the speed of light. *She didn't want his number. She wanted him!*

You just don't get it, do you? She didn't speak aloud, but her sulky glare spoke volumes.

Her mind whirled even as she fought for control. How could he be so calm, so infuriatingly rational? It maddened her that his body wasn't bloated, that his emotions weren't in turmoil. Her whole life was changing and he was acting as if his wasn't and as if they still ought to be playing by the same old rules.

Not that it occurred to her that *she* had made the rules. In that self-pitying instant she hurtled over some precarious emotional edge. Suddenly she wanted to stomp up and down like a spoiled child and scream wildly. When her bottom lip curled sullenly, she bit down hard on it.

"Surely," he continued in that same, very male, hatefully rational tone, "you can see that your coming would just make this whole impossible situation more difficult—for all of us."

That did it!

Some tinsel-fine thread sheared at her emotional center.

"Impossible situation?" she shrieked. "I— Is that how you see our marriage? How you see me?" Then she began to weep, thinking even as the thick tears flowed down her puffy cheeks that the last thing she had wanted to do was scream and weep.

"And how do you see it, Kate?" he thundered, losing his patience at last. "I've often wondered. You made it damn clear that you didn't want a real marriage with me. Never—not once...except when we're in bed...have you ever acted— You're always so cool...so controlled." He started to say more and stopped himself. "I'd better go—before I do or say something we'll both regret!"

"Say it! Do it! What could be worse than the way you've been torturing me with your fake kindnesses, with—"

"Fake— Damn you, I'm not your robot, Kate—though I've tried to be. I'm a man, and I'm sick and tired of playing your game. You think you own the world...that you own me. You've told me about your father buying women. Are you really so different from him?"

"How...how can you say that?"

"Kate, I don't know if I can take another three or four months...." He turned to go.

"How can you just walk out?"

"With two feet, one after the other—darling."

"Oh, I—I do hate you."

His black eyes narrowed. "Is that really how you feel?"

She was too wild with her own pain to deny it. "Yes! Yes!"

His handsome face darkened. "Well, cheer up," he said quietly. "You will be rid of me soon enough. I regret this sham of a marriage every bit as much as you do." Without another word he stormed out, so anxious to leave he did not even bother to shut the front door.

She rushed after him and slammed it. Then in the next moment she pulled it open again. She wanted to call him back, to tell him that she didn't hate him, that she could never hate him, that she had only said that because he'd accused her of being like her father and because she was too proud to admit the truth—that she loved Keith and couldn't contemplate life without him.

But a savage pain tore through her middle and cut her in two. Gripping her distended abdomen in agony, she sank to the floor, calling after him helplessly.

Chapter 11

"Where did you put my suitcase, Kate?" Keith called from the living room.

The long-expected question jolted through Kate as if it were a bolt out of the blue.

The sun was sparkling outside. Houston looked lovely. Kate had been leaning toward her mirror, running a brush nervously through her hair. At his simple query, every warm feeling inside her turned to ice. Her brush fell from her shaking fingers and clattered onto the bureau, scarring the fine glossy wood.

So today was to be the day he would walk out of her life forever.

Why today?

Heidi was four months old.

Kate had lived with the dread of this moment every day since Keith had brought her home from the hospital, her fear having intensified until that terrible third-month birthday.

But the dreaded date had come and gone, and although the day had been tense and she'd felt hysterically close to losing control, Keith had said nothing and done nothing. She had been too afraid to ask why because she might cause the very thing she feared most. And three days later Keith had even lovingly given her red roses on Mother's Day.

And now, suddenly, he was leaving her.

For a long moment she couldn't trust herself to answer in that cool polite manner that had become their custom— except for that one fight—ever since she'd gotten pregnant.

With the uncanny timing all babies are born with, Heidi started to cry.

Thank goodness! Relieved at the excuse not to answer him, Kate rushed to their daughter, only to find that Keith had gotten there first.

Kate paused at the door, unable to join him by the crib. "I just fed her and changed her." Her voice sounded lost and far away, not so carefully controlled—a stranger's voice.

Keith nodded absently and then grinned at the tiny red-headed being he gently lifted into his arms. "There, there, my sweet darling," he said to the baby in that husky, warm voice he never used with his wife—except in the dark when they made love.

Keith held the little girl close and continued to whisper soothingly. Only when Heidi began to coo did he speak to Kate again in that coolly polite tone. "I don't think she wants anything but love."

Dear God. Kate struggled to smile bravely in that cool way he was smiling at her, but her lips quivered.

Her heart was breaking. She was flying to pieces inside. The Karlington control, which had been her first line of defense against loneliness and despair, seemed to be shattering forever.

Not that he noticed. He had looked down at Heidi

again, his entire cherishing attention focused on their daughter, who had wrapped her tiny fingers around his larger one.

Kate was not jealous of his love for Heidi. Kate simply wanted his love, too. And seeing how wonderful he was with their daughter always made Kate all the more sharply aware of his indifference to her.

Ever since Keith had brought them home from the hospital, he'd treated Kate as gingerly as she were made of eggshells. As if she were a stranger he was forced to live with and make polite conversation with. And she had played along, careful not to expose all her vulnerable new needs.

Not that he hadn't been wonderful. Those first weeks when she'd felt too weak and sick from the surgery, he had done practically everything for her and the baby. He allowed Bobby Lee to come more often now—to visit his sister. While Kate had been overly anxious about the baby because Heidi was her first, he, the more experienced parent, had been self-confident and relaxed. With every passing day, Kate had come to rely on his help and upon his steadiness and strength.

With every passing day she craved his love more.

"It's going to be hard not to see her every day," Keith murmured.

His low, polite voice sent a searing flash of pain through her. *It's going to be horrible not to see you every day, too,* she thought.

"I—I'll get your suitcase," Kate whispered and then stumbled upstairs to her hall closet, where she'd stashed it neatly all those long months ago. Frantically she began tearing boxes down from the packed shelves until she found it. Feeling wild and desperate, she tossed the hateful thing onto the landing, not caring when it rolled to the edge of the top stair, teetered and fell, end over end, banging loudly all the way down the winding stairs.

Miserably, Kate watched Keith come out of their daughter's room, lean down calmly and pick it up.

"Thanks. I guess I overstayed my welcome," he murmured mildly, not bothering to look up at her.

Thanks? After they'd lived together for more than a year?

Just go, if you're so anxious to! She wanted to shout at him. She wanted to run down the stairs and throw him and that awful suitcase out. But she was determined to avoid another wild humiliating scene like the one that had brought on her premature labor when he had said that he regretted their sham of a marriage.

Knowing she was on the verge of tears, Kate ran into her bathroom and locked the door so he wouldn't see. There she hugged herself against the wall and wept soundlessly as she listened to him throwing things into his bag. But as the tears rolled down her cheeks, in an odd way she was almost glad this thing she had dreaded had finally happened.

Because only now, when he was actually leaving, did she realize how unbearable the silent explosive tension between them had become. How had she borne needing him and wanting him this long while pretending that she was an aloof creature made of ice?

It seemed an eternity later that he uttered a muffled curse as he slammed his suitcase closed. Then she heard the sounds of his footsteps coming up the stairs.

She held her breath, struggling for control when he hesitated before her door. After a long time he knocked gently.

"Kate—"

"Go away!" she whispered.

"I wanted to say...goodbye."

"Fine. Goodbye."

"You were the one who said that all you wanted from me was the baby."

"Yes," she whispered desperately, sinking to the floor like a broken lump, dying inside as she wondered how she would live without him.

"And that is still all you want, right? You want your perfect, neat life back, right?"

She choked on a sob. "Yes! Yes! Just go," she ground out in an agonized tone.

He hesitated and then she heard his retreating footsteps. They sounded like leaden weights going down.

The minute her front door slammed behind him, she unlocked the bathroom door and came flying out of it. Stepping onto the landing, she saw the heap of tangled boxes and hangers she'd thrown out of the closet. The silence in the vast apartment held a new and crushing loneliness. Gone were Keith's clothes thrown messily over the back of her couch.

Her gaze ran fondly to the plastic newspaper wrapper he'd left on the floor. More hot tears filled her eyes. It was the dearest thing in that room filled with priceless Karlington antiques.

Without Keith, the baby she had wanted so desperately would never be enough. The Karlington money meant nothing.

She hadn't ever wanted him to go. She had always wanted him. As much as she had ever wanted their baby. *More*.

Then why hadn't she broken down and begged him to stay?

Because from the first she had been the one to chase him. Because she didn't want him to stay for any other reason except that he loved her. Because he had once said,

"I regret this sham of a marriage...." Because she loved him enough to sacrifice her own happiness for his.

She was reasonably sure she could have used the baby and several other arguments to get him to stay. She had the Karlington money after all. She could have offered him the use of it, the power that came with it for as long as he stayed married to her.

She thought of the nights they shared in bed together. Of his final tendernesses to her when he'd taken her in his arms only the night before. Of his seeking mouth and roaming hands, his flaming passion. Of her own. But such passion was not love. Hadn't he told her she could have his body anytime—but never his soul?

She wanted all of him—desperately.

She wanted him to stay because he loved her.

Heidi began to cry.

Never again would she rush to her child and have the added pleasure of finding Keith there, too, to share her joy.

After a long moment Kate ran down the stairs. But when she opened the door to the nursery, Keith stepped coolly out of it.

Startled, caught completely off guard, she felt terribly vulnerable—exposed. Her voice came out harshly, defensively. "What are you still doing here?"

But he was different, too. The cool stranger was gone. She saw an agony as wild and profound as her own in his piercing black eyes as he stared at her tear-streaked face.

"Why are you crying?" he demanded in a gentle, compassionate tone.

"I—I'm not...cry...ing," but the words came out in a horrendous very un-Karlington-like blubber. "I don't want you to pity me...."

In the next minute, his arms came around her, and his

searching mouth claimed hers hotly, passionately—adoringly.

"God, Kate, I tried to leave you—"

Heidi made a muffled, indignant sound.

"What about the baby—" she whispered brokenly as he propelled her into the hall and slammed the door.

"The baby is fine. We've both spoiled her—that's all."

"I don't understand. Why…why are you still here?"

"Because, damn you, I'm not a high-class Karlington who can say goodbye to you through a locked door. Because I can't play by your rules another miserable second," he said brokenly, angrily. "Because I want you too much to let you go without a fight. I don't care if you despise me because I'm poor…and you're rich. If you despise me because you think you bought me or because you think I'm a failure or because I made this stupid idiotic deal. Or because your family thinks I'm a gold digger—"

"But I—I don't think any of those awful things. I—I don't despise you. I—I made all those stupid rules to protect myself…because I'd been hurt before. I—I thought you regretted our marriage."

He didn't seem to hear her. "I want to help you raise Heidi. I feel like a heel leaving you to face it all—practically alone—even if it is your idea. I don't go for the mother of my kid raising my kid alone when she doesn't have to."

"You don't have to go," she said, no longer caring that she was chasing him again. "I never wanted you to."

"I thought you just wanted me to serve as a baby machine."

"No. I love you, Keith. I've always loved you. That's probably why I wanted your baby that first night, why I asked you to marry me. Why I did all the stupid things I've done."

"I'm glad you did those things. Because I love you, too," he said simply. "I have for a long time."

"Are you sure you want me...and not my money?"

"Damn your money and your father and Edwin for making you think money is everything. I wish you were poor. That we were equal."

"We are equal," she whispered. "More than equal. I think you're wonderful."

He kissed her mouth softly, reverently. "I love you for yourself alone. You are everything to me."

A long time later, after many fervent kisses, she asked, "If you loved me so much, why didn't you ever tell me before?"

"Because I was playing by your rules. Suffering under them. Dying under them. When I gave you that ring, you reminded me we wouldn't have a real marriage. After that... Then the one time I broke down, we had that terrible fight and you went into labor. I was so afraid you might die...that the baby might die...that it would be all my fault...that I decided to stick to your stupid rules till you told me to go. I did it for you. I didn't want to ever hurt you like that again."

"Oh, my darling. I thought...you were just marking off the days till you could leave me."

"After you got pregnant, I hated every day and every night we had together, because time was our enemy. Then, when Heidi was three months old and you didn't throw me out, I began to hope you felt something for me, too. But you never said— Not even when I gave you the roses on Mother's Day. You were just this exquisite polite stranger who said, 'Thank you, darling.'"

"You didn't say anything, either. Why did you pick today to leave?"

"Today?" He raked his hands through his hair. "I just couldn't take it anymore. I couldn't live with you—loving you, wanting you to love me. And I could see what this was doing to Bobby Lee. Every time he came to stay, he begged to stay. He feels left out.''

''I do love both of you. I wanted him with us so much. But I was afraid to show it...especially after you left me on our wedding night. I thought maybe I'd chased too hard and been too eager....''

''I left because I realized I was madly in love with you, and I didn't know how I could live with you and not let on. I left because I loved you, but I came back for the same reason. It's why I couldn't walk out the door today.''

''And I was too proud to confess how much I loved you partly because I'd chased you so blatantly, so shamelessly.''

''Honey, I want you to chase me—for the rest of our lives. I like it when you're shameless.''

And the incredible warmth in his voice lit a tiny spark of happiness within her that soon grew into a fire that raged out of control when he carried her up to bed. For the first time in a long time they made love in the middle of the day with the sunlight streaming through the high windows. And she lost all control, gave herself to him more shamelessly than ever before.

Afterward she wouldn't let him go until he admitted that at last she did possess every part of him—not only his body but his soul, as well.

And he possessed every part of her, too.

Keith loved her. She was the mother of his children.

But most of all, she was his beloved wife.

* * * * *

THE BABY INVASION
Raye Morgan

To Marie Ferrarella,
for trying hard to understand the secret life of dogs.

Dear Reader,

Motherhood is a strange career. "They" don't pay you the big bucks, but nothing else gives you so much pride, so much fear, so much joy. The only thing I resent about it is the lack of sleep. They tell you how you won't get any sleep that first year, when the baby wakes up, every hour, all night long. But they don't warn you that it's déjà vu once your child has his driver's license, as you lie awake until dawn, praying for the sound of a car in the driveway. I've already been through that stage with all four of my boys.

Still, being a mother is usually my favorite part of being alive. It's the most wonderful thing in the world, and from the very first "What do you mean, gas? I *know* that's a smile!" to "Look, he's pulling himself up! I think he's going to walk. I think he's going to… Oops!" right on into "You'll get the keys back when those grades come up, young man, and not before!" until you hit "Darling, if you really love her, we love her, too," time goes so quickly. Too quickly.

Motherhood — catch it while you can!

Raye Morgan

Chapter 1

MANY CONDOLENCES DEATH OF BROTHER.
BABY'S THERE ONE WEEK. INTERNATIONAL AIRPORT,
NEXT SATURDAY.
NURSE'S DELIVERY. THANK YOU.

Matt Temple sat at his desk and stared at the telegram for a long time. Cryptic though it might have seemed to some, he knew exactly what it meant.

"It means," he said aloud, more in wonder than in fear, "I'm about to have a baby."

"Did you say something, Mr. Temple?" Shayla Conners, administrative assistant extraordinaire, was passing his open office door. She stuck her head in and looked at him questioningly.

"No," he said slowly, then looked up and realized she was the very person he needed. "I mean, yes. Come in, Conners. I have a little problem. Maybe you can help me deal with it."

Shayla stepped into the oak-paneled office, pulling a pencil out of the bun at her nape. She took a seat across the wide, cluttered desk, her pencil poised, her notebook ready. She was used to judging her boss's mood and could tell there was something different about him today. That put her on edge and on her toes, like a tennis player ready to receive the serve and deal with it brilliantly.

Matt turned in his seat and pinned her with his steely ice-blue gaze, using a stare that often turned opponents into blithering idiots, shaking in their expensive loafers.

"Well, Conners," he stated firmly, his rock-solid jaw jutting. "Tell me this. Have you ever had a baby?"

Shayla Conners did not quail under his piercing stare. Actually something close to amusement was flickering behind the owl-shaped lenses of her glasses. A personal question—and this from the man who treated her as though she had no existence outside of this office. She lifted her chin and said calmly, "No, Mr. Temple. I've never had a baby."

"Damn," he said, grimacing, his wide, exquisitely chiseled mouth twisted, his blue eyes troubled. "I was hoping you could help me out here." He frowned, searching her clear gaze. "Are you sure?"

Shayla nodded her neatly coiffed head, wanting to smile but holding it back. "It's not something a woman easily forgets," she advised him.

"I suppose not." He gave an exasperated sigh and sat back, flexing his wide shoulders beneath the expensive Italian suit, his square, expressive hands flattened against the desktop as he contemplated his options. "This is damn awkward, Conners, but I've got baby problems."

"Have you, sir?" The amusement died in her violet gaze and something frosty took its place, directly mirroring the chill that had crept into her heart. A quick glance into his eyes told her he wasn't joking. "Is it the Carbelli woman you've been dating lately?" she asked, attempting to keep up a cool, disinterested front.

"What?" He looked at her blankly. "What does Pia Carbelli have to do with this?"

Thank goodness for that, she thought to herself. Pia Carbelli had the motherly instincts of a half-starved cobra. "I see," she said quickly, keeping the stiff upper lip intact. "Then it's one of the others."

He stared at her for a moment as though he were afraid she'd lost her mind, then realized what she was getting at and barked out a short laugh. "No, Conners. None of my girlfriends are in the family way." He looked slightly offended. "I don't do things like that, you know. Any man with half a brain knows how to keep that from happening."

Shayla uncrossed her legs and crossed them again, a burning curiosity shining just behind the bland expression she kept on her face as if it were a mask. It was no secret her boss dated beautiful women. And it was also pretty plain he wasn't the marrying kind. So just where babies fit into his life, she couldn't imagine. "Then I'm afraid I don't understand, Mr. Temple," she said simply.

But Matt wasn't really listening. Instead he was studying his assistant as though he'd never seen her before. His attention had been caught by her tone and suddenly, he began to notice things about her—things such as her pale, strangely colored eyes with the heavy fringe of dark lashes and how the line of her neck curved gracefully into the white collar of her sensible blouse. She was a woman, and that was a fact he hadn't really registered much in all the months she'd worked for him. And not a bad one at that, in a chilly, reserved sort of way.

Not his type, however, and that, of course, was fortunate. He wouldn't want to be distracted by having stray thoughts about his assistant—especially this one. She was too important an employee to risk losing that way. He shoved the thought away immediately.

"Never had a baby, huh?" he mused, still examining her and wondering why he hadn't ever paid this much attention to her as a person before. "Are you married?"

She stared at him, and now outrage was beginning to form in that misty place behind her eyes. She'd been working for him for almost a year, noticing every single detail about him and about his life. She'd always known he basically saw her as an extremely efficient android. But this was taking things too far. He was looking at her as though he couldn't quite remember why she was here. Where had he been all this time? "No," she told him icily.

He shrugged. It wasn't the sort of thing he would have noticed. To him, work and play were entirely separate, and that was the way he meant to keep things.

"No baby, no husband." He frowned, his gaze taking in her flawless skin, her red, perfectly shaped nails, and the modest cut of her linen suit and cotton blouse. "And yet I have this feeling that you have a whole secret life I know nothing about."

She held his gaze and didn't waver. He was a tough boss but she'd never knuckled under to him. Their relationship was a precarious balance between his barked orders and her tart replies, but it seemed to work for them. Still, she resented the fact that he hardly seemed to know she existed in any capacity other than as a well-oiled part in his business operation. It stung to think he hadn't even bothered to remember if she were married or not.

"I have no other life, Mr. Temple," she said sweetly, leashing her irritation for the moment. "What I do when I leave here is go home and hang from the ceiling with my wings folded and wait for the dawn, like a reverse vampire bat."

He grimaced quizzically. He was used to her quick rejoinders. "You joke, Conners. But I think you're covering up for something." His eyes narrowed, assessing her in an infuriating fashion. "Care to comment?"

No, she did not, and now she was beginning to think he was toying with her. Snapping her notebook closed, she rose and turned toward the door. "Will that be all, Mr. Temple?" she said evenly.

He hit the flat of his hand on the polished mahogany of his desk with a smack that echoed against the walls. "No, dammit, it won't. I want to confide in you." He blinked rapidly for a moment, then looked up at her again. "I'm sorry if I've offended you, Conners, but I'm not thinking very clearly this afternoon. My brother has just died and I feel the need to unburden my soul. Unfortunately there is no one else around to unburden to. You'll have to do."

"Oh." She dropped back into her chair, horrified, her cheeks burning. She'd had no idea. The two of them often sparred. It seemed to be part of the natural rhythm of the way they dealt with each other. But now she felt nothing but remorse for having treated him so coldly.

"Oh, Mr. Temple, I'm so sorry," she said, her eyes misting, her compassionate nature coming to the surface without hesitation. She just barely resisted the urge to reach out and touch him with a sympathetic caress. "I...what can I do to help you?"

His mouth twisted. "That's very kind of you, Conners. But there's no need to get maudlin."

She sat back quickly, feeling rebuffed.

"He was a half brother, I should add. That's not to say I'm not upset at his loss," he said quickly, and a faraway look clouded his eyes. "We never spent much time together, but he is my flesh and blood. Partly. And he didn't deserve to go that young."

He paused, shaking his head, and she steeled herself against feeling sorry for him again. It was tough not to.

He had a look on his face she hadn't seen before, and it touched her deeply. Why was he trying to put up this facade of unconcern? Was he afraid of appearing weak in front of an employee? She wouldn't put it past him, and she bit her tongue, holding back the sympathy.

"Are you with me, Conners?" he asked softly, glancing at her again.

She nodded, holding her notebook closed in her lap.

"Okay, here's the deal," he said, leaning forward, his eyes strangely veiled. "Remy had been fooling around in South America for years and he finally got himself killed in a plane crash. His wife died with him, but according to the lawyer who called me last night, there was a baby left at home, and therefore very much alive. I'm this baby's oldest living relative. So I'm elected. I get custody."

It took a moment for the details of the situation to fully form in her mind, but once they did, the horror of it all overwhelmed her. What on earth was this confirmed bachelor going to do with a baby?

"You, sir?" she murmured, thinking fast. She was his administrative assistant and he was used to turning to her for advice. He was asking for her help, so he must be trying to think of a way to get out of taking the baby. And that was exactly as it should be. Matt Temple with a baby in his arms—it didn't work for her. And it certainly wouldn't work for the poor baby.

"Yes, me," he responded. "And I guess I'll have to keep the little tyke. Family feelings and all that. So there's only one question. And that's what I want your help with."

She blinked at him, thrown a bit off guard again. "And what is that, sir?"

"Why, it's obvious." He looked at her expectantly. "I

need a wife. Do you know where we can get one quickly?''

Shayla's mouth dropped open. For once, he'd floored her. She was speechless.

But Matt didn't notice. He went on, looking thoughtful. ''I figure she ought to be good-looking, because after all, if I'm going to be married to her, I'll need to feel some sort of attraction, don't you think? And educated. I like a woman who understands the issues of the day and can hold her own at dinner parties.'' He shook his head. ''But other than that, I just don't know. You're a woman. Maybe you know these things. Why don't you make up a list of specifications and call an agency and round up some candidates. We can start holding interviews....'' He flipped through his calendar. ''How about Thursday?''

She was still finding it difficult to react. She'd always thought he needed the right kind of woman to take care of him. Though he was a bold, decisive man who overcame obstacles and challenged danger constantly, she thought she could see a hint of sadness in his eyes at times, a suggestion of a loneliness that seemed to touch a chord in her. He needed someone. But not this way!

He wanted to hire a wife. In all the months she'd worked for him, she'd always considered him a very smart man. How could he have gone so wrong? Coughing to buy time, she came up with the most delicate solution she could think of offhand.

''But, Mr. Temple... If you really think you need a wife, wouldn't you prefer to pick from among the women you see socially? Someone you know?''

He looked at her as though she'd suggested sending away for a mail-order bride. ''Hell, no. Those women aren't domestic. They're only for dating.''

She opened her mouth and then closed it again. This was impossible. *He* was impossible—one of the original

Neanderthals still in existence. There was no point in feeling outraged. He was what he was and she certainly wasn't going to change him.

"Mr. Temple," she said, more in despair than anything else, "why are you taking on this baby? Don't you have a sister or something?"

"No sisters. Only brothers." He raised an eyebrow and gave her a questioning look. "Why? What's wrong with me taking on this baby? Do you think women are the only ones who can nurture?"

She licked her upper lip and tried to be diplomatic. "I think they have a heck of a lot more practice at it than men do."

He grinned at her suddenly, as though she'd said something that tickled him. But he challenged her. "I consider that a sexist remark," he said. "But I'll overlook it for now." He looked at her sharply. "Besides, how would you know? We're both in the same boat. You've never had a baby and neither have I."

"True," she responded. How could she deny it? "But I grew up in a large family and took care of plenty of babies in my time."

"Ah-hah!" His smile was triumphant. "I knew it. You're going to come in handy after all. You always are my best resource." She tried to protest, but he didn't give her time. "Okay, argue with me on that later. We've got too much work to do to get tangled up in that right now." He glanced at the clock. "I've got a meeting with the Bradley people at two. Get right on this, would you? Get me a list of prospects by say…four this afternoon. We'll go over them and…"

"Wait." She put up a hand as though to stop the flow of this river of words. "I'm not sure that's possible. Agencies don't handle things like that. They're not matchmakers. They don't find partners for people."

He was not convinced. "Oh, sure they do. They must. There must be men who need them all the time. Nowadays, with all these mothers going off and leaving their husbands stuck with the kids..."

Stuck with the kids. She groaned. This entire situation was doomed. It would never work. This was a man who worked long, hard hours and partied seriously whenever he got the chance. A little person was about to come into his life, a baby who needed constant care and lots of love. He didn't have a clue about what raising a child would entail. Shayla looked at him and shook her head. She'd helped him out of scrapes before. She was going to have to help him out of this one—even if he didn't think he needed help at the moment. He would, soon enough.

"You know, there's something about your attitude," she told him severely. "I think you'd better mull this over again. You don't seem to realize what you're getting yourself into."

But then she looked into his face again, and her asperity melted. For once, his blue eyes held a candid look. She saw things there she'd never seen before, things that surprised her. The hardness was gone, the tough, biting intelligence was muted by something else. He was thinking about the baby who was coming, and his face held a look of wonder that set her back on her heels. She'd never realized he might have a tender side, and for once, she seemed to be getting a glimpse of one.

"I have no choice, Conners," he was saying softly. "The baby is as good as mine already." He shrugged. "I'm going to have to learn how to live with it."

That stumped her. He really meant what he'd said, she could see it in his face, and immediately, her instinct was to soften toward him. But she fought it this time, kept it inside. He was a complex man, and over the past few months, she'd learned the best way to handle him was to keep her guard up at all times. Instead of giving in to sympathy, she hardened her heart and tried to think of some way to convince him he could no more raise a baby than she could swim the Atlantic. There had to be a way to get through to him.

Matt was waiting. He could tell she was against his plans and he often trusted her judgment. So he waited for what she had to say, and while he waited, he looked at her again, gave her a good scan in a way he almost never did. She wasn't bad looking, despite the glasses and the severe attitude. He noticed the trim line of her ankle. She was wearing dark stockings and conservative pumps with only the barest suggestion of a heel. She dressed, he realized suddenly, to turn male attention away.

"Don't you like men, Conners?" he asked. He was accustomed to saying what he thought when he thought it, and he saw no reason to hold back now.

"Sir?" she asked, startled, and shocked at the fact that her heart was suddenly beating very hard.

He frowned, puzzled by her. "Do you date much? Do you ever try to make yourself attractive to men?"

That was enough to raise permanent hackles. She gritted her teeth and gave him a frigid smile. "You've asked an awful lot of personal questions today, Mr. Temple," she noted icily.

"That's right." He gave her a quizzical look. "And you haven't given me a satisfactory answer to one of them."

She shifted her position, unconsciously broadcasting how uncomfortable he made her. "What kind of answer are you looking for?" she said evasively.

He smiled. For once, he'd put her on the defensive. It was an unusual moment for him. "I want to get to know you, Conners," he said smoothly, picking up the first thing that popped into his head. But then he went on more sincerely. "You're the best administrative assistant I've ever had, and I realize I hardly know you."

The compliment seemed to smooth back her ruffled fur, at least a bit. "Thank you, Mr. Temple," she said quickly.

He leaned toward her, giving her his most sincere look. "No, I mean it. You're darn good at what you do."

To her chagrin, two bright spots of color appeared in her cheeks. She could feel them glowing there warmly, and she cursed them silently. But it didn't seem to help.

"Thank you very much, Mr. Temple," she said, averting her eyes and hoping for the color to die down.

He was still staring at her and suddenly she realized he was waiting for something. "Well?" he said impatiently.

She looked up, blinking at him, bewildered. "Well, what?"

He shrugged, looking hopeful. "What about me? What do you think about me as a boss?"

"You?" She hesitated. He was just so darn sure of himself, she could hardly stand it. He wanted her to drool all over him, and she flat refused to do it. "I'd prefer not to answer that question," she said at last, rising.

"What? Why not?"

She smiled at him, enjoying the look of surprise in his eyes. "The evaluation is still pending," she told him briskly. "I'll let you know. Stay tuned." And with one last flip smile in his direction, she strode out of his office.

Matt sat back in his chair and laughed softly. He wasn't used to a woman who didn't use flattery to get her way with him. *But wait a minute,* he told himself. How could he say that? Conners always acted that way. Funny. He'd accepted it without question as a co-worker, but he couldn't quite handle it as a man-woman thing. Mainly because he'd never thought of her in those terms before. Why was that?

But he had no time to puzzle it out. His mind was

already shifting gears. Picking up the telegram, he frowned at it, his gaze cloudy. For just a moment he saw the silver plane, flashing in the sunlight, plummeting to earth as if it were a wounded bird, and he winced.

"Hey, Remy, old man," he said softly, as though his half brother might be nearby, just waiting for a word from him. "We were never close, but we were brothers." Something burned in his throat and he paused, trying to swallow it. But it wouldn't leave and he accepted that, thinking of Remy again.

"I'm going to do this for you," he told him. "You didn't get a very long run in this life, but your kid is going to be taken care of." He clenched his fist, crumpling the yellow paper in his hand. "And he's going to be raised a hell of a lot better than we were." He ground out the words, his eyes lit with an icy fire. "That much I promise you."

Chapter 2

Shayla Conners sat at her desk and stared at the telephone. She'd already called four employment agencies. At each one, she'd had exactly the response she'd expected—plus a few guffaws. The question was, would Mr. Temple accept four rejections and call it quits? *She* was certainly ready to.

Shrugging, she turned to her computer keyboard and typed up a complete report, every word of the answers she'd received, including the obscenities, and put the memo on his desk, just as she would have done with any other project.

And that made her realize the flaw in this entire operation once again. Finding a mother for a baby was not an office project. You couldn't treat it like a new assignment. There was just something missing.

"Heart," she mused aloud, balancing her pencil on her finger and watching it wobble. That was it. Where was the heart?

Only Matt Temple would come up with such a crazy scheme. You didn't hire a wife the way you hired a re-

ceptionist. But surely he knew that. He made a distinction
between the women he worked with and the women he
dated. It was obvious. He worked with a lot of women,
but the women he worked with were all business while
the women he dated were all entertainment. He saw the
difference and used it to his advantage. His dates were
young, shapely and utterly brainless. His employees were
nothing like that. Shirley, his secretary, was a grand-
mother many times over, and had an advanced degree in
abnormal psychology. Carol, the receptionist with the
motherly attitude, had a loving husband and five children
who called constantly once school was out in the afternoon. And if that weren't enough, she was taking legal
writing at night school. Shayla herself had a degree in
business management and was probably the youngest on
his immediate staff.

"And I suppose he took one look at me and thought,
'I'll never be attracted to this one,'" she mused as she
packed up her things and prepared to leave for the evening. And he was right. He hadn't been. She'd worked
there for months and he hadn't shown one spark of interest. "And I haven't shown one spark of interest in
him," she lied to herself.

She stopped, as though something in her conscience
were chiding her. She knew what she'd just told herself
wasn't true. She'd seen potential in Matt Temple from the
first time she'd interviewed with him. How could a
woman not respond to those eyes that were as blue as
northern lakes, that wavy dark hair that sometimes fell
boyishly over his forehead when he got excited, the tall,
strong body of an athlete, the engaging grin, the dangerous scowl, the...

"Stop it!" she told herself fiercely, tearing a stack of
papers and dumping the remnants into the trash.

She was a thirty-year-old professional woman without

a husband or a family of her own, and the last thing she was going to let herself do was begin fantasizing that there was something going on with her boss. She knew women who did that, women with no real lives of their own who lived in a dreamworld, pretending some movie star or singer or some man they worked with would someday fall in love with them. She wasn't going to let herself fall into that trap.

"Even if I *don't* have a life of my own," she muttered to herself as she restocked the paper in the printer and began to plot out a schedule for Matt Temple's next week.

That was a bit of an exaggeration. She had friends and plenty of brothers and sisters nearby. Her life wasn't entirely empty. But there was no man in it, hadn't ever been.

"You're just too picky," her happily married sister said at least once a week.

"Yeah," her brother would chime in. "There comes a time, you know, when you have to settle for reality."

And they would look at her and she would be sure they were noticing a few new wrinkles around her eyes, a certain tiredness to the set of her mouth, and thinking, "Gee, she'd better jump at what she can get, poor thing. She's not getting any younger."

All done in love for her, she knew, but it was annoying as all get-out. She had to admit, she had once had a stray thought of what their faces would look like if she walked into Sunday dinner, just once, with Matt Temple on her arm.

All in all, he was quite a man and she knew it. But he certainly wasn't the type of man she would ever end up with. Even if he had been interested in her, she would have had to put a stop to it. Her goal was a big, happy family, just like the one she'd grown up in. It was that or nothing with her. And Matt wouldn't ever fit into a picture like that. He was the sort of man who was wedded to his work, and she was not about to end up with a husband who hardly remembered her name except on weekends. She'd seen the heartbreak that kind of union could inspire in the marriage of her best friend, as well as one of her sisters. He was not right for her. No, not her type at all.

And that was just fine because actually, when you came right down to it, there were a lot of things she didn't like about him.

"What I mean is," she told herself, overanalyzing as she always did. "My hormones have no trouble responding to him on a physical level. If we were still at the stage where we were running around in the jungle, I'd want his genes embedded in my children. But we're not running around in the jungle. We're living in modern America, and his type of gung-ho masculinity is just a little too much to bear."

Besides, he'd never shown a spark of interest.

The elevator doors opened and there he was, striding down the hall toward her, glancing at his watch as he approached her desk.

"Listen, I'm running late," he said after a piercing look at her. "Miss Carbelli will be stopping by to pick me up any moment. We're going to that new play at Warren Theater." He looked into her face again and hesitated, as though something had thrown him just a bit off his stride. Then he frowned and went on. "Have Shirley make me a dinner reservation at the Station House out on the wharf, will you?" He glanced at her again, then headed for his office. "For six," he called back as he went. "That ought to give us time...." His voice faded as he disappeared in through the doorway.

Shayla nodded as though he could still see her and put in an intercom message to Shirley. But all the while, she was puzzling over the way he'd looked at her. "It was as though he'd actually seen me," she mused. "I guess he's never really noticed me before."

That had annoyed her earlier, but now that she thought about it, it was hardly surprising. What had she ever done to draw his attention, after all? He might as well have a robot working for him. She'd never shown him any other side than the industrious workaholic who did a little talking back, but not enough to ruffle any feathers.

"And do I really have another side?" she asked herself caustically. She certainly didn't do much with her time other than work.

But she didn't have much time to analyze her thoughts, as she heard the dulcet tones Pia Carbelli tended to emit come slicing through the late-afternoon hum of office work. The woman was a vision in mink and rhinestone, her red hair a flame that crackled around her pretty, pouty face.

"He's waiting for you, Miss Carbelli," Shayla said, smiling stiffly at the woman as she flounced into the area. "Go right in."

The door opened and the woman disappeared inside, trailing perfume like a wake in water, but before the door closed again, Matt Temple's voice exploded from his office.

"Conners!"

He'd seen the memo. Shayla smiled to herself as she rose and complied, obedient but unbowed.

He was standing at his desk, waving the paper in the air, his brow furled. "What is the meaning of this?" he demanded sternly.

She met his glare and shrugged. "As you can see, the..." She glanced quickly at Pia and realized she didn't want the woman to know about this. Maybe he'd told her, but then again, maybe not. "The, uh, category you requested is in short supply these days.'' She caught his gaze and waited.

He swore under his breath, obviously unhappy that this was turning out to be such a problem. ''I'm afraid you're going to have to try a little harder to find the source of that supply, Conners,'' he noted coolly. ''Or you're going to find yourself pitching in to help me.''

She blanched. What on earth did he mean? Would he set up a day-care facility here in the office? And assign her to it? Over her dead body he would!

''I'll see what I can do, sir,'' she told him quickly.

He nodded, somewhat mollified. ''Good.'' He glanced at his date for the evening. She was sitting in a chair, humming to herself and checking out her manicure, totally ignoring them both. He looked up at Shayla again, then away, and Shayla blinked. Was it her imagination, or did he look slightly uncomfortable? She gazed at him curiously. He was acting in a way she'd never seen him behave before, and she couldn't figure out why.

Pia seemed to sense something out of kilter as well, and she tossed her flaming head, batting her enormous eyelashes at the man. ''We better get going, sweetie,'' she reminded him. ''Time's a wastin'.''

''Yes,'' he said quickly. ''We're leaving,'' he told Shayla, closing up his ledger and putting it away.

She nodded. ''Shirley made your reservations,'' she told him, handing him a slip of paper with the information on it. ''Have a nice evening.''

She left the inner office quickly, but not quickly enough to avoid hearing Pia chirp and coo. What was that he'd said earlier? He wanted a woman who understood the issues of the day? That certainly wasn't the woman he was about to traipse off with. From what she'd gathered, the young lady's conversations consisted mainly of squeals and giggles, punctuated by the occasional low moan of pleasure.

"*Ooh,* Matt," she heard as the two of them prepared to leave the inner office. "Oh, you bad boy!"

That was followed with excessive giggling and the two of them emerged, arm in arm.

"I know what you're thinking," Pia was saying flirtingly to Matt, "and I'm going to have to make you pay for that, you little devil." She tugged on his arm, obviously planning to whisk him away as quickly as possible.

Shayla couldn't help it. She had to react. And she didn't think either of them would notice, they seemed so wrapped up in each other. So she made one little comment.

"Yech. Gag me with a spoon," she muttered, turning away from them in her swivel chair.

Matt came to a dead stop before her desk and suddenly the office seemed very, very quiet.

"What's that, Conners?" he demanded, glaring at her. "You said something?"

She looked up, surprised he'd noticed. "Uh... No sir, nothing at all."

His blue eyes held hers for a long moment, throwing daggers, and she held her breath, staring right back at him. Finally, his head went back and his eyes narrowed. Taking Pia's arm again, he turned toward the elevator. But he'd heard her, and her words and her look of disdain stayed with him as he left the building with his date. It had been a long time since he'd allowed another's criticism of his life or anything about it to cut him. And for some strange reason, this did. He couldn't imagine why.

Dinner tasted like dust and Pia's pouting was suddenly very boring. The play went on before his eyes, but he hardly saw it. His mind was a sea of seething images, from Remy's young face to memories of his father to the way Conners had looked as she glanced at him leaving with Pia on his arm. The pictures kept coming, he couldn't hold them off. The calm, even pace of his days was about to take a jolt of change, and he was going to come out of it a different person. That sudden insight hit him as he walked back to the car with Pia, and when she asked if he was coming up to her apartment, he stared at her as though he'd never seen her before, then made an excuse and left her to her own devices.

This was it. He was going to be a father.

My God, he thought, staring into the midnight sky studded with a million stars. *What am I getting myself into?*

Shayla's attitude still rankled in the morning. He respected her and usually, he respected her opinion. But he was seeing her a little differently now, noticing things about her he hadn't noticed before.

"Good morning, Conners," he said gruffly, eyeing her without smiling as he stopped before her desk at nine sharp. "I trust we'll get through this day without another critique of my behavior from you."

Shayla looked surprised. "Wh...what?" she stammered. The incident from the night before had completely slipped her mind.

He fixed her with a steady glare. "The comment concerning the insertion of a dining implement into your esophageal region was spectacularly ill timed. If you disapprove of the women in my life, or anything else for that matter, please keep it to yourself."

It took her a moment to digest exactly what he was talking about, but once she had it firmly in mind, her heart fell and she nodded quickly. "I'm sorry about that, sir," she told him sincerely. "I didn't mean for you to hear it. Really. I won't let it happen again."

Her remorse was genuine, and his resentment melted

like spring snow. He liked the look of abject regret in her eyes. Suddenly he felt much better about it all.

"All right, then," he said, appeased. "Come into my office and we'll discuss what to do about this baby problem."

He turned and she took a deep breath and gazed after him in wonder. Their relationship had always been stormy, but it had been a superficial sort of tempest. Somehow things seemed to be going deeper all of a sudden. She wasn't sure if that was good or bad.

"I can always count on you, Conners," he added from the doorway to his inner office, and she shook herself, getting back on track immediately. "I want to hear what you've come up with."

The answer to that was not much, and she followed him into his office rather reluctantly. Sitting across the desk from him, she outlined the agencies she'd called already that morning, all of whom had given her the same answer she'd received the day before.

"This obviously isn't going to work, Mr. Temple," she told him as he frowned at her detailed report on the calls. He was going to have to admit defeat on this one. You can't hire a wife. So here went her own big idea. She sat forward. "You're going to have to hire a nanny. Maybe someone full-time who can live in and—"

"No."

She lifted her head and blinked at him from behind her owl-shaped glasses. "What do you mean, no?" she asked, hoping he'd decided to find a better home for the baby.

But he wasn't about to give up on raising his brother's child. "The nanny business is okay," he began, leaning back in his chair and gazing at her from beneath half-lowered lids. "I realize I will need someone to care for the tyke in the daytime." He paused, then added in a measured tone that left no doubt about his intentions, "But I'm going to raise this kid, Conners, even if I can't find a wife. No matter what, I'm going to do it."

She stared at him and wondered if she really knew him at all. Insanity. That was what it seemed to her. But what could she do? "Help him all you can," her conscience told her. "And hope for the best." Aloud, she said very calmly, "I can see that you feel very strongly about this, Mr. Temple. And since that is the case, we had better approach the situation from another angle. We're going to have to find you someone who can teach you baby-raising skills."

She expected a frown for that, but he only looked at her quizzically. "Do you really think I need to be taught?"

"Of course. It doesn't come naturally, you know." And she couldn't resist adding, "Especially not to men."

His head went back, but he smiled. "There you go with the sexist comments again, Conners."

It occurred to her that he seemed to be in an awfully good mood for someone who was running into brick walls at every turn. "Sorry, sir," she said, studying him curiously. "Now there are agencies that hire out people to teach new mothers what they're doing. I'm sure we could get one of them to—"

"No."

He'd said it again. She frowned, searching his blithe face. "What now?" she asked.

He smiled at her, his widest, most seductive smile, the one he used when closing a business deal, the one he used when charming the most beautiful woman at the party, the one that came naturally to him when he really meant it, the one that made her heart beat just a little faster.

"We're not going to have to hire anyone at all. I want you to do it."

Her eyes widened and a shock ran through her. "Me?" she croaked.

"Yes, you." He leaned forward and held her gaze with his own. "Didn't you say you came from a large family? I'll bet you raised lots of little ones in your time."

He would have won that bet, but she wasn't ready to concede. Something inside her was shivering and she wanted to make it stop, very quickly. "They were sisters and one little brother. And that was years ago."

He smiled again. "There you are. You know all about it."

He had her cornered and she knew it, but she was going to go down fighting. "But I don't know the latest techniques, the latest theories," she said, feeling desperate. "I don't know if they're advising you to put your baby on a schedule or let it dictate the rhythm of the day. I don't know if you should begin cereals at twelve weeks or twelve months."

She would have gone on chronicling her deficiencies, but he shook his head and waved her to silence. "Give me a break, Conners. You and I were raised without all that claptrap. We survived. We can do this."

Her heart skipped a beat. She was a goner.

"*We* is hardly the issue here," she snapped, though most of the zing had gone out of her tone. "*You* are the one who is going to have to do this."

His smile was infuriatingly smug.

"Exactly. But *you* are the one who is going to teach me how."

"But..."

"Pack your sports togs, Conners. We'll have the whole weekend at my place out in Marin County. You can re-organize my house and teach me what to do. Do you think one weekend will be enough? I'm a pretty quick study."

Shayla didn't say anything at all. She was too stunned to speak.

Chapter 3

Matt Temple gazed around his sunken living room and tried to imagine a child playing on the thickly carpeted floor. The picture wouldn't come clear. What the hell did he know about babies, anyway? His life was in for a big change. Was he up to it?

He'd put on a face of confidence when talking to Shayla. She'd arrived a half hour ago, dressed as though she were spending the weekend in the office instead of here at his place in the country. Luckily she had brought other clothes, so he'd sent her up to the room he'd had the housekeeper prepare so that she could change. She ought to be down any minute, and then they would begin the lessons. Baby-raising lessons. For some strange reason, he was nervous.

He'd never thought about having children. It was one of those things that either happened or it didn't, as far as he was concerned. He hadn't avoided it, but he hadn't planned for it, either. Here he was, halfway through his thirties, and settling down had never been an issue for him.

He'd spent most of his adult life creating his business and driving it to the success that now seemed almost dizzying. Though he'd started out with a nice cushion of wealth in his inheritance, he'd definitely taken that nest egg and turned it into a thriving enterprise that had bought him respect and even awe in the marketplace. The next step should be to marry and pass on all this empire he'd built. But he'd never thought of things quite that way. Perhaps that was because he'd never known what it was to have a happy family when he was young. How was he supposed to replicate something he knew nothing about?

His parents had been very rich, but they'd also been very absent from his life. Proverbial jet-setters, they had been more at home in European nightclubs than in the nursery they'd left behind in San Francisco. His mother had died when he was nine. The headmaster of his boarding school had been the one to tell him about it. He'd been sent home to go to her funeral, but through some oversight, no one had come to pick him up at the airport. He'd finally taken a bus that had ended up in Santa Cruz and he'd missed the funeral entirely. But it hardly mattered. He hadn't really known her very well.

After that, his father had gone through a succession of wives, each younger than the last. Remy's mother had been about wife number three, if he recollected clearly. He remembered her as a shy, pretty woman, somewhat overwhelmed by his father's booming personality. She'd been very nice to him, even made a short-lived attempt to mother him in ways none of the other wives ever had. He'd been about twelve or thirteen and, as he remembered it, he hadn't been very nice to her, had shrugged aside her attempts to get closer. But memories of her kindness stuck with him, and even now, he often thought of her rather than his own mother, when the subject of mothers came up. His father had divorced her a few years later, and she'd died of cancer not long after, leaving behind a young son who'd had his own turn at boarding-school life. But Remy had inherited his mother's sweetness and had kept in touch with Matt over the years. Now he wished he'd made more of an effort to reciprocate.

"But I'm going to make it up to him," he told himself firmly. "I'm going to raise his baby. I'm going to do it right. No boarding schools for this little guy."

A sound on the stairs told him Shayla was coming down and he turned impatiently, ready to get on with the work he'd set out for them. But what he saw was a stranger, and he reared back, appalled.

"Conners?" he asked, staring at the woman coming down his stairway. "Is that you?"

Shayla wanted to laugh at his stunned expression, but she managed to hold back the impulse. "You're the one who insisted I dress down for this," she told him as she came up beside him, feeling like a teenager in her jeans, tennis shoes and soft sweater. "I was perfectly happy in heels and a suit."

He frowned. It wasn't the casual clothing that bothered him, he decided, although it did make her appear much younger and shorter than before. It was mainly her hair. He'd never realized that she had so much of it. She usually wore it pulled back tightly into a nice, professional bun, but for some reason, she'd taken out the pins and let it go wild. Gold with light blond highlights shimmering here and there, it cascaded around her shoulders in a very disturbing way, looking as if it belonged to a woman of free, impulsive habits, not the careful, controlled assistant he was used to. Somehow it brought up thoughts of passions and hot looks and other things he had never associated with her before. And yet when he looked into her eyes, they were still the cool, clear violet eyes he was used to. She hadn't really changed. Strange. Very strange. And he wasn't sure he liked it.

She could read his mind. Laughing softly, she reached into a pocket and pulled out a band, quickly pulling back her hair and making a casual ponytail. "There," she said, challenging him with the look in her eyes and the tilt of her head. "Is that better?"

He didn't answer. He really didn't want to get into it with her. And yet, it wasn't better at all. Now, wisps of hair curled around her face, making her look younger than ever, and very, very pretty, while the full, rich substance of her hair still swung from the back of her head. After studying her for a moment out of the corner of his eye, he turned as though ready for some purposeful enterprise.

"Let's get to work," he said gruffly. "Got a game plan here? Or are we playing it by ear?"

She looked up at him and took a deep breath. She hadn't wanted to come. She was very shaky on what was going to happen. But here she was, Matt Temple's guest for the weekend. And now he was looking at her as though *he* wished she hadn't come.

Paradoxically that rather cheered her. Maybe things weren't going to get as dangerous as she'd feared.

But it was best to be careful. "What we need, first of all, are guidelines," she told him, glancing around his extravagantly beautiful living room. "We have to maintain the employee-employer relationship. This is a working weekend. Not a vacation."

"Okay," he said, shoving his hands into his pockets and looking at her as though he were going to wait for her cues. "No problem."

She glanced at him quickly. He was being uncharacteristically agreeable. He looked very different, too. At work, he usually wore the most expensive suits, the whitest shirts and everything looked crisp and serious. Today he wore a soft, open polo shirt that clung to some nicely chiseled shapes and slacks that were casual and slightly snug. Something fluttered inside her chest and she frowned, not pleased. No, there was no reason he should look this good. No reason at all.

"Now tell me this," he said, unaware of her scrutiny. "How do I fix up this place so it's okay for baby raising?"

She turned slowly, biting her lip. "Number one," she said once she'd cased the joint, "we baby proof everything." Reaching into her pocket, she pulled out a sheet of brightly colored stickers and waved them at Matt. "I'll put a sticker on each object that has to go."

He raised an eyebrow. "You certainly came prepared," he muttered as he watched her go to work. But what had he expected? She was always prepared. Why would she change just because she'd suddenly revealed beautiful hair and become too short?

And she hadn't. She was a whirlwind, dashing through his house, putting stickers everywhere. He had only the foggiest notion of what she was doing at first. But as she continued her work, he began to frown.

"Wait a minute," he said as she slapped a sticker on his four-foot statue of an Etruscan love goddess that stood on the hearth of his massive fireplace. "What exactly is going to happen to these things?"

She looked up at him brightly. "They'll have to go," she said, seemingly quite cheerful about it. "Put them in storage, sell them off, whatever. But they can't be here when the baby arrives." And she popped a sticker on the marble coffee table without wasting an extra glance on it and went on to his dagger collection hanging on the wall.

He watched her, appalled, then turned and examined the statue thoughtfully, his hands shoved deep into the pockets of his slacks. "Uh, why is this, exactly?" he asked. "I mean, what does this piece of art have in common with the coffee table, since I notice you've pegged it for removal as well?" He turned to glare at her. "Are you making your judgments on the basis of taste or personal preference? I don't quite get it."

"Not at all," she assured him breezily, reaching back to refasten the band in her hair. "It's all a matter of safety. Look at this." She pointed out the square corners of the coffee table. "Sharp corners. Babies are always falling against sharp corners. And this." She nodded toward the statue. "Tall and heavy. A baby could easily pull it over and get bashed by it."

He looked pained. He loved that statue, and the coffee table had been one of his first selections when he'd decorated his own place.

"Next thing I know, you'll put a sticker on me," he grumbled. "How about if we just tell the little tyke, 'no'? Wouldn't that work?"

Her laughter came echoing back to him as she sped down the hall, slapping a sticker on his poisonous houseplant as she passed it.

"No matter how hard you try," she advised him, "you can never watch them every minute of the day. So you have to think ahead. The moment you turn your back is the moment they climb up and try rolling in the embers of the fireplace or diving off the kitchen counter into a fishbowl or eating the dog's Crunchy Beef Nuggets."

He frowned. Why would a baby do all these things? Something wasn't jibing here. "Wait a minute. When I think of a baby, I think of a cuddly little thing wrapped in covers and sleeping in a basket."

She looked back at him and grinned, shaking her head. The poor man was in for a rude awakening. "No such luck. In retrospect, they're only like that for about five days, and then they're off and running and they never sit still again.''

The prospect was daunting and he lapsed into silence, watching worriedly as she littered the house with tiny iridescent signals of doom.

''Aw, not my baseball trophy,'' he complained as she made her way through his den.

''You can put it up on a high shelf where you can still see it,'' she told him, biting back a smile at his stricken look. ''Come on, take it like a man. Having a baby is serious business.''

''So I'm beginning to realize,'' he muttered, following her.

Once she was finished demolishing the artifacts of his life, he called the housekeeper rather grumpily and asked her to assemble a crew of workers to put everything Shayla had tagged into storage. ''Don't bury anything too deep,'' he said sadly, watching his Etruscan love goddess being carted away. ''I may want to visit these things from time to time.''

And then they climbed the stairs to the room that was to be the nursery. The floor was littered with books of wallpaper samples and paint swatches and fabric ideas.

''Boy or girl?'' Shayla asked as she sank to the floor and began to flip the pages.

''You got me,'' he answered, sinking beside her.

Her head swung around, the ponytail bouncing, and she gaped at him. ''You don't know the sex of your baby?''

He shook his head and patted his flat stomach. ''Just like most people, I'll find out when it gets here,'' he quipped.

She shook her head in wonder and another thought came to her. ''How about the age?''

''I don't know that, either.''

Unbelievable. If she were awaiting the arrival of a baby

and didn't know the sex or age, she would be going crazy, but he didn't seem to care. Shayla sat very still and watched him as he went through a book of wallpapering ideas. A feeling of dread was welling up in her. This was so crazy, him trying to take on the raising of a baby. It wasn't going to work. And it was going to hurt so much when it all fell apart—both for him and the child. But how was she going to convince him?

"Hey, what do you think of this?" he asked, showing her a sample that portrayed pirate ships and tiny cannons going off. "Isn't that great?"

She had to smile back at him. When he wanted to, she noted somewhat resentfully, he had one heck of a charming smile. "It's awfully cute," she agreed. "As long as the baby turns out to be a boy. If it's a girl..." She held up her own choice, tiny ballet slippers against a pink background.

Matt's face fell. "How about something in yellow?" he suggested, going back to the book. "Maybe cartoon characters."

They compromised on a darling pattern in both blue and pink, with teddy bears of both genders cavorting on clouds that transformed into spaceships and magic carpets.

"With drapes and a bedspread to match," she suggested, and they rose from the floor to take some measurements.

He held the measuring tape while she jotted down sizes, and he found his attention straying to her lush hair again. He frowned.

"I can't get over how short you are," he said as she stood next to him while he measured the window opening.

She glanced up at him and quickly moved away. "I'm just as tall as I've always been," she protested.

"No, you're not," he said, following her. "I mean, at

the office, you seem taller. And it's more than just the heels.''

She turned and looked into his eyes. Why did he seem to resent everything about her today? ''At the office, I *am* taller,'' she said softly.

That wasn't exactly what she meant and she wasn't sure why she'd said it that way. Maybe because she felt taller at the office. Taller, more in control of things. Here, she was feeling very vulnerable—as though he could reach out and change her life with the flick of his wrist.

He was standing very still, caught by something in her gaze, caught and confounded again. She wasn't supposed to be able to get to him this way. *What way?* He didn't have a clue. All he knew was, she was making him nervous. She wasn't all business as she was at the office. And she wasn't a piece of whipped cream fluff as his girlfriends were. She was something else entirely and he didn't have the slightest idea how he was going to handle her.

''Why are your eyes that color?'' he demanded suddenly, happy he'd found something else to complain about. ''Is it contact lenses?''

No matter how prepared she thought she was, he always surprised her. ''What?'' she said, dropping her pencil and not even noticing as it skipped across the floor.

''It's not natural, that violet color you've got.'' He peered into her eyes as though they offended him, though the truth was, he was enchanted by their shade. Fringed with black lashes, her eyes had a sparkle that would do a diamond proud. He'd never seen anything quite like it, and to his chagrin, he found himself responding in definite physical ways. ''How did you get that?''

''Witchcraft,'' she snapped, turning away in disgust. ''My mother put a spell on me.''

''You ought to wear your glasses,'' he muttered, feeling ridiculous, but bound and determined not to let her see how she affected him. "It's not as noticeable when your glasses are in the way."

Whirling, she confronted him, her hand on her hip, her chin in the air. "Listen, mister," she said as crisply as she was able, though she was shaking inside with anger at him by now. If he really hated everything about her, she might as well get out of his way.

"I arrived here dressed for the office. You're the one who made me go up and change. Now you don't like anything about me. You don't like my hair." She yanked the band out defiantly and let it fly around her face. "You don't like how short I am. You don't like my eyes." She pounded one small fist against her chest. "This is me. This is who I am. If you really can't take it, I'll just go and leave you to handle this thing all by yourself."

He'd tried to frown fiercely about halfway through her speech, but he found he couldn't really maintain the front. She was beautiful with her hair a golden mist around her face and her lovely eyes glistening with anger at him. He wanted nothing more than to sweep her up into his arms and take possession of all that effervescence.

"Listen, Conners," he began, trying to be stern, and then his armor crumbled. "No, dammit. I can't call you Conners." He shrugged, looking almost helpless, his eyes troubled, his mind fogged by this unexpected reaction he was having to her. "You're not Conners anymore. Maybe I should call you...what is your name again? Sheila or something like that?"

For just a moment, she was sure he had to be joking, teasing her, trying to get her goat. But then she caught his gaze and read the complete sincerity in his eyes and knew this was for real. He was just a jerk. A complete and utter jerk. What the heck was she doing here?

"Oh!" she cried, turning on her heel and starting for the door. "Let me out of here!"

She was escaping, and despite all his complaining, that was the last thing he wanted her to do.

"No, wait," he called out. "It's Shayla, I remember now."

His legs were longer, which made him faster and he reached the doorway before she did, grabbing her by the arm and pulling her back around to face him. "I'm sorry. I'm not very good at names." His smile was oddly endearing. "But you know that. You know me. All too well, it seems," he added softly, almost under his breath, as his gaze searched hers. "And I don't know you well at all."

"Good," she said, trying to pull away, avoiding a look into his face. She was angry and she wanted to stay that way. She knew one look at his smile would do her in. "Let's keep it that way, shall we?"

"It's too late for that," he said, and suddenly his free hand was touching her hair as though it were spun gold, something magical.

Her heart leaped into her throat, beating there like a wild thing, and she could hardly breathe. "No." She managed to grate out the words, and she reached up to push his hand away. "None of that," she warned, her eyes filled with wary apprehension.

She was right and he knew it, so he didn't push it. But he didn't move, either. Standing there, one hand on her arm, he looked down into her eyes and stared just a beat too long, as though he could read her mind if he looked long enough. She looked back, startled by the depth of something dark in his gaze, the strong pull of something she didn't recognize and couldn't identify.

"Okay," he said at last, and his hand slipped away

from her arm. "Okay. We're all business. But you've got to stay. I need you."

She could have sworn her knees had melted. She wasn't going anywhere, and she hated herself for it. But she was here for the duration. If he needed her, she wouldn't let him down.

Silly, she chided herself silently as they moved on to choosing paint colors. *You're a fool if you think you mean a thing to this man. And an even bigger fool if you care.*

But she couldn't help it. Not only did she feel a duty as his assistant, but she felt a bond with him that she couldn't break at the moment.

"Like a woman in chains," she scoffed to herself melodramatically, but she followed him to the kitchen and began pointing out cupboards that would need protective latches.

He paid strict attention, but at the same time he was watching her, watching and wondering. Who was this woman he'd invited into his house? And how long could he get her to stay?

Chapter 4

The day passed more quickly than Shayla expected. She threw advice around as though she actually knew what she was talking about, and she had to admit, he took it all very well, jotting down notes, considering her opinions, compromising without his usual arrogance when they disagreed.

His house was amazing. She'd never been in such a gorgeous place before. The azaleas were blooming in the yard, white ones along one bank, pink along another. The swimming pool sparkled like a turquoise jewel in the sunlight, studded with rocks and small waterfalls so that it seemed to be a mountain pond, which Matt might have found on a hike and brought back as a souvenir. The house itself had an aging elegance, like a debutante from the twenties, all dressed up and still waiting for the right beau to come along.

Like Sleeping Beauty, Shayla thought to herself as she studied the rooms, breathing in the ambience. *Waiting for the prince to appear and awaken her.*

"Your house is so beautiful," she told Matt later when

he joined her on a balcony overlooking the lawns and the swimming pool. "Have you had it long?"

"Since before I was born," he told her, leaning against the railing and looking more at her than at the view.

"Then it must be full of memories for you," she said, glancing at him and then back out at the azaleas.

He shook his head slowly, straightening and turning to look out as well. "Not really. I spent most of my time in boarding schools, so this was just a place I came on holiday. A place to sleep, somewhere to store things. No real emotional attachments here."

That sounded very sad. She looked at him sharply, wondering if he were pulling her leg. "But your parents... Surely you had good times together here."

He shrugged as though it hardly mattered. "I was hardly ever here. And neither were my parents for that matter. No one much was here but the caretakers."

She leaned on the railing, biting her lip. That explained the waiting atmosphere, as though the house had been built for great things but they hadn't happened yet. The place was almost like a museum. What was a baby going to do here? Matt had ordered a sandbox and swing set and monkey bars for the yard, but that was like putting a bonnet on a dachshund—it wouldn't change the essential character of the place at all.

Still, things would have to change with a youngster around.

"The baby might just bring this place to life," she murmured, more to herself than anything else.

"You're right," he told her. That was just what he'd been thinking. "And if it doesn't..." He shrugged and smiled at her. "I'll move to somewhere that's better for the kid."

His words astounded her and she wasn't sure she believed him. "You would do that for this new baby you haven't even seen yet?'' she asked him, skepticism unmistakable in her voice.

But he didn't seem to notice. "Sure," he said. "When I go into a project, I go all the way."

She knew him well enough to know that was true. Still, he was Mr. Playboy, Mr. Don't-Tie-Me-Down. How could he possibly contemplate making a shift like this? He was dreaming. It just couldn't be done. "You may say that now," she began, her doubt in her eyes.

"You don't understand," he interjected before she could go on. "My life is going to change completely. I know that. And I'm ready for it."

She stared at him, searching for something that would convince her and not finding it. "But why?" she asked him softly.

He gazed into her eyes, his own clear and honest. "Because it has to be done," he said.

No. He couldn't go the distance. He just didn't realize the enormity of what he was getting into. He had no idea what it was going to be like, that this new being would demand his soul as well as his every waking moment from now until it left home. He was fooling himself. She had to find a way to make him see reality.

And yet—why? At first she wouldn't face that question. But finally, it nagged her down. Yes, why? Why did she care what happened to this man? Why didn't she just sit back and let nature take its course? He'd find out all these things soon enough. Why get involved?

"He's my boss," she told herself, tossing her head. "I...I care about him. I hate to see him make such a painful mistake if it can be avoided."

She thought about it for the rest of the afternoon, and when they finally sat down to dinner on the terrace and watched the sun set, she had some ammunition up her sleeve. But she waited, biding her time, hoping the wonderful meal of poached salmon, curried couscous and sautéed sugar peas would sweeten the way for her.

Little did she know, he might as well have been eating sawdust for all the attention he was paying to his food. There was no room for taste and texture—his mind was on Shayla. She'd changed for the evening meal and the changes were as disturbing as the previous metamorphosis had been. The white gown she wore was light, filmy and sort of Grecian, and his attention was on her luscious hair and her bare feet in the light sandals and the way her breasts filled the bodice of the dress. She was downright beautiful. Why hadn't he seen it before? What was he, blind?

But he didn't want her to be beautiful, dammit. She was supposed to be efficient and smart and loyal, a perfect administrative assistant. He knew she was all those things, but somehow being beautiful was beginning to obscure them. It was clouding his mind, and the last thing he needed at this point was a clouded mind.

She was clearing her throat. He glanced at her and saw that she was preparing to launch into a lecture of some sort. Silently he groaned. He didn't want any lectures right now. He was too busy lecturing himself to stay put for lectures from others.

"About this baby," she began.

"About *my* baby." He corrected her, smiling as the concept danced before his mind's eye. He was beginning to like the sound of that.

"About your baby," she amended. "I know you're excited about starting this new phase of your life." She hesitated, looking at him, and then launched. "You know, it's very odd, but you're very much like a teenage girl who's just found out she's pregnant. Her first reaction is shock, but once she's decided to go ahead and have it, she starts to dream about how it will be. She starts to imagine dressing the baby up and playing with her and showing her off to her friends." She paused. This part was harder. "And...and she starts to believe that now, she'll have someone who...who loves her."

She glanced at Matt, wary and ready for fireworks. After all, she was implying that he was expecting, even needing, love from this baby. And yet, there was no evidence to support that, and she knew it. He got plenty of love. Half the women in San Francisco were ready and willing to give him all the love he needed. So she waited for his retort, but to her surprise, Matt seemed undaunted. He took another bite and chewed slowly, watching her as though he were truly interested. So, hesitantly, she went on.

"Then, when the baby gets a little older and starts to make all sorts of demands on her, she has regrets," she continued. "She begins to see what she's given up just to have this baby. And she begins to wonder why she gave up her life for this."

He nodded. He agreed with her. That sort of thing seemed to happen all the time to young girls. He could see that she was really concerned and it amused him somewhat. He wasn't a young girl, and he wasn't looking for love. He knew what he was doing. And anyway, what was the big deal? Didn't she know that he was usually successful at just about everything he tried? He had supreme confidence in this new adventure. After all, what could be so hard about raising a baby?

"Nice story, Shayla," he said, taking another bite of salad and making a face at her. "And I appreciate the spirit in which you told it. But that's not it at all."

She cocked her head to the side, looking at him. "Isn't it?" she asked softly, hoping he would think about her words, take them to heart and maybe glean a little understanding from them.

"No. I'm raising this baby because it's something I just have to do. For my brother. For...for my family." Odd, he'd never thought he had family feelings, but a strange emotion was welling in his chest. "And hey, for father's rights," he added with a grin, papering over the emotion he didn't know how to deal with. "That's it. Father's rights. Every man has a right to a kid, don't you think?"

She shook her head slowly. "What about baby's rights?" she said softly. "What about a baby's right to have a mother and a father? A real family?"

He avoided answering that one. Savoring the salmon for the first time all night, he glanced down at her plate. "You know, you haven't eaten a bite, and it's very good."

Shayla frowned, not hungry and unable to think about food right now. There was an edginess to the man at the moment, and she knew it wasn't the best time to push this, but she didn't have any choice. It was pretty much now or never.

"Mr. Temple," she began again.

Swinging around, he stopped her with a sharp look. "Mr. Temple is for the office," he told her. "If I'm going to call you Shayla, you'd better call me Matt."

That was precisely what she didn't want to do. She longed to get back to the more formal discourse between the two of them. Every time he said her name, his voice sort of rolling it in his mouth, she felt prickles down her spine, as though they were already too close, too intimate.

"All right," she said quickly, then avoided using it. "Please listen." Reaching into her pocketbook, she pulled out a handful of brochures. "I've got information here about a wonderful adoption agency. Just sit and listen for a minute, let me show you the details."

Glancing up, she could see a storm cloud gathering in his eyes, but she pushed ahead quickly, ignoring it as she spread the brochures out before him. "I want you to think about it, really think. There are thousands of couples out there who can't have babies of their own. There are waiting lists a mile long for any child under a year."

He was sitting very still and his knuckles were white, but he kept his voice steady and low. "Philosophically I agree with you. But I'm not going to do it."

Anything short of a shouting match was positive, she told herself. She was making progress and that spurred her on. "All those girls I was talking about want to raise a child without a father, which usually ends in disaster," she told him earnestly. "And now you want to raise this child without a mother. I have a feeling that will be even worse."

She held her breath, knowing she'd probably gone too far, waiting for him to explode. But that wasn't at all what she got. As she watched, he looked down at his plate and played with his fork in his food for a moment before answering.

"I haven't totally given up on the wife idea, you know," he said softly, looking at her.

"You haven't?" Her eyes widened in surprise.

"No. As a matter of fact, Pia actually volunteered." He smiled at her smugly. "And you thought I couldn't get anyone to take the job."

"No," she breathed, horrified. Pia Carbelli with a child? "Oh, no. Oh please, you wouldn't…"

His smile drooped, and the storm was back in his eyes. Pushing his plate away, he crumpled his napkin and threw it on the table.

"I'm kidding," he said shortly. "I didn't really tell her. I just wanted to see your reaction."

"Oh." Annoyance followed quickly on the heels of the relief she felt. "I'm so glad I can be here to provide you with entertainment,'' she said evenly, tossing back her hair.

"Shayla..." His large hand covered her. "Don't try to talk me out of this. I have to do it. There's no choice."

She stared into his deep blue eyes and for just a moment, she got lost there. She had a strange sensation of walking through icy caverns, with stalactites hanging and a cool blast of wind tearing into her hair, and she pulled back, yanking her hand from his and blinking to avoid his gaze. "Don't," she protested, though she wasn't sure if she was talking about his hand on hers, or the mystery of his gaze.

"No problem," he said, but his tone made it clear that his words weren't sincere. Rising and turning away with barely a glance in her direction, he said, "I've got some papers I have to go over. See you later." He started to stride off, then turned back and added, "Meet me in the den at nine if you feel up to it, and we'll go over plans for tomorrow."

And with that he was gone. She sat where she was, sitting very still. She had a feeling she knew why he'd left so abruptly and it wasn't because he resented her trying to make him face reality. It was a lot more than that. They weren't comfortable with each other the way they'd always been before. And he didn't know what to do about it any more than she did.

She wasn't sure. Should she stay or should she go? If she left right now, things might get back to normal at the office on Monday. The house was awfully far out of town. He'd sent a limousine to her apartment to bring her here, but there must be buses, taxis, something she could take to get back to the city. She had a feeling it was going to be dangerous to stay. There was a sense of electricity that simmered between them now, something that had never been there before, as though neither of them knew exactly where he stood with the other, and each was stepping very carefully so as not to break too far out of old patterns and find that there was nothing left to bind them together in any way.

She should go. That might be the only way to rescue her relationship with him, and her job. Lifting her face to the cool evening breeze, she let the power of the lovely estate wash over her, and thought again, drowsily, "Yes, I should go."

But she didn't move an inch.

Matt wandered down to the creek that ran through a small stand of aspen barely visible from the house. This was where he'd often come as a child, whenever Fate had left him here, usually alone. This was where he could get away from housekeepers and gardeners and people telling him to practice his tennis. No one ever thought to look for him here.

Funny how his childhood was coming back to him more clearly than it had for years—forever. He'd never been one to dwell on the past. But now, with the baby about to arrive, the past was a source he would mine to find a guideline. How was he going to be sure he was doing the right thing by this baby?

Shayla will know, a small voice inside his head tried to assert.

"No," he said aloud. He couldn't depend on her that way. Her help was only meant to be short-term. On Monday, he wanted her back in the office, back in her suit and sneer, back to work. She was his most valued employee. He couldn't risk losing her.

But as the reality of the baby became clearer, he was beginning to realize she was right about one thing: That kid was going to need a mother.

"And Shayla already has a job," he reminded himself,

with a sad smile. The mother was going to have to be someone else.

He moved restlessly along the banks of the creek, throwing in a stick to watch it wash its way downstream. His mood seemed to be on a pendulum. One moment he was on top of the world and looking forward to his new direction, the next, he was wondering if he was losing his mind. He wasn't used to this sort of uncertainty. He was the guy who always had all the answers. He didn't know why he was wavering at the moment. He only knew it had something to do with Shayla.

"Maybe if I call her Conners again," he muttered, turning back toward the house. "Maybe that would put things back in proper perspective."

But it was too late for that. She was Shayla to him now. And he wasn't sure if he would ever be able to revert to the Conners relationship. Looking back toward the house, he sighed. Life hadn't been this complicated since he was a child.

"As soon as the baby comes, things will get back on an even keel," he told himself. But his confidence was finally beginning to show hairline cracks.

Chapter 5

In the end, of course, Shayla didn't leave.

She strolled through the garden, breathing in the scent of sweet peas, and browsed through the library, then went on and wandered through the exercise room, lifting a weight or two, and stopped by the kitchen before she realized the house seemed strangely empty. Earlier, there had been a gardener repotting plants in the gazebo and a housekeeper organizing the removal of the dangerous items and a cook who'd fixed that delicious dinner. Now there seemed to be no one. It was almost nine, and she went quickly to the den to meet Matt.

He was pacing the floor when she arrived, holding a glass filled with a rich brown liquid, and he saluted her with it as she entered the room.

"There's no one in the kitchen," she said before he had a chance to speak.

"That's right." He nodded, one eyebrow raised quizzically.

She shrugged. "Where are they all?"

"It's their night off. They usually leave on Saturday

afternoon. They only stayed this long in order to serve you some dinner." His charming smile engulfed her. "Wasn't that nice of them?"

Alarms were going off all through her system. "When will they be back?" she asked warily.

"Monday morning."

Was it her imagination, or did his eyes seem to gleam in the shadows? "That means we're all alone in this house."

"That's right." He smiled again. "Hey, there's nothing to be afraid of. I'm here to protect you." He gestured toward the bar. "Would you like a drink?" he asked.

"No, thank you," she said automatically, glancing at the counter along the side of the room where an array of half-empty bottles sat cluttering the surface. Her eyes widened. Matt Temple had never been much of a drinker as far as she knew. She turned to him questioningly.

"I'm going to quit drinking," he announced.

"I see," she said, looking at him skeptically. "And you're swilling down every last drop as quickly as possible so that you can begin right away, is that it?"

"Right." He gazed at her with exaggerated wonder. "My God, you are perceptive, aren't you? That's exactly what I'm doing." He took a sip. "I don't want any liquor in the house while I'm raising the kid. So I'm getting rid of it."

He seemed awfully happy about it. She sank to the couch and watched him, her brows drawn together. "Do you have to finish the job tonight?" she asked him.

"Why not?" He stopped before her, considering her with his head to the side, his blue eyes veiled. "Why not wipe it out in one big blowout?"

Why not, indeed? She wasn't sure she had a good argument on that subject at the moment. Without waiting for her answer, he went to the bar and poured a glass of liquid that caught the light and glowed, returning to offer it to her.

"It will go much faster if you help me," he said. "Here. Have some wine."

She looked up at him from under lowered brows. "I don't want any wine, thank you. I don't drink." At least, not often and never much.

He regarded her with annoying good humor. "Any allergies? Medical problems? Religious considerations?"

"No, it's nothing like that. I just don't drink."

He set the glass before her on the coffee table. "You will drink tonight," he announced, as though he'd received a special message with that information enclosed.

She pulled her arms up, hugging herself and stared at the glass. "I don't like liquor."

He laughed and gestured with his glass. "Think of this as medicine. You need something to cure that terminal starched collar you're plagued with."

Her head jerked up and she would have laughed at that if she weren't so startled and appalled at being thought of that way.

"You took your hair down, you put on grungy clothes." He went on, as though he hadn't noticed her outraged reaction. "But somehow you missed the heart of the matter. We've got to do something to bend that concrete exterior you wear like a shield."

"Mr. Temple," she said icily. "I think you've had too much to drink yourself."

He sank into the couch beside her, shaking his head as though he were exasperated by her. "Okay, now this is serious," he said. "You've got to stop calling me that. My name's Matt. Use it."

"Mr. Temple…"

"Ah-ah." He held up his hand, warning her. "Say it."

She didn't make it on the first try, but finally she choked the name out. "M...Matt," she said.

He nodded happily. "See? That wasn't so hard." Sitting forward and reaching out, he took the wineglass from the table. "One drink," he coaxed.

"No." She shook her head obstinately.

"Okay." He put the glass back down and put his hand up in the manner of one taking a solemn vow. "I swear to you, I won't take advantage of you or anything like that. You can feel perfectly safe if you get a little tipsy. Hell, you can get downright drunk if you want. Your bedroom is only steps away. You're not going to get hurt. And I promise, I will not do anything to tarnish your good name."

She was weakening. She wanted to laugh at his play-acting, wanted to soften her stance. After all, she was tired and one glass of wine couldn't really hurt. "You promise?" she said softly, searching his eyes.

"On my honor as a scout. There will be no threatening behavior." He smiled as she took up the glass. "Kissing is all," he added as an afterthought.

"What?" She paused with the glass halfway to her lips, her violet eyes wide. "What did you say?"

His look was one of pure innocence. "Kissing." He shrugged. "I thought we might have a little innocent kissing. Why not?"

She put the glass back down on the table very carefully. "Mr. Temple!"

"Matt."

He was giving her that smile that melted ice on sight. She opened her mouth to protest again, but somehow her own lips were curving, and then she was shaking her head and laughing along with him.

"Matt," she said. "There will be no kissing."

He shrugged. "I didn't say there *had* to be kissing. I just didn't want to rule it out."

She stared at him for a moment, knowing she should be resisting his charm, his handsome face, his overwhelming masculinity, and knowing at the same time that she was enchanted by it and that there was very little hope her enchantment was going to dry up anytime soon.

Okay, she found her inner voice saying in her ear. *Go ahead. You can relax a little. Just as long as you never let him see that you...*

No, she told her inner voice silently. *Don't say it!*

But she found herself blushing, laughing and reaching for her glass of wine, all at the same time. "There will be no kissing," she announced, taking a sip. "But we could talk." She glanced at him. "Tell me about your brother and what you know about the baby."

"About the baby, I know very little," he said, sinking back beside her on the couch again. "And I must admit I don't know much more about Remy, either. His mother was my father's...let's see...second wife? Or was it the third? My mother was the first." His eyes sparkled as he went on, half teasing her. "I always felt like that made me the real crown prince. The others were more like pretenders to the throne. You know what I mean?"

He was joking, but there was just enough conviction behind what he was saying to make her wince. She rolled her eyes at him. "Oh, brother."

He grinned, glad she'd reacted. "You find that crass?"

"I find that pathetic."

"Hey. Nobody gave you permission to pass judgment on my private life."

"Then don't tell me about it."

"Well, I've got to tell you about it."

"Why?"

"Because I've got to tell somebody and you're here."

''Thank you so much.'' But she was feeling very warm and very happy. Maybe too warm and happy. Looking at the half-empty wineglass in her hand, she frowned distrustfully, and set it down as far away as she could reach. ''Tell me about the younger ones,'' she suggested. ''Your brothers.''

He noted her interaction with the wineglass and suppressed a smile. ''There are only two. There's Jared who's living it up on the French Riviera with a plethora of Continental starlets, and Michael, who's gone native in Bali and refuses to wear clothes or speak English any longer.'' He gave her a superior look. ''You see, it's quite clear that I'm the only responsible one.''

''Ah, yes.''

His slow smile seemed to curl around her. ''What do you mean by that sarcastic tone? You don't think I'm responsible?''

Her violet eyes sparkled. ''I think you're responsible for a lot of things. Mostly bad.''

''Ah, the lady jokes. But tell me this, Miss Comedian. Why haven't you married in all these years?''

Her smile grew more studied. She hadn't counted on the conversation turning to her quite this soon. ''It hasn't been that many yet,'' she said evasively.

''You know what I mean. What are you, twenty-six, twenty-seven? Most women are married by that age, aren't they?''

Thirty was more like it. She hid a smile. Either he was being tactful, or he really thought she looked that young. Either way, she liked him for it, even though age didn't matter to her a bit. The only problem with age was the way a woman's window of opportunity began to close— the opportunity to have a family with lots of children. That had always been her goal, though it was beginning to seem a distant one.

"I'll tell you the truth," she said, turning to face him on the couch.

"Ah, the truth. You mean, rather than a wisecrack?"

She nodded. "Rather than a wisecrack," she echoed. A thrill ran through her. She didn't do this very often. Her fingers were tingling.

"The unadulterated truth."

"Exactly."

"And you think I can handle it?"

She gave him a baleful look and continued. "Okay, here it is. I've never married, because..." She risked looking directly into his eyes. "Because I've never been in love."

His teasing tone evaporated and his gaze grew serious, holding hers in thrall while he considered what she'd said. "Never been in love?" he said softly at last. "I thought women fell in love all the time."

She continued to stare at him, her wide, black-lashed eyes brilliant with candor. "Some do. I don't."

He frowned, looking her over. She was so unlike the women he usually dealt with. A Pia or a Faith or a Darlene would have made up a story rather than admit to having no real love life. Shayla was a beautiful woman— a warm, bright, intelligent woman. Why wouldn't she have a man in her life? It didn't seem to make sense. "But, you do date men, don't you?"

She nodded slowly and reached for her glass, taking another sip of wine. She was telling him things she'd never told anyone else, and she wasn't sure why she was doing it. The miracle was the way he was listening. Most men would be laughing or yawning or changing the subject. But he really seemed interested.

Still, she wasn't going to tell him everything. She wasn't going to explain that she wouldn't fall in love— couldn't fall in love—with a man who didn't want a big family. And these days, it seemed too many men were afraid of that sort of commitment.

"I did date for a while" was what she told him. "It got more and more depressing, though." For just a moment, she flashed back to all those years of hopeful dates made, and disappointing mornings after. "One broken man after another," she said softly, remembering. "I...I finally gave it up."

"Really? When did you do that?"

"Oh, about..." Suddenly she realized more truth. It had been about a year ago that she'd given up on men. Right after she'd started working for Matt. Before she could stop herself, she was blushing and she had to turn her face toward the fire to hide it. "A while ago," she said evasively, then turned back and gave him a bright smile. "I've told you a truth. Now it's your turn." She gazed at him speculatively, head to the side, debating what to ask him. "I know," she said. "Tell me about your childhood."

To her surprise, his face changed very quickly. The open, friendly expression was replaced by a mask of indifference, a look she immediately interpreted as a protective ruse.

"I don't like to talk about my childhood much," he said, pouring himself another drink.

She watched him as she asked, very softly, "Is it too close, too personal?"

He glanced at her, ready to deny it vigorously, but something in her face stopped him. "Something like that," he admitted reluctantly.

She smiled. "Then talk about it in the third person. Talk about that little kid named Matt as you remember him."

He laughed. "In the third person?"

"Try it."

He struck a pose and spoke out of the corner of his mouth. "It was a dark and stormy night..."

"You don't have to begin with the night you were born," she said, smiling. "Five would be a good age."

He looked at her and hesitated. Did he really have to do this? No, he didn't have to do it. He never did things like this. Spilling his guts was not his style. Better to stick with the jokes. And much safer.

"He was a lonely little boy with few friends and no one to love him," he tried in his best melodramatic voice, cocking an eyebrow for her reaction.

She knew he was still kidding around and she didn't believe it for a moment. She had every confidence he had been a charmer then, as now. "Maybe seven would be better," she suggested quickly.

"Seven." He tilted his head back and thought for a moment, and as she watched, his face changed, as though he were remembering something.

"Okay, here's a little story," he said, his voice normal at last. "Once when he was seven years old, little Matt Temple came back unexpectedly from boarding school." His eyes took on a distant look, as though he could see the past, see that little boy. "Whether his parents had mixed up schedules or there was a sudden outbreak of scarlet fever at the school, I don't know. But he was sent home to an empty house." Frowning, he settled back in the corner of the couch, retreating into his own history. "There was no one home but the servants, and to them, he was just in the way. Taking up a few of his toy cars, he went to play in the dirt along the side of the driveway, and as he played, a car rolled up with his father driving. His father stopped the car and leaned out, frowning furiously."

His mouth twisted for a moment, but somehow it didn't look much like a smile. He stared at the fire for a moment, then seemed to remember where he was. Smiling quickly at Shayla, he went on.

"The boy was surprised that his father didn't seem at all glad to see him, surprised that he looked so angry. 'Hey, kid,' his father yelled, glaring at him. 'What are you doing here? Don't you know this is private property? Go back to the village where your kind belongs.'"

Shayla stared at him. "Your father didn't recognize you?" she asked in wonder.

He gave her a reproachful look. "We're not talking about me, remember? We're talking about that weird little Temple kid."

"Oh." She sat back, properly reprimanded. "Sorry. Please go on."

"If I must," he said, making a face at her. But finding no relenting there, he continued. "The man looked down and did not recognize the little boy. You see..." He winced as though the thought was not an easy one to face. "You see, he didn't see the boy very often. To him, the boy was something of a nuisance. All boys were something of a nuisance. So when he saw the boy playing there, his instinct was to drive him away."

She shook her head, appalled, and wished she could ring the neck of that callous man. Matt was trying to make this a lighthearted story, but the depth of his pain was clear. From the look on his face, she imagined it was surprising him, too.

"What did you do?" she asked softly, tears threatening and choking her voice.

He sat still for a second, as though he were trying to remember, then turned and looked at her. "Threw rocks at his car," he said with a sudden, happy grin.

"You didn't!"

"Yes, I did. I'd forgotten that." He laughed, giving his thigh a sharp slap. "That got me grounded until the next day. Then they left to go skiing in Vail, so I got a reprieve.''

Shayla could hardly believe it. This was like no family she'd ever known. In the household where she grew up, there was always someone nearby who loved you, no matter how big a fight you might get into from one moment to the next.

''They left while you were still home from school?'' she asked.

''Sure. While *the boy* was home from school,'' he reminded her. ''We're talking impersonally here.''

''Matt…'' She wanted to reach for him. This was not the macho, disdainful man she thought she knew so well. This was someone else entirely. She blinked quickly, holding back emotion.

He smiled at her, wanting to dismiss it. ''Hey, listen. I probably exaggerated a little. Don't go getting all weepy over my childhood. My parents weren't the greatest as parents, but I survived. And turned out pretty damn well, if I do say so.'' He shrugged it away. ''It didn't hurt me that much.''

Yes, it had. It had hurt him deep inside. There was no way for him to deny that. Even if the wounds didn't show, they still bled.

''But I do know one thing,'' he said, his resolve evident in his voice and in his eyes. ''This baby isn't going to be raised that way. Remy, his father, was a good guy.'' His smile was rueful. ''He even tried being nice to me. I'm afraid I didn't make it very easy for him.'' He looked at her, that pain she'd been sure he had showing plainly in his eyes for just a moment. ''That's why I have to do this. I'm going to love this baby. I'm going to be the best father this baby could possibly have—other than Remy, anyway.''

Shayla sat very still. She was touched, deeply touched,

but also, deeply frightened. He was expecting so much, asking so much of himself and of the baby. What if things didn't turn out the way he thought they were going to? How would he accept still more pain? She ached with an agony of longing to help him somehow. And yet, she knew this wasn't something she was going to be allowed to do. This was his journey through life, not hers. She was a bystander, with no rights in the matter at all, and she couldn't even offer any meaningful advice.

But finally, she thought she understood. And she knew she wouldn't be trying to talk him out of taking the baby any longer.

They sat and talked for another half hour as the fire consumed itself and fell to embers. Shayla had another glass of wine, and Matt made her laugh. The room was warm and as the fire flickered out, the shadows grew around them, so that it almost seemed they were in a small circle of light that held them together, like ancient travelers around a campfire. The talk tapered off, and even the silence was companionable.

Like a dream, she thought as she luxuriated in the delicious sense of well-being. She stared into the coals in the fireplace, but all she saw was the man on the couch beside her, and she longed to slide slowly into his arms and...

"Uh, it's getting late," she said quickly, before the thought could fully form in her mind. Putting down the wineglass, she smiled at him. "I think I'd better get to bed."

He didn't say a word, but he rose as she did and went with her to the door of the den, holding it open for her. She hesitated in the doorway, smiling up at him.

"Good night," she said. "It's been very nice."

He smiled back and breathed in the scent from her hair and the next thing he knew, his hand was taking hold of the back of her head and his mouth was coming down on hers as though it were the most natural thing in the world.

She made a sound, but he didn't think it was a protest, so he went on, deepening his kiss, exploring the warm depths of her mouth and holding her closer to him so that he could feel the imprint of her breasts against his chest. It was all a part of a whole, the room, the fire, the wine, the sense of friendly attraction, the underlying desire that had smoldered in them both all day. She felt good against him, wonderful, all heat and flesh and sudden surrender. He was already glancing over at the couch and thinking of how he would carry her back there when she broke away from his embrace, surprising him with the sharp accusation in her eyes.

"This isn't part of our deal," she said, wiping her mouth with the back of her hand and glaring at him, shaken by how quickly and completely she'd responded to his embrace. It had been so long, after all, and she'd forgotten what a man felt like, how seductive human contact could be. "You can't do this."

"Shayla, I didn't do anything but..."

"Kissing, I know." She calmed as quickly as she'd come to anger, and almost smiled, despite herself. "But kissing leads to harder stuff, and we both know it." She'd noticed the glance toward the couch and she'd read his mind. "With you, it seems to happen almost instantaneously," she noted, a touch of light derision in her tone. "Haven't you ever heard of gentle wooing?"

His lopsided grin gave him a boy-next-door look, but there was more than casual friendship shining in his deep blue eyes. "Is that what it takes to win you, fair lady?" he teased.

She considered for a moment, challenging him with narrowed eyes. "No," she told him once she'd thought it over. "I just wondered if you'd heard of it." She was out the door and hurrying down the hall before he could react. "Good night," she called back. "See you in the morning."

He stood watching her disappear around a corner to-ward the stairway and he laughed softly to himself. It was probably just as well she'd stopped things. Losing his best assistant would have been a high price to pay for one night of passion. Shrugging, he returned to the den and poured himself a drink. He put another log on the fire, and settled into the big leather easy chair. He was tired, but there was tension in his shoulders and he knew he wouldn't be able to sleep if he went to bed right now. Better to use this time to think some things through. He had a lot of things to think about—starting with the baby who was set to arrive in one short week.

Chapter 6

Shayla woke with a start and stared into the darkness, listening hard. What was that noise she'd heard? Or had she dreamed it? Right now she could hardly hear anything but the wild thumping of her heart.

She'd only had a little sleep. The clock beside the bed said two. Lying back against the snowy white sheets, she stretched beneath the warm covers and waited for her pulse to slow. No sound. Nothing. But she was fully awake and she knew it was going to take a while to change that back into drowsiness. She let her mind drift for a moment, and the dream she was having when she awoke returned. What she remembered jerked her eyes wide open again. Matt. She'd been in his arms....

She groaned and beat her fists into her pillow. This was not supposed to happen. She was too smart to let this happen. She was not one of the women he dated for entertainment. She was hired for business, and the lines were firmly drawn between the two. She'd let the lines blur in the den in front of the fire. No wonder she was dreaming about him. The question was, did he realize how she felt? Could he tell she'd cared about him much too much for much too long?

She groaned again, knowing she'd let her guard down. It was this house. The place was seductive. She'd known from the moment she'd walked in the door that she couldn't stay too long. You couldn't let yourself linger in a place like this. That would be like taking drugs or eating too many rich foods. Such behavior might tempt you into changing your whole way of life, your whole way of thinking. And that wouldn't do.

Sliding out of bed, she began to pace her room, walking in and out of the silvery moonlight. No, that wouldn't do at all. And what was going to happen in the morning when they met over breakfast and he smiled at her and she went weak in the knees and...and...

She stopped dead and stared out the window into the night. Memory flooded back, memory of how she'd felt when he'd kissed her, how her defenses had melted away for a moment, how hard it had been to stop, to pull back and deny what they both wanted.

Could she do it again? Would she be strong enough? She had to be. She had no choice.

Turning, she knew she was in too much danger to ride on hope. No. This was not the right thing to do. She knew where she was going, where her life was headed. This would provide a very ugly detour if she let it happen. She had to leave. She had to get out while she could.

Breathlessly she changed out of her nightgown and back into the jeans and sweater and packed her things away in her bag. She thought of leaving him a note, but there wasn't any paper in the room, so she gave up on that. Making her way down the stairs, stepping as quietly as she could, she headed for the front entryway. But as she rounded the corner of the living room and turned into the hall, the light from the open door to the den fell across her path, and she stopped, paralyzed, holding her breath.

He was still up. Moving slowly, very slowly, she positioned herself to see into the room, and there he was, sitting in the enormous easy chair, staring into the embers of a fire that was still crackling. She drew back quickly and closed her eyes. She was going to have to pass by this doorway to get out of the house. That was, unless she wanted to try breaking a window to escape, and that didn't strike her as a particularly clever plan. Moving with glacial dispatch, she eased herself up to the doorway again and looked in.

He hadn't moved. There was a cup of coffee sitting next to him on the end table. His face was dark and brooding, his eyes troubled and filled with some cloudy torment, and with a jolt, she realized that what she was seeing was very likely the real Matt Temple—without the mask of control he usually wore. She saw naked heartache, naked longing that took her breath away.

Her first impulse was to go to him, to reach out and make it better, whatever it was. He was in obvious pain of some sort, and she ached to help him. He needed someone—or something—so badly. And yet, how could she be arrogant enough to think she could provide what he needed? No, there wasn't a chance of that.

She looked again, and the shadows from the fire danced across his face, making her wonder if what she'd thought she'd seen was real or an illusion of smoke and firelight. Because whatever it had been was gone, and he looked quite normal.

For all she knew, her own mind was playing tricks on her now. For a moment she felt as though the whole world was conspiring to force her into his arms. Her determination strengthened. She had to leave.

Holding her breath, she tiptoed quietly past the door,

not letting herself breathe again until she was in the middle of the living room. She let herself out of the big front door, easing it shut. Starting down the path, she shifted her bag from one hand to the other and crunched quickly through the gravel. The long, winding driveway seemed to go on forever, but finally she'd reached the gates, and then she was out on the road. She knew it was going to be a mile or two into the little crossroads at the highway where she'd noticed an all-night coffee shop. Once she got there, she would find a phone and call a cab....

She felt the perfect fool, walking down the road with her suitcase in the middle of the night. Now that she'd left the house, she was beginning to wonder what had seemed so threatening, so dangerous, that she had to flee into the dark without saying goodbye. And what was she going to say to Matt on Monday morning? Regret welled up in her throat and she wished she'd stayed right where she was, safe and warm in the bed in Matt's house.

Suddenly there were headlights, coming up fast behind her. Her heart skipped a beat, halfway between relief and fear. Should she hide? Should she try to hitch a ride? What kind of person would be out here on this country road at three in the morning, anyway? And what sort of person would pick up some stray woman walking along the side of the road way out here? There was no time to do anything. The car was pulling up alongside her. The driver had seen her. Her heart was thumping wildly. She could pretend to live nearby, she planned a bit frantically. She could say she'd had a flat tire. She could—

"Shayla. What the hell are you doing?"

It was Matt. She hadn't recognized the car. It wasn't one he usually used.

She paused only a moment to bend down and look in at the driver. Once she saw his face, she remembered why she couldn't stay anywhere near him.

"I have to go," she told him firmly, pushing aside the hair she'd neglected to tie back. "It's way past time."

He didn't buy it. "Get in the car, Shayla."

"No, thank you. I'd rather walk." And she started off again, her bag bumping against her legs.

The car cruised along beside her.

"If you really feel you have to leave, I can take you. Get in."

"No."

"I'll take you anywhere you want to go. Honest."

She shook her head, staring straight ahead as she walked, not looking at him. *This is called resisting temptation,* she told herself silently. *Get used to it.* "You can't take me where I want to go," she told him aloud.

"Why not?"

She glanced at him and then away, still walking. "Because it's away from you," she admitted, feeling herself slipping to the edge of desperation. "That's where I have to go. Can't you tell?"

"Okay." He pulled the car to the side, slamming on the brakes and turning off the engine. In another moment, he was striding beside her. "If you want to walk, we'll walk."

Swinging around to face him, she felt all her energy draining away. "Matt, please," she said. "Don't do this. Let me go."

"But why?" His eyes looked black in the moonlight. "Shayla, tell me why."

She stared at him for a long moment, then dropped her suitcase and sank to sit on it. He went down on his haunches beside her, still waiting for his answer. He looked young and appealing in the big, open leather jacket he'd put on, and she longed to run her fingers through his unruly hair. Wincing, she turned away from him.

"I don't want to be here anymore," she said as firmly

as she was able. "I...I don't want to be whatever it is that we're becoming."

"Shayla." He reached out to take her hand and then thought better of it. "We're not becoming anything. We don't have to, anyway."

She shook her head, not accepting his weak reassurances. "I want to go back to being Conners to you," she said, turning back to look into his face, her eyes filled with a smoky sense of regret. "I want to go back to calling you Mr. Temple. I want to be in my suit with my hair pulled back and my glasses on and you yelling out orders and me throwing back thinly veiled insults. And..." Her voice faltered. "And I'm just afraid we can't do that anymore. It's too late. Can't you see that? We've gone way beyond that."

He looked back at her silently for a long moment, then slowly rose, holding out his hands to help her up as well.

"I know what you're scared of," he told her softly.

She searched his eyes, but it was too dark to see into the shadows there. "What?"

He still held her hands in his and he pulled her closer. "It's the same thing I'm scared of."

Despite what she'd thought she'd seen in the den a little earlier, she didn't believe he could be scared of anything. She'd never seen any other evidence of it. She shook her head vigorously, wanting to deny what was undeniable. "No."

"Yes." He pulled her even closer and his arms brought her body against his. "You're scared of this," he murmured, and he kissed her again, kissed her gently, slowly, with all his desire leashed and barely showing.

She melted into his kiss as though she were sinking into a warm bath. There was no resistance in her. His touch set her pulse racing and his taste poured through her like hot, rich brandy. The kiss only lasted a moment

and was gentle, unthreatening and sweet, but it proved
her case. Proved it, and demolished all the defenses she'd
built up against it.

"There now," he said as he drew back, sounding a bit
breathless himself. "Was that so frightening?"

She looked up into his face and she told him the truth.
"Yes."

"I know." He half laughed, half groaned, pulling her
back into his arms. "Me, too."

She started to laugh and they laughed together, holding
on, and when he turned and began to lead her back to the
car, she didn't stop him.

He stowed her suitcase in the trunk and drove her back
to the house. Taking her into the big, gleaming white
kitchen, he brewed her a cup of tea and sat across the
counter from her while she drank it. Her hair had frizzed
up in the late-night dew and it flew around her head like
a golden halo and her eyes shone violet in the bright
kitchen light.

An angel, he thought. *That's what she looks like. And
everybody knows you can't seduce an angel.*

"Feeling better?" he asked her aloud.

She nodded and smiled at him, and he groaned, because
this untouchable angel was all too tempting.

"Think you can sleep now?" he asked.

She looked down into her teacup. "I don't think so,"
she admitted. "I'm just so wound up." She looked up
quickly. "But you go ahead. Don't mind me. I can..."

"Come on." Rising, he stretched out a hand to her.
"Come with me."

She seemed to have lost all will of her own. As she
rose and let him take her hand, she made a feeble attempt
to remember all those times she'd reacted to everything
he said with a smart remark. But that spirit seemed to be

dormant at the moment. She couldn't rouse it. She didn't want to, either.

He led her into the den. The fire was barely flickering, but he threw another log on and turned to her.

"Come here," he said, his eyes luminous in the shadowed light.

She came, trusting him beyond all reason.

He drew her close. "Don't worry," he told her softly. "I promised you no threats to your virtue, and I meant it."

She nodded. She knew he was telling her the truth. He always told the truth.

Taking her to the huge leather chair, he pulled her down into it with him, and she came, trusting him completely. He held her to him as if she were a child, her head cradled to his chest, her legs curled up in his lap. Stroking her hair, he told her gently, "Close your eyes. I'll watch over you tonight. You just relax."

She closed her eyes, squeezed them tightly, but two small tears rolled through nonetheless. She didn't know why she was crying. She only knew she had never felt so protected before, so completely safe. Every muscle let go, every nerve went dull, and she felt herself melt against him like butter on a hot plate.

How did he know to do this? How did this man who had never experienced the sort of love every child deserves know to hold her this way, to treat her so tenderly? It was a miracle, as far as she was concerned. A perfect miracle. And in no time at all, she was asleep.

He must have slept at some point, but it didn't feel like it. Dawn was painting the sky purple outside, and the fire had finally gone out in the fireplace when he became fully awake. She was still asleep in his arms and he shifted a little beneath her, restoring circulation to areas that had been cut off. Her hair was still a mop of spun gold, but it smelled like fresh flowers after a rain shower.

For a long moment, he enjoyed the feel of her against him and puzzled over the changes that had come between them in the past few days. He'd always liked her, respected her, found her completely necessary to the smooth running of his office. But on Wednesday, he'd begun noticing that she was more than the woman who kept him on his toes at work. He'd resisted it at first, but it wasn't long before he'd realized she was probably the most attractive woman he'd ever known. And now, here they were—at a crossroads. What came next would determine a lot of things for both of them.

He moved restlessly, annoyed with himself. After all, he had a baby coming to live with him. He really didn't have time to embark on a new romance now. He had enough complications in his life. He didn't need this one.

No, he was going to be strong and tough and responsible, for a change. He was going to do what was right for everyone involved. And just as soon as she woke up, he was going to tell her so.

"Matt?" She was stirring, stretching out her arms and smiling up at him.

"Hi," he said softly, looking down at her and forgetting all his good intentions. "You've been asleep for hours."

She smiled, nodding, loving the way his hair fell over his forehead, the way the morning light exposed the craggy nature of his handsome face. This man, this bear of a boss, this arrogant, conceited ladies' man, had held her while she slept, had watched over her protectively to make sure she wasn't afraid and wasn't harmed. She could hardly believe it had really happened. Was it a transformation, or had he always been this way and she just hadn't noticed?

Both. A little of both. She'd seen his tender side now, as well as the side that put shivers down spines all up and down the boardroom. And she knew two things: First, he might just make it raising this baby after all; and second...she loved him.

Reaching up, she cupped her palm to his cheek and looked at him. Her look said it all. His heart began to pump, though he was shaking his head, warning her.

"Shayla," he began, "I promised you..."

She stretched luxuriously and began to inch her way up to where she could reach him, wrap her arms around his neck, press a kiss against his cheek. "You can make all the promises you want," she murmured huskily. "I never promised a thing."

Looking at her, he laughed softly. After all, what could you do if the angel decided to seduce you?

And the angel turned seductress, indeed, with long, slow kisses that turned the heat up and a lazy, gliding hand that slipped beneath his shirt and quickly found how sensitive his skin was. He could only take so much coaxing before he'd turned from reluctant companion to a hard, aggressive male who was used to taking the lead in these matters. The kisses grew quicker and they slid down off the chair onto the thickly carpeted floor, rolling together and shrugging out of the constraints of clothing. Her breath was coming very fast and when he saw her naked body in the morning light, his stomach fell away as though he'd been slugged there, and he couldn't breathe at all.

She turned to him, reached for him, needing to feel like a woman in a way she never, ever had felt before. She'd never found what she was looking for and she didn't really expect to this time, but she had to hope. After all, no man had ever been like Matt, no man would ever be like this again.

She wrapped around him and reached for a fulfillment she could only dream of. He took her to him as though she could make him whole in some way, heal something deep inside him he hadn't realized was aching until he'd looked at her. She cried out as he thrust his way into the bond that would join them. She lifted to meet him, urging more from him, taking and giving at the same time, until they moved together, harder and faster, clinging as though they couldn't live without the touch of skin on skin, flesh to flesh. And finally, they fell, breath completely spent, into the shallows of an illusionary sea that lapped around them, calming the storm in their blood, the heat in their veins, the hunger in their bodies, and leaving them entangled in each other's arms, skin shiny with sweet sweat.

Chapter 7

So now it was done. Shayla had taken that dangerous, irreversible step that drove their business relationship forever out of reach. And she didn't have a thing to show for it.

"Fool," she told herself as she showered in the plush bathroom off his bedroom. "You crazy, idiotic fool."

But her regret was only skin-deep. It barely scratched the surface. And down where it counted, she was a woman in love, a woman fulfilled as she'd never been before. She was happy.

They'd made love again, on his bed this time, and it had been even sweeter than before. They'd spent an hour tangled together, murmuring silly things and laughing. And then, reluctantly, she'd left him to take a shower. Now she was about to rejoin him on the terrace for a breakfast he'd fixed. What was she going to see in his eyes when she walked out into the sunshine? Slipping into slacks and a lacy top, she stopped to slash some quick pink color on her lips, fluff her hair, and then turned and went out to face the music.

He'd set the wrought-iron table with yellow china and put a handful of blue irises in a glass with some water and stuck them in the middle of the table. A pitcher of orange juice sat to the side, and a huge plate of crispy bacon joined some warmed muffins to fill out their meal. She stopped, mouth open, to stare at what he'd done.

"Wow," she said, gazing at him in wonder. Who would have guessed her demanding boss would have these hidden talents? "Where did you ever pick up these domestic skills?"

He shrugged, looking endearingly embarrassed. "Most summers and vacations when I was a kid, I hung out in the kitchen," he told her. "The cook was my best friend some years. I picked up a few things." He pulled out the chair for her. "Would you like some eggs? I'm great with omelettes."

"Oh, no thanks, a muffin will be fine." She sat and turned her head to smile up at him. His gaze was open and amused, without a hint of regret or impatience, and her heart lightened. The scent of honeysuckle filled the morning air, and birds sang in the trees. It was going to be a wonderful day.

They didn't eat much and they spoke in fragments, but the feeling between them was warm and happy. She laughed at his jokes and made a few herself, but all the while, her left hand lay in her lap with her fingers crossed. It was wonderful, but it couldn't last. It never did, did it?

"A week from today, the baby will be here," Matt said as they began to clear away their dishes and carry them to the kitchen. "I guess I'll be taking a few days off work while the baby gets settled in," he mused.

Shayla suppressed a smile. He would be taking off more than a few days unless he found himself a good nanny by then.

"I can hardly wait to hold the little guy in my arms,"

he said, his hands full of dishes but his eyes on the future.
"To see those tiny feet. To see those little eyes gazing
up at me, that little tiny mouth making baby bubbles, the
little hand grabbing my finger…"

His voice broke and Shayla swung around to look at
him, stunned. "You really are looking forward to this,"
she said softly, searching his face and finding only candor.

He nodded, looking slightly abashed. "Yes. Yes, I am.
I've always wanted a child."

She looked away from him as they entered the kitchen
and began to load the dishes into the sink. "You just
didn't want to lay the groundwork and marry someone to
get there," she suggested rather caustically.

His wide mouth twisted. "Always looking for ulterior
motives, aren't you, Conners?" he challenged. "The fact
is, I never really thought about it. But ever since that
lawyer called, I've realized how much I want a son or
daughter. It's only natural. I'm at that age. It's time."

She stared at him. For almost a year she'd been studying him, watching every move he made, and she'd
thought she knew him so well. But she'd never dreamed
of these things that lay at the depths of him. He was much
more than she'd ever thought.

They shared doing the dishes, then sat down at the
breakfast nook and began to talk over other things that
had to be done to prepare for this baby.

"You're going to need to fence in the pool," she told
him, making a mark on her checklist with a big black
marker. "You'll need gates on all the staircases, top and
bottom. The gardening tools need to be stored away in a
locked shed. The cleaners and other chemicals in the
kitchen should be stored up higher, out of reach of little
climbers."

He leaned back in his chair and groaned. "My God. It

would be easier to start from scratch and build a child-proof home.''

She grinned at him. ''Millions of people have babies every year. They manage. You will, too.''

His eyes darkened. ''I hope so,'' he murmured.

She set down the list and looked at him. There was a lot to do and little time to do it. She wanted to help him all she could. And at the same time, she felt a restless need to get away from him for a bit, to put things into perspective. ''We don't have much time. Maybe we should each go our own way today, so we can get twice as much done,'' she suggested.

''Okay.'' He nodded. ''I'll get a hold of the contractor and get plans going on the pool fence and some other things.''

''And I'll go looking for baby furniture and order the wallpaper and drapes.'' She jumped up. Things had moved awfully quickly in the last day or so. She needed some space, to stand back and see what was really going on here. ''I'll go to the mall. Where are the keys to your car?''

He watched her drive off and waved until she was out of sight. ''Don't be gone too long,'' he muttered, then turned back into the house and listened to the silence. Just twenty-four hours and he'd already grown used to having her around.

But that wouldn't last. It never did. He had a lot more faith in his ability to give lasting love to a baby he'd never seen before than to a woman he had every respect and affection for. It had been his experience that these things just didn't last.

He called the contractor and made an appointment, and he was searching for the number of a good iron worker when the front bell rang. He frowned, realizing he'd left the gate open, but it was with no trepidation at all that he sauntered to the front door and opened it. There on his doorstep stood a harried-looking woman. A limousine was parked behind her with the engine still running. She seemed to have a large basket at her feet. It looked like the sort of basket some people put dogs in when traveling, and he had already begun to form the words of refusal— "I can't keep a dog, I just don't have the time"—when the woman cried out, "Señor Temple? Is you, no?"

"Uh, yes, I'm Matt Temple. What can I do for you?"

"I am sick, Señor Temple," the woman screeched, clutching at her throat. "Baby's here, but I am sick. Please, please, you have a room for me?"

"The baby?" He stared at the basket and every nerve in his body was suddenly tingling with anticipation. "Remy's baby?"

"Si, Señor, but I must have a room. I am very sick."

The woman's tone of desperation finally penetrated his consciousness and he looked up, noting her extremely green pallor. The woman was definitely sick. There was no doubt.

"Are you the nurse?" he asked.

She nodded. "Please, please," she moaned, swaying and turning a chalkier shade of green.

The nurse. The baby. He could hardly believe it. They weren't supposed to arrive until the next weekend, but here they were.

"Hey, mister." It was the limo driver who called out. He was taking baggage out of the car. "Better get her to a bathroom. She's been like this since I picked her up at the airport."

"Bathroom." He glanced at the basket curiously, hesitating. But then again, this woman looked very sick. First things first. "Sure. Of course."

He had ordered the housekeeper to set up a room for the nurse he'd been expecting to accompany the baby, and she'd done so, at the back of the house. The room had its own bathroom and even a little office on the side. He led the poor nurse to it now.

"Here you go. Let me know if you need anything," he said as he escorted her into the room and shut the door. But his mind was still on the doorstep with that basket, and he hurried back.

The basket hadn't moved. He looked down at it and his mouth went dry. There was something inside, something making a noise. This was it. His baby was here. He was a daddy.

Carefully he pushed back the visor. A little round face stared up at him with gray eyes as big as saucers, and his heart nearly stopped. This was the most beautiful baby he'd ever seen. Devon said the name on his little bib.

"Devon," Matt whispered, staring down and hardly daring to breathe. "Hi, Devon," he said, his gaze taking in every detail, from the wispy golden hair to the feet in little yellow socks that were kicking away a blanket. Two fists began to wave at him and a determined look came over the round face. He let out a sound that was somewhere between a coo and a grunt, and Matt blinked, surprised at such a big voice coming out of a baby.

"Hey, you're a big boy, aren't you?" he noted, beginning to frown. This baby was bigger than he'd imagined they were, bigger and—

"Say, mister," called the limo driver, interrupting his thoughts. "Better get this one, too."

Matt rose to his feet and looked out at where the driver had piled the luggage. There was another basket, identical to the one at his feet. For just a moment, his mind refused to assimilate that information, and he stared at the second basket as though he were seeing things.

"Wait a minute," he said slowly at last, frowning suspiciously. "What is that?"

The limo driver grinned, unwrapping a stick of gum as he watched Matt's face. "What do you think it is? Can't you hear him fussing?"

Matt lost all power of speech for a moment, and his voice was as rough as ground glass when he finally did speak. "No. That can't be. There are two babies?"

The limo driver nodded, unwrapping a stick of gum. "You got that right. The nurse said they're twins."

"Twins?" he echoed stupidly. "Twins? Two babies?"

The limo driver looked concerned at his tone as he popped the gum into his mouth. "Hey, mister, are you okay? Listen, that nurse knows what she's doing. Once she gets better, she'll help you, don't worry. There were two of them, you know."

"Two?" The word was echoing in his brain and he wasn't sure if the limo driver had actually said it again, or he'd just heard his own brain repeating it.

"Yeah. Two nurses, I mean. Two got off the plane. But the other one hated everything she saw and she turned right around and got a ticket on the next plane back to Argentina. They had a big long argument right there in the airport. And Lola—that's your sick nurse there—she came on out with the babies, even though she's sick as a dog. The other one's going back."

Matt couldn't quite get all this information straight in his head. "Two?" It had almost become a mantra with him now.

The limo driver frowned. "Listen, you go on and carry that one in, I'll get this one. Where you going to put them?"

Matt watched the driver lift the second basket and then he bent down and picked up Devon. The little fist waved again, hitting him square in the eye as he took hold of the basket, but he hardly noticed. The word "two" kept reverberating through his head. He was numb.

They stowed the two baskets in the living room, and Matt gave a lingering look at Devon before turning to take a look at the other one. The driver pushed back the visor and there was a carbon copy of the first baby, fists waving, feet kicking, face turning red as though he were making some major effort at something. David said the name on the bib. Matt stared at him, still stunned. "Two," he repeated softly.

The driver gave him a baleful look. "You got some woman around here who can help you?" he asked doubtfully.

That brought Matt back to life. He swung around and glared at the man. "What do I need a woman for? I can handle this," he insisted stoutly.

"Sure you can," the driver said, backing toward the door. "Listen, I didn't mean anything by it. Uh...you'll do great with the kids. I guess you've had a lot of experience, huh? You know what you're doing. I'll just be going, then."

Matt handed him a large bill as a tip and ushered him out the door with hardly a thought. His mind was consumed with his two arrivals.

"Two," he repeated as he turned back to them. "What am I going to do with two?"

Two pairs of gray eyes stared up at him. Two little mouths were open, one forming a perfect circle, the other stretching wide in a yawn. They were awfully cute. Matt started to smile, first at Devon, then at David. Twins. Twin boys. They were his now. Pride tried to shoulder out terror in his heart, but it wasn't strong enough yet and his smile faltered. He still wasn't sure what he was going to do with them.

As he watched, Devon's face started to crumple. The fat lower lip began to quiver. The eyes squinted almost shut. A whimper came out of the tiny mouth.

"Oh, no. Don't cry." Terror was definitely going to win this round if that happened. Matt looked at the baby, then looked at his own hands. He was going to have to hold it, wasn't he?

The whimper had become a wail. Matt worked fast, undoing the seat belt that held Devon in the basket, pulling away the blankets that were stuffed all around him, and pulling him up by his shoulders. The wail became a howl. Matt held him out the way he might hold a soaking wet towel and stared at him. He was crying hard and waving his arms. This kid was mad. What now?

The nurse. She would know. Grabbing the child to his chest, he raced through the house to the room where he'd led the nurse.

"Excuse me," he called, knocking on the door and raising his voice so that she could hear above the din Devon was making. "What do I do when they cry?"

"You must hold him, Señor. Or feed him. The bottle is in the blue bag." Her voice disappeared into a fit of coughing.

Matt's heart sank. He'd been hoping she would be well enough to come out and help him. She sounded worse than before.

I'd better call a doctor for her, he thought as he turned away, the child still screaming in his arms. A doctor. Yes. They knew what to do with babies, too, didn't they? It was a professional duty of theirs.

He went back into the living room. Devon was not only screaming, but he was now wriggling as though he wanted to break free and make a run for it.

"Hey, you're awfully strong for a baby," Matt muttered, putting him down on his back on the floor near the basket where his brother was still staring out at the world with big eyes. "You stay right there. I've got to go call the doctor."

He made his way quickly to the den and found the doctor's number, dialed it and got his service.

"Please give me your name and number. The doctor will call you as soon as he can."

"Make that semi-immediately," Matt ordered, a note of hysteria in his voice. "We've got an emergency here."

"Would you like me to call 911 for you, sir?"

Matt considered for a moment, but decided this wasn't quite that much of an emergency. "No, thanks. Just get the doc to call me back."

"I'll do what I can, sir."

Matt hurried back to the living room, following the sound of the wailing child. The crying was going strong, but when he reached the room, there was a very empty spot where he thought he'd left the baby. He stared at it for a moment, as though the baby had turned invisible and would reappear if he just looked hard enough. Then he glanced around the room. No baby. The crying was coming from David now. He was waving his arms and legs and turning a bright red as he screamed out his annoyance at still being strapped into the basket while his brother was off having all the fun.

"Wait a minute," Matt muttered, tearing his hair distractedly. "How can this happen? Where the heck is he?"

The answer came in the sound of a crash coming from the dining room. Matt raced to find Devon sitting in a pool of water and broken daffodils, the hem of the tablecloth in his hands.

"Oh my God. Are you okay?"

The happy smile and bubbling gurgle that came from the baby answered that question. Matt scooped him up, ignoring the mess, and carried him back to the living room. David was roaring like a young, angry lion, and Matt hesitated. Devon was happily kicking his heels against Matt's stomach. At least he wasn't crying. But if he put him down while he picked up David, would Devon head out for more disaster? He looked down into the happy face and met eyes brimming with adventure. There was no doubt about it.

Did babies follow orders like dogs? That was probably too much to hope for. But he had to try. What else could he do? He set Devon down in a sitting position on the floor and held out the flat of his hand as though he were a terrier. "Stay!" he said firmly. "Stay!" Devon looked up at him with eyes full of wonder.

Turning quickly, he began to unbuckle David from his basket seat. Out of the corner of his eye, he saw movement. Devon was scooting along the floor, heading for the doorway.

"Stop!" Leaving David half unbuckled, he raced after the fleeing tyke. Grabbing him around the waist, he lifted him and brought him back. "Stay!" he said again, though he didn't think his message was really getting through.

He tugged at the strap on David's basket, freeing him, but Devon was off again, gurgling happily as he went. Matt crossed the room in three strides and scooped him up again, turning just in time to see David scrambling out of the basket and heading for the opposite door on all fours.

"Hey!" he called out, dashing back and scooping up that baby, too. Now he had them both, two wriggling, fussing babies, one for each arm. What now?

The nurse had said something about bottles in a blue bag. The luggage was still sitting outside, but there was the blue bag, stashed in the entryway. He maneuvered himself into position to reach down and grab the strap and pull it back into the living room. Both babies were struggling harder, each determined to get away and explore the house. He contemplated putting them back into the baskets, but he knew they'd scream if he did, and besides, while he was buckling in one, the other would head for the hills.

But there were bottles inside the bag. Maybe if they got a look at those bottles, they'd calm down. He carefully put down the babies on the couch and pulled the zipper open on the bag. Bottles and other supplies were neatly stowed inside. He pulled two bottles out and waved them at the wiggling boys.

"Look, guys. Food!"

They both stopped, stared for just a moment, as if they didn't really trust him to fork over the real thing, and then two pairs of arms reached eagerly for sustenance. They each took a bottle and lay back, drinking greedily, their eyes half closed.

For the first time in half an hour, Matt felt as though he could catch his breath. He sank onto a chair and leaned back, exhausted. This baby stuff was rough going. He just needed a minute to relax, to regroup. The babies drank, and every muscle in his body went limp, and in a moment, his own eyes were drooping. He just needed a minute…

He didn't know what woke him, but something did, and for a moment, he didn't remember why he was here, sitting in a chair in the living room in the middle of the morning. Then he heard something that sounded almost like a giggle, and his head snapped around in time to see two little toddlers disappear down the hallway toward the kitchen. For three seconds he sat still, paralyzed. The figures he'd seen had been upright, wobbling, arms in the air for balance, but moving fast on chubby, sturdy legs.

His mouth dropped open and he groaned, his head in his hands. "No. They're walking!" he cried.

And then he was up and after them again, reaching them just as they reached the swinging kitchen double doors, grabbing each around the waist and holding them to his chest, as they let their outrage be known and kicked and wrestled as hard as they could. They'd seen the promised land of pots and pans and cupboards and they wanted to go on in. He'd caught them just in time.

That was when he began looking at the clock rather desperately and wondering where Shayla was. She should have been back by now. But that meant she should be back any moment. If he could just hold out until she returned, maybe he could survive this.

But it wasn't easy. He spent the next hour in a state of constant motion, chasing one while holding the other, quieting one while the other got into mischief behind his back, learning that Devon had a wicked laugh that usually meant he was about to dive off the couch onto his head or climb the drapes, and David didn't smile much, but he watched every move Matt made, moving his eyes without moving his head, until he saw his chance and he made another run for the kitchen every time. Matt stopped by the nurse's room twice to make sure she was okay, and he tried calling the doctor again, but Devon pulled the cord out of the wall in the middle of the call. He felt like a man on a hamster wheel, running like mad and getting nowhere.

Finally he had an idea. Taking the two of them into his arms, he went into the den and flopped down on the big leather chair, sinking down with the two of them held closely. And then he rocked. At first, they both struggled, whimpering to be let go. But the rocking seemed to soothe them very quickly. First Devon began to relax, then David, and soon two little blond heads were resting against his chest. They were asleep.

Matt sighed with relief, and then went stiff with the realization that he'd only sealed his own fate. They were quiet, but one false move and they would be wide-awake again. He was a prisoner of his own cleverness.

Well, this was what he'd wanted. Only, this was a bit too much of a good thing, wasn't it? He closed his eyes. Maybe he was dreaming. Maybe if he fell asleep again, he would wake up and it would all have been a dream.

Shayla returned, her car filled with wallpaper and drapery fabric. She drove up the driveway and looked curiously at the pile of luggage near the front door. Guests? He hadn't said anything about guests. And then she had to smile at the vague feeing of disappointment she felt. She'd wanted to be alone with him again and she might as well admit it.

"Ah, yes, ain't love grand?" she muttered to herself as she parked the car, turned off the engine and went into the house.

The place was as quiet as a library. She frowned, looking up and down the hallways from the entryway. There was an eerie silence.

"Matt?" she said, but not too loudly.

There was no answer. She walked through the parlor and peeked into the kitchen before heading for the living room. The two baskets and the blue bag spilling out its contents from the couch brought her to a halt. Frowning, she turned slowly, wondering where to search next. Something drew her to the den. She could see the top of Matt's head over the back of the chair, but instead of calling out a greeting, she approached slowly, instinctively careful.

What she saw stopped her heart in her throat. Matt was sound asleep, and so were the two babies he held.

"Two?" she gasped softly, realizing this must be Remy's child—or Remy's twins, at any rate.

Matt twitched, but he didn't wake, and she stood there filling her soul with the sight of them. His handsome face was relaxed, and the babies were gorgeous beyond belief.

He looked like a father, looked like a man who could build a family, and she almost wished that she could freeze this moment in time. If he could be like this, if he could commit to the babies and...

But she didn't want to think that way. She was here temporarily and they both knew it. Reaching out gently, she ran her fingers through his thick hair, pushing back a stray lock that had fallen over his forehead. When his eyes opened, she smiled into them.

"Who are these?" she whispered.

He groaned, throwing his head back. "Thank God you're here," he said. "It's been a nightmare."

An icy shiver shook her heart, and disappointment filled her. "It can't be that bad," she said softly. "They're the most beautiful babies I've ever seen."

He stared at her dully. "The lawyer lied. About everything. Not only are there two instead of one. These aren't even real babies. They walk."

"Oh." She held back a short laugh. "Yes, they look about ten months or so. Some do walk by then."

He looked mortally offended. "I never bargained for walking. I expected a nice little baby in a pram. Something that wouldn't move."

But now the two of them had begun to stir, yawning and frowning and stretching their pudgy little bodies.

"Look out," Matt warned, tightening his hold on them. "They take off like rockets." He frowned down at them. "And to top it all off, they hate me."

She couldn't hold back the laughter any longer. It bubbled up and spilled out like champagne, and it continued, even while Matt protested, even while she picked up David and propped him against her shoulder, rocking him and holding him tightly. She laughed while she taught Matt how to change diapers and she laughed while she prepared the bottles and found where their toys were

packed and she laughed while she showed him how to
hold a baby—even a big, walking baby—on his hip while
doing other things.

And then she tried to hold back the laughter while she
checked on the nurse and got through to the doctor and
pulled together a quick lunch for the two of them. But it
came back every time she remembered the look on Matt's
face.

"You seem to take it all so personally," she explained
when he complained about her sense of humor.

"It *is* personal," he grumped. "These babies are now
a part of my life. I feel like I've been invaded."

She could have said "I told you so," but she held it
back. Instead she stopped laughing, and she asked him,
"What are you going to do?"

"Do?" He looked at her blankly. "I'm going to raise
two babies instead of one, that's what I'm going to do.
What else can I do?"

She'd made her suggestions and she wasn't going to
make them again. Right now, she only wished he looked
happier about his decision.

The doctor came and checked over the twins after he'd
seen Lola, the nurse.

"It's my opinion that the nurse's illness was provoked
by traveling more than anything else, and that being the
case, the babies shouldn't be harmed in any way. Keep
an eye on them. If they begin to exhibit any symptoms,
give me a call and I'll come out again."

"A doctor who makes housecalls." Shayla marveled
as he left them. "I thought they'd gone the way of the
dinosaurs."

"My father and he were close friends," Matt told her.
"I don't think he does this for just anyone."

But he'd pronounced the twins hale and hearty and as
healthy as young horses, and when Shayla looked at them,

something seemed to bubble in her heart. They were so adorable! And so full of mischief.

"Grab him!" was a phrase heard often that afternoon, as the two of them chased down the little ones. A desperate plea from Shayla brought an express delivery of two cribs from the furniture store. The nurse's supply of diapers and baby food was enough to hold out for the night. Matt and Shayla fed them, gave them bottles and walked them, until the babies' eyelashes dropped reluctantly to brush against their rosy cheeks, and their little round heads drooped against the adult shoulders, and they were laid carefully in the cribs. Matt and Shayla lingered just a moment to smile at how lovable they looked while they slept, and then the two of them tiptoed out of the room.

Once in the hallway, Matt stretched, twisting his back and grimacing. "My God. The first day of boot camp must feel a lot like this," he grumbled.

"Tomorrow will be better," she promised, then glanced at him curiously. Under the original plan for the weekend, she would have been home by now. Nothing had been said, but she'd assumed he would want her to stay. But just to be sure, she probed him. "Think you can handle them by yourself now?" she asked lightly, smiling at him.

A look of pure panic crossed his face. "You can't go," he told her firmly. "You can't leave me alone with them."

She shrugged and pretended to be considering. He grabbed her by the shoulders. "Don't forsake me now, woman," he demanded. "What do you want from me? An admission that I, an ignorant and incompetent male, can't do it alone? You've got it. It's true. I need you as badly here as I've ever needed you at the office."

She laughed and pushed back his disheveled hair.

"With these two, I would have a hard time myself. And you've been doing a wonderful job." Her hand brushed his cheek. "I'll stay until the nurse feels better," she offered.

He pulled her close and kissed her soundly. "Thank you," he said, his voice husky. "Let's go to bed."

She laughed again, feeling warm and toasty but very much aware he might just be pleading exhaustion rather than passion.

He disproved that theory soon enough, seducing her quickly with words and kisses. They tangled together as though they'd been kept apart too long, reaching for an ecstasy that stayed just tantalizingly out of reach, and then swooped down to engulf them in a wild ride that left them gasping for breath and laughing in each other's arms. It took a few minutes to recover, and to lose the laughter. Finally they lay side by side, breathing easily and enjoying the feel of companionship they shared.

Lying back against the pillow, Matt stared at the ceiling and thought about the day to come with trepidation.

"We'd better get hold of a nanny right away," he said.

Shayla propped up on one elbow and looked at him. "No," she said gently, stroking his chest.

He turned and glared at her. "What do you mean, no?"

She shook her head firmly. "It's not right, Matt. You have to get to know them first, before you hire someone to take care of them. They're your babies. If you want to farm them out to someone else, you still have to be the prime parent to them, and they need to know you first. And you have to know them."

She was right and he knew it, but that didn't stop him from uttering a harsh curse under his breath.

"All right then, I'll take a week off," he said, compromising.

"At least," she murmured, smiling.

But he paid no attention. Instead he reached for her and began dropping sizzling kisses along her collarbone. "But you have to promise to stay," he muttered between nibbles.

"You won't need me," she teased. "You'll have the nurse."

"The babies will have the nurse," he said, running his hands down her naked back and settling at the base of her spine. "I'll have you."

She sighed happily, sinking into the tempting heat of his embrace. No man had ever made her feel the way he did so effortlessly. His touch was magic. She knew this wasn't meant to last, but while it was there for her, she was going to grab it with both hands.

Over the next few days, their lives were saturated with child care. At first, Matt made some effort to stay in touch with the office, but he abandoned all that soon enough. There just wasn't time. There just wasn't the mental space to think about work. Babies filled their thoughts and dictated their every action.

The nurse was fine in the morning and she took over some of the more mundane routines, but Matt and Shayla were involved in every aspect of the babies' daily existence. Matt learned very quickly how to play patty cake and "Itsy Bitsy Spider" and "Monkeys on the Bed" but diapering came hard to him. In no time at all, he had bandages on all his fingers from where the diaper pins had struck home.

"We'll go to disposable diapers," Shayla told him soothingly when he showed her his wounds. "They're easy. No problem."

A man with a degree in engineering and a knack for woodworking should have been able to get the hang of disposables, but Matt seemed to have a blind spot there, too. He put them on backward and sideways and inside out, until Shayla began to suspect him of doing a bad job on purpose.

"You just don't want to do it, so you're making sure you're incompetent at it," she accused him, laughing.

He looked at her, shamefaced. "That's not true," he said dejectedly. "I'm really trying. It's just that there's so much else going on every time I try to put on a diaper."

It was true, they didn't sit still for it. They had to be held down with one hand and cooed and coaxed and sometimes ordered to quiet down in a stern voice, but Shayla and the nurse could manage it. Why Matt couldn't do it was a mystery.

He was good at the game playing, and when he swung them into the air, they each came back and begged for more, raising their arms to him and crowing with delight. He played hide-and-seek until they were rolling with baby laughter, and he carried them around easily, showing them the stream and the fields and the deer in the woods.

Shayla watched him and her love grew, until she was almost sick with it. She loved him and there was no hope for her. She was also growing to love the babies, and that was going to turn around and hurt her as well. She knew all that. But she didn't shy away from it. It was all a part of life and she would handle it. Somehow.

The nurse was a godsend. She'd worked for Remy and his wife and, devoted as she was to Devon and David, she would be the link to their past. She'd brought along with her a huge scrapbook full of pictures and anecdotes about the twins' past and about what their parents were like, a resource that was going to be invaluable as the boys grew up.

"Nina Castillo—she was the best friend of Remy and Marta—she got all their friends together and they wrote these little stories about what they knew," Lola told

Shayla when she showed her the scrapbook. "Nina put them into this book for the babies, so that they could know what their parents were like."

"That's wonderful," Shayla said, tears springing to her eyes as she thought of Marta and all that she was missing. The boys were settling in beautifully and didn't seem to realize that something very important had been ripped from their lives, but she knew that deep down, they felt the loss, and that their pain would come back to the surface at some time in their future. And when it did, this book would help sustain them.

In the meantime, she was worried about Matt and how he was adjusting to his new lifestyle. He was trying very hard. He played with the twins, talked to them, fed them, cared about them. But there was an edginess to him that wouldn't go away. When the two of them were alone, he lost it, and he was a lover any woman would dream of. Lover, boss and friend. It was an odd combination and she wasn't sure it could work for long. But for now, it was heaven.

He loved the babies—she thought. He liked them, anyway. He enjoyed the playfulness. Now and then he made gestures of affection, such as dropping a kiss on a fat cheek or patting a blond head. But there was something missing. Something was not quite there yet.

"It's just not the way I pictured it," he admitted when she finally got up the nerve to confront him about it. "One would have been easier to get used to. The two of them seem...almost like they're a closed front against me sometimes."

"They love you!" she protested.

"Do they?" His gaze was hard and unrelenting. "How do you know that?"

Her heart sank. It wasn't working. Chiding herself, she realized she'd been dreaming. In the dream, Matt would turn into an instant family man, Father of the Year, and that maybe, just maybe, he might want her to join their little family. But it wasn't working out that way. She could see it in his eyes, hear it in his voice. If it didn't come together for him soon, he might start asking to see those brochures she'd brought about adoption.

Well, wasn't that what she'd wanted all along?

No. Oh God, no. Not anymore.

He was so wonderful with them. Why couldn't he see that? What was making him so uneasy?

At one point, she wondered if she ought to go and leave him with them—that maybe she was part of the problem. Used to babies as she was, she'd fallen for these two right away, had picked them up and held them and bonded as naturally as if she'd been their mother. They turned to her when they were hungry and they turned to her when they were sleepy. They clung to her when strangers came around. And she'd opened up her heart and taken them in from the beginning. There was no question about it.

But Matt was another story. Something in him resisted, and the babies seemed to sense it. He often got bogged down in the mechanics of things, such as why the baby carriage didn't run smoothly and why the crib creaked and why the baby food processor liquefied peas instead of mashing them. The twins were still objects to him, challenges to be overcome, things to adjust to. He hadn't fallen in love.

And it was hard to figure out why, because he acted very loving to her. His touch, his casual glances that met hers, his smiles, all told her that the feeling between them was growing all the time. Still, something wasn't quite right.

One day, after the babies had been there for almost two weeks, she prepared a picnic lunch and they took the babies and hiked out into the hills behind the house, sitting in the sun and watching the little ones play. When clouds began to gather, a rolling round of thunder came crashing into their little scene, and the two boys ran screaming for Matt, throwing their pudgy bodies against him, hiding their faces into his wide shoulders, hanging on for dear life as he comforted them. For just a moment, he looked pleased, and Shayla held her breath. She watched the way he dealt with them and hope was rekindled in her breast. Tomorrow. Surely each day would bring him closer to them. Tomorrow would be better.

But it wasn't.

Things seemed to go pretty well in the morning, but in the afternoon, she realized the cupboards were bare and she would have to run in to the market to do some grocery shopping, and the nurse was taking the afternoon off.

"I'm going to leave you alone with them," she told him. "Do you think you'll be okay?"

"Oh, sure," he said, all confidence. "I've learned how to handle these guys by now."

She left a bit doubtfully. But after all, what could happen in one short hour?

Not much. Just disaster.

Things started out quietly enough. Matt played with the boys, having them sit opposite him and rolling a ball to each in turn. David laughed uproariously and Devon quickly learned to throw the ball, though it didn't go anywhere near his target, if he actually had one. When they tired of that, he placed them in the mesh playpen that had been set up in the living room, but they weren't in the mood for that sort of confinement, and they fussed until he took them back out again and set them down to play with cups on the floor of the den while he went through some bills. Somehow his attention drifted away from them as he puzzled over some sums that weren't coming out right. Their play was background noise, and he didn't notice when it faded from two voices to one. He didn't know what made him glance up and look out the window, but when he did, he saw Devon running far out across the grass as though demons were behind him, his fat little legs churning. David was still absorbed in stacking cups, but Devon was out of control and racing down the hill toward the stream, his blond hair shining in the sun.

Matt swore and ran out through the living room and out the French doors to the garden. A stiff wind was blowing and it caught his hair as he ran. He reached the top of the hill and Devon was nowhere in sight. He'd already made it to the trees and any second, he would reach the stream. Matt ran faster, pounding the ground, his breath ragged in his throat. Visions of a little blond head floating in the swirling water loomed like doom in front of him.

His eyes, used to the bright light, were blinded when he went into the gloom in among the trees. "Devon?" he called. There was the stream, but where was the baby? Had he already fallen in? Was he being swept down toward the river? "Devon!" he called again, running alongside the water.

Suddenly there was a giggle and he stopped dead, turning around on a dime. There was a flash of blond hair as the tyke scrambled in among the rocks. Matt closed his eyes, holding his heart. Devon was okay and it was all right to breathe again.

Erasing the distance between them in a few long strides, he grabbed the little devil around the waist and swung him up into his arms, holding him tightly and kissing one fat baby cheek. Then he held him away and looked at him sternly. "Don't run away like that, Devon," he ordered. "Don't you ever do that again!"

The lower lip began to tremble and the little eyes filled with tears and he groaned, holding him close again, feeling manipulated. Why couldn't he get this right? Maybe...he hated to let the thought surface, but it had been lurking in his mind for a long time now. Maybe he wasn't cut out to be a father. He loved these little guys, but he just didn't feel as though this was working.

He carried Devon back up to the house and into the den. The cups had been abandoned. David was gone.

Before he had a chance to get excited, a high-pitched screech of joy told him what direction David had gone in. Still carrying Devon, he headed for the kitchen. The double doors swung open and there was David. He'd found the flour bin and pulled it over on himself, and now he sat on and under a huge pile of flour, taking handfuls of the white powder and throwing it into the air, creating his own flour mist. He was flour from head to toe, and his eyes were mere slits in the flour mask he wore. Matt stopped, stunned, and Devon slipped from his arms, crowing with delight as he tumbled head over heels into the flour to join his brother.

For a long moment, Matt stood and stared at them, hardly breathing. It was just too much. There was always something. He really wasn't sure he could handle it any longer.

"I've go to get back to work," he told Shayla when she'd returned and the boys had been cleaned up and put down for naps. "I'm going crazy here."

She nodded. The way things had been going, she'd been expecting this. "What about the babies?" she asked softly, not looking at him.

He hesitated, and she turned and confronted him. "There are plenty of wonderful couples who are waiting for babies like these," she said, though it broke her heart.

A look of pain shot through his gaze and he winced. "No," he said quickly. "No, I'm not ready to do that." He tried to read her face and failed. He hated this. "It's time to go ahead and hire a nanny, though,'' he said. ''You'll help do that, won't you?''

She nodded. ''Of course. And I'll stay with them until they get used to her.''

He frowned. ''Oh. Sure. But I'm going to need you at the office, too.'' He ran a hand through his hair, grimacing. Hell, he needed her everywhere. And he wasn't too happy about that, either.

But she smiled sadly and shook her head. ''I won't be going back to the office,'' she told him firmly. ''We can't go back to that. Not now.''

She was right and he knew it, but anger rose in him and he wanted to smash something. Turning from her, he made his way out and down to the stream, and he stayed there a long time, but he didn't make much progress in finding solutions, no matter how hard he stared into the water.

Monday morning, he drove off to work and she watched him go. It wasn't that he was going back to the office that filled her with such melancholy. After all, most fathers did that, didn't they? It was what it meant, what it symbolized—and the fact that he'd done it as a way to get away from the babies. The dream was fading away, and she might as well admit it.

Matt spent a week getting back into the swing of things at work. He felt himself drifting farther and farther away from what was going on at his house. He returned from the city late and left early, and his relationship with Shayla was falling apart. He felt like a man in a maze— no matter which way he turned, he was only getting himself farther and farther from where he wanted to be.

Despite all that, Shayla put off interviewing nannies. The babies weren't ready yet. She couldn't bear to think of leaving them. And yet she knew she was going to have to.

"Are you sure you won't come back to the office?" he asked her one night. "The place is going to hell without you." He stroked her cheek with his thumb. "I'll call you Conners again. You can pin up your hair and throw around the old insults."

She twisted in his arms and kissed him. "No," she told him bluntly. "It wouldn't work and you know it." Besides, though she didn't know how to tell him, her interests had changed. She was reading everything she could about babies, about food, about exercise for toddlers, about teaching methods. She was into raising kids right now, and it felt right. *This is my time,* she told herself. It was just a shame it couldn't last.

Two weeks after Matt went back to work, she forced herself to do the right thing, and she called an agency to arrange for prospective nannies to start coming by for interviews.

"There are three of them coming today," she told Matt the next morning as he arranged things in his briefcase and prepared to leave for the city. "Do you have any preferences I should know about?"

He looked up and saw the shadows in her eyes. Frowning, he looked away again. "No. You make the decision. You know more about these things than I do."

His admitting it depressed her more than ever, and as she waved him off, she felt a cloud developing, a bit of gloom that was going to stick around for quite some time.

Matt was in a surly mood as he drove across the Golden Gate Bridge. He wasn't looking forward to his day. Meetings and more meetings, a call to the East Coast, lunch with his accounts lawyer. Work just didn't seem to have the same spark to it these days. When you came right down to it, things were downright boring.

Part of that was because Shayla wasn't with him. He'd never become so dependent on an employee before and it puzzled him that her absence could make such a big dent in things. He knew he was crazy about her. But it was more than that.

He pulled into the parking garage below his building and waited for another car to pull out of a space so he could pass.

It was a warm morning and he hadn't put on the air conditioner, and now he was sweating. Reaching into his pocket, he pulled out his handkerchief and began to wipe his brow, but it felt funny, rough and strangely shaped, and there were little straps flopping on his nose. He drew it down to take a look. He did a double take. He hadn't pulled out a handkerchief at all. Instead he'd wiped his forehead with a bib that had a small blue teddy bear embroidered on it.

"How the heck did that get in there?" he muttered, laughing to himself. What if he'd pulled it out in the middle of a board meeting? That would have turned some heads.

He looked at it again, then put it to his face and drew in the fresh, baby smell of it. Was it Devon's or David's? He couldn't tell, and for just a moment, a picture of them both swam before his eyes and he smiled. They were his babies, a part of his life. His. Something twisted in his heart, something broke open and left him gasping. His. The emotion that word conjured up took his breath away. He loved them.

Shayla's beautiful face swam into the picture as well. He loved her, too. What was the matter with him? Why was he risking losing everything that he loved this way? What was he doing here?

Someone was honking for him to get out of the way, but he didn't hear a thing. The people he loved were all still at home. And here he was, pursuing—what? He'd made his fortune. He had a smooth-running company that didn't really need him any longer. And yet he was here instead of at home where certain people did need him. Was he crazy?

Yes. He was crazy. And it was time to put a stop to it.

Ignoring the honker, he put his car into reverse. As if he were a man in a dream, he backed out of the garage and turned his car toward home. That was where he really wanted to be. So why didn't he go there? There were a thousand things he could do there. He could start a new company, work on improving baby products, do something related to this grand new adventure he'd begun— and then almost turned his back on. Why had it taken him so long to wake up to the truth? The babies were his. He wanted them. And he wanted Shayla. And he was going to get what he wanted. Didn't he always, in the end?

Shayla was taking the babies outside to run in the grass when his car rolled up. She shaded her eyes as he got out, smiling at him.

"Did you forget something?" she called.

"Yes, I did," he called back, striding quickly toward her. "I forgot you," he said, taking her up and whirling her around so that her yellow sundress sailed out around her.

She laughed and when he dropped a hot kiss on her mouth, she kissed him back.

"I was just sitting in my car," he told her, still holding her, enjoying the look of her outdoor freshness against his impeccable suit, "when it occurred to me that I would rather be with you. So I came back."

Before she had a chance to respond, the twins caught sight of him and they both came streaking back across the lawn, crying out.

"Hey, guys," he said as each grabbed a leg and held on, little faces turned up toward his.

"Da-da," Devon said softly, looking eager. "Da-da."

Matt's jaw dropped and he looked up into Shayla's face. "Did he just say…?"

She nodded happily. Something told her this was the key. "Yes, he did," she told him. She grinned. "They're very precocious you know."

That seemed to strike him as a very wise thing to say. "Of course they are. They're my babies."

Her heart swelled at his words, and something choked in her throat. Was she imagining things, or was something happening here?

He looked at her slyly as the twins ran off again. "You want them, too, don't you?" he noted softly. Turning, he took her in his arms again. "Admit it."

She looked up at him, not sure where he was going with this. "What?"

"You want them. You've wanted them from the beginning." He kissed her hard, then drew back and said firmly, pinning her with his hard gaze, "Well, there's only one way you're going to get them."

She stared up into his eyes, confused. "What are you talking about?" she murmured.

"How you can have them, too." He went on, talking as though it were all quite sensible. "You can marry me."

The world was spinning now, the sky where the grass should be, and she was giddy with it. Leaning back in his arms, she shook her head slowly, staring at him. "What, so you can have a nanny without having to hire one?" she teased.

"No," he said, dropping a kiss on her neck, and then another behind her ear. "So I can have the woman I love at my side," he growled huskily. He looked into her face for a moment, then threw out an arm grandiosely. "So we can raise these babies together. So they can have the best mother they could possibly have, and I can have the best lover who—''

''Don't you dare!'' she warned, putting a finger over his lips to stop him.

''Why not?'' he said, his words muffled. Reaching up, he took her wrist in his hand and pulled her fingers away. ''It's true. Lovemaking is important to a good marriage.'' He smiled at her. ''That's why we have to practice it a lot.''

She laughed. ''So it will be perfect?''

His eyes darkened. ''It's already perfect,'' he said, stroking back her hair. ''Everything is perfect. As long as you say yes.''

''Yes.''

''Yes, you'll marry me?''

''Yes, I'll marry you.''

His kiss was tender, sealing their bargain, but the sound of galloping babies drew them back to reality. Turning, they saw David and Devon coming toward them, blond hair bouncing as they ran on their stout little bowed legs.

''Da-da!'' Devon shouted as they came.

''Da-da,'' David called out as well.

''Da-da, Da-da,'' they cried in unison.

Matt looked at her, his face full of a special light. ''They really are saying Daddy,'' he told her, incredulous. ''I didn't believe it at first. But I think they really are.''

She nodded, her eyes sparkling with tears. ''Of course they are.'' She smiled. ''I've been training them for days,'' she whispered to herself.

She watched as he leaned down and took both babies into his arms and began to swing them, talking to them as they shrieked with pleasure. And then she closed her eyes as happiness began to crest in her like a wave, and she let herself sink back into the dream. It was coming true after all. In the final analysis, the baby invasion was a complete success.

* * * * *

New York Times bestselling author

ELIZABETH LOWELL

brings a sensual tale of unrequited love starring her reader-favorite Mackenzie family!

FIRE AND RAIN

Carla McQueen had loved Luke Mackenzie for as long as she could remember. But bitter rejection had caused her to flee the Rocking M ranch, leaving Luke with only memories of the girl he secretly loved. Now, years later, Carla has returned, determined to realize all of her dreams.

***Look for Fire and Rain in May—
wherever books are sold.***

Where love comes alive™

SPECIAL EDITION™

From *USA TODAY* bestselling author

SHERRYL WOODS

TREASURED

(Silhouette Special Edition #1609)

After a series of tragedies convince him to
abandon love, Matt Carlton has retreated
to his farm in brooding silence, vowing
never to risk his heart again. His only solace is
his work…until his aunt introduces art gallery
owner Kathleen Dugan into his life.
Can this luminous woman brighten the
shadows cast by Matt's painful past?

**The final installment
in the popular miniseries**

MILLION DOLLAR DESTINIES

Three brothers discover all the riches money can't buy.

Available May 2004 at your favorite retail outlet.

A captivating story of love, loss and faith regained,
by acclaimed author

LENORA WORTH

"Lenora Worth orchestrates...romance in her classical, emotionally rich style." —*Romantic Times*

Alisha Emerson is drawn to Dover Mountain, situated in the beautiful
north Georgia mountains where blue spruce trees reach up to heaven.
There, she feels a sense of healing and communion, and she hopes
she and her unborn child will thrive in this idyllic setting.

A man without hope and without God, Jared Murdoch is attempting to
flee his demons when unforeseen circumstances compel him to help
Alisha deliver her son safely, and he decides to stay in Dover Mountain.

But when they encounter the darker elements of village life,
Alisha and Jared begin to wonder—is Dover Mountain
really the sylvan sanctuary they thought initially,
or a much more sinister place?

Available May 2004.

Steeple
Hill®

SLW514-1

New York Times **Bestselling Author**

LISA JACKSON

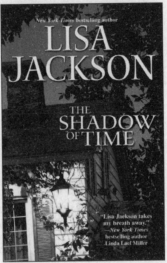

THE
SHADOW
OF TIME

After four long years, Mara Wilcox had finally accepted that her lover, Shane Kennedy, had been tragically killed overseas. But now, inexplicably, he was back—as handsome, arrogant and sensual as ever! Can Mara and Shane overcome the shadow of time and give in to their long-denied passion?

"Lisa Jackson takes my breath away."
—*New York Times* **bestselling author Linda Lael Miller**

Coming in June 2004.

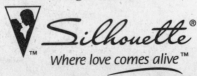

PSLJ824-TR